DOMINIC NOLAN

PAST LIFE

HEADLINE

First published in 2019 by
HEADLINE PUBLISHING GROUP

1

Cataloguing in Publication Data is available from the British Library

Hardback ISBN 978 1 4722 5465 8
Trade paperback ISBN 978 1 4722 5463 4

Typeset in 11.25/16.25 pt Adobe Garamond Pro by Jouve (UK), Milton Keynes

Printed and bound in Great Britain by Clays Ltd, Elcograf S.p.A.

HEADLINE PUBLISHING GROUP
An Hachette UK Company
Carmelite House
50 Victoria Embankment
London EC4Y 0DZ

www.headline.co.uk
www.hachette.co.uk

LEABHARLANNA FHINE GALL
FINGAL LIBARIES

Items should be returned on or before the given return date.
Items may be renewed in branch libraries, by phone or
online. You will need your PIN to renew online.
Damage to, or loss of items, will be charged to the borrower.

Date Due:	Date Due:	Date Due:
03 JUL 2019		

For Val and Jim Nolan

liberty givers

How can we live without our lives?
How will we know it's us without our past?

John Steinbeck

La vie que j'ai menée
M'empêche de me suicider

Blaise Cendrars

Whatever was happening was already receding, departing from her mind quicker than she could gather up its wool. It surprised her that she was lying down. There was a bare mattress beneath her and she faced the wall. In the low light her eyes slid round the room seeking something familiar, anything that might tell her where she was. Planks neatly boarded up the window, bolted into the wall either side. Walls of cheap Anaglypta, once white but now maroon and bubbled with damp, peeling away at the corner to reveal older laminae beneath like decorative strata.

Evidence of bygone peoples.

She was exhausted. No, more than that – *drained*, as if it was something done to her, making her bones weary and her head light and daffy. She was scared, felt it low down in her guts, but didn't know what of. Didn't know anything, in fact. That icy realisation set off a mild panic. It would come to her, she told herself, it would all come to her. Just lie here a minute, wait for the obvious stuff to occur.

Such as your name.

Her body began to make itself known. Head pounding, mouth coarse and spitless. One eye was barely more than a slit, her face tender to the touch, and new pains were cropping up faster than she could identify them. She couldn't have chosen this, whatever *this* was. Movement was a trial, and battling to sit up she drunkenly toppled sideways before pushing herself up onto her knees.

She wasn't alone.

In the far corner a half-dressed girl sat slumped against the wall, legs stretched out before her with bare feet turned inward.

Trying to speak to her, her voice snagged awkwardly. Working up some saliva in her mouth, she cleared her throat with a rasp.

'Hey.'

Nothing.

'Hello?'

Crawling towards the girl, she discovered bruised knees and shins along the way. Late teens perhaps, childlike body appearing younger, skin the colour of sand at low tide. She noticed her arm, little bug bites along the veins, and on the floor a needle and spoon, all the makings. Leaning over, she held her hand under the girl's nose.

'Shit.'

Finding no pulse at her neck, she pressed her ear to her chest, just above the little top that covered her small breasts. There was nothing, the skin stone cold.

Deep breaths now. Resist the urge to call out.

The door was locked and had no handle on the inside, a brass plate screwed over the hole. One of the planks across the window had been worked loose and, scuttling over on hands and knees, she pulled away the slack end. Peering through the dark glass she saw it was boarded from the outside too. She sat back against the wall beneath the sill, where an unpainted patch and small holes cut in the carpet suggested a radiator had once stood.

The room was ill-lit by a low-wattage bulb in a lamp on the floor, its fuchsia shade grubby and tasselled. It wasn't plugged into a socket in the room but rather an extension cord that disappeared out beneath the door. The ancient carpet had probably sometime in the seventies been a tangy shade of orange. Now dark and dirtied, it had worn right through in places so soot from the disintegrated underlay spilled out like scorch marks. An accumulation of stains covered it, the nature of which she didn't care to speculate on.

She was alone and she knew a few things. What a radiator was, and wallpaper and doors and locks and the absence of heartbeats. And, when she heard them, the sound of footsteps. She froze. They came from outside the room, on exposed floorboards she guessed. Edging towards the door, she cocked an ear. Old white paint peeled from the frame, little curls of it on the floor like nail clippings. Her breath was quick and shallow, her heart the loudest thing. She tried to listen over it. Voices, human voices, indistinct through the walls but definitely two voices in another room.

Please God be speaking in the same words I'm thinking.

The footsteps were right outside the door, the voice clear as he passed – she knew it was a man – but none of it made sense, gibberish to her. Another one followed, calling out from further away, his noises as incomprehensible as the first's.

What did that mean? She'd forgotten how people spoke to one another? Maybe wherever she was, she wasn't from there. A foreigner, lost and stupid in some faraway place.

The first voice stopped outside. At the sound of a key in the lock she scooted back over to the mattress and lay exactly as she'd woken, back to the door. She heard it swing open and felt eyes on her, but nobody came in. The other one was shouting from afar, the closer one replying. The door pulled to again, this time unlocked.

She chanced a peek over her shoulder, then moved quickly and quietly to the door. It was open a crack and she could see one of them through another doorway across the hall a few yards down. His feet and legs, his bulk resting on his thighs where he sat on a stool. He held a tray on his knees and wore gloves, thin disposable ones. With a fork in his fist, a balaclava rolled up over his chin, he heaped tangles of tinned spaghetti into his mouth, loose ends whipping about, leaving a trail of sauce across his full lips.

She almost laughed. Spaghetti. She knew what that was too.

A third voice in the other room, a woman's. Not speech, but other noises.

Noises of fear. Noises of pain.

Putting the tray on the floor, the man heaved himself to his feet and moved deeper into the room, out of view. His size was such that he listed from side to side, more of a lumberer than a walker. The noises of someone being struck, of a woman pleading.

She slipped out of the door into the hall, where power cables trailed up and down the floor. A door down the end, past the room the rumpus was coming from, looked like the entrance to a flat. There were two other rooms the other way. The first, almost directly opposite, was a bathroom, frosted glass in the door. The other was a kitchen. A camping stove was heating a pan of water on the side and another pan, smeared with congealing sauce, sat in the sink. The window was boarded up like in the other room, but the various power cables came together and went out through a hole cut in the bottom plank to wherever the electricity was being siphoned from.

She crept back to the bathroom, leaving the door open enough to see the door of the room she'd been locked in. Key was still in it. The bathroom was small and windowless, served only by the cataracted light from the sandblasted door panels. A newspaper hung over the edge of the bath and she squinted in the dark, stifling a cry of joy as she read and understood the headlines. She scrambled around for anything else she might read, but the room was bare.

A small cabinet above the basin was empty, but closing it she caught sight of herself in the mirror and didn't recognise the face. Not because it was marked and bruised, but because she was certain she had never seen it before. The mouth was doing strange things in the glass and she didn't know the colour of the eyes. Trembling, she got down on the floor, sitting beneath the basin with her knees drawn up. The plaster walls had been stripped, the plumbing exposed, and the bath was without its panel. A broken shard of tile lay on the floor. She picked it up, clutched it close to her.

Through the wall the other woman cried out again. She listened to her and, pressing herself further back into the gap between the cold ceramic pedestal and the crumbling wall, listened to the sounds of the things they did to her.

Heavy footsteps approached down the hall. Forcing herself up, she hid behind the door in a sprinter's crouch. When the dark shape moved across the pearly glass, she hurled herself out and crashed into the mass, jamming the fractured tile deep into it.

He roared and arched his back, reaching for the tile. Her hand had slipped, slicing her palm on the sharp edge, but the tile stuck fast in him under the shoulder blade. The impact staggered him into the room and she pulled the door closed behind him, locking it and removing the key, sending it skating across the hard bathroom floor into a dark corner beneath the tub.

No way the other man didn't hear the commotion and the big one was already shouting. He kicked at the door but it opened inwards, so the frame held against his boot.

In the kitchen, the pan was boiling over furiously, water spitting in the flames. She took hold of the end of the handle, hot but not too hot, keeping it on the heat. Hopping from foot to foot, she could hear the other one in the hall.

Closer, closer, let him come to you.

She lifted the pan and jumped out.

Baseball cap and a bandana around his mouth and nose so she could see only his eyes, dark and implacable with black brows. A brush of dark hair sprouting out around each copper ear. His jeans were undone, the open flaps and unbuckled belt ends clutched together in one fist.

They stared at one another, and she flicked the pan.

Boiling water scalded his face and he gave a peculiar shriek, dropping his jeans and clawing at the steaming bandana. He collapsed into a sitting position, jeans pooled around his ankles, and she tossed the remaining water into his lap, drawing another scream.

The big one had booted the panelling out of the bottom half of the door and on his hands and knees was trying to force his way through a hole that needed to be twice as big.

Telling her he was going to fucking kill her.

Dirty little bitch.

She understood his words perfectly now.

A woman tottered into the hallway from the other room,

moving gingerly on the balls of her feet. Wearing only a grimy white vest, her blonde hair darkly streaked with blood, she wiped more from her eye as it trickled down from her scalp.

Grabbing the pan, she strode over to the burns victim and clouted him about the head again and again. Making strange noises, he grabbed at her ankles but she smashed his elbow with the heavy bottom of the pan and his breathing could barely keep pace with his cries.

When she spoke, it made no sense, like the men before but different. She went into the pockets of the burnt man's jeans and rooted around, coming up with keys. As she got the front door open, the big one was almost through the hole, splintered bits of door tugging at him. A wooden panel hung across the doorway outside, but was affixed by only one corner and swung aside easily.

Clambering through after the other woman, she covered her eyes. Though grey and overcast, the light was still blinding and she blinked into the sun as if it was something new. Having expected the baked ochre bricks of some desert place, as the kaleidoscope faded from her eyes she found herself on the external deck of the first floor of a low-rise housing block in a distinctly British town. Flats up and down the way were similarly boarded up, the car park beneath them almost empty. Maybe half a mile away the tubular crown of a stadium squatted on the skyline, and nearer than that, standing at staggered intervals, three tower blocks. Giant tombstones facing the dying sun.

Something struck her hard on the back of the leg and she tumbled sideways.

The big one was coming out through the door and had hold of her.

'Run,' she screamed at the other woman. 'Don't fucking stop.'

The woman was frozen for an instant until yelled at again, then she was off in a sprint towards the stairwell at the end of the deck.

Him, she kicked out at with her heel, catching him in the side of the head and flat against his shoulder. He lost his grip on her leg and she fell back into the shadow of the balcony wall, scrambling to her feet and making off in the other direction to the woman. It was a dead end, a granite wall beyond the door to the final flat. She could hear him coming after her. The other woman was in the clear. She didn't have the legs for a chase anyway. She pulled up as he was upon her, a big hand round each bicep, thumbs digging painfully into her armpits. He slammed her against the balcony wall, back bent over the edge. She turned her face away, expecting him to hit her, but he did nothing.

Looked at her through his mask.

Studied her.

Then lifted her up and threw her over the side.

Backwards she went, feet coming up over her head, spinning out into gravity. Something hard and immovable caught her across the hip and thigh. She was looking at the sky, and then suddenly the ground, like getting punched in the face with a mountain.

The sky was back again. She remained perfectly still, assessing her options. There was a car beside her. She tried to crawl under it – it was important she not be found until she had fully gathered herself. No part of her was of a mind to obey, however. Something in her mouth, bits of hard stuff she tried to spit out, but it was like syrup in there.

Voices came and faces along with them, hovering above her.

Someone touched her shoulder, offered comfort. Their words were familiar.

They told her to stay still, don't move. Help's on its way.

She wanted to laugh. Where'd you think I'm going to go? Can't even get under this car.

Far above the faces, curls of black smoke quilled to the top of the sky, kiting on the breeze that ushered in the end of day. Tongues of fire darted into view where the boards over the windows ignited, the flat alight now along with the horrors it concealed.

Her leg hurt in a way she couldn't quite figure. It was beneath her, or beside her. Something billowed out above her, a jacket, and floated down to cover her. She realised she was shivering. People were saying it was going to be okay, saying it like a question. She thought maybe she knew them, or she wanted to.

Other voices came, more authoritative. She wanted to speak, to tell them.

Reassure them she was still alive in there, and she still knew a few things.

Tell me your name, love.

That one wasn't supposed to be difficult.

Tell me what happened.

I don't remember, she said, or probably just thought.

It's okay, love. It's okay.

They didn't get it. It wasn't okay. She didn't remember what had happened. She didn't remember anything that had happened before waking up in that room, not even her own name.

She didn't remember anything about anything.

ONE

I WAS ABIGAIL BOONE

I

The shower was a generous cubicle, plenty of room for the moulded plastic stool with adjustable legs and rubber feet. Soft water, something fitted to the supply. It had all been done specially for her coming home, an en suite in the biggest bedroom. They'd moved house, actually, but that bathroom was the first thing done. A new start. Not that she remembered the old house at all.

Boone sat and took a pumice to the white skin on her heel. She shifted her weight. Sometimes she could feel the pin at the top of the bone digging into her buttock. It had been almost a year, and she still didn't quite trust the leg.

Stepping out, she fetched a towel from the rail and turbaned her wet hair. She left the shower running. Wrapping another towel around beneath her arms, she listened at the bedroom door. From downstairs, Jack called, 'Bye.' He waited before trying again.

'Bye.'

Then the boy. 'She can't hear you, the shower's on.'

She waited until she heard the front door close behind them before turning the shower off. Rage had assembled itself silently within her, as it so often did. She crept into the hall, even alone in the house trying to hide that she favoured the hurt leg. Doctors told her it had healed just fine, outside of the discomfort caused by the screw, and there was no reason she should be limping.

Boone considered herself outside the wheelhouse of most of these quacks. Moving into the front guest room (precisely decorated in floral monochrome like a boutique hotel), she stood to the side of the window with her head between wall and curtain, peering down at the Lexus in the drive. It gleamed immaculately beside her twenty-five-year-old Saab 900SE.

The Goose.

Iridium blue, only rusting in a dozen or so places.

They'd tried to convince her to get rid, but there was no way. There was something oddly comforting about it. Maybe because it stuck out beside this beautiful home, with its polished wooden floors and sea views and luxury Japanese automobiles. Maybe because it looked as battered as she felt. It was the only thing in the world that made any sense.

Jack was behind the wheel of the Lexus already, the boy – Quin – half in, half out, his dad telling him to sort himself out. Jack had told her that they'd named him for the home village of her grandmother's people, farmers from near Ennis in County Clare before they came shilling-chasing after the war. Boone thought that was probably a yarn she'd fed him, as studying the bookshelves in what Jack called the study she had found a copy of Ann Quin's *Berg*.

Quin's door closed with a satisfying clunk as he fiddled with his backpack.

How did his packed lunch get done? She hadn't noticed if he prepared it himself or Jack did it. Did she used to do it? It felt like mum territory. She watched the car slowly back out of the drive and disappear away down the road out of sight. Left alone and in peace, the anger would disperse as quickly as it gathered.

In her own bedroom, she fetched her bridge from the glass of solution on the nightstand, rinsed it off under the tap and slid it into her mouth. She rolled her jaw, tongued around her gums until it felt right. She pushed out her top lip with the tip of her tongue, under the scar that ran along one ridge of her philtrum. Barely visible now, it was the only outward sign that her teeth had been smashed out. She rubbed in a little moisturising cream. Didn't seem to be making much difference at this point, but it had become ritual. She did the same with the scars on her leg.

Plodding downstairs in her towels, she left a trail of damp foot-prints in the duck-egg carpet. The large kitchen was housed in a rear extension. South-facing, its skylight captured the sun and radi-ated it off the white furniture. She filled the kettle and flicked it on, fetching a cafetière and a vacuum canister of ground coffee beans from a cupboard above the counter. She ground her own, keeping fresh beans sealed in the freezer until she was ready for them.

The press was enough for two cups, the first of which she took with a splash of milk. She liked it either muddy or black. Jack said the coffee was a new thing.

He also said she used to take two sugars in her tea, but she couldn't imagine it.

Sitting at the breakfast table, she flicked on the tablet Jack had bought her. There was an app that gathered news from all sorts of sources and she browsed through with glazed eyes, skimming the headlines and guessing the rest. News and politics were things she hadn't yet found the will to engage with. Best to pretend the whole thing wasn't happening and leave the making of decisions to those who turned up.

She took her time with the coffee, having the second cup black. The day, like all others, stretched out before her as a wide avenue of opportunity. She had time, means and transport. She could do anything, and so invariably did nothing. Taking her coffee upstairs, she dressed in jeans and a thin sweater. She'd inherited wardrobes of stuff from her previous life, but rarely wore anything that couldn't be folded.

Lounging in the hulking club chair Jack had spent a fortune on for the study, she read for a spell. The chair nearly filled the bay, which was north-facing and therefore bright but not too bright. She was still deciding on her tastes. Not wanting to merely inherit, she'd made Jack promise not to tell her which books were hers and which his, but let her find her own way through the library. Turned out he rarely read fiction and she wasn't for keeping up with the latest ideas in psychology, so the exercise was moot.

Finding her place, she continued with Richard Stern's *Other Men's Daughters*. It had been the only volume she'd found on the shelves with a bookmark, probably what she'd been reading at the time of her accident (as she'd come to think of it). For months she'd left it untouched, a totem to some previous existence, but the temptation to find a connection to the past had proved too great. Starting over from the beginning, none of it had been familiar.

The card bookmark bore the wild crayon designs of a child and had been laminated. A tin eyehole had been punched through it, looped with a stringy pink tassel. Despite its plastic sheath, it was creased and dog-eared with age and use. After a few chapters, she marked her place and shut it. Having two or three books on the go at once was what she had found worked, different kinds of stuff, and she switched to a detective story, *The Laughing Police-man* by Sjöwall and Wahlöö.

She was most comfortable in that room. It wasn't littered with photographs like other rooms – gleaming, grinning faces huddled together for the camera in places she couldn't remember visiting, their emulsive eyes roving, searching her out as she slid around the house like their ghost.

She'd looked up all the places they'd gone on holiday, read so much about them that she wondered after a while whether it mattered that she didn't recall going to any of them. What was the half-life of memory? The gradual decay of remembrance must at some point intersect with received knowledge such that the two were indistinguishable.

The phone rang and she ignored it. No message was left. Ten minutes later it rang again and she knew it was Jack. She grabbed keys and went out into the garden so she couldn't hear it. The yard was small, with decking sporting a small table and chairs, but beyond its fence only a road and a thin strip of beach separated it from the sea. A gate led out to the grassy verge of the coast road, where the salt surprised her every time.

They were on the outskirts of Lark, a medieval port and Victo-rian tourist resort now surviving off the dregs of both industries, and the shore there was usually deserted save for the odd jogger or dog-walker. There was a bench, which Boone considered her bench, and she sat there in the stiff breeze communing with the Channel, studying its grey undulations, France a dark finger on the horizon.

2

If there is no memory, what is time?

Boone's recollection of that day at the boarded-up flat and the things that happened there had distorted bit by bit, the way a mirror unsilvers. She remembered coming to in the hospital and feeling like she'd been there for a million years. It was her strong belief that there had been many hundreds of people talking to her over that time, all saying the same things, more or less. Repeating their words like the chanting of spells in dead languages. She couldn't clearly remember any of their faces but they'd surely been there, above her somewhere, looking down. She recalled snatches of what they said.

Distal radius.

Comminuted femoral shaft.

Zygomaticomaxillary complex fracture.

Intramedullary rod.

It had the foggy familiarity of a poem recited in childhood, the sense that she'd always known the words but couldn't fully comprehend them now. Lacked the context in which to put them to work.

At one point she swore her mother was there, and though she felt the side of the bed sink beneath her weight when she sat, she was less of a person, as Boone understood people to be, and more of a presence.

When she came around enough to make out faces and actual bodies, recognise their workings even if she didn't know their identities, she was deeply suspicious of everything they told her. Two days, the doctor told her she'd been there. Sedated at first, then under anaesthetic for the operation on her shattered femur, and a few more hours to fully come round. Sounded like bollocks. Nothing these people said could be believed until checked against verifiable quarters.

Only Boone had none. No way of getting her bearings. Nothing before that day at the flat existed. She knew the past only by its absence, and even then had no sense of its shape or volume.

She was presented with two people who apparently were glad to see her. A man leaned in for some kind of hug that he turned into an awkward clutch halfway through and, perhaps realising exactly how much of a mess she was, kissed her on the forehead. A boy hid behind him somewhere, awaiting instructions on how they were all supposed to behave.

Married with a teenage son.

It took a while to convince all parties involved that she hadn't a clue who they were. The doctors said short-term memory loss wasn't that uncommon after major trauma, so confusion was to be expected. The heavy dose of benzodiazepines found in her system wouldn't help either.

They asked her questions, establishing a baseline of what she did remember. The autobiographical stuff, she drew a big blank.

Zero recall. No clue who she was, where she came from or who anyone in her life was.

Her semantic memory was better, but still patchy. She understood the world in theory, knew what a hospital was, knew what the various uniforms people wore meant. They showed her an array of objects and pictures of objects and she identified as many as she could be expected to. Specifics were sketchier.

Some things she knew, and some things she didn't.

She knew what an astronaut was and knew mankind had been to space, but she couldn't tell them who the first man to walk on the moon was.

Some things she half knew.

They asked her about books from her home and she knew that Simenon had written the Maigret novels but couldn't remember the plots to any of them. Jack confirmed she had them all and had obsessively read them in order.

Other things she wished she didn't know.

'Who is the current prime minister?' a doctor asked.

'Oh Jesus Christ,' Boone said.

When things showed no signs of improvement after a few days, there was a lot of frowning and sharp inhalations of breath, like plumbers just before delivering the bad news. Jack and Quin, father and son, wore their concerned faces and adopted a position of wait-and-see. Only a matter of time before she remembered them, remembered herself. They were positive she was in there somewhere.

Until that time, she held court. Doctors, consultants, surgeons, psychiatrists and experts of every stripe paraded through her room thinking aloud but committing to nothing, waiting for a consensus to coagulate. Numerous scans showed concussion but no serious injury that would impair brain function, and certainly nothing that could result in total retrograde amnesia. They were settling on some kind of dissociative state, a stress reaction to physically and psychologically traumatic events.

Then there was the other option, but nobody was going to call Boone a malingerer to her face.

She was a stranger upon the earth. Less than that. A specimen, something to be studied, something to be known only from a remove. She made a point of not asking questions but acquiring information cavalierly, letting it stick to her like burrs, were she walking through fields.

Her parents were no longer around, and she had no siblings or any family at all other than Jack and Quin. She lay awake at night, eyes wide in the darkness, unable to construct her father's face, or her mother's hands. Everything was present and crowded and confused beyond any imagining.

So she embraced the procedure and routine of the place as something concrete. There were pill regimens, doctors' visits, and physio sessions, the muscles in her leg needing rebuilding before the fractured bone could take any weight.

And there were daily inquisitions by detectives from several constabularies.

Four days she had been missing.

One hundred and two hours.

Nobody could be certain how many of them she had spent in that flat. The questioning bore little fruit. Her descriptions of her captors were vague, muddied by violence and narcotics.

She thought they were dark-skinned, darker than her anyway.

She thought they were tall, taller than her anyway.

And spoke a language she didn't understand.

She wondered how many times she'd listened to witnesses tell her the big black men did it.

More troubling was why she was even there. A detective sergeant, she had been detailed to long-term missing persons, the kind of cases that had gone well beyond a constable dealing with them but had never raised the right traction or concern for a full-blown high-risk misper investigation. Usually troubled teens with a history of running, cautions for drugs or soliciting.

She had been riding solo and there was no entry in the diary on her computer for that day, though she had mentioned to a colleague that she'd received a lead regarding a particular case but didn't expect much to come of it.

Sarah Still, born 1995 and reported missing October 2010 by her grandmother Molly Still, who had raised her with her husband Rodney after Sarah's mother had abandoned the infant and fled the country. Social services had a file on Sarah, a frequent runaway, and nobody had been surprised when she eventually left and never came back.

No notebook had been found on Boone, and nowhere else had she recorded details of what the new lead might have been. There was also the awkward issue of having been found in east London when she worked for Kent Police, and nobody having any record of being notified of her travels.

Her unmarked police car was found on the first day in a residential neighbourhood four miles from the flat where she was held. The area had been searched as it was near to the last sighting of the car on CCTV. The residential area was a CCTV dead zone, and a close study of hours of footage from cameras in surrounding streets produced no leads on what had happened after that. For weeks, hundreds of officers canvassed the areas around the flat and where the car had been found, taking thousands of statements that produced no viable leads. Nobody had seen Boone with her car; nobody had seen her get into another vehicle. Nobody had seen her taken into the flat, or seen anyone else leave it. CCTV around the estate was vandalised so often, most of the cameras were eventually left out of order, hanging from their mountings like the snapped necks of dead birds.

Security cameras outside a local gym in a refitted warehouse captured two men leaving the estate on foot. Dark, grainy footage of a large man lumbering along with a smaller man clutched to his side. Officers found the video seventeen hours after Boone had been discovered. The area was cluttered with half-empty high-rises and apartment blocks, lock-ups and work yards, dozens of abandoned commercial premises, and a six-track railway trunk with a vast network of sidings. There was no further trace of the pair.

Drenched with accelerants, the flat had gone up like a summer wildfire, destroying whatever evidence there might have been. Months later, Boone had returned to the site for a walk-through with detectives. The rooms were blackened like the inside of a railway tunnel, and the outside walls were darkly streaked around the windows like the flat's mascara had run.

The dead girl found in the flat was burnt past identifying, and dental records proved fruitless. Police theorised she had been trafficked from overseas. An autopsy revealed she had died of a heroin overdose and bore signs of an ongoing habit. The other girl who had escaped was picked up by police hiding behind the wheelie

bins on the housing estate. From Bulgaria, she apparently had little English and even less enthusiasm to help the police. All things
said and done, the investigation was at a dead end.

The police Boone could handle, though. Recovering in her
bed, it was the family visits she found the hardest.

Jack and Quin came to see Abigail Boone, and she couldn't
help them with that. They flicked through photos on their phones,
told tales about family dinners or days out or just the silly jokes
that make life bearable. Their ways, so certain to them, were lost
on her. She had no commerce with that common past, was unable
to spend her own memories.

Identity can be proven with papers, but how do you prove self?

How do you measure a person, seek evidence of what they
might be? Only in the past, Boone concluded, and in that thing
constructed by the past that we call a mind.

3

When Quin came in from school, Boone put her book down and stood up. Every day when he returned she'd stop whatever she was doing – be it reading in the club chair or watching women's tennis on the satellite – and loiter in the hall or one of the wide, doorless arches connecting most of the ground-floor rooms (the study had a door, for propriety's sake). It felt presumptuous to be found doing something. They exchanged heys. He had started calling her Mum again, but endearments felt awkward in Boone's mouth. She'd wondered if she and Jack had pet names for each other but hadn't asked, afraid he might take broaching the subject as the first step towards giving them a try.

Quin was a darter, whipping in and out of rooms, foraging for snacks or filling his arms with mysterious electronic gadgets. He'd taken to settling at his father's desk in the study as soon as he got in to complete his homework, a monkish devotion to education that Boone suspected was designed to keep them in close proximity.

As he worked, she returned to her seat in the bay and continued reading, the two of them barely sharing a word until they heard

Jack's car pull up outside. The hunter home from the hill. Boone remained in her chair, picturing him from the sounds he made, the same every day – key in the lock, door shutting, keys landing in the bowl on the hallway sideboard, briefcase clonking on the parquet floor, jacket sliding off and dropping onto the chair. 'Hi,' he said, hovering in the door to the study. 'Hi,' she said.

'Hey, Dad,' said Quin.

'Christ. That was a day. Calls for a snifter.' He made a face like, want one?

She nodded and followed across the hall into the front lounge, where he stood at the oak drinks cabinet. It contained an array of bottles ranging from the mildly to the ridiculously expensive, a direct correlation between their cost and how much remained in the bottle. Only a few fingers left in the one he selected, pouring them each a healthy measure. Drinking was another thing she didn't want to be caught at during the day, so liked it when he was after one when he came in.

Jack finished his drink quickly, standing thoughtfully at the cabinet.

'Thai chicken?' he said.

'Sounds good.'

Though cooking had stayed with Boone, the recipes and technique, she had no recollection of how that had previously presented itself in her life. How often had she cooked, what had she especially enjoyed preparing, what were the meals she knew to be unspoken favourites of her husband and son? Jack seemed to enjoy having the run of the kitchen when he came home, a salve to his day's work, so it was easier to let him do it. She set three places at the dining table and then sat at the smaller kitchen table as things were chopped and sizzled, listening to him talk about his day in vaguenesses – he was very proper about his patients' privacy. 'You went out today?' he said. 'I called earlier and there was no answer,' he added quickly.

Boone was never sure if he was laying traps or saving her from them. They'd met at university, she had learned, and he'd turned his doctorate into a stint heading an NHS department and now a profitable private practice as a clinical psychologist, with some forensic consultancy on the side. Though he obviously couldn't treat her himself, she found his natural conversational manner to be probative. A few times since her return from the clinic, he had pushed her to see someone.

'I had months of cognitive therapy, Jack,' she had told him. 'Talking, drugs, hypnotism, more talking. It didn't do anything.'

'It's about more than the remembering,' he had told her. 'You should see someone about reintegrating. Someone who can help you with just getting used to the world again.'

'I live with a shrink,' she had told him. 'I need another one like I need throwing off a balcony again.'

He hadn't raised the issue since. Still had his questions, though. 'Just down to the beach,' she said, watching him squeeze a lemon into the pilaf he had prepared.

Nodding, he clapped his hands with cheffish satisfaction and reached for three large bowls from a wall cupboard.

'Call Quin?' he said, stretching.

Shouting through the house was too much of an exuberance for Boone, something you only did when you felt at home. She walked soundlessly to the study, where the boy was still working.

'Dinner,' she said.

He raised his eyebrows in approval and followed her out.

'Maths?'

He nodded. 'Simplifying rational expressions.'

Fuck me, she thought.

'Your father will be all over that,' she said.

Piping bowls of Thai chicken and rice laced with onion and shredded peppers were waiting for them on the table. Jack was fiddling with the small kitchen stereo, and they took their places and waited for him.

An odd fifties-sounding thing about dancing with Eskimos came on. From what Boone had picked up in her brief time in the house, Jack was more of a My Bloody Valentine kind of guy, his taste for shoegazing indie rock ambering during his sixth form and uni days. She felt him studying her until she was compelled to comment.

'Interesting choice,' she said.

He only nodded. She didn't know which little things were of importance, so they all became important. Which is how paranoia starts.

He'd left a bottle of red to breathe and poured them half-glasses. The wine was always good, she'd give him that. They tucked in. The dish was a favourite of all of them and they'd had it a lot since Boone came home. She suspected Jack hoped it was imbued with magical properties, that if they ate it enough it would somehow draw out the old Abby in place of this invader. It was a lot of stock to put into food.

'You walk far?' he said.

Boone shook her head. 'Just to the bench, really.'

'Felt a bit nippy today.'

She shrugged. She was trying to sip her wine when he did, so she didn't finish before him. Often, she felt like she was on best behaviour before visiting dignitaries from a foreign land. Observe all the protocols. Absurd, she knew, but nonetheless.

'There are some good walks on the Downs,' Jack said. 'I don't think I have much on in the morning. It's only a short drive.'

'I told Tess I'd drop round,' Boone said. It was true, but she immediately felt guilty.

'Sure. We can do it any time.' He turned to their son. 'Homework all done?'

Quin nodded, taking a big mouthful of rice. It was hot and he tried to hide the fact.

'Rational expressions,' Boone said.

Jack considered that quietly for a moment.

'Useful for engineering,' he said eventually. 'Or aerodynamics, because you can—'

'Just need to pass the exam,' Quin said.

'Right. Any other news to report?' Quin shook his head.

'Good then,' said Jack. 'Great.'

They finished the meal without further comment, which was becoming the norm. Boone knew it was hard for Jack, as if he was dealing with two teenagers. In hospital, she had dreaded the family visits, the relentless cheeriness and bravura optimism.

Don't worry.

It'll all come back.

Things will return to normal before you know it.

The picture they painted of normality was no less strange than the alien world in which she had found herself. That chipper early attitude, as if at any moment the old Abby would return, had gradually given way to resignation and strained smiles. Forced conversation over the dinner table. Silences.

Jack could deal with it, he was an adult. With Quin, it was different. What was she supposed to think of him? He was her son. He had grown inside her. That much, the fact of her motherhood, was indisputable. The reality of being a mum was something else. Where emotion should be, there was biology. She knew he had gestated, but what of his nurturing? Initially the boy had been cautious, slinking about behind his father in the hospital, wary of this stranger who looked like his mother. Boone had been almost nine months in a clinic after that, and returning home had taken some adjustment. But Quin was making the effort and she knew she wasn't meeting him halfway.

It was as if she denied having feelings of any kind about Jack or Quin, not even curiosity. Her life felt like her own and nobody else's, something to be stowed out of sight and protected from the meddling of others.

Those were big issues, though, so big she didn't know where to start dealing with them. She didn't even have a handle on the little stuff yet. What time dinner was each evening; how long people spent in the bathroom, and when; how fresh towels were folded; what cupboards things went in; whether apples were kept in the fridge or the fruit bowl.

Life was habits and systems, and Boone had to learn them all anew.

4

After dinner, Quin disappeared upstairs and Jack put the telly on. Evenings were tricky. So much of conversation is made up of what we've said before, either to the same person or to others, massaged and whittled down to its smoothest form. Boone had nothing laid in, no cache of old favourites to fall back on, and she didn't recognise the routines of others. Stories once guaranteed to bring a smile to her face now elicited looks of bewilderment. The telly offered them both sanctuary. In those first days she was home, Jack would offer her the remote or flick over to what he called 'your programmes'. They made an awful discovery one night when Boone wanted to watch the Liverpool match. Jack got excited, telling her that her father had taken her to games as a little girl, in the paddock after the seats went in. Awful, because he took it as a sign that she was remembering, but in truth Barb had told her she was a Red. Even Boone knew the last thing you abandoned was your team.

Jack had the news on.

'We could flick through the movie channels,' he suggested.

'Think I'm going to lie down,' Boone said.

'Okay. See you in the morning.'

'Yeah. See you.'

Leaving Jack basking in a bluish glow, Boone went upstairs with the rest of the bottle of red. She had her own room, had laid the foundations for that on one of Jack's visits to the clinic. She'd told him she'd need to ease into things. As far as she was concerned, she'd never shared a bed with anyone. Jack wasn't bad-looking, but she couldn't remember why she was attracted to him and didn't feel anything now, didn't even know what those feelings would feel like. Nothing chemical was occurring.

The room was large, spanning the rear of the house. Even with the new en suite, there was plenty of space for a sofa and a table and chair, as well as bedroom furniture. A colossal wardrobe stood in the alcove made by the bathroom. It was hung with garments from her old life, skirts and trouser suits and dresses, the kind of clothes she didn't know to where she would ever have worn them.

An iPod sat in its dock on the low chest of drawers, a gift from Quin when Jack got him an upgrade. Since she had returned home, he had delved into what he thought was the music she would have listened to around his age, and had stuffed the player with albums from the nineties. *Endtroducing, Slanted and Enchanted, Siamese Dream, 36 Chambers, Dummy, Bee Thousand, OK Computer, If You're Feeling Sinister*, et cetera. Boone had no way of knowing if she'd actually listened to any of this stuff when she was younger, but, illusory or not, it offered a kernel of comfort.

She undressed and showered. Wrapped in a towel, she sat on the bed and dried her hair listening to *Loveless*. Into the corner of two windowless walls she had pushed a table. Across its surface, and pinned to the walls above, were fugitive pieces from her previous life – photographs, police notebooks and files, maps, printouts from social media (Quin's mostly – Boone apparently had been a digital hermit), paperwork from school, university and work. There were newspaper clippings from the handful of times she had made it into ink. Local press mostly, a few national clippings illustrating the meagre coverage the Sarah Still disappearance had received. If she had ever been a keeper of diaries, they hadn't survived.

It seemed to Boone that everything in her life had happened to someone else. She had married and she had borne a child but remembered doing neither, and it seemed the only major event remaining was death. It may have already begun.

She had questioned Jack about her life, taken copious notes from his answers in the hope that sense might be made of her existence. Her enterprise lay in neat piles, handwritten sheets of A4 covered with events and details, written and rewritten in some attempt to percolate experience out of data, each word only further degrading its likeness to reality. The map is not the territory. A copy of a copy of a bootleg next to being at the concert itself, it lacked the smell of sweat and stale beer. It was pitiful what a life could be reduced to on paper. It lay open before her less like a book than a box of rusty needles.

An only child, Boone's parents separated soon after her birth, her mother moving to Canada never to be seen again. When she was nine, her father was killed in a car crash and her paternal uncle took her in. They were from the Wirral, but he'd moved for university and had an accountancy firm in Canterbury, so Boone was transplanted south.

By the time her uncle died, the summer after her first year at uni, any trace of an accent had been scrubbed. She met Jack at university in London and they were married before they graduated, already pregnant with Quin when she collected her certificate at the Barbican. Four years, later she joined the police force. Probation, plod, detective, Serious Crime Directorate, detective sergeant, and finally mispers. Mostly girls, mostly vulnerable, mostly presumed dead. Examining old evidence, tracking cold leads. It was work she apparently had an appetite for and was good at.

These were the facts of the life of Abigail Boone, née Kelly. She existed as a being in the world and these were the things she did, reduced now to the model of a person's life in the mind of the person inhabiting her body. She had gone over it so many times it was getting so she could easily be convinced her life had been made up. Truth is the first victim of narrative.

The past was inert, a still thing. She picked over it like a crow, like a scavenger on an ancient battlefield hoping to find some good teeth to pull from the mouths of corpses. Yet this scavenged past was all she had. Her present, like the future, was an impenetrable murk in which she blindly stumbled around. One thread of everything she'd pulled together still resonated with her, still tied her to her past – the fate of Sarah Still. Boone had never met the girl; she had always existed as an idea, as a name on a piece of paper or on the lips of other people. She couldn't honestly say whether she now genuinely cared for her, as maybe she once had, but what she knew for certain was whatever had happened to Sarah Still was inextricably linked to what had happened to Abigail Boone. Almost by accident at first, an unforeseen consequence of trying to map her old life, Boone had started to haphazardly assemble what information she had into a review of the Sarah Still case. The few sightings there had been of her were marked on a map of the south east. The only promising lead had been three years after she went missing, an old school chum spotting her in a nightclub in east London. Not a million miles from the flat where Boone found herself two years later. She didn't know if there was a connection, because what was missing from all this information was any clue as to what had led Boone back to London.

Her focus had by now zeroed in on this one aspect of Abigail Boone's life, the link with Sarah Still. A link that felt crucial to her, albeit in ways she couldn't clearly articulate. It wasn't that her life had become merely unbalanced, some slippage in its calibration. It was unrecognisable, a world where nothing was familiar, not even her own face. If there was anything that would spare her forever living in that murk, that would gift her peace in her own skin, she was convinced it hid somewhere on those walls among the recapitulated pieces of her life.

Not long later, she heard footsteps on the carpet in the hall, saw the shadows of feet in the light beneath the door as someone hovered out there. Clutching the foot of her crossed leg in the towel where she had been drying it, Boone remained perfectly still, her breathing shallow and silent. At the same time, she willed herself to invite them in, whoever it was, to say goodnight like you should with family. But she didn't, and the feet padded away down the hall.

Boone dried off and pulled on a robe. Opening the French doors, she sat out on the balcony with the bottle of red, feeling the breeze off the water. Alone now, the drink steered her to melancholy. How much of what she had forgotten were essential pieces of her? She couldn't recall a single face from before that day at the flat, but she knew she had thin ankles and she knew that was a good thing. Were the things she remembered too small to make a difference, or were the things she had forgotten too large to?

In the clinic, after the hospital, a therapist had asked her about her faith, as they arranged various visiting clergy and there were meetings run by patients. Boone had no idea what she was talking about. The word itself she understood in the broader sense but she had forgotten, literally, Him. For a while she read all she could on the matter, and when she lay in bed unable to sleep, the night thrummed with the engine of godly works.

Sometimes, on the balcony with a glass in her hand, she fancied she could hear it still.

5

Then there was Tess.

Boone had been considered at risk when they brought her into the hospital. Uniforms swarmed the wards and two AFOs were stood outside her door twenty-four hours a day. The first person she spoke to when she properly regained consciousness was Barb, who told her she was fucking disgusted Boone couldn't remember her. She'd been in the room when Boone woke up enough to talk, said she was on security detail. She'd been reading to her, thought the sound of something familiar would help when she came to.

'Helen Foster, 42, Thomas Vaughan, 67, Tony Sepple, 29, of Snodland, Sittingbourne, Sheerness, all suicides: the nerves, leukaemia, bedroom tax. Four thirty in the a.m., an as yet to be identified gentleman of east Asian descent was accosted by two men in Gillingham. One broke his left leg, the other his right.'

She'd collated daily police reports for Boone during the time she'd been away. Sweetheart, Barb. She offered herself as a friend, which is a difficult thing to accept at face value when you don't know your own mind. As the official daily visits from Met detectives slowed to a trickle and the appearances of concerned Kent Police colleagues dried up, Barb kept coming. The only one who didn't treat Boone like an alien life form who'd crashed into the middle of an investigation. They'd talk about things of no consequence, and she'd listen to whatever Boone had to say. She didn't expect anything from her.

'Detective Constable Barbara Bowen,' she said, every time she came in the room. 'Just in case you forgot again, dozy cow.'

Barb made regular deliveries of various magazines and books. They were trying to locate Boone's misplaced tastes, so *Hello!* lay next to *New Scientist*, Barb's *Fifty Shades* beside the Elizabeth Taylor and Henry Green she'd found at Boone's house: 'Maybe you like completely different stuff now . . .'

One day she also brought with her a letter that had been handed in at Gillingham nick. It had been opened and read, she told Boone, a precaution against threats or abuse. People hear a police officer has been hospitalised and are thoughtful enough to offer unsolicited advice, or touching romantic overtures. This was different.

It was from a young woman, someone Boone had come into contact with through a case some years ago. Someone she'd clearly had an effect on. The letter was personal and sincere, and Boone instinctively valued the woman's concern. It was signed Tess Boxall and, after some cajoling, Barb brought in a copy of the file and collected Boone's old notebooks from home.

It amounted to this: eight years earlier, Boone had arrested one Michael Boxall, a known face who went by Mickey Box, for a punch-up in a pub in Canterbury that had left a lad deaf in one ear and prone to seizures. There was history between the two men and CCTV showed Boxall striking the victim as he lay defence-less on the ground, so he went down for GBH with intent, six years. A couple of years later, she received a request from Mickey Box to visit him at Elmley. His daughter had got herself caught up with a guy and he was worried for her. She'd missed a visit and he couldn't reach her, and nobody he had called had seen her. Boxall was a thug and the daughter, who had a history of disappearing through her teenage years, was more or less an adult, and Boone had no idea why she had agreed to help. Perhaps the oddness of him reaching out to the woman who had put him away.

'Uniform doesn't seem to have turned you into a complete knob yet,' was how Mickey Box put it.

Turned out the guy, Clifford Ingram, had taken Tess to Bruges. Nice romantic week away with two other young women in a cara-van near a truck stop, where he plied them with benzos and sold them to drivers. Boone eventually found the girl in a bedsit in Folkestone, barely coherent, along with the heroin Ingram had bought and dozens of boxes of paracetamol in bags from different pharmacies and supermarkets.

Faced with the full gamut of charges, including people-trafficking, false imprisonment, rape, and intent to distribute, Ingram pleaded guilty to a host of others and still only got a dozen years. Not in the files, but in scratchy cursive in her notebook, was how Boone helped Tess afterwards, with finding a survivors' group and with securing a place on a care assistant course.

Tess was someone Boone had liked. So she wrote to her, giving her the number of a phone Jack had got her, and Tess texted and visited a few times. Boone was kept in a private room as a precaution, but it quickly got to the point where her physical recovery could be done anywhere, and the hospital wasn't staffed for her particular psychological needs. It was agreed she should go to a specialist clinic, far away from what she was told was home. During the months she was there, she and Tess messaged each other every day, spoke on the phone every few days. Boone felt unguarded talking to her. She shared her fears about the stunted recovery of her mind and, paradoxically, her trepidations about what it would mean should any of her memories begin to return. Things she couldn't confess to Jack or Quin without them sounding like a betrayal. On her return from the clinic, she visited Tess at her caravan every week.

In a field of snakes, she beat a path.

6

The caravan sat alone in a field on a wet headland jutting into the Medway, an hour's drive from Lark on the Channel coast. Boone tooted as she pulled up in the Goose. Tess was inveterately crap at feeding herself, so Boone had stopped off for supplies and now hauled the shopping bags off the back seat and up onto the decking built round the caravan.

'Tess?'

She rapped on the sliding glass door and pulled it aside, lurching in under the weight of the bags and swinging them up onto the kitchen counter. Half the caravan was an open living space with a kitchen and breakfast bar along one side and the rest given over to a huge battered couch and armchair sitting by a telly. Outlaw utility pipes siphoned water and leccy from Tess's father's nearby cottage.

'Tess, it's me. With the bounty of my travels.'

She started packing the cold stuff into the fridge, including an array of chocolate bars and cans of pop that Tess considered essential sustenance.

'Tess?'

The place was a tip. Dishes filled the sink, bottles and food containers lining the counters and coffee table. Boone moved into the thin hall leading to two small bedrooms and the bathroom. In Tess's room drawers were half closed, a wardrobe door open. Clothes breadcrumbed a path from door to bed – socks pulled inside out, twisted knickers, lime cords, a thin sweater – where Tess had discarded them thoughtlessly behind her.

Her mobile was on the bedside cabinet, battery gone. Boone plugged it in. She went round picking up clothes, pulling socks through, folding them neatly on the bed. The laundry hamper held more stuff than the wardrobe.

'Jesus, Tess.'

She turned the phone on and her own three messages about her impending arrival sat there unread. It was a scorcher, so she unzipped her hoodie and left it on the back of the sofa. Stuffing a can of drink and some chocolate into a bag, leaving the rest of the caravan as she found it, she cut across the marshes behind the cara-van to the path running along the shore of a Medway creek. In the next field lived a lone sheep who harboured a deep interest in eve-ryone else's business, monitoring their comings and goings with Calvinist scrupulousness. Its long face was narrow-eyed and pious and it bleated as Boone passed.

The cottage was a quarter mile further up the headland. It had stopped being a working farm long before Mickey Box bought the plot, bringing Tess there from coal country after her mother passed. Well hidden from the public road, it stood at the end of a winding drive lined with a selection of mature trees. His Mercedes was parked outside, but the back door to the cottage was locked and there was no answer to Boone's knocks. Nobody ever used the front door.

Beyond the cottage, a few hundred yards to the east where the land fell into the estuary, piles of stripped and rusting cars hove into view like grounded ships. The scrapyard was one of Mickey Box's more legitimate endeavours. Heaps lined the dirt track leading to it, wingless junks baking in the heat, burning to the touch. The ground glimmered in the sun with tin twists and cusps of broken bulbs half buried in the weeds. Stacks of dead cars piled four or five high loomed over thin corridors where grass and weeds only grew in window- or door-shaped patches of shadowless relief on the ground.

To one side a clump of thin birches stood on uneven earth that had been pushed aside when space for the yard was cleared. They sprouted in a thatch at cross-angles. Beneath their sparse canopy had been built a two-room hut of corrugated iron, serving as office and tool shed.

'Mick?' Boone said, standing out front.

From the shadows inside the hut emerged a face like the back of a well-used shovel, rusted slits for eyes. Fifties, but body still hard and wiry, hands like cast iron. Boone thought of Mickey Box as a battle, one petering out, its ending inevitable. Valiant defeat the best that could be hoped for.

'Sarge,' Mickey Box said, tipping an imaginary hat.

'Caravan's open but nobody's home.'

'Out by the water,' he said, looking off in that direction.

'She okay?'

'Bit of a week. She's being a bigger bastard than usual.'

'Good that she can rely on such understanding and support.'

'Thought maybe you could have a word.'

'Yeah?'

'Seeing as you both – you know.'

'Have a vagina?'

'Are a bit fucking loopy, I was going to say.'

Fitz, Mickey Box's shadow, was suddenly there, an exhibit of studied indifference, leaning against what had once been an automobile. She and Fitz weren't big buddies. Boone was an interloper, a strange addition to an established dynamic, and he wasn't sure about her. He had an annoying habit of eating sunflower seeds from a bag in his pocket, tossing the empty shells down wherever he was. He was a few years older than Boone, forty probably, not unattractive but the charm of youth behind him. He always looked to her like something was almost amusing him, which was to say he always looked punchable.

'There's a boy,' Boone said.

'Thought so,' said Mickey Box. 'Who?'

Boone shrugged her chin. 'Dunno. She hasn't said. I got the feeling, though. Texts, going out at odd times.'

'Which is funny,' he said. 'Usually she gushes about that sort of thing. She's always told me about the fellas. Started off as some form of torture, I suspect, but she was always open about it.' He turned to Fitz.

'I don't notice that shit,' Fitz said.

'Feels an avuncular kind of loyalty,' Mickey Box said. 'Pretends he doesn't know what his eyes see when it comes to Tess.'

'She's on the path?' Boone said.

Mickey Box nodded.

Boone moved warily between the great rows of wrecks, out to

the shore path. Before the war there had been a boatyard nearby, hundreds of men assembling barges. Their hulks still littered the shore, skeletal remains all but sunken in the muddy flats.

She spotted Tess out at the tip of the headland, standing with her arms crossed. She was wearing a full-length dress under a cardigan, even in the heat, and the breeze off the Medway drove its skirt onto her like a marble statue. She was partially sheltered by a small copse that grew out there like a challenge to the waters, though not enough that the wind didn't hide Boone's approach from her.

'Hey, kid,' Boone said.

'Hey, old man,' said Tess, eyes on the sea.

'Thought you could do with a bite.'

Boone dropped down onto the trunk of a fallen tree, surface worn smooth by time and the elements. Wind whipped her hair about her face. Tess sat beside her and took the Milky Bar and can of Dr Pepper she offered.

Tess was sleek, feline. She had a mole like a daub of chocolate at the corner of her mouth, and eyebrows fair to the point of being invisible, often giving the impression something was wrong with her. People would frown as they searched her face for the problem.

'You got something too?'

Boone took out a Kit Kat. Tearing the end, she pulled back the wrapper and bit straight across three fingers.

'Barbarian,' said Tess.

The can of pop opened with a hiss and she sipped quietly before heeling it in the soft earth at her feet.

'How are you, kid?'

A tear ran down Tess's cheek. She made no noise, no attempt to wipe it away.

'Fine,' she said.

'Yeah, looks it. I stopped by the caravan. Keeping the place shipshape, I see.'

'Fuck off,' Tess said softly.

'Keeping an even keel?'

Tess met her eyes. 'You can count the pills back at the caravan if you want.'

'I don't want.'

They went quiet, watching the tinfoil glint off the Medway until the sun began to dip. Boone straightened her leg, working away at the thigh muscles with her thumb. All this rambling about looking for Tess, sitting on hard wood, it was reminding her she was old and had been broken into pieces not so long ago and shouldn't treat her body like she was eighteen. Mousing away at the chocolate, Tess watched her furtively.

'I'm cold,' she said. 'Home?'

She helped Boone up and they made their way back in silence, Tess walking pigeon-toed in heeled sandals. Practising this since she read somewhere it made your legs look thinner. Reaching the cottage, they saw Mickey Box approaching from the opposite direction. He had a gun bag with his .177 in one hand, the other holding the rear legs of two dead rabbits, which he held up by way of waving to them.

'You cooking?' Tess said hopefully.

'Aye. Enough for all.'

The kitchen was the heart of the cottage. A large oak table took pride of place, its drawers hung with darkly burnished handles, its scarred top ringed with black halos from cups and glasses. During the day it was usually where you'd find anyone home, the lounge at the front of the house strictly a room for evenings or company.

They removed their boots, socked feet silent on the stone floors. Mickey Box was precious about shoes in his home. Boone and Tess sat at the table as he skinned, gutted and deboned the animals, putting the meat from one in the freezer.

Fitz joined them and Mickey Box decided there were too many people in his kitchen and shooed them out into the living room. Although – 'Not you, Boone,' he said.

Boone shrugged and sat back down. Tess dallied in the doorway waiting for an elaboration. When none came, she sloped off to join Fitz in the lounge, closing the door behind her.

A knife rat-a-tatted on the wooden chopping board as Mickey Box diced up the veg, sliding them into a pot with the rabbit.

'Couple, three hours, that,' he said, sitting across the table from Boone.

'She didn't say much,' Boone said. 'Could be the drugs, but she says she's keeping up with them, and I believe her.'

'I have half an idea what it is.'

He rooted about in the drawer his side of the table and produced a typed letter, slid it across the table. Dated several months earlier and addressed to Tess, it was from Victim Liaison, asking her for a personal statement to submit to a parole review.

'Ingram?' Boone said incredulously.

Mickey Box shrugged. 'Hoped you could tell me.' He counted years off on his fingers. 'Where are we? Beak who sent him down said he had to serve six before they'd even think about it.'

'She gave you that?'

'God, no. Found it in the caravan. She never said a word, and

I've not seen anything else. Don't they have to let you know, someone gets released who did things like that? Excuse me, remember that time you were abducted, well the piece of shit what did it has paid his debt to society.'

Boone examined the letter again.

'I'll look into it,' she said.

Mickey Box had recorded the previous night's match and they watched it while the stew bubbled away. Neither Jack nor Quin were football guys, and watching games at home Boone felt like she was inflicting something upon them. She didn't remember being a fan before her accident, and being one since was a choice she deliberately didn't scrutinise. She was aware there were other aspects of her past life she could choose to embrace more thoroughly but didn't. So they hooted and sucked breath and generally reacted to the delayed action as if they might still psychically affect its outcome in the way deep down all fans believe is possible, and when it was over they made their way to the kitchen table. Tess laid covers consisting of simple place mats and a spoon each, and Mickey Box ladled the broth into big steaming bowls. Mickey Box's coney stew was one of those things, first time you had it you realised you'd been missing it all your life. They ate in silence, like it was feast or famine, slurps and wet chins. Last to finish, Tess wiped her bowl squeaky clean with little bits of bread as the others watched, then belched when she was done.

'Tess,' Mickey Box said.

'Seal of approval,' she said.

He shook his head. 'Wolfs them down fast enough, but should have seen her face when I took her hunting the first time. Wouldn't even shoot at bottles after she'd seen me plug a bunny.'

'I like black pud too,' Tess said. 'Doesn't mean I need to know how it gets to my plate.'

'Boone here knows her rifles,' Mickey Box said, 'and she don't hunt.'

The first time Boone shot a gun after her accident, Mickey Box had taken her out to a shady yew grove in a field between the cottage and the scrapyard, gun case under one arm.

'When you were with *them*, you did your guns?' he'd asked.

Them was Mickey Box for the police.

He had strung empty bottles from the branches of a tree to see what she was made of. The gun case held a Browning pistol-grip .22 rifle, which he'd quickly fitted together, clunking in a magazine. Boone had accepted the rifle awkwardly, holding it out before her like someone else's baby.

'Get your eye in, few shots at the trunk. Then see how many bottles you can take out.'

The face on him when she skipped the rehearsal and took them out quickly and methodically, *kish kish kish*. Not a single miss.

'What?' she'd said.

'What? What, she says. Looks at the gun like she's never seen the likes. Some alien technology. Harquebuses to the Aztecs.'

Boone had shrugged.

'I can shoot.'

Secretly, it had excited her. She had known she could shoot, or rather she had known that in a previous life she had been qualified. Actually doing it, it felt like new information. Something thrilling.

'Boone is a badass commando,' Tess said, clearing the table. 'I don't want to shoot.'

'Course you do,' Mickey Box said as he served coffee and Italian biscuits. 'All sorts of reasons to know how to shoot a thing. Impending caliphate, post-Brexit apocalypse, and God knows how long we can rely on the Boche reining in their baser instincts.'

Tess looked helplessly at Boone, who shrugged.

'Might be useful to know how to shoot Fitzy one day,' Boone said.

7

Driving the Goose, Boone took the M20 and the coast road home as they were well lit and she was sleepy after the meal.

Jack was in the front hall when she came in.

'Hi,' he said. 'You're back.'

'I'm back.'

She shrugged off her jacket and hung it on the rack.

'Have you eaten? We had prawn and mango curry. There was enough for all of us, loads left over. Not sure how it'll reheat, but . . .'

'I ate. Thanks.'

'I texted to see what time you'd be back.'

'Shit, I meant to put it on vibrate,' Boone said, checking her phone. Her go-to excuse.

'Amazes me,' Jack said, 'people who have phones but keep them on silent the whole time.'

'I have it so I can make calls, not so people can call me.' Boone shrugged. 'And to google stuff surreptitiously so I can appear smarter than I am.'

'I didn't realise you'd be so late.'

'I told you I was going to see Tess.'

'Yeah. It's just . . . it's almost ten o'clock.'

'Jesus, Jack.'

He raised his palms. 'Hey, you're absolutely free to do whatever you want. I'm saying I don't think it's unreasonable for us to know if you're going to be out until all hours.'

'Maybe this is why I stayed out.'

'*This?*'

'This. Crowding me at the door like the family Lab, only with ulterior motives.'

'Ulterior – seriously?' He went sotto voce, as he always did when mad. 'I sit down to eat with our fourteen-year-old son and what do I tell him? Oh, you know how Mum hides away from us most of the time and barely talks at mealtimes? Well, she's off to see her other family. She's probably there, hiding away in quiet rooms and not talking to them either.'

'Fuck this,' Boone said, brushing past him and gimping up the stairs at pace.

The pile of her bedroom carpet was too deep for the door to slam but she gave it a vigorous closing. Her hands were clammy and her heart thumped, and in the black window she could see the vein in her neck pulsing. Taking deep breaths and feeling a bit of a twat, she closed her eyes. She knew exactly what Jack had meant, and his upset was understandable.

Boone had not found love for them yet, this husband and son. Inside her was a yawning space where love should be, a dark aperture through which she felt only hard, knotty guilt. Love you shared, but guilt you hoarded alone, like precious gems. Guilt you treated in your own special way.

A quick rapping on the door brought her round, and Jack looked in without waiting for a response. He slipped in through the door and pushed it closed behind him. Boone couldn't remember him having been in her room before.

'A minute ago, when I was being an idiot,' she said, looking at his reflection in the mirror. 'I'm not doing too well with this, you see.'

She turned, without looking directly at him, and sat gingerly on the end of her bed. Jack sat down beside her, not too close.

'I didn't mean to get on you,' he said. 'I don't enjoy being a nagger, but you have to see it from our point of view. When you're gone that long . . . We lost you before. You went out and didn't come back and you were gone for four days. And when they found you, you were . . .'

'A mess?'

'Hurt. Really badly hurt. And I really can't do that again.'

'I know. You're right, and I knew you were right when you were saying it. Among every other thing, probably I forgot how to apologise properly.'

'That's not a new development,' he said, faintest trace of a smile. Noticing the corner, with the photos and the documents and the copious notes, he stood up for a closer look.

'I didn't realise,' he said.

'Trying to make sense of stuff,' Boone said.

'And?'

She shook her head.

'Did I tell you about your holidays in France, with your dad?'

'Look, Jack, I've been over this stuff a million times and—'

'No, I know. This is a short thing, though.'

Jack remained looking at the wall, occasionally glancing back at her. 'He loved France. As soon as you were out of nappies, he took you there every year until his . . . until the accident. There are probably pictures here somewhere.'

Boone had seen them. Her grinning face covered in ice cream in a valley-side restaurant, Rocamadour clinging to the cliffs behind her.

'Your dad liked to drive. Which is crazy, as it has to be the best part of a thousand miles from Liverpool. You used to say he liked to pack the kitchen sink though, just in case. He'd take his time. Drive down, spend the night in a B and B. Get a morning ferry, but only go as far as Paris, spending the night. Maybe stop again, like mini holidays along the way. Then you'd have two weeks in a gîte.

'The whole way, you'd be in the back, munching crisps and playing computer games. Those little cheap hand-held ones, kind that only had the one game? Your dad, he had these tapes, like the collections you used to see advertised on the telly. Hits of the fifties or sixties on ten cassettes. That's where your perverse preference for Jan and Dean over the Beach Boys comes from. You used to joke that some of those old tunes left deep psychological scars. "Tell Laura I Love Her" can fuck up an eight-year-old. Pulling his body from the twisted wreck, with his dying breath, what have you. It must have been the Ricky Valance version. But the real treasure was "Never Do a Tango With an Eskimo". Those long drives, you'd get travel sick sometimes, and years later just hearing the opening chords of that one would make you queasy.'

Boone nodded. 'So that was a test, at dinner yesterday?'

'Not a test, exactly. I wanted to see . . . Your body seems to remember things your mind doesn't. Procedural stuff. Muscle memory. I wondered if it might have taken in stuff like that too. Like how a song can remind you of a place sometimes.'

'It would have been a good thing, me throwing up?'

'It would have been something.'

'I'm not a fucking lab rat, Jack. I'm not here for your field tests.'

He raised his hands in truce.

'I know. I'm sorry. I handled that all wrong. My thinking was, if it stirred something in you without you knowing beforehand what it meant, then . . . I don't know.'

'Then the old Abby would come back.'

'You *are* the old Abby. Don't you see that? This isn't Jekyll and Hyde.'

'Isn't it? All that time at the clinic, talking to doctors, cognitive therapy, the drugs. The focus was recovery. Recover from my injuries, but also trying to recover something I'd lost. Some*one* I'd lost. Now I'm not so sure that any of what was is ever going to come back.'

'And yet there's all this,' Jack said, gesturing to the wall. 'It seems all this time you've been trying to do what I was doing with the song.'

Bending at the waist, he leaned in close to a picture tacked to the wall. A girl with dark hair and eyes darker still.

'Is this her? The missing girl?'

'Sarah Still, yeah. Well, it's how she looked a long time ago, anyway.'

'And you think she's still alive?'

Boone shrugged. 'I must have thought so a year ago. She's been missing six years now. Everyone thought she was dead years ago, then a girl she went to school with saw her in London. That was three years ago, the last solid sighting. The only sighting, until whatever sent me to London last year.'

'You've collated a lot of information.'

'Everything there was. Everything I could get from Barb, anyway.'

'You cared about this girl. About Sarah Still.'

'I guess.'

'And you still care now.'

Boone stared at the case file plastered all over the wall.

'Something the old Abby and I have in common.'

'Can you speak to Barb? Who have they got looking at these cases now?'

'Nobody, probably. I was working it between other things apparently.'

Jack raised his eyebrows.

'You think I should look for her?' Boone said.

He waved at the wall. 'Aren't you already?'

She stood up, looking at all the data. A makeshift investigation board.

'You're right. I could do this.'

'Let's take things one at a time,' Jack said. 'Treat it like an exercise. Almost certainly this case was the reason you went missing. You're not doing anything that's going to put you at risk again.'

The act of vocalising it, of talking to someone about it; for the first time she could remember, Boone was excited. The constant guilt she felt wasn't just for the distance between her and her family, but was also the guilt of inaction as her life drifted along on rails she had not laid. Though she resisted the past and feared the restoring of her memory like a rupture the other side of which she wouldn't emerge, she had also been expecting some other point or purpose from her former life to make itself clear to her. Now she suddenly felt on the brink of rediscovering something vital, a moment of limitless destiny.

'No, but you said it yourself, Jack. This is a live link to the past. I've been holed up in this room reading all this stuff and it's got me nowhere. I need to look out there, out in the world. She's out there somewhere.'

'So are the people who hurt you.'

'Yes,' Boone said. 'They are.'

8

Boone awoke in a sweat, the pillow damp and her hair painted to her head, pulse racing like a bird's heart. She showered and washed the sheets, sitting down in the kitchen with a coffee. She had a second and then washed the mug in the sink, procrastinating rather than calling Barb.

Since her accident, she hadn't been the greatest at keeping in touch with people from before. Tess and Mickey Box didn't feel like part of her old life; all they knew was the new Boone and had no expectations of the old Abby. Jack had arranged a few dinner parties with friends soon after she returned home, but she found it weird. All couples, Jack had called them 'mutual' friends even though they had mostly been met through his work. They had private jokes with her she didn't get, knew more about her than she did. She could never shake the feeling they were watching her, making a note of things they could discuss among themselves later.

Barb hadn't been invited to any of these soirées. From what Boone could tell, Barb had been perhaps her only close friend before her accident. Certainly the only close one she knew exclusively on her own terms. There were a few people from university, but it became apparent she had spoken to them only sporadically in the years since graduation, and when they visited after the accident she felt no connection with them.

Though Barb had visited regularly in the hospital, Boone hadn't seen her since she'd come back from the clinic. Barb had found Boone's relationship with Tess and Mickey Box strange. A betrayal of sorts, given their shared police history and Mickey Box's criminal lifestyle. Walking away from what she didn't remember to accept counsel from wolves. On this matter, Boone was conflicted. Barb was important to her, but she felt no loyalty to the police. Sometimes it felt as if she existed in a twilight of ideas, where she was no longer beholden to broad notions such as law and justice.

Dialling, she wasn't sure how she'd be received.

'Bowen.'

'Barb, hey. It's Boone.' There followed a pause, begging to be filled. 'Uh, Abby. Abigail. Former Detective Serg—'

'I remember who you are, Boone. That was your particular problem, as I recall.'

'Right. I thought with the name thing. Some people still call me Abby even though—'

'I got your email about it.'

Boone had emailed people to let them know she was going just by Boone, rather than Abigail. For reasons she could never explain, she felt more comfortable with her husband's family name than any of her own.

'How's life?' Barb said. 'Settled in?'

'Yeah. You know. Quiet. One day at a time.'

'Good.'

'Is this a good time?' Boone said.

'For what?'

'Just a quick word.'

'Sure.'

'I can call back if you're tied up. This evening or something, if it's better.'

'Boone.'

'Wondered about getting a spot of lunch.'

'Sure. Today?'

'I . . . uh. I hadn't really . . .'

'Thought that far ahead? Today works for me. I'm out now, but there's a thing later in Gillingham. Not exactly your neck of the woods, I know.'

'No, it's fine.'

'Noonish?'

'Yeah. Definitely.'

'I'll text you a place.'

Three hours later, Boone was sat in a high-street caff in Gillingham across from Barb, who ordered a plate of chips, as eventually did Boone when a cursory examination of the menu revealed it was the dish least likely to kill her. The plastic furniture was moulded to accommodate no human Boone had ever seen, and the lights gleamed too brightly off the white tiled walls. It felt like an abattoir.

'Knew it. Absolutely fucking knew it. How about lunch, Barb? Are you free this week, Barb? How are you doing, Barb? How's work? Congrats on making detective sergeant. How about your love life? How about a fucking favour, Barb, first time in months I see you?'

Boone ate a chip, letting her get it out of her system.

'Could have bypassed this part,' Barb said. 'Just asked me on the phone. I don't mind missing the dinner and dance if I'm not getting a reach-around at the end of the night anyway.'

'And miss the delight of your company?' Boone said. 'Seriously, though. How are you doing, Barb? How's work?'

'Sod off.'

Boone held up another chip. It bent sideways before snapping under its own weight, only a flap of skin holding it together.

'I thought what made a good chip good was a crunch that came from it containing enough grease to drown your heart. What are we doing in this place?' The café was long and thin, the narrowest in a jumbled row of shops wedged together like bad teeth.

'Because it's near something for work. You remember that? Kent Police? The people who ask me to do detective work for them and then pay me in legal tender with which I can buy things. Things that I like.'

'Like shit caff chips. Should have brought my own coffee, too. This tastes like it was brewed in someone else's shoe.'

'How have you become a snob when you dress like you do?'

Boone stretched a leg out from beneath the table.

'Hey, these jeans are older than my marriage. I know because I have a photo of me wearing them at uni.'

'How is the good doctor?'

'We're working through things.'

'Well, since you're such a sorry sight, I'm inclined to help you out of pity.'

'That works.'

'Hit me with it. What information can I get for you, no doubt breaking countless laws in the process?'

Boone explained about Tess, and Barb remembered the basics of the Ingram case. Said she'd have a word, check on his status. She popped outside to make a call and Boone forced down a couple more chips.

'This for him?' Barb said, sliding back into her chair.

'Who?'

'Boxall. You know what he's capable of. And it's not like he doesn't have cause here.'

'It's for me. For Tess. I'm not looking to set anyone up, Barb.'

'He's out,' she said.

'Shit.'

'She knew, your friend.'

'I found a request for a statement from her, before the review.'

'They'd have written again. He was released on licence seven weeks ago. I didn't ask where he was.'

'No, of course. Thanks, Barb.'

'Do you think he's made contact with her? Because that would breach his terms.'

'I don't know. She wouldn't say even if I asked. It might just be her being a moody cow.'

'If he has, don't you go doing anything Boonish about it.'

'Fuck does that mean?'

'You're the only person who doesn't remember you accidentally-on-purpose tripping Matty Scargill down a flight of metal-nosed stairs after he threatened to kill the girlfriend whose teeth he'd earlier knocked out.'

'Sounds like he tripped himself down the stairs.'

'Aye, that's what we said. But you don't have a blue wall to protect you any more. If Ingram is taking the piss, you let me know. I'll have it handled.'

Boone nodded. 'Sure. Listen, there's something else too.'

'Course there fucking is.'

'That day. The day of my . . .'

'You call it an accident one more time and I'll scream.'

' . . . incident. The other girl. Eastern European.'

'Bulgarian.'

'Yeah. Do you have any idea what happened to her?'

'Uh-huh.'

'Willing to share?'

'Why?'

'I don't want to cause her any trouble. But I think I'd like to speak to her.'

'Saw this coming.'

'What?'

'You wanting to look into what happened to you. Work the Sarah Still case again yourself. Kent Police never did handle it to your satisfaction.'

'It's not really that.'

Barb snorted. 'Boone, private dick. Half right.'

'Shut up. I just want to talk to someone who was there. In the file it said she didn't speak much English anyway, so it probably won't go anywhere.'

'Yeah, well that was bollocks. She understood perfectly, just pretended otherwise. She had previous with British coppers and decided keeping shtum was her best course of action. I spoke to her a few weeks later, though, to see how she was doing. She wanted to see you back then, but you had an armed detail. Only police and family. Plus, you were all fucked up in the head, back before we knew you permanently had a sieve for a brain.'

Barb was the only person from before whom Boone knew why she had liked. 'So you can look her up?'

'Actually, I had a hunch when you called that this was what you'd want. Rumena Zlatkova. Likes to be called Roo. Now, I haven't spoken to her in a while, and I don't have an address. But she works here.'

Barb pushed a slip of paper across the table.

'It's a small restaurant in south London. They do a fantastic eggs royale for brunch, and you get mimosas with it.'

Boone frowned at the plates of chips on the table.

'We can do posh when you're paying to make up for this flagrant abuse of our friendship,' said Barb.

'Done.'

'You ready for this? Looking into this stuff?'

Boone shrugged. 'I've been staring at pictures and paper so long, but nothing connects. Time to get in the sandbox.'

'I didn't push her too hard, a year ago. She was terrified. People wanted to. A cop gets abducted and seriously hurt, it tends to ruffle a few feathers. Maybe she knows something she held back.'

'Something about east London, maybe.'

'East London?'

'Where I was found. And where the last sighting of Sarah Still was. Could just be coincidence, but . . .'

'My position on coincidences is the same as it is on UFOs. Or socialism. I know other people believe in these things, but I've never seen them myself.' Barb looked past Boone to the café's front window.

'Oh Christ.'

Boone turned to see why Barb had dropped her head into her hands, finding a smartly suited young man, late twenties, outside the window searching through the glass between cupped hands. He waved at Barb, making a gesture like, come on. He looked at Boone, maybe nodded.

'Barry,' Barb said.

'I know him?'

'Detective Constable Barry Tayleforth. Rising star. Qualified barrister. You called him Canter, but you were the only one who called him that.'

'Take it he didn't bring me get-well flowers.'

'He thought you were a knob.'

'It's fair.'

'Wants in at the Met. Thinks he's going to be the first black deputy comm.'

'What, doesn't think he'd cut it as commissioner?'

'I better go. Bollocks. He's big on community policing, there's some sort of meeting.'

'You lot really do need to stop killing people in your custody.'

'Do you know what a hero we could have made of you if only you'd died?'

9

In the Goose, it was a straight shot through from Gillingham to the Peckham Road. Calling Jack, she explained to him where she was and what she was doing and promised to be careful. She could see Cassie's from the spot she found. A four-storey Victorian town house on the main drag, the first and second floors had been knocked through and housed tables and chairs, seats built into alcoves, and a small roof terrace on top of the rear extension. The semi-basement was the kitchen, magical smells wafting up from below.

Boone didn't know if there was a Cassie, but a middle-aged Englishwoman seated her at a small table in the front bay. A good crowd was in and several waiting staff glided between tables with plates. She wasn't sure she'd recognise Roo, having only seen her once, a year previously, half naked and covered in blood. She needn't have worried. Roo had no problem remembering Boone and, spotting her from the rear of the house, strode right up and sat down opposite her. She glanced at an imaginary watch on her wrist.

'Only one year you have made me wait.'

'Uh . . .'

'My shift ends in one hour.'

'I can come back, or—'

'I wait a year. You can wait one hour. You can order from the menu and leave the big tip.'

Boone ordered eggs royale and a mimosa.

TWO

WHAT REMAINS OF A MAN

10

Roo's father never had what you'd call a career. He worked farms and fields amid the forests of the western Rhodope Mountains in southern Bulgaria, scratching out enough to get married and start a family in a hamlet not so far from Satovcha. That was where Roo was born, the summer before the Iron Curtain fell, a year before the country's first real elections brought Bulgarians' illusions in line with those of the rest of the Western world. Two brothers were already on the scene, and eighteen months later, her sister Penka was born.

They were schooled in Satovcha, but her brothers worked from an early age, joining their father growing grain and raising livestock on the private lots he had taken over following the forced exodus of ethnic Turks in the years before communism ended. All in all, things could have been worse.

Try telling a thirteen-year-old girl that. Desperate to escape rural life and see the cities, Roo and a couple of her friends were mesmerised by the stories told to them by an older girl who had returned from the resorts on the Black Sea, towns fattened by the wealth of foreign tourists, towns that offered excitement, night-life, young people and a future.

The girls signed up to work at an eastern resort, sneaking out one night with a small bag of clothes, leaving notes for their families. They piled into a truck outside Satovcha and before the sun had ushered in the new day they realised the terrible mistake they had made. The men in the van said they were Pomaks, but Roo knew Pomaks. She knew the sound of their language, their accent. These men weren't Slavic, and their names made no sense for Pomaks. She thought maybe they were Turks or Kurds. The truck had no windows and no light, and as they jounced around in the back they had no idea where they were being driven.

When finally they stopped, at a small, isolated house they were told was a halfway point to the Black Sea coast, they were fed a weak stew and tepid water. One or the other was laced with something, as what followed she remembered only in fragments. Days, it felt like. Taken alone into a room, stripped and humiliated, and then taken in other ways. A longer drive followed. They offered her water along the way and she took it gladly, embracing the fog. It didn't clear until Italy, where she worked in a brothel for two years before being driven to London in the back of a goods lorry.

She was seventeen when the police raided the house she was kept in. They treated her as as much of a suspect as the men who pimped her. Out of fear, she didn't tell anyone the extent of her plight. She wanted to stay, but they deported her back to Bulgaria. Her father barely spoke to her and her mother hid her away with cousins in a different village. But she was a commodity now and her owners wanted her back. They found her sister, Penka, dragging her from the shop in Satovcha where she worked, and three of them took her to the woods. They left her with her front teeth missing, a broken arm, and pregnant. That was the warning.

Roo gave herself up to them the next day.

After recovering from the beating she got, she spent a year in a brothel in Tel Aviv before returning to Italy for a spell and finally on to Britain, once more behind the panels of a white van. The life of her sister rested on her compliance. She was used in a London brothel before being sold to a man in Kent for three thousand pounds. She never saw him, only those who worked for him. After a couple of years, she was told she was too old and was driven back to London, where she was used at parties, no longer fetching the same money she did as a teenager. She lived in one of four rooms that had once been a single room, and was periodically shown pictures of her mother or sister, entering a shop or walking near their home village.

It was all the tether they required to keep her in line.

That was when she saw a girl killed. Slovenian, seventeen, eyes black buttons like a Hopper painting. Her face never lost its blank expression no matter what went on. That was probably the reason, if there was any reason at all, a man losing patience with her zombie demeanour and demanding a reaction. Her neck broke where it landed across the polished outer hearth of the fancy fireplace. That was where Roo found her, and finally caused more fuss than anyone was prepared to tolerate. By their best reckoning, a week later Boone came to in that flat with Roo bound and gagged, having been bundled out of her room one evening with a bag over her head and driven there in the trunk of a car.

After she escaped, she knew the laws had changed, that she could remain freely in Britain. She refused to speak to the police, claiming she remembered nothing. Barb thought she might be hiding some connection to Boone and helped her out, put her in contact with another Bulgarian girl she knew in London who got her a bedsit and some shifts at the restaurant. She called home but was unable to reach anyone. Eventually, through the same cousins she had stayed with before, she found out that her father had passed away and her mother and sister had moved to Germany, while her brothers now lived in Sofia.

She wrote to her mother and learned that the gang who had taken her had forced Penka to have the child, before taking it from her to sell into adoption. Her mother said her father had died of shame, and soon afterwards they packed up and made their way by train and bus to Germany, where her mother's cousin had years earlier moved when she married a butcher. There, beyond the reach of the gangs, her sister was recovering and had returned to education.

II

Roo told Boone all this at the table when her shift was over. Boone had asked her to start at the beginning, hardly expecting such a tale of anguish. They were still talking when they left, and Roo invited Boone to her home.

'It is not more than half an hour walk,' she said. 'Skipping the bus, I have an extra twenty-five pounds a week.'

'Today you ride the Goose,' Boone announced, to Roo's bewilderment.

Home was an imposing block of Victorian town houses by the railway in Lewisham, knocked through so its once spacious rooms were carved up into a warren of separate units. Roo had an upstairs room, by no means the smallest in the place at ten by ten. A bed against one wall, the opposite wall tiled and featuring a basic kitchenette and a shower cubicle in the corner. A balsa chair was pushed beneath a small table at the only window. She shared a toilet off the hallway with three other tenants.

Boone fiddled with a coin meter behind the door. Beneath it

was an awkwardly positioned electric heater, its plug pulled from the wall.

'Electricity,' Roo said, meaning the meter. 'One in every room. I have cheap wine. Red as I don't have to chill it.'

'Go for it,' Boone said, and they sipped plonk from coffee mugs. Roo offered Boone the only chair, perching herself on the edge of the bed.

'I have a picture I'd like you to look at,' Boone said.

'You think it is something I know?'

'I think something brought me to that flat, and something brought you to that flat, and I have to start somewhere in figuring out if those somethings intersect.'

'Okay.'

Boone laid a photo of Sarah Still on the table. Long dark hair and big dark eyes, pretty but unsmiling. Roo tilted her head, placed a finger on the picture.

'You know her?' asked Boone.

'Maybe. She looks different.'

'She may have been several years older when you saw her. She went missing when she was fifteen, but she'd be twenty-one now. It's the case I was working on, the case that took me to that flat.'

'If it is her, it is a girl called Sarah.'

No such thing as coincidences.

'Well, that's Martians and the Labour Party fucked,' Boone said.

'Martians?' Roo said quizzically.

'Go on,' Boone said. 'This Sarah.'

'I don't know what was her second name,' Roo said.

'Where do you know her from?'

'A place they took us.'

'Where you saw the girl die?'

'It was a hotel.'

'Where?'

'London. This is all I know. I was picked up in a van, like with seats in the back, but windows were blacked out. We would get out the back doors, open near the entrance to hotel, and walk straight in. It was across from a park. Through a window, I saw this. Hotel was like a house, a big house. Not like normal hotels with much rooms.'

'You knew the men? The . . . clients?'

'They did not say what are their names.' She shrugged. 'Men. Men in suits. Men in jeans. Fat men. Thin men. Old men. Young men. Men who stink. Men with shirts that turn yellow under their arms. Other men are clean.'

'This was quite recently?'

'Not so long. She was there the night the girl died. Not much over a year then?'

'So Sarah was alive a year ago?'

Roo nodded and shrugged. 'If it is the same girl.'

'And they brought her to the hotel like you? In a van?'

Roo shook her head. 'Not like me. She came maybe with a man. She was not nice. Mean. I did not like her.'

'She was mean to you?'

'No. Mean to Czech girls. She talked to the man who brought them. She knew him.'

'He was Czech?'

Roo nodded. 'Brought young girls who are here to work on farms. Picking fruit. That is what they say, but they are brought to hotel. Young-looking girls, how the men like them.'

'The girls were all young?'

'Yes.'

'Uh, younger than you?'

'Ha. I was not so young. I was kept there for younger girls. How you say? Like nanny. They were Bulgarian also, but did not speak much English, so I help with the talking.'

'The men didn't sleep with you?'

'Yes, that too. Or watch me with other girl.'

Roo's candidness caught Boone unguarded and she felt herself blush.

'Right. But this Sarah, did they sleep with her?'

'I did not see. I think maybe she was like me. There were other girls there too, very young. I can say, twelve or thirteen?'

'Foreign? Eastern European?'

Roo shook her head. 'English girls. They were on something, or had been drinking. I think this Sarah, she saw to them.'

'But she knew this Czech man.'

'Yes. She talked with him. Like they were friendly.'

'So she was there by choice?'

'Nobody is there by choice. Even if they think they are.'

'You know this Czech guy's name?'

'Maybe . . . Milan? I do not know second name. This is helping you?'

'Yeah. Yes. A lot.'

'You are thinking to follow your old footsteps? Do the investigating again?'

'Maybe.'

'Why? Why do this?'

Boone blew out her cheeks. 'A lot of reasons, I guess. To find

Sarah, for one. The police don't find missing people. Missing children is one thing, but a missing girl, young woman now, with a history of running away, and a certain reputation with the police? A woman who has been missing for six years already? That's quite another thing. There aren't the resources for that.'

'What if she does not wish to be found?'

'I'd like to give her the chance to tell me that. I also want to know what happened. Need to know what happened. How I got to that flat with those men, with you. Fill in the missing gaps.'

'You want to investigate to help you remember your old life. But it is the same investigating that broke your head and made you forget in the first place.'

'What else have I got?'

'Same as me,' Roo said, pointing at herself. 'Life. Second chance. We were taken to that place to die. To be killed. And here we are, in shit English flat, drinking shit English wine. But better than dead.'

'I need shit English food to soak up shit English wine,' Boone said. She checked the refrigerator, but the door was propped open, the power off. 'No food?'

'Costs pounds,' Roo said. She nodded at the meter on the wall. 'For refrigerator, for heater, I have to put in pounds every day. Dink dink dink. Much pounds. So I turn them off. I have light. Kettle for black coffee. And the shower. Still pounds, but not so much. And I have microwave, I plug in to cook cans.' She waved at a selection of tins on a shelf over the sink. 'I can eat at work sometimes. The chef likes us. He hides food for us.'

'How much do they charge for the electric?'

Roo shrugged. 'I am not told price. Just put in pounds. Pound after pound after pound into little hole. Dink dink dink. He comes every month to empty it.'

'The landlord?'

'That is his very favourite thing. Sound of the pounds landing on the other pounds in his sack. Whistles when he collects them from every room. Tells me, this is his best day. Collection day.'

'Sounds like a prince.'

Roo shrugged philosophically.

'What else I can do? Flats in the newspapers, they cost too much. I cannot get references. They tell me, pay six months advance. Who has this money? So I am here.'

'Well, I'm not eating out of a can. I saw an Indian round the corner.'

'English and your curry.'

'You'll be sticking with the cans then?'

'If you find . . . is vegetable. We call it *patladjan*. Big, black . . .'

'Aubergine.'

'Yes. Something with aubergine.'

'You're vegetarian?'

'I don't eat much meat. I don't give it a name.'

Boone walked round to a street of low, stout buildings, single flats above shops. Half an hour later, she returned with vegetable tandoori and a lamb and pumpkin saagwala for herself. She bought another bottle of wine from the offie, too. The smell of the food when they opened the foil cartons was delicious, though less so when the small room was still festooned with it two hours later. Roo had been doing most of the talking, so it was only fair Boone shared her own story, her life as far as she had reconstructed it.

'You made big changes,' Roo said. 'Leave police. Move house.

I made my world smaller. Here to the restaurant. Restaurant to here. No driving licence. No Facebook. Nothing they could see me with.'

'Why didn't you go to Germany, to your family?'

'I don't speak German, for the first. And for the second, I don't like to disturb them. It is not so easy for the gangs to threaten people in Germany, so they are safe now I think. But maybe I go there and they find me, things would be different. And for the third, I like your London. I am poor and this room is shit and I hate my job, but is better than a farm.'

'You have plans?'

She shrugged again. 'Right now, I am water. Run away wherever it is easiest. I get enough hours at the restaurant to just pay for this place. Nothing else. I go to the library. Books are free.'

She held up a worn copy of *Lolly Willowes* that lay on her bed.

'She leaves her family and moves to the country to be witch. This I can understand. But you English have too many words for the same things. Spoil yourselves even with your tongues.'

'I apologise for my people.'

Roo waved a hand. 'I am drunk.'

'Me too,' Boone said, thinking about the drive home.

'You will stay tonight. Or you will drive this Goose into a tree and kill yourself.'

Boone looked around the cramped room.

'We share bed. No need for to be shy. You are not *obratna*?'

'I don't . . .'

'Lover of women,' Roo clarified.

'Oh. No.'

'But then, how do you know this? You could have been doing anything before.'

'When you put it like that . . . I need to ring the husband, otherwise he'll think I'm getting myself killed again.'

Boone retreated into the hallway on her mobile.

'Jack?'

'Hey. You on the way home?'

'I'm going to stay here the night.'

'Here? Where's here?'

'With Roo. She has a room in town.'

'You're staying in a room in London with a Bulgarian prostitute? Jesus. I mean, stop me if this all sounds familiar.'

'She's a waitress, Jack. And it's not . . . there's no danger here. I'm
fine. Just had a few drinks and don't think driving is a great idea.'

'I can come and get you.'

'Jack, it's late, and I'm in Lewisham, and what about Quin?'

'When you said you were going to be looking into this . . .'

'I haven't gone looking for the bad men, Jack. I'll text you the
exact address. And I'll call you when I get in tomorrow.'

Roo had cleared away the containers when Boone came back in.

'He is nice man, this husband of yours?'

Boone shrugged. 'Seems to be. He knows me in a way I'll never
know him, though.'

The room was cold. Boone wrapped her jacket round herself
under the blankets and pulled on the thick socks Roo had offered.
Eventually she got up and put all the pound coins she had into the
meter and plugged the heater in. 'Now I will think of you when
he comes with his sack to collect, this thief,' Roo whispered.

Roo had described herself as water. Water was defined by the
vessel that contained it. Seemed to Boone that everyone was like
water in a way, the vessel that contained them being their pasts.

Roo had stopped making decisions and allowed her existence to be the product of circumstance. Barb had put her in contact with a girl, another trafficked Bulgarian, who had got her shifts at the restaurant and secured her the room. These were things that happened to Roo, as much as choices she made.

Boone didn't feel so different. She was a woman with no more past; her vessel no longer had a defined shape. Now everything felt like circumstance. What Roo saw as big changes were things that had happened without Boone having much of a say. Kent Police pensioned her off, citing the leg but meaning the inexplicable amnesia. Jack was the one who earned the real money, and when the police suggested protection at home might be an idea, he decided a new home was a better one.

Reading over her previous life as she had, she wondered if it had ever been much different, if she had ever really made a decision. How much of her life had merely happened to her? Her mother leaving; moving to London with her uncle after her father's death; growing close to Jack while she watched her uncle fade away; marriage and a child, starting a family to replace the one she'd lost. It was what people did. Was something really a choice when it was the expected norm? Nobody held the lien on their own life. One cosmic snap of the fingers and they were in foreclosure, everything they ever knew forfeit.

None of which was helping Boone get to sleep.

Every bed was strange to her. Beds in hospitals, beds in private clinics, beds in palatial seafront houses, beds shared with Bulgarian sex-workers-turned-waitresses in extortionate hovels. She couldn't remember a place that felt like home, couldn't even imagine what such a thing might look like.

She got up, putting her jacket on, and sat at the table. The night was clear and the moon shone through the small window, boxing her in its pale light. Roo's face was just visible beneath the blankets, her sharp features and pointed little nose. In the soft rasp of her sleeping, Boone heard that engine of godly works.

Books were stacked neatly on the window ledge. Alongside the Warner were similarly well-thumbed library copies of *The Heat of the Day*, *A Hell of a Woman*, *The Vet's Daughter*, and an obscure English/Italian phrasebook donkey's years old. It was this last one she flicked through, its polite and cheery scenarios accompanied by neatly inked illustrations of perpetually happy tourists and locals. Transactions at coffee bars were conducted in lira and smiles. She checked the edition notice at the front of the book. Same age as her.

'You could not sleep?' Roo said, squinting out from beneath the covers.

'Don't seem to much any more.'

Roo nodded.

'Do you ever think about it?' Boone said. 'Or dream about it? What happened to us.'

'I have dreams of many things. That is just one more thing that has happened.'

'It's the only thing that has ever happened to me.'

'You have dreams?'

'I don't remember my dreams any more. But I know that's what they're about.'

Between pages towards the back of the book Boone found two passport photos, still together but cut from a longer strip, of a young woman bearing a remarkable similarity to Roo. Her sister, Penka, presumably. It marked a page of Italian idioms that readers had added to over the years. Three or four different hands in pencil and biro.

'I was going to learn,' Roo said. 'Where they kept me in Rome, the building had a janitor, Francesco. His mother was Ethiopian, Oromo. His father was Italian, had stayed in Africa after the war. Francesco was born when his father was very old, and he had no memories of him. Did not even speak his language. But he was left enough money to go to school and become an engineer, and later he moved to Rome, where he could only be a janitor. He taught himself Italian, and then he taught himself English. He says to me, Rumena, you speak English. It is easy to speak the Italian. It is a language dogs could speak. I do not know the same dogs as him. I never did more than read the pages at the back.'

She sat up and turned the book on the table so they could both see. 'I like the sayings,' she said, running her finger beneath one. '*In bocca al lupo*. Into the mouth of the wolf.'

' "May the wolf die", ' Boone responded, reading from the book.

'And here someone has added, "Up the whale's arse", ' Roo said, delighted with the addendum.

'That'd get us a long way at the Pantheon,' Boone said.

'*Questo è un altro paio di maniche*,' said Roo.

' "This is another pair of sleeves", ' Boone read.

And so it began, the secret language by which they would communicate, the colourful idioms of a foreign people appropriated into their private shibboleth. The code by which they might better express themselves.

12

Soft oak-aged light reflected greenly through the open blind, shimmering across Boone's face. Blinking it away failed so she draped an arm over her face before eventually surrendering. There was no fighting stars. Climbing gently out of bed, she stood on tiptoes and stretched, her spine clicking in resentment of the new day.

Her breath was awful and she'd need coffee to mask it.

On her front with her knees somehow tucked up beneath her, Roo slept like a contortionist. She wore a fierce expression, and above the neck of her vest Boone could count the notches of her spine, moving as she breathed like some alive and limbless thing inside her.

Boone put the kettle on and was disgusted to find only instant coffee in the cupboard. She filled two cups, ringed inside as they could only be washed by hand, and placed one on the table by the bed.

'I should have every morning a coffee bringer,' Roo said, a sleepy smile softening her face. Pulling the sheets up about her ears, she sat up cloaked in them and reached for the cup. 'You have to leave?'

Boone shook her head. 'What have you got on?'

'I have shift at noon,' Roo said. She looked at her watch. 'I cannot believe what is the time. You keep me in bed all day.'

'I'll drop you off. There's ages yet. I thought, if you're up for it, we might take a little road trip. You could show me where this flat you used to stay at is.'

Roo lowered the cup from her lips, alarmed.

'Just a drive-by,' Boone said. 'You show me where it is, nobody will see you, and we jet right off.'

'You are thinking it is still used for girls like me?'

'Worth a look. If it is, and they still pick the girls up in cabs, I could follow one.'

'Maybe this time you make sure to follow them all the way to roof for when they throw you off. These first-floor falls, they are only getting half the job done, *da*?'

'Strictly a surveillance job,' Boone said.

'I will come with you because I want to see up close how it is you are stupid in way planets are big.'

'Cool.'

'But first, I am needing shower.'

Getting up, Roo slung a towel over the back of the chair and reached into the corner cubicle to turn the water on, testing it against her wrist. Without a second thought, she peeled off her vest and shorts, starkers in the small room.

'Oh, okay then,' Boone said, averting her eyes.

There didn't seem anywhere else to look. Boone tugged her sweater down firmly past the waist of her jeans and busied herself with a book until Roo disappeared behind the frosted glass.

'I'm going to use the bathroom quickly,' she said, and scurried down the hall. Using a bunch of toilet paper, she lowered the toilet seat lid and sat in the cold and scuzzy closet checking her phone. No new messages from Jack. She smiled at the idea of him restraining himself. After a couple of minutes she flushed the chain and returned to the room.

Roo had dressed, a damp towel hanging from the chair, drips on the faux-wood flooring. Her hair was dark with wet.

'You need?' she said, jerking a thumb towards the shower.

'I'll get one at home,' Boone said.

Roo shrugged, suit yourself.

In the Goose, they took Tower Bridge north of the river to Bethnal Green. It was a large end-of-terrace house that had been extended into the loft and looked recently refurbed. They couldn't park anywhere with a view of the house, so Boone told Roo to stay put while she had a quick look.

'No way you are leaving me on my own,' Roo said. From her bag she produced big sunglasses and a summer hat.

'Nice *chapeau*,' Boone said. 'Very incognito.'

She retrieved a hooded jacket from the boot.

'Take that get-up off and put this on,' she told Roo. 'Pull the hood up. Nobody will see your face.'

With a pack of Lamberts bought from the corner, they sat across the street on a bench at the edge of a small square struggling to grow green grass in the shadows of surrounding tower blocks.

'Marvellous thing about smoking being outlawed everywhere,' Boone explained, 'is you can hang around outside just about anywhere with a fag and nobody asks what you're doing there.' She offered the pack to Roo.

'I do not smoke,' she said. 'Live longer without them.'

'Only feels that way,' Boone said.

Jack told her she quit after Quin was born, but Boone suspected she had snuck illicit ones at work. At the clinic she'd bum
fags from staff and they'd gone down like she had a twenty-a-day
habit. Tess had got her a Zippo with her name etched on the side.
'In case you forget again.'

Lighter and a pocket knife; she never left home without them.

An hour and too many cigarettes later, a fifty-grand Volvo 4x4
pulled up and a smartly dressed man and a young boy got out and
climbed the steps to the front door.

'That was your one?' Boone said.

Roo nodded. 'But was all single rooms. No families.'

'Probably got rid of it, your pimp friends. Made an absolute
killing selling it to someone who turned it into luxury flats. We're
not going to find a lead here.' Probably they panicked when she
and Roo escaped, Boone surmised, and got rid of properties that
could be identified. She could ask Barb to look into the sale of the
place, but it wouldn't have been owned under anyone's real name.
They drove back to Peckham and parked near Cassie's. Hungry,
Boone went in with Roo.

'We do breakfast to go for busy types,' Roo said.

Sometimes it was a smell, Boone found. Catching a scent in
the air that shook a tambourine. Something from earlier in her
life, but specifically what, she didn't know. Haunted by olfactory
ghosts.

This time it was the breakfast muffins, stacked with bacon and
eggs. She bought one and they stood on the pavement outside,
Roo with a few minutes before her shift started.

'You need vegetables and fruit,' Roo said, watching as Boone tucked into her food. 'Probably you also forgot it is possible to have solid shit.'

'You should do a wholewheat one,' Boone said with a full mouth.

The muffin didn't last long.

'We will talk again?' Roo said.

'Fuck yeah,' said Boone. She lunged forward, surprising Roo with an awkward embrace.

'Oof, is certain you forget how to hug,' Roo said. She squeezed back. 'But I am very glad to have met you again, Abigail Boone.'

13

Boone was in a great mood when she got back to Lark. The Lexus was still in the drive.

'Jack?' she called, almost skipping through the door.

'In here.'

He was sat behind his desk in the study, glasses on.

'You not working today?'

'Decided to work from home this morning,' he said. 'I only have appointments in the afternoon.'

'Jack.'

'I was curious. I wanted to hear what you'd found out.'

'Wanted to check on me.'

'That so wrong? Might not seem it to you, but you're my wife. Worrying about you is what I'm supposed to do.'

'You're right,' Boone said.

Jack eyed her suspiciously, not used to such concessions.

'I'll tell you about it after a shower,' Boone said. 'I stink.'

Upstairs, she showered and changed into fresh clothes. Back down in the study, she dropped into the big club chair, her favourite furniture in the house, and recounted her lunch with Barb (leaving out the Ingram business, as she didn't want to go over what he'd done to Tess) and how she'd gone on to meet Roo. She left out the finer details, any names Roo had told her, telling herself she was protecting him with plausible deniability.

'So Sarah was definitely alive a year ago,' Jack said.

'Looks like.'

'You going to tell Barb?'

'Maybe.'

'Ab— Boone.'

'They had to already assume that I thought she was alive a year ago. I told someone there was a lead and then I was poking around in London, near where she was last seen. They knew that and they didn't get anywhere with it.'

'Nothing Roo told you would be of interest to them?'

'Probably. I'll see. I want to see Sarah's grandmother, Molly. I think she deserves to know her granddaughter was seen alive. Take my cue from her.'

Boone made them both tea and sat in the club chair with her laptop as Jack worked at his desk. There were more pressing concerns than Sarah Still. Such as locating the newly-released-from-prison Clifford Ingram and making it clear that Tess was out of bounds to him, before Mickey Box decided to take matters into his own hands and create a whole new missing persons case.

It didn't take much googling to draw up a list of places where Ingram might be found. His mother lived in Lark, and he'd grown up there. Just out of nick, needs somewhere to stay, most likely he goes where he knows. He'd have a day job, satisfy his supervisor, but she was dealing with a career shitehawk here. She jotted down addresses for places calling themselves bed and breakfasts, but really they were doss-houses, surviving on the council and probation sending people their way.

Jack eventually surrendered and said he was going into the practice for a few hours. They agreed plans for him to pick up a fish supper on his way home, from what they called the posh chippie (it didn't have plastic furniture inside, and sported a classy wood and brushed-metal sign above the door).

'Quin will be late, remember,' he said at the door.

'Late?'

'He's got his thing after school. For the play.'

'Play?' Boone said blankly.

'At the theatre group. He's on stage crew.'

'Right.'

'He'll be finished by about five.'

'Okay.'

'Might be that he'd appreciate a lift.'

'Yep.'

He stared at her. 'To be clear, I'm suggesting his mother goes and gets him when he's—'

'Yes, I got that, Jack. Thanks.'

'Well then,' he said, before nodding and disappearing through the door.

When his car was well gone, Boone jumped on the phone and started calling places, asking for Clifford Ingram. She got lucky on the second one. A Mancunian, with more of a snivel than an accent, informed her calls couldn't be forwarded to rooms, and anyway Ingram was out.

'At work?' Boone asked.

'Who wants to know?'

'Mr Ingram is on licence, and—'

'Yes, he's at work. On the six-to-twos this week.'

Boone thanked him and hung up. Shift work, probably a warehouse or big all-night supermarket. Zero hours contract, zero dark start.

With several hours to kill, Boone polished off what she had been reading and moved on to a Dorothy B. Hughes novel. At half four, she got in the Goose and drove across town to fulfil her mumly duty.

A down-on-its-uppers seaside town, Lark was rebranding itself as an alternative for those who didn't have a spare half-million for a three-bed in almost-London. The shops and hotels of the seafront promenade had been freshly painted in pastel tones, the town's chin wiped clean for visitors. The kind of place that people not from there called charming.

Near the low remnants of the ruined castle, the old pier stretched out precariously into the waves, the ballroom at its end shuttered for good now. A hardy few braved the pebbled beach to watch the grey waters. Gulls circled above, laughing. They dipped and dived, scavenging for dropped chips, occasionally attacking small children and the elderly. Behind the promenade, rows of Victorian villas gave way to winding streets of matchbox Georgian terraces and fishermen's cottages, and further back still the style became less monarchial, the architecture of sprawl.

Quin's theatre group met in a hall in that direction, on an otherwise quiet street. It was set back from the road with a car park out front. Across the street a disused gasometer squatted in a padlocked site, rusted ladders reaching up above it, stairways to nowhere.

Boone parked away from the other cars and remained in her seat. There were no other parents around yet. If she'd been there before, she didn't remember it. A modern building erected on brownfield land; Jack had explained it was paid for by the developers who'd turned the old theatre in town where the group used to meet into apartments.

With her hood up, she got up and slunk around the front entrance. A poster box advertised that month's events, mostly live music and the upcoming run of the play. Double doors opened into a small lobby, bathrooms off one side and private rooms the other. A small box office booth was closed. Another set of double doors led to the hall itself. She sidled up to them, close to the wall, and peered through the glass.

There was no permanent seating or stage. Chairs were stacked against two walls and at the far end stage blocks stood in no particular arrangement. Spigoted aluminium trusses had been rigged from six towers and criss-crossed the space almost twenty feet above the floor. Teenagers in school uniforms, blazers and ties discarded and sleeves rolled up, were busy around the place, a couple of adults supervising. One of the teachers from school organised the whole thing.

When Boone spotted Quin, atop a wheeled scaffold tower in the middle of the hexagon and attaching lights to the truss above, she shrank back from the door slightly. Another boy sat up there with him and Quin was showing him how to correctly use the O-clamps. He was in his element. She smiled to herself, watching him work.

The headlights of a car swept across the lobby, scattering brightly through the frosted glass. A door clunked shut and another parent pushed through the double doors. Hood still up, Boone turned away slightly as the woman opened the interior doors to the hall. She hovered for a moment, perhaps expecting Boone to follow her, before letting the door slowly pull itself closed.

Boone went back outside and found a couple more parents milling about chatting, one nursing a cigarette. She slipped back into the Goose at the far end of the car park and sank low in her seat, watching over the dash. Gradually other parents gathered, waving and laughing. Jack insisted Boone had been friendly with some of them, a notion she found about as plausible as ghost stories. She dreaded being noticed, someone coming over and knocking on the window, and began thinking she should have parked down the road and only come into the car park when she saw the kids were out.

She didn't notice Quin until the passenger door opened and he jumped in.

'Hey,' he said.

'Hey.'

'Didn't know I was getting a lift.'

'Surprise.'

Boone pulled herself up in her seat and turned on the engine.

'You should have come in,' the boy said.

'Hmm,' said Boone.

'Who were you hiding from?'

'Oh, you know.' She waved a hand at the other parents. 'All that.'

'Dad said you spent the night with a Bulgarian hooker,' Quin said, pulling on his seat belt.

'That's not exactly . . . We don't call them that. And she's a waitress now.'

'Wow. I thought he was kidding me.'

'You know your father can't tell jokes,' Boone said, reversing out onto the street. 'Anyway. How was your . . . thing?'

'Stage crew.'

'Right.'

'We're doing *Godot* in the round, so it's different. The lighting is unusual. We're rigging a scaffold up over the whole thing.'

'Ah. The beauty of the way and the goodness of the wayfarers.'

The recollection stole up on her like a static shock, its origin and existence a mystery.

'I set the lights and man the cans,' Quin said. 'So what's she like?'

'Who?'

'This Bulgarian waitress.'

'Roo.'

'Roo,' the boy said. 'Roo.' He rolled it round his mouth, elongating the vowels. 'Is she pretty? Do they have to be? You know, for what they do. Is she young, or more like your age?'

'She's . . . Wait. More like my age?'

'You know. Not old, but like . . . older. You're older than Dad, right?'

'By a month. That's the kind of older that only brings with it wisdom.'

'So she's younger, Roo?'

'I think I carry it better,' Boone said, pulling down the visor and glancing at herself in the mirror. 'I don't look older than your father, do I?'

Quin shrugged.

'Do I look older than I did before?'

'You used to dress smart. People in suits and stuff always look older.'

Boone frowned. 'So I look younger?'

'There's Dad,' Quin said.

They were at the junction to their road and Jack's Lexus approached from the opposite direction. He tooted his horn and waved as he turned in ahead of them.

'He should have fish and chips with him,' Boone said.

'From the posh place?'

'Yep.'

'Nice.'

Boone pulled into the drive beside the Lexus, Jack waiting for them with the door open.

'Why don't you set the table so it won't go cold?' she told Quin.

The boy skidded off into the kitchen and Jack followed him, bringing into the house with him the glorious aromas of deeply fried foods.

Over dinner, Jack steered table talk away from missing girls and trafficked women and kept Quin on his crew work.

'We made a tree from bicycle frames,' the boy explained. 'In the second act, we attach the wheels.'

Boone was making a careful examination of the chips and found them wanting.

'Is it possible that the chips of my mind do not and never have actually existed?' she said, holding up a spineless and drooping example.

She unscrewed the mayonnaise and spooned a great dollop onto her plate, digging into it with another chip. Jack watched, she felt, like he was witnessing the scourge of the Hun. She considered dipping one straight into the jar.

'Quin's production sounds interesting,' Jack offered. 'Must be some task, all the work for the lighting.'

To which Quin replied, 'Vladimir is a girl.'

'Well,' Jack said, 'that's interpretative.'

'I mean, he's still a bloke, but he's played by a girl. Otherwise it was going to have to be Pozzo or Lucky, and Mr Archibald wasn't comfortable with that. Plus, it works out because Vladimir has prostate problems.' When Jack didn't reply, Quin said, 'That's a joke, Dad.'

'Nothing to be done,' said Boone.

Probably drunk with this much conversating over a family dinner, Quin carried on with abandon. 'Is she going to help then? Roo?'

'Help what?' Boone said.

Quin shrugged. 'I don't know. Help you catch the men who hurt you? Help you remember what happened. Remember old stuff.'

'I wanted to meet her. See what she was like.'

'I think you should catch them.'

'Quin,' Jack said.

'It's been a year,' the boy said, 'and the police haven't done anything. Mum could do better herself.'

'Thank you, Quin.'

Father and son exchanged a look that Boone couldn't quite decipher. So much of Quin was a mystery to her, not least his face, which she often tried to read but found empty of telling expression. She felt sure she must once have known his looks and sounds, some physiognomic forensics she now lacked.

After dinner, Quin went upstairs and as Boone made herself coffee she watched Jack neatly fold the wrapping and cardboard boxes the food came in and put them in the recycling.

'I'm not sure anything with grease on it is meant to go in there,' she said. 'Clogs up the doobrey that shreds them. Or clogs up the shredded bits. Something.'

He stopped and looked up at her. She'd turned back to her cafetière and was steadily pressing down the plunger. She poured herself a mugful and splashed in a little milk. Bringing it to her lips, she slurped at it loudly. He watched all this without comment.

'What?' she said.

'What what?'

'Well, I clearly wasn't eating chips in the expected manner earlier, and now I seem to be fucking up the making of a hot beverage.'

'I didn't say anything.'

'No, you communicate by other means.'

He nodded, like, here we go.

'Oh, and by the way,' Boone said, 'Bulgarian hooker?'

'What?'

'The first thing Quin says when I picked him up, he asks me about the Bulgarian hooker. So clearly you don't have any difficulties articulating your thoughts to him.'

'I didn't use that word.'

'No. You wouldn't. Was it prostitute? Or would that be too much? Sex worker, was it?'

'Well, what was I supposed to call her?'

'She's a human fucking being, Jack,' she said, her voice rising.

'The horrors of whose life would make you weep. And you of all people, the work you do, should know better.'

'All right, all right. Just calm down.'

'Don't do that,' she said.

Jack glanced out to the hallway, towards the stairs.

'Oh, what? In case the kid hears?'

'He's not *the* kid. He's *our* kid. Yours and mine. And I'm sorry. I shouldn't have told him, not the details. But he is *our* kid and we are a family. And when you're off and about seeing these people and coming home telling us about their problems, well it grates. What about our problems? How about we try to fix them instead?'

'*I* am our problem,' Boone said. 'And I'm sorry I can't fix things to your satisfaction, Jack. Can't just bring Abigail back with a snap of my fingers.'

'You're not giving this a fair chance.'

'No?'

'No. Sitting up in your room alone, poring over notes and photographs. How about sitting downstairs and talking to your husband for a change? Search for whatever it is you're looking for in some actual human interaction. Talk to your son, or take him out and do something. How do you expect to reconnect if you hide yourself away? It makes things worse. Makes the gulf between you and the past wider.'

'I'm going to lie down,' Boone said.

'Come on, don't walk away,' said Jack. 'This isn't a debate where one of us wins and the other loses. We have to find a way forward. I want to help. I want whatever is best for you.'

'And what if what is best for me and what is best for the family aren't the same thing?'

'How can you know if you don't even try to be part of the family?'

Boone huffed her way upstairs. She didn't have any answers for Jack, couldn't really explain even to herself why she felt the way she did. How did any person justify themselves on that level? She went to put on some music but the iPod wasn't in its dock. She didn't remember having it in the car earlier, but perhaps she'd left it downstairs. Couldn't show her face back down there now. She stood still, rage pulsing through her, oscillating just beneath the surface and quickening the blood. She'd spoiled for a fight and then fled, not for the first time either. She approached the marriage like guerrilla warfare, nipping in and starting little skirmishes before hotfooting it to duck the consequences.

'Hey.'

She'd left the door open and Quin stood in the frame.

'Hey. Did you . . . Were we being loud?'

Again, she found herself unable to read between the lines of his face. Expressions of cunning or daring or fear or joy, they all melded. The only one she could ever pick out, the one she feared, was anticipation. The prospect of his mother emerging from this strange hibernation.

He shrugged. 'I have this,' he said, holding out the iPod. 'I was putting more stuff on it.'

'Oh, right. Thanks.'

'Check out *You'd Prefer an Astronaut*. And maybe *Ruby Vroom*.'

This was his spare time now, scouring the internet for albums from another time. Her time. She noticed his exercise was expanding beyond its original parameters, accumulating albums from her earlier years that no child would have listened to. Building a musical biography of a life that in many ways had never existed. He was on a search that had no attainable object.

She took the little white box, stared at it.

'Cool,' she said uselessly.

'Night,' he said, withdrawing from the door.

'Night,' she said. As the door closed, she added, 'And thanks.'

Turning the lights off, Boone lay down and stared into the darkness before her eyes adjusted. Even when she closed her eyes and was alone with herself, she couldn't be sure of who that self was. All that was certain was that she was alone.

14

The Mercedes was parked outside the cottage, but there was no answer at the back door. It was unlocked and Boone let herself in.

'Mick? Tess, you here?' She hung her head down the hallway. 'Am I talking to myself?'

No response. On the side was a French press, full but with the plunger up. It was hot to the touch.

Coffee had become a matter of some interest. Boone had gone out and bought a none-too-cheap machine that took little pods and turned them into something that resembled, more or less, what they passed off as coffee in the chain stores. Mentioning this one day to Mickey Box, he told her she was an idiot. When she visited Tess, the pair of them usually ambled over to the cottage as the caravan's cupboards were invariably bare, and by some tacit understanding, Mickey Box had started leaving the good beans out in plain sight. One morning, Boone had found on the kitchen table a bag with her name on it containing a small packet of beans, a burr grinder and a five-quid cafetière. The bean was the thing, he always maintained. And a rigorous commitment to consistency of process.

'Black, please,' Mickey Box said, appearing from within the cottage somewhere.

'Hey. You put this on?'

Mickey Box nodded and sat at the table. Boone poured them both coffee and took a pew. Fitz appeared at the back door. He glared for a moment before pouring his own mugful.

'You get anywhere with that other business?' Mickey Box said.

Boone exhaled. 'He's out,' she said.

Mickey Box nodded. He sniffed. Pushing the coffee away from him, he got up and went to the Welsh dresser, took down a tumbler and a bottle of Scotch. He fetched ice from the compartment in the fridge and the cubes chimed in the glass before cracking as he poured on the Scotch. He sat down at the end of the table, where he always sat, and took a long sip. Swallowed. Drew his lips back tight against his teeth.

'I'll be needing a conversation with him,' he said finally.

'Mick . . .'

'Told him when he went in. And had him reminded when he was in, lest there be any lingering confusion.'

'Mick, all we know is he's out. We don't know he's contacted Tess. He'd be mad. It's a condition of his licence.'

'Best I have a wee chat and find out. Peace of mind. You find out where he's staying?'

'Mick, you asked me to help. So let me help.'

'You did then. Where?'

'Why do you think Tess didn't tell you about any of this? What do you think she's going to do if she finds out you've been round there and bashed him up?'

'Thank me profusely, I should think.'

'Aye? And when the police come round for a word? You've one stint already for GBH; reckon there'll be much leniency a second time? You'll be a two-time shitehawk and Tess'll see her father go away again.'

'Police won't get near him for it,' Fitz said.

'Let me find out if there's even been contact,' Boone said. 'Let me do that.'

Mickey Box weighed it up. 'Mind you don't dally.'

He got up, following Fitz to the door, but came back as if with an afterthought. 'With Tess, be sure to tell her there's nothing to worry about. Whatever's going on with her, I'm not mad. Not with her. Never with her. Whatever it is, we'll deal with it. And we'll deal with it however she sees fit. Entirely up to her.'

'O-kay,' Boone said.

Conversations were prone to oblique turns with Mickey Box. She watched through the window as he and Fitz headed for the shore path behind the cottage, and Tess followed her nose into the kitchen looking for coffee.

'It's all gone,' she said miserably.

'Didn't realise you were here.'

'Had a bath. What're you doing here?'

'Came to see you,' Boone half lied. 'Had to have coffee first, obviously.' She cleared the ground beans out and made fresh coffee as Tess sat playing with her damp hair.

'I found the woman,' Boone said. 'The one from the flat, the day of my accident.'

'I wondered how long it would take you to get around to that.'

'I'd been thinking about it for a while. And then Jack encouraged me.'

'Really?'

'Sort of. We talked about Sarah Still's disappearance, how caring about it is something the old and new me both have in common.'

'So you're going to look for her again? On your own?'

Boone shrugged. 'I don't know. I want to know what happened to me. And that probably means knowing what happened to her. I showed Roo a picture of Sarah Still and she recognised her. Meaning she was alive not long before I was at that flat.'

'Roo? That's her name?'

'Rumena. She's Bulgarian. Sarah Still went missing six years ago. I don't remember doing any of that misper work, but looking back over the cases, so many of them were gone for so long that I'd taken it as given that I was just looking for, you know.'

'A body.'

Boone nodded. 'Even if they hadn't been abducted, the life they likely fell into after running away. Living rough. Drugs. Prostitution.'

'Not conducive for.'

'Right. But if she was alive a year ago, having been missing five years . . .'

'Good chance she's still alive now.'

'Seems more likely, anyway.'

'Dangerous, though, digging into it all again.'

'Yeah. That's what Roo said.'

'Sounds like a smart lady. You should listen to her.'

'Probably. Might be I forgot how to listen too well, though. Regardless, I want to see Sarah's grandmother. She lives in a village back near Lark. Read in my notes that she was in a bad way when I saw her last. Drinking. I've called the number I have, but there's no answer. Thought I'd pop over.'

'What village?'

'Hold on,' Boone said.

She dug around in the battered messenger bag she'd nicked from Quin to keep some of her files in.

'You could keep all that in the cloud, you know,' Tess said.

'I could learn Spanish and move to Barcelona and make new friends with whom I'd dine and dance for the rest of my days.'

She flicked through a knock-off Moleskine pad.

'Here we are. Kearswood.'

'Went to school near there.'

'Nice place?'

'Probably was in the thirties.'

'Fancy a trip? Fresh air, bit of nostalgia. Save me from the whims of the maps app.'

Tess sipped her coffee and pulled a face.

'I'll throw in a bacon double cheese.'

'Well, if you're going to play hardball,' Tess said, getting up and slinging a cardy over her shoulder.

'What's the best way?' Boone said when she got the Goose going.

'M2/A2. Then we'll cut into coal country. I'll tell you when.'

'Didn't realise you lived down that way.'

'It was a long time ago. I grew up down there, but we moved when Mum died.'

Tess watched out the window, half a smile on her lips. A memory? She puzzled Boone sometimes. Smiled at the strangest things, or at nothing at all. Boone didn't push it and instead fiddled with

the radio, finding a middle-of-the-road station that she recognised
as almost always playing 'Bette Davis Eyes' whenever she tuned
into it. She turned it off.

'Tell me about Roo,' Tess said eventually. 'Is she a tom?'

'Yeah. No. It's complicated.'

Boone briefly recounted Roo's story, how she was trafficked,
what happened to her sister.

'Well, that's horrifying,' Tess said. 'And now you're taking me
to see the alcoholic gran of another abused girl. What would I do
without you to brighten up my days?'

Kearswood sat on a ridge half a dozen miles from Lark, an old
mining village now missing a mine. The high street was a clutch
of takeaways and a tanning salon – 'Defeatist attitude for the garden county,' Boone observed – with the post office now in the
small convenience store.

Molly Still didn't live in the village proper, but on an estate
called The Groves, built on the fringe of the village just as the
mines were closing. A pattern of cul-de-sacs with arboreal names,
lined with two-storey boxes of maisonettes. Coal hadn't been
pulled out of the ground in thirty years, and the chemical plant
and cement works that had offered lifelines when the shafts were
capped had also long since closed down. A warren that offered no
work and no future, you couldn't give the houses away now.

'We should park here,' Tess said, indicating a gravel yard beside
a pub at the end of the village.

'She lives in the new bit,' Boone said.

'Exactly. You don't want to leave the pride and joy there for any
amount of time.'

Molly Still was a small woman who wore a shapeless tracksuit and no make-up, and whose thick eyebrows were the same grey as the ratty hair she tied back in a ponytail.

'I'll put the kettle on,' she said, showing them to a Formica table in the kitchen. The decor and furnishings were dated, but everything was clean save for a rumour of dog. She threw tea bags in three mugs and conducted a hurried rather than covert tidying job on the empty bottles she found on the counter, sweeping them into the bin beneath the sink. Budget cider, fortified wine and cheap whisky, the kind that came in plastic bottles. As far as drinkers went, she had egalitarian standards.

She found posh bickies in the cupboard, ones kept for company, and struggled with the plastic seal inside the box before setting them out on a plate. With the back of a spoon she pressed the bags against the inside of the mugs and took them out. She searched the cupboards for something to add a nip to her mug from, finding nothing.

Boone caught Tess's eye and slid a twenty-pound note across the table to her. They spoke in facial gestures, Tess widening her eyes and Boone frowning, before Tess took the money and got up, leaving the flat. 'I've made tea,' Molly said. 'She's left the door open.'

'She'll be back in a minute,' Boone said.

Putting everything on a tray, Molly carried it across to the table, but her hands were shaking and it made an ungraceful landing.

'Sorry,' she said.

'No harm done,' Boone said, distributing the cups. 'You remember me, Molly?'

Molly sipped her tea and shrugged. 'Maybe. Shorter hair.'

'That's right. I came to see you before, about your granddaughter. About Sarah. When someone reported seeing her a few years ago in a nightclub.'

'Police?' Molly said, the word laced with suspicion.

'I was. I'm not any more.'

'So is she dead, Sarah? Have you found her?'

'No. Yes. I mean, she's not dead as far as I know. She was seen alive about a year ago.'

Molly nodded. Clearly this wasn't new information.

'Have you heard from Sarah?'

Molly shrugged. 'Maybe.'

'Maybe?'

'A young man come round.' She shook her head, as if ridding it of cobwebs. 'About a month ago now. He was after money, said Sarah had sent him.' Molly was distracted by a scratching at a door down the hall.

'Did you give him any?'

The scratching continued.

'Molly, did you give him money?'

A malodorous dog nosed out of a bedroom and trotted through the kitchen, waiting at the back door. Molly reached back to open it. The animal gingerly took the small step down to the grass, lolloped over to the fence and pissed up against it, before returning to the bedroom and curling up on the bed in a nest of its own hair.

'I told him, if Sarah wants money, she can ask for it,' Molly said. 'I'll give it her. Told him she could call me even, and I'd give it him. So long as I heard her voice.'

'What did he say?'

'Got upset. Yelled at me and shoved me. Called me names.'

'Was that the first you'd heard from her?'

Molly nodded. 'I figured he knew the story and was trying it on. Told him, all she had to do was call. Once. Say, "It's me, Nana," and hang up. That's all.'

'Did he give you a name, this fella?'

Molly closed her eyes. Knuckles pressed to her temple, she rubbed them in small circles.

'Molly, you okay?'

She opened her eyes as if she'd been caught at something.

'I remembered his hair,' she said. 'Terrible. Twisted up like the black boys used to have it. Filthy.'

She started at the sound of the door closing. Tess came in with one arm weighed down by shopping bags, hoisted them up onto the side.

'I got white bread, not sure what you like. Bacon and eggs. Milk for tea.'

Molly watched in pained anticipation, like a child at Christmas. Boone got up and found what she craved, a half-bottle of unbranded whisky, marked only Special Reserve.

'Could use a tot,' Molly said, sliding her mug forward on the table.

Boone sat with the bottle. 'His name.'

Molly looked at her with exasperation. 'I don't know,' she said. 'He didn't say it.'

Boone waited.

'It'd be in one of them books most probably. He never told it me though.'

'Books?'

'From the school. He always had that hair. Used to be they wouldn't allow it, get you sent home.'

'He went to school with Sarah?'

'Not the same year. Same place, though.'

Boone unscrewed the bottle, hovered it over Molly's mug. 'You going to eat something?'

The older woman looked at her like she was simple. Boone lifted the bottle away.

'Okay. All right.'

Boone poured in a dram. Added a bit more off Molly's look before she replaced the cap.

'You can leave it,' Molly said.

Boone slipped it into her coat pocket. Tess got a pan heating over the hob, and Boone went through to the second bedroom. There were posters on the wall like a teenage girl would hang, bedding and curtains trimmed in pink. Though the decoration was untouched, it was no shrine to the missing girl. Boxes were stacked on and around the bed, and there was an extra wardrobe filled with coats and jackets Boone suspected were Molly's.

Scanning the shelves, she found a few Penguin Classics (spines unbroken – for school, nothing suggesting reading for fun), and a handful of CDs, but Sarah would have been the digital generation. A few neatly arranged trinkets, mementos from trips to the coast and the like. The bottom shelf housed A4 folders, school stuff. The covers were creased and heavily scribbled.

Tucked between them, Boone found what she was looking for. Yearbooks of a sort, glossy-covered but stapled without proper spines. More like brochures for the year's events at Kearswood Secondary, photos of teachers and students having improbable fun, kids engrossed in extracurriculars.

She flicked through them, studying the pictures, finding him in the second book she tried. A group of boys in rafting gear, a school trip to an Olympic training facility. His hair was tied back but was clearly in fawn dreadlocks. The names were listed beneath, left to right. Luke Rayner.

Taking the opportunity, Boone peeked in the living room. Small, with a sofa and a chair, a coffee table with more empties and an ashtray that hadn't been seen to in a while. There were photos on a shelf. Sarah with an older man, her grandfather, Boone supposed. Molly and Sarah in deckchairs in a park, a boy crouched at Sarah's side. Older than her, a cousin maybe. Another one with Sarah hugging the dog when it was a puppy. Boone closed the door silently and headed back to the kitchen.

'This him?' she said, showing the picture to Molly. Molly squinted at the photograph. 'Hair's bigger.'

'It's tied back here. But is it him?'

'Yeah. He was around sometimes, when Sarah was still here. They ran away together.'

'You know where?'

Molly shook her head. 'Different places, I suppose. Sleeping rough. There was a pub they squatted in, The Sink. That was ages ago, mind. I used to look for her, first few years. Go round the closed pubs. Weren't illegal to squat in them because they weren't a house.'

Boone carefully tore the page out and folded it into her pocket. Molly had taken a few bites of the sandwich Tess had made, small mouthfuls whilst avoiding the crusts. Boone sat with her again.

'I'm backslid,' Molly said. 'My Rodney, he was the drinker. When he got the blackouts, that's when I knew. Friend of his stopped him, from the cement works, took him to meetings at a church. They'd both been down the mine before. Didn't believe in no medicine but the Bible after that, him. He tried helping me, but I never bought it. Felt like madness. When he died, I wondered if that weren't his sickness, the first signs of it.'

She leaned forward suddenly, teeth clenched, heel of one hand pressed into her eye.

'Molly?' Boone said.

Molly raised her other hand. She was quiet a moment, before sitting back once more.

'Sorry,' she said.

'You all right?'

'Yeah. Comes some days. Might go weeks without one.'

'What, headaches? You seen a doctor?'

Molly laughed. 'Worked years at the chemical plant, making perc for the dry cleaning.' She shrugged. 'People got it worse.'

'There's others, maybe it's something you can look into. With a solicitor, I mean.'

The old woman shook her head. 'My boss was good to us. Kind man, he was. Handed my notice in once. We figured we could get by on Rodney's salary, and it'd be better for Sarah if I was here. I had her mum young, you know, and it never really worked out.'

Sarah's mother had bolted soon after she was born, Boone recalled from her notes.

'You hear from her at all?' she said.

'Australia, I heard. Never got so much as a Christmas card, though. Dunno where she is now. That's part of why I wanted to be home for Sarah, why I handed in my notice. Rodney got ill though, and the boss let me back, even moved me into the offices on account of the headaches. Didn't have to. I didn't have no skills

for that sort of work. He was a kind man, fond of Sarah, showed
an interest in her after my Rodney passed. But it's not the same, is
it? And he had his own family.'

The dog returned to investigate the kitchen smells, sitting
patiently by the table until Molly put the plate with her crusts and
leftover bacon bits on the floor, the animal wolfing them down.
Molly drank the rest of her tea, the liquor getting her back to an
even keel.

'You're not a copper no more, you said.'

'Right.'

'I don't get it. Why are you here?'

'Something happened to . . . someone I know. I think it's connected to your granddaughter, or at least to people she was seen
with. I wanted to tell you that Sarah had been seen. I wanted to
tell you someone was still looking for her.'

'You?'

Boone shrugged.

'Ghost of a chance,' Molly said, eyes fixed on Boone's pocket.

Boone pulled out the bottle and pushed it across the table.

'She'd be a woman now,' Molly said, half filling her mug.

15

Boone drove Tess home, picking up burgers at the Medway services along the way.

Tess got two.

'I love them cold, later,' she explained.

'Strange child,' said Boone.

At the caravan, Tess was busting and flew off to the bathroom. Boone set about laying the food out on the coffee table before calling Barb.

'Detective Sergeant Barbara Bowen, your go-to police source.'

'Hey, Barb. You got my text?'

'Yeah. Luke Rayner. Obviously I'm happy to help, because police feeding information to private investigators has never gone badly in the history of the police, or information.'

'I'm not a private investigator.'

'Well, what would you call it?'

Boone thought about her notes pinned to the wall.

'I'm a biographer. A historian.'

'Oh, well. Heaven forfend I should besmirch thee.'

'We getting to the bit where you're going to tell me you can't tell me?'

'Kent Police cannot and do not release information to civilians.'

'Right. Look, I'm sorry, Barb. I know what it looks like, asking you for stuff. It's not how . . . I'm just a little caught up in this and—'

'Boone?'

'Yeah?'

'Shut up.'

'Yeah.'

'He has a record. Petty stuff, shoplifting, minor bit of aggro. Nothing for a while, though, and we don't have a fixed abode for him.'

'Molly said he and Sarah used to squat.'

'Economically prudent strategy in these dark times.'

'Thanks for this, Barb.'

Tess had left her mobile on the coffee table. Keeping an eye on the bathroom door, Boone had a peek, scrolling through her recent messages.

'You still owe me mimosas,' Barb said. 'My luck, you'll probably wander blindly into a world of shit again pretty soon and get what little remains of your mind bashed out of your noggin and won't remember any of this.'

'So touching, your concern.'

Shit. Bit of texting to and fro with an unnamed number, whoever it was telling Tess he was staying at the Regency Guest House. Had to be Ingram.

'Boone, who is this Rayner character?'

'He went to school with Sarah. Molly Still told me he dropped by to see her recently, trying to hit her up for money. Saying he had seen Sarah. Sounds like bollocks, but I want a word with him.'

The flush went and Boone put Tess's phone back as she'd found it. Barb was saying, 'You find anything that resembles evidence, Boone, you bring it to me. We'll do things the right way, yeah?'

'Yeah.'

'Yeah, bollocks.'

Tess came back in and set about the bacon double cheese, dipping fries into her strawberry shake.

'Absolute bloody savage,' Boone said, shaking her head in wonder.

'Who was that?'

'Barb.'

'Your copper mate?'

'Yeah.'

'She give up the goods?'

'Nothing to give up. You online here?'

'Got a data dongle thing. It's plugged into the laptop.'

'Molly said Sarah used to stay with Rayner when she ran away before. Closed pubs are his favourite. She said a place.' Boone was on the laptop, googling. 'The Sink. I can't find it. Got a bar in Shoreditch. A pub in Middlesbrough. A restaurant in Vancouver.'

Tess chuckled.

'What?'

'It's not with an S.'

'What do you mean?'

'The Cinque Ports. It's on the Oak Road coming out of Lark. Big old place out on its own. Used to go there in sixth form. One of those places people used to say, if you can't pull there . . . Everyone calls it The Sink. Times I spent there.'

'Oh aye?'

'You wouldn't know it now, but for all my primness, I spent the nights of my youth knees up in the back of Fiestas and Astras doing things a lady should never talk of.'

Boone looked the place up on the map, finding it not far from where they'd been earlier. That could wait for another day, though. There were other things to run down first.

She went over what information she had on Sarah Still, which remained paltry even after six years. The police file had a name and number for someone at social services who had handled Sarah's case when she was a teenager. Boone called, asking after a Jerry Killock, but was told he had passed away. She was put through to a Harry Eustace, a colleague who had taken on a lot of Killock's cases. He told her he wouldn't be able to tell her anything, but did confirm he hadn't had any contact with Sarah since Killock's death and presumed he never would as she would be an adult now.

Then Boone tried the number for the school friend who had seen Sarah at a nightclub in London three years earlier. The girl's mother answered and told Boone she'd since moved to Australia.

'Here, what are you like on the internet?' Boone asked Tess.

'I can download all the Netflix shows or porn you could possibly want for free.'

They looked up the witness on Facebook, finding pictures of a tanned and smiling girl on the beach, all bikinis and martinis. Boone decided against contacting her. If she was half as happy as she pretended to be for the internet, then she didn't want to be responsible for interfering with that. Probably wouldn't be able to add anything to her statement after all this time anyway.

'Roo mentioned this fella, Milan. Czech. Runs some sort of agency for farm workers coming over. Could be a new angle.'

Tess searched online for the names of a few agencies, looking up the details of their directors without any luck. Following a thread of posts on an agricultural forum threw up the name of the AnyFarm Agency, which seemed to have gone out of business, its telephone number coming back as not in service, but Tess found a Companies House entry with a Milan Jedinek listed as director. There was a correspondence address in Lark: a flat in The Carlton, a once-fashionable development.

'I don't even want to imagine what sort of grot you could track down on this thing,' Boone said, making a note of the address.

'Gonna go see him?' Tess said.

'No,' Boone lied. 'Just information-gathering. Field trip to Kearswood is as adventurous as I get.'

Boone drove home brimful of bacon burger to find Jack had cooked mushroom risotto, which she forced down, not wishing to appear ungrateful. After dinner, she and Jack sat up in her room before her wall of evidence and she told him about Molly Still, and that she had tracked down Rayner.

'You're doing this then,' Jack said.

'I told Barb I'd keep her informed, but I'm not a detective any more.'

Jack chuckled.

'What?'

'You might think you're a completely different person, but I still know your looks. You're into this, no matter how hard you protest, and nobody's going to tell you otherwise.'

'I'd like to be able to tell Molly Still that her granddaughter's still alive.'

'That's what you would have said before.'

'I thought you weren't keen on me getting too involved? Just have enough of a sniff about to see if I catch the scent of the way things used to be.'

Jack shrugged. 'I'm not saying you should run off and arrest the bad men by yourself. But you used to be a detective.'

'I used to be a lot of things. None of which I remember being.'

'The woman I married, the woman who is Quin's mum, she would want to know what happened to this girl. You say you're a different person, but you remember how to drive that clapped-out old bird of yours parked on the drive. Can't remember learning, but you know how. You remember how to cook paella. And you remember how to shoot a rifle. You were a detective. Detect.'

It was like the Thai chicken. All of Jack's hopes were coalescing around this idea of forging physical connections to the past, striking a mnemonic spark by wading around in the same waters she used to before the accident. He was right about one thing, though: she did want to find Sarah Still. She also wanted to find the men who had her in that flat and see about them too.

Sometimes her life had the elliptical texture of a dream half remembered. Her life before and her life now, connected by this missing girl in ways she didn't yet understand. When she thought about giving herself over to the logic of that dream, accepting that she was in fact Abigail Boone – detective, and wife, and mother of one – a deep fear took hold of her.

A fear that upon her awakening from the dream, her identity as Boone would instantly cease to exist.

16

Rain purring against the window woke Boone, the sheets shot through with sweat again. Her leg was stiff and she did some stretching exercises that she didn't do nearly often enough. She yearned to run. She'd asked, and it wasn't something she did before with any great glee, just to keep fit. Perhaps her leg preventing her now had crystallised the want inside her.

Jack and Quin had left already. Over coffee and toast, Boone fiddled about on her tablet. There was no telephone listing for a Milan Jedinek at the address Companies House had. The firm, AnyFarm Agency, wasn't listed as wound up, but there weren't any returns on file for over a year.

Showered and dressed, she was sitting in the Goose on Bewsborough Road, across from the Regency Guest House, before two o'clock. It wasn't long before she spotted Ingram, recognising him from pictures. He wore a baggy black beanie, shoulders hunched in a fleece bearing a supermarket logo. White cable from earbuds hung down and disappeared into his trouser pocket.

There was a droop to his right eye that wasn't in photographs of him from before the trial. Boone remembered what Mickey Box said about sending Ingram a reminder. He had a hitch to his walk too, like a skip where one foot hopped along twice for every step taken by the other. For just a moment, despite everything she knew the man had done to Tess (and, in truth, perhaps partly because of it), she felt a jolt of kinship with him.

He scuffed quickly up the steps to the tiled porch and pushed through the door, disappearing inside. He was quicker on his gammy leg than Boone was, probably because unlike her he didn't try to mask his limp. He'd simply worked out the quickest way of getting about with it. Crossing the road, Boone balled her hair and pulled up the hood of her sweater as she pushed through the front door. Saw Ingram's feet turning at the top of the stairs in front of her.

'Hey,' said a voice from a window in the wall on the left.

The Mancunian she'd spoken to on the phone. Keys hanging behind him, he sat on a revolving chair, face pinched into a murine frown, hair hanging like it had been taped on.

'He's already paid me, knobhead,' Boone said, hurrying past.

The man stood, face against the Perspex window as she took the stairs quick as she could, feeling the leg on each one.

'Oi,' he said, before deciding she wasn't worth the bother.

Boone heard Ingram fiddling with the lock on the second floor, saw the door shut as her eyes came over the landing. The carpet in the hall was loose offcuts laid on the wooden boards and it moved underfoot.

Two quick knocks.

'Fuck's sake,' he said before coming to the door.

Peering through the gap, it took him a second.

'Jesus,' he breathed.

'Need a word, Ingram.'

'I ain't done nothing. You got no cause being here. I seen my PO. Stacking shelves there with the kids and the muppets. This is harassment is what this is.'

'I'm not a copper any more.'

Emboldened by that, he opened the door wide, stepped forward.

'Should have sacked you years ago, way you did me.' He jabbed a finger in her chest, then again for emphasis.

'Conversation's better had with me than Mickey Box,' she said.

'Fuck you,' he said. 'And fuck Mickey Box.'

He dug his finger in, twisting her flesh. Boone didn't think, she just reacted. Snatching his finger in her fist like you'd hold a microphone, she jerked upwards violently. It snapped the way celery does. Ingram yelped but stopped short as she stood on his foot and shoved him hard, sending him tumbling back into the room.

She followed him in, closing the door behind them.

'You broke it,' he said, looking up at her like she'd started explaining multivariate polynomials, finger pointing now in roughly the same direction as his thumb.

'Lay a finger on me again, I'll give you a whole hand of them. Like a retired wicketkeeper.'

When Boone had first got home, first thing she did was go looking for lessons. However it was she had ended up in the flat that day, she wasn't going to let it happen again. Not without someone losing an eye, or the ability to shag. Looking into various martial arts, she settled on a place not too far away that taught Krav Maga. She wasn't in it for the belts, just the fight. Even dragged Tess along a couple of times but she lost interest quickly, claiming if she ever got in trouble again Boone would be there to fetch her out with fancy new violence.

Ingram got up, cradling his hand, and sat on the bed. The room was small, just enough space to walk round the bed, with a wardrobe pushed into an alcove, a dresser in the bay window, and a tiny bathroom to the side, with a toilet and shower. A laptop stood open on the dresser.

'Earning already?'

'Second-hand. Easier than having a telly.'

'How's Tess?'

'Fuck should I know?'

'Even you can't be dumb enough to think Mick won't come after you.'

'Fucking Mickey Box. Bollocks. Tell him that.'

Boone got her phone out. 'Tell him yourself.'

His eyes went from her to the phone, back and forth. 'All right. I seen her.'

'You stupid . . . When?'

'Got her number off a friend of a friend after I was released. Thought it was dumb, but. She told me to get lost. I text her, didn't get a reply much past go fuck yourself, but then she comes to me, see. Couple, three weeks ago. Just turned up, no warning.'

'Bollocks.'

'God's honest,' Ingram said, holding up the hand with the bent finger.

'Why would she?'

'Dunno. She never said. Comes up, had a couple bottles of

cider, them big ones like. We have a drink. And then, you know. Do it.'

Boone snorted.

'Think what you want,' Ingram said. 'But she was here. Only it was . . . it weren't like before.'

'What, she wasn't doped out of her gourd getting pimped to God knows who?'

'Not . . . I mean when we was together. The sex, like. After, she never said nothing.'

He was an odd creature, Ingram. As many years past forty as Boone was thirty, he'd never been much to look at, and with his eye and his limp his prospects hadn't improved. The notion of him with Tess would be laughable if Boone didn't know it had happened before.

'And what? She just ups and leaves?'

'She gets a call, some fella, took the phone in the bathroom. I listened, like, but she was whispering. Sounded like – not a fight, but you know, a whisper fight. Left straight after.'

'Didn't say who he was?'

He shook his head. 'I thought her old man maybe, but he'd have paid a visit if he ever knew. And why was she whispering?'

'A lover, you think?'

Ingram laughed. 'It weren't a boyfriend. I mean, if she had a fella, fuck would she want to come to me for? I ain't stupid, fella like me and a girl like her. But you know she's a bit messed up. You know this.'

'You hear from her again?'

'Nah. Text a few times. Didn't hear back.'

'I'm you, I think I'll cut the texts out from now on. Permanently. That type of behaviour, it's not conducive to healthy living. Leads to Mickey Box finding out where you live, complications of that nature.'

'Mickey Box is a cunt.'

'I might not be a copper, but I still know plenty. How fast do you think you'll get hooked back inside for busting your licence if anyone sees those texts? You ready for another six years? Ready for another reminder when Mickey Box finds out why you were sent back in?'

Brandishing his crooked finger, Ingram made threats his heart wasn't in. He wasn't going to tell anyone, wasn't going to advertise the fact he'd been unmanned by a woman.

The rodent behind the window in the wall stood when Boone left, as if he might enquire about her services but thought better of it. The police wouldn't come, Ingram wouldn't talk, and everyone would go on with their day as if nobody gave a shit what happened in the Regency.

Which was pretty much the size of things.

17

The Krav lessons were conducted in a safe environment. Whilst there was contact, and the odd bloody lip when things got too enthusiastic, there was never any real threat. Boone's understanding of violence all stemmed from that day at the flat and was born from her being the one who was hurt, not the one doing the hurting. She had worked hard in the intervening months at thinking of herself not as a victim but as a survivor, and at developing the tools with which she might continue to survive.

This with Ingram was different. It was the first violence she had actually done since her accident, and she was surprised to discover a tranquillity in the aftermath, something that attuned her to her surroundings and instilled confidence instead of fear or guilt. Made her wonder if she'd felt it before, what kind of a friend she might once have been to violence.

Taking advantage of this new-found sharpness, she decided to go looking for the Czech labour agency guy, Milan Jedinek, immediately. Needed to do a spot of shopping first, though. Doing the twenty-minute drive to Dover in just over ten, she stopped at an independent plumbing supplier and picked up the following: a box of disposable nitrile gloves, a small carbon-steel crowbar, a dust mask, and a bag of assorted copper elbows so it didn't look completely like she was going on the rob. Back in Lark, she parked the Saab at home. Packing her new gear into a rucksack, along with other bits and bobs like pliers and a wire coat hanger, she walked the couple of miles to where The Carlton stood on the seafront. Hardly noticed the leg at all.

A six-storey horseshoe, shopping units on the ground floor surrounding a plaza, The Carlton had once been a solution for modern urban housing problems.

Now the plaza was gated off, chains around the bars, and the shops all boarded up.

Been that way for a while, looking at the hardy weeds sprouting from the concrete in the quadrangle.

Higher up were other boarded windows, enough that it seemed as if the council had tried decanting the place and lost interest halfway through. The flats featured ensconced balconies arranged in pairs, apart from the top two floors, each of which was set back from the floor below it and sported uncovered terraces, also in adjacent pairs.

Her hair scraped back into a tight ponytail, dark hood of her sweater pulled up, Boone found the door to the flats. There was controlled entry, so she buzzed a few numbers, hoping someone would just let her in.

They didn't.

Lighting a fag, she stood outside for half an hour until a courier came with a package. She caught the door when he was let in and, leaving him to ride the lift alone, took the stairs up to the fourth floor.

The stairwell was decorated with graffiti – swastikas and anthropomorphised genitals – and the landing at the top was piled with junk. Bulbs were out in the corridor, and near the bend, where it turned down one of the legs of the horseshoe, it could have been night.

Milan's flat was the last but one. Boone rapped on the door, loud enough to be heard inside but not so much that she would attract the attention of whatever neighbours there might be.

She knocked again.

Nothing.

The corridor dead-ended after the last flat, leaving nowhere to go if she was spotted levering the door open. Subterfuge was the answer. She knocked at the last flat with half a story about knowing Milan and being worried, wondering if they'd seen him or, if their terraces were next to each other, whether she could peer round into his flat somehow. The story wasn't needed, however, as the door pushed open a crack under her knock. Gently she opened it further, seeing the frame was splintered at the lock where someone had forced it.

The flat was empty, all the furnishings gone or stolen. A fouled mattress was bent into one corner of a bedroom, and crushed beer cans and fag ends carpeted the place. The wall between bedroom and living room had been kicked through in several places, gypsum and shards of wood filling a couple of plastic buckets. The doors out on to the terrace had been boarded, but the plywood was cracked and pulled away, rotten now where the break was swollen and feathered by rain. Boone snapped on a pair of the disposable gloves. Idly she wondered how whoever had originally boarded it up had got back inside afterwards.

The terrace balcony was separated from Milan's by a brick wall that curved down away from the building, but even at its lowest part it was taller than Boone. No climbing that with a gammy leg. Emptying the buckets in the flat, she set them upturned beneath the window ledge and, with her good leg, boosted herself up onto the highest part of the wall (though not without making the mistake of looking five floors down to the concrete plaza). Milan had plastic patio chairs in a stack against the wall and clumsily she used them to clamber down.

The flat was dark inside. Cupping her hands to the glass, Boone peered through the back door into a living room with a kitchenette at the far end. A hallway off to the left was in darkness. She tried the handle, but it was locked. A two-lever mortise slapped in on the cheap, the lock was bullshit. Height lends the illusion of security. Groaning as she got onto her knees, Boone took the pliers and coat hanger from her bag and shaped one end of the wire into a rude approximation of a mortise key.

It wasn't pretty, but with a bit of back and forth the lock turned with a clunk. Any worry about noise was muted by the ungodly smell.

'Oh, Christ.'

Fearing being spotted, she went in quickly and pulled the door shut behind her. The stench was hideous, and as invasive as smelling salts. Boone covered her mouth and nose with the neck of her sweater. The light switch flicked up and down uselessly – no electricity.

Sparking her lighter, she held it out against the darkness like a shield, edging her way down the hallway, the black snapping back into place behind her. The first door was ajar, a small bedroom with a sofa and a desk. Cardboard boxes were stacked against one wall.

With her back to the hallway wall, she walked slowly behind the lighter. Across the way the door was open into another room, its curtains closed but the murky shapes of a bed and wardrobe just visible. The other door, between the bedrooms, was closed.

Treading on something, she stepped back and froze. Crouching, in the flickering light she found a wire, an extension cable loosely coiled on the floor. One end was fixed to a wall socket in the hall, the other snaked beneath the closed door at the hinge-side corner. Boone closed her fist around the handle. She counted her breaths, then turned it and opened the door.

The rank stench of the dead washed out over her and she gagged, almost vomiting down the inside of her sweater. She dropped the lighter and fell away from the door, sliding down with her back to the wall until she sat on the floor.

'Ah, fuck,' she said, fingering tears from her eyes.

She felt about on the floor, finding the lighter, and flicked it again. Holding her breath, she entered the bathroom. The sight in the bath was ghastly. A body, presumably Milan, bloated and larval, buoyant upon the water, maybe a third of a tub's worth. The power cord trailed over the edge and into the water, but to what exactly Boone couldn't see. A portable heater maybe.

The blued skin of his exposed hands was lifeless, maceration pulling meat from bone. Nails were missing. The water was barely identifiable as such, and it was as if someone had dropped dollops of yellow and brown loam into the tub. The face was fat and twisted, the mouth a bowl for maggots, the eyes dull like chalk. The hair seemed to have slipped off, a bloodless scalping. The whole form had steeped into human soup. He still had his shoes on.

Boone stepped back out, pulling the door closed.

The bedroom was neat, everything in its place. It had almost certainly been searched. The clothes in the wardrobe were caught up on each other, as if someone had angled them out on their hangers to search the pockets and pushed them back in any way they could. There was an en suite shower room with a toilet. Behind the folding door was a rattan corner laundry basket. Boone opened it and sifted through pants and socks before she found a pair of dark cords.

Something in the pocket.

She groped about for the opening and pulled out a car key on a large silver fob. Not real silver. It wasn't heavy enough and it rattled when she shook it. There were no signs of a struggle anywhere, so it was probably put in the wash by mistake rather than being deliberately hidden.

She relocked the rear door on to the terrace and shut the bathroom door fast. She scoped the corridor through the fish-eye peephole before leaving through the front door, closing it behind her. The stink would make its way out eventually, offending someone enough to call the police, though hopefully not for a while yet.

There was a residents' car park behind the block, overlooking the old tidal swimming pool, whose walls were now barely visible in the dark sands even at low tide. A colossal jack-up rig stood with grallatorial defiance, too close to the shore for Boone's liking. The wind was up, whipping spume into her face, but she closed her eyes and let the salty breeze cleanse her nostrils. She suspected she'd never fully rid herself of that smell.

Like some mad dowser divining for water, Boone roamed about with the key before her, pressing the button wildly. Nothing beeped. The key was for a Honda so, on the off chance, she scouted the surrounding streets, clicking the button in her pocket every time she saw an H badge and sometimes just for the fuck of it. She'd been at it an hour when she heard the clunk of central locking, finding a tarped-over ten-year-old Accord tucked away in an alley between two abandoned brick sheds near the railway line.

Lifting the tarp, she opened the front passenger door and slid inside, letting the tarp fall down again, engulfing the car in a clammy dampness. The smell sparked something off in her brain. It was how she imagined a cheap tent to be, which raised the horrifying prospect that she'd once been the outdoorsy type, or possibly even a girl scout.

In the glove compartment she found the manual and service log, along with a lighter-plug charger and a phone holder with sucker pads. Nothing was stuck in the sun visors. Running her hands under the seats and on the floor in the back, she found used tissues and a chocolate wrapper. Finally, in the driver's door compartment under an ice scraper, she found a phone.

Pulling the cover off, she shook out the battery and removed the SIM, not wanting it to ping a tower. Even the police knew dead men couldn't make phone calls, and she didn't want anyone to know later that the phone had been examined. Battery was dead. Turning on the engine, she hooked up the charger and waited for it to boot. There wasn't much on there. No stored numbers, but the log showed calls going to and from three separate mobile numbers, though none for several weeks. She took a picture of the log with her own phone's camera. There were no pictures or other files on the phone, and no memory card.

She examined the key fob again. It was a silver square, less than half an inch thick, with a picture of what appeared to be a Mediterranean beach embedded in the front. Fooling around with it, she found the cover rotated, revealing a space inside to keep things. In Milan's case, a micro SD card. She turned the phone off and popped the battery to install it. Turning it back on, she found the gallery populated with pictures of girls, posed shots, some of them dressed and others not so much. She recognised some of them as being taken in Milan's flat, but others were in a different place. Hundreds of the things. There were video files too. She turned the phone off and removed the memory card, slipping it into a zip pocket.

Thinking better of it, she turned it back on and checked the maps app. One place was listed in the saved locations. Scraycroft, some sort of farm the other side of Canterbury. She turned the phone off once more and replaced the SIM, returning it to the door compartment. Then, leaving the car tarped over just as she found it, she took a circuitous walk home and posted the keys through a slot in a random surface sewer grille.

Police could find their own way in when it came to that.

18

The farm was set deep in woodland off the A2, behind an abandoned housing development. The access road passed a honeycomb of concrete foundations the colour of fish-belly, the tarp now torn or stolen so the perfect squares pooled with rainwater and seepage.

The road thinned to a track through a densely packed silver birch corridor, the Goose's wheels struggling in the deeply rutted mud. Fifty yards down, she saw a rusted sign on the ground that read *Horton & Son at Highdene*. Wrong name but right place, according to the maps.

The woods rolled over the shoulder of a hill before abruptly opening up onto a flat expanse bounded on all sides by trees. The open space was lined with polytunnels, though none of them looked as if they'd produced fruit in some time. Polythene cloches were drawn over the hooped frames, many of them torn and tattered and flapping in the breeze, snagged like the sloughed skins of giant and departed reptiles. Snapped hoops had sprung apart like half-buried ribcages.

Boone parked the Goose at the mouth of the passage through

the woods. The farm had probably been somewhere Milan had supplied with cheap migrant labour, but what she couldn't figure was why he might have been there recently. It was obvious the place hadn't been operational in some time. She walked out among the dead rows, beneath the hoops. The ground was lined with black plastic, though in many places the earth came through great rips in the sheets.

In one tunnel, lengths of two-inch board were stacked in piles of various heights ranging from knee to chest. They'd been laid as walkways through some other tunnels, a job left unfinished. On the drive, Boone had stopped off at a supermarket and bought a cheap prepaid voice and text phone. She sat on the woodpile and dialled the numbers she'd found in Milan's phone. All three were no longer in use.

Listening to the automated out-of-service messages, she didn't hear the dog until it was almost upon her and began barking. Taking her weight on her good leg, she scrambled up the planks onto the tallest pile, having to duck her head beneath the tunnel's roof. The stack of wood swayed slightly and she grabbed the nearest metal hoop to steady herself.

The Alsatian snapped and barked just below her feet. A hundred pounds of black and bronze, the animal could easily have cleaned her off the top of the stack if it so desired.

'Kaz!'

The call was deep, guttural, and at its sound the dog spun away and fell in beside a tall man with an easy farmer's gait. He wore a navy gilet and faded jeans over oxblood riding boots, a herringbone cap pulled low against the noon sun. 'Private property, miss,' he said, a statement of fact rather than an accusation.

'I'm sorry,' Boone said. 'I didn't realise it had closed down.'

'Would have been private all the same.'

'I was looking for someone who might have worked here. One of the fruit pickers.'

The dog, Kaz, was going garrity again, bounding back and forth a couple of tunnels down the line. He barked and growled and clods of earth were thrown in the air as he tussled with the black ground lining between his teeth.

'Kaz! Kazak!'

The animal's reaction to his full name betrayed an understanding of human syntax that all hounds would rather keep disguised for reasons of mischief. He sloped back to the man's heel, whining until he was offered a hand for a quick lick.

'Always finding a field mouse or something about the place,' the man said. 'He'll learn himself when he finds a badger one day.' He looked up at Boone. 'Safe to get down now.'

She scooted down the stacks in a sitting position and brushed off her jeans. 'Didn't mean to trespass,' she said. 'When I saw the place was closed, it just looked strange somehow. I took a walk.'

'Looking for someone, you said?'

'I wanted to be at Scraycroft. The sign I saw back there said Highdene?'

'Horton at Highdene. That's what my father called it, what the company was called. Never really stuck as far as the land went. People still call it Scraycroft, and always will, I'd bet.'

'You'd be the son of Horton and Son?'

'Geoff Horton, aye. Was my father's place really, though. The fruit and everything was his idea. More of a cereal man myself. Closed the place down when he passed.'

'Sorry.'

'I'm still not clear on what it is you're doing here.'

'There's a man, Milan. A Czech.'

'They were most of them Czechs or Poles. Poles by and large. But it's been shut almost two year now. Milan, you say?'

'Milan Jedinek. He wouldn't have worked in the fields, mind. He ran an agency, AnyFarm?'

'Aye, brought the workers over. Dad paid them, and then they paid the labour. Seasonal, like. I never had anything to do with it, though. Dad handled all that. I never knew any names.'

'I don't suppose your father had any paperwork?'

He shook his head. 'Have to appreciate the nature of the business.' Code for he should have but he didn't, or he did but couldn't be bothered.

'You police?' Horton said.

'No. This is more personal. I'm looking for a missing woman. Milan, or anyone who worked for him, might be able to help.'

Horton shook his head again. 'Can't be any help there, I'm afraid.'

Kaz had skulked off again and was growling and snouting about.

'Better see to him,' Horton said. 'Stick his nose where it don't belong and lose it sooner or later. You all right getting back out of here?'

'Straight shot through,' Boone said, pointing down the avenue through the birches.

'Well then,' Horton said, touching his cap.

Boone spun the Goose round, pausing at the edge of the field to watch Horton in her mirror. He had to drag the dog away, but never once looked back.

19

It was still early afternoon. Boone phoned Roo and found she wasn't working so took a drive into Lewisham. She stopped by a supermarket and paid cash for a cheapo French press, a less inexpensive burr grinder, and a bag of very acceptable Toraja beans.

The main entrance to the house was propped open with the kind of plastic bottle crate that had gone out of fashion with milkmen, and the hallways of the place were in bedlam. Caked with yellow clay from the farm, Boone removed her boots and carried them. She clambered past a chattering brood of old men sitting in facing doorways taking tricks with German suited cards. Children chased a ball in and out of rooms, one pale and pitiful young girl tugging a wooden train behind her on a string.

Upstairs, she found Roo sitting on her bed reading, door to her room ajar. 'It's chaos,' Boone said.

'It's collection day,' Roo explained. 'Landlord comes to empty meters of our pounds and to collect security.'

'Security?'

'People do not pay deposit when they move in. You live here

because you have no spare money. What comes in goes right out. So we pay security every month. Cash.'

'A shakedown.'

Roo frowned. 'Huh? What is shakedown?'

'A scam. A trick. He's taking advantage.'

Roo shrugged, as if this sort of exploitation was only to be expected.

Boone dropped her boots just outside the door and shrugged off her jacket.

'Hey, I am liking the shirt,' Roo said.

Boone held out the hem of her top, a maroon Sonic Youth T-shirt with the band as cartoon astronauts, emblazoned with Japanese script. She turned this way and that.

'It was a present from my son,' she said. 'I think it's about twenty years old and Christ knows who wore it before. I try not to think about it. You like?'

'It is the saint's shinbone.'

'It is indeed. Your coffee, on the other hand, is shit,' Boone said, plonking her haul down on the kitchen top. She swiftly cooked up a brew, highlighting the importance of burr grinders over charlatanical bladed models, and Mickey Box's oft-stressed rigorous commitment to consistency of process. Roo placed her open book face-down over a knee and listened delightedly to Boone's prattling.

'This strength bean, two cups, five and a quarter minutes,' Boone said. 'Some people would say that is too much and that you should never stray from the orthodoxy of three and a half minutes. Some people also second-filter when they pour. We call these people animals, and you never let them near your beans. Other people add sugar. We call them savages. Milk is a matter for your conscience. Sometimes I have it black, sometimes I like a splash, leave it muddy like the Medway. Muddy enough to find old boots and broken bicycles down there.'

As Boone kept time, Roo took a leaf from a newspaper on the small table and laid it on the floor folded over, retrieving Boone's boots from the hall and placing them on it.

'Anything you leave out there, you lose,' she said. 'Where is it you have been to get dirty like this?'

Boone told her about Molly Still and about Milan and the farm.

'Why you didn't call the police?'

'Breaking and entering is generally frowned-upon behaviour in these parts. And I want a little more time to look into what I found.'

She slotted Milan's SD card into her phone and showed Roo the pictures.

'What do you make of these?'

'How you say, with the menu when you pick the different things?' Roo said.

'A la carte.'

'*Da*. A la carte. Men see the pictures, they pick what they want.'

'Some of them are dressed.'

'Men like Milan lie. They say there is jobs, be a hostess or work in a bar. So someone needs to see what you look like. But is always the same job, and if you change your mind, they convince you.'

'Threats?'

'There is a man, he is Kurdish. This is where they get the heroin. You remember from the flat. The girls who make trouble, they make them take it, and then it is different. They are addicts. And if there is still trouble, then they are overdose.'

'Fuck.'

Roo nodded. 'How long you think he is in the bath, Milan?'

'I dunno. Weeks probably, the mess he'd become. Someone will smell him sooner or later. I'm not going to needlessly involve myself in those complications.'

Roo shrugged it off. Boone stood to the side of the window watching the road, where a Jaguar had pulled up. A man got out, suit and open collar, probably fifty but with a softness to his edges that lent him the illusion of youthfulness. He beamed and waved at the tenants already congregating at the front door, before retrieving a brown leather overnight bag from the back seat.

Roo made more coffee, adhering strictly to Boone's hermetic methodology, and they waited for the landlord. He whistled as he worked and could be heard throughout the house. Boone was amazed. Roo was jittery, couldn't control her knees. Finally the man arrived at the door like a blind date, smelling of perfume and with his nose free of hairs. He offered Boone a soft hand, delicate almost.

'Harry Winter,' he said.

'Boone.'

He smiled. 'Any friend of Rumena's.'

His straw hair probably looked just as it had in his school days: free of product, its parting and brushed-back sides as naturally a part of him as his dark eyes with their dwarf lashes, or his long tapered fingers.

The overnight bag hung heavily from his shoulder, and from within it he produced a small cloth sack into which he released the pound coins stored up in the meter.

'Isn't it a beautiful sound?' he said, cocking an ear to the chime of the coins. He looked into the sack before putting a clip round its throat and depositing it back in his bag. 'Rumena is the most frugal of my tenants, but she always has her maintenance.'

He smiled at Roo as she took an envelope from a drawer in the kitchenette and handed it to him. He was conspicuous in its counting before jotting a note on its back and it too disappeared into the bag.

'What about her receipt?' Boone said.

Roo made wide eyes.

'Her receipt?' Winter said. He held his arms out, palms showing. 'We all trust each other here. All my tenants and I. We don't need receipts here, do we, Rumena?'

Winter weighed up Boone but addressed his words only to Roo.

'You really ought to notify me if you have guests staying,' he said. 'Conditions of the lease. Insurance. Things of that nature.'

'Yes,' Roo said. 'Sorry.'

He nodded. Looked round the room, examining high corners. Then he was gone, his perfume lingering in his wake as his whistling faded into the next room.

'You're sorry?' Boone said.

'What is it I can do?'

Boone sighed. 'You're right.'

'He can remove me, and then where will I be?'

'I'm sorry, Roo. Of course, you're right.'

'Maybe I call council. I hear they're falling over themselves to give me free home and money.'

'How much does he charge?'

'One fifty.'

'A month?'

'A week. And fifty a month cash security.'

'Jesus, Roo. I can get you a flat near me for that.'

'And deposit and references? You can get me these too? Is not so easy as you say.'

Boone looked about the room.

'You should look for a job,' she said. 'Out of London. You're working on the minimum anyway, might as well be somewhere rent is cheaper. Get away from this shithole. I can give you a hand with a deposit on a new place. First and last month, what have you.'

'I am not taking handouts.'

'A helping hand isn't a handout.' A thought occurred to her. 'I might know a place, actually. Not a palatial estate, but waterfront views. What stuff do you have? Not the food or anything. Belongings.'

Roo slid a small case out from under the bed. Inside, her clothes were arranged in immaculately folded piles.

'It is it,' she said. 'A few dirties in the bag.' She toed a laundry bag creeping out from beside the case. 'And a wash bag. My toothbrush.' She bared her teeth.

'So you could clear out lickety-split whenever you wanted. That's good.'

'Yes, lickety-split,' Roo said, confused.

20

In her bedroom in the caravan, Tess was naked and towelling herself off after a shower when Boone came in.

'Jesus, Boone!'

'Shit, sorry,' Boone said, hiding behind the door again. 'The sliding doors were open.'

'All right, I'm good.'

In jean shorts and a tee, Tess sat at her dresser drying her hair with a towel.

Boone sat on the bed.

'Must be nice, though,' she said.

'What?'

'Not needing a bra.'

Tess threw the towel at her. 'Fuck off, you big bender.'

Tess brushed her hair and poked around with her face in the mirror, Boone watching her quietly.

'I'm all right, you know,' Tess said.

'I know.'

'There's no need to worry.'

'I know.'

'I'm taking my pills.'

Boone nodded. 'Should you be?'

'What does that mean?'

'Not pre-natal vitamins, are they?'

Tess froze. 'Shit. How'd you know?'

'Something Mick said. And I put other things together.'

'Bollocks. He doesn't know. How could he?'

'He knows.'

'Jesus, he's going to murder me.'

'Hasn't yet.'

'He's going to murder me and then he's going to resuscitate me and murder me again for sport.'

'The fella, maybe. I'd keep that information to yourself. But he told me that he's here to help you deal with anything, and how-ever you want.'

'It's a trap.'

'I don't think so.'

'He asked me to move back into the cottage. Until I was feeling better, he said.'

'There you go.'

'I don't want to. That would be unbearable.' She looked about. 'Although I do love a good bath.'

'You seen a doctor?'

Tess shook her head.

'Well, we should do that. See what's what inside there.'

Tess was quiet.

'I saw Ingram,' Boone said.

Tess made a face and then buried it in her hands. 'Does Dad know?'

'Knows he's out, but doesn't know you've seen him. And he won't.'

'Stupid,' Tess said, eyes damp and nose running.

'Snapped one of his fingers in two,' Boone said. 'Ingram, I'm saying.'

Tess brightened up. 'Really?'

'Sounded wet and dry at the same time.'

'*Mazel tov.*'

She blew her nose loudly and peered miserably into the mirror.

'Great. Look like a slapped arse now. Can we change the subject?'

'With pleasure,' Boone said. 'I didn't come here to talk about your problems anyway.'

'No?'

'Only things more boring than other people's problems are other people's dreams and other people's gym stories. I want to talk about good stuff, like I've been thinking about trying dresses again. I have great ankles, you know.'

Tess laughed, a child's laugh. 'Weirdo.'

'I have a favour, actually,' Boone said.

'In exchange for the finger-snapping?'

'No. Because of your deep and abiding respect for me.'

'I'm all ears.'

'The woman I told you about, Roo. She needs to get out of the place she's in.'

Tess nodded. 'And you're thinking here in the caravan?'

'I'm asking what you think. Fancy a roomie?'

'She's knows it's not huge?'

'For her, it's an upgrade, trust me on that. And I sold her on its waterside charms.'

Tess shrugged and nodded. 'What the hell. Have to run it by Mick, but probably he'll be happy if there's someone here with me.'

'Cool. Thanks, kid.'

'Give us your iPod,' Tess said.

Boone dug it out of her pocket and handed it over, examining the array of beauty products on the dresser as she did.

'You got any moisturiser?'

'This you and your feet?' Tess said.

Boone sat back on the bed and pulled her socks off, picking at her heels.

'Here,' Tess said, tossing her a tub. 'Avocado with shea butter.'

She plugged Boone's iPod into a portable speaker, Automator beats leading in the sci-fi screwball of *Dr Octagon*, before fetching two cups of lukewarm coffee from the kitchen.

'So much better than mine,' she said. 'So much cool old shit on here.'

'Fuck off, old shit,' Boone said. She'd rolled her jeans up and was rubbing cream into her feet.

'I'd barely started infant school when this came out.'

Boone wiggled her toes.

'You want to wear dresses, better sort those things out,' Tess said.

Boone examined her legs.

'Japanese soldiers hiding in that undergrowth. Still think the war's on.'

Boone shrugged and sniffed the cream still on her hands. 'This stuff smells bloody amazing. Listen. There's something else I need to tell you,' she said, holding up the SD card.

'Where's that from?'

'Milan.'

Tess stared at her. 'Thought you said you weren't going there.'

'I lied. I found him at his flat.'

'And he gave you that?'

'Not exactly. He was dead, in the bathtub with – something. A heater. Fucking toaster. I couldn't see.'

'Jesus, Boone.'

'Yeah.'

'So it was suicide?'

'Made to look that way, I reckon. Dunno. Place felt like it had been searched, but I found car keys in a pair of trousers. Found the car eventually, and the mobile inside. Memory card was in the key fob, though.'

'You looked on it?'

'Pictures, mostly. Of girls.'

'You tell the police?'

Boone shook her head.

'Boone.'

'I want time to figure this out. Roo said Sarah knew this guy. So we have Molly saying that someone claiming to know Sarah came to see her, what, a month ago? Six weeks? Almost as long as Milan had been in his bath, from the state of him. Let's see what we have before we start complicating matters.'

Tess turned the iPod off. 'Come on. We'll look at this on the laptop.'

In the living room, she slotted the memory card into the computer and made herself fresh coffee, graduating Boone to a bottle of Scotch.

'This is what remains of a port-finished single malt from Arran that Mick gave me for Christmas. I can't stare at it for nine months waiting for sprog-dropping. You'll have to drink it.'

'Well, for your sake then.'

'Of course.'

Tess settled down on the sofa with the laptop. 'Girls is definitely what we have,' she said, bringing up the pictures from the memory card.

'Roo reckons it's like a catalogue.'

Tess screwed up her face. 'People are bastards.'

She cycled through dozens of images, did some pointing and clicking.

'Other stuff on here. Couple of videos. Oh God.' She covered her mouth with her hand.

'What?' Boone sat next to her.

The video was dark and grainy, artefacts and blocks looming out of the black before the screen flashed a brilliant white. The camera adjusted to the light, the cool radiation of an LED source of some description, a torch or lantern maybe. The shape of a woman emerged, lying on a low bed on her back with a mostly dressed man on top doing things to her.

Tess turned the volume up. The woman was crying out, and from somewhere in the murkiness behind the light, another man laughed. There was something large behind them, but in the dark it was just a shape.

'That's rape,' Tess said. 'They're filming a rape.'

The woman, girl really, was British and had long dark hair. For a moment Boone thought it was Sarah Still.

Reading her reaction, Tess said, 'Is that Sarah?'

Boone shook her head. 'No, I don't think so.'

Tess paused the video and went frame-by-frame until there was a clear shot of the girl's face. Boone got a picture of Sarah from her bag. It was a photocopy of a picture from the police file, but was enough to tell it was clearly a different girl in the video.

Boone clicked play again. After a while the girl stopped crying and turned her head away, staring at nothing. Dissociating. Until he flipped her over and started doing other things, and the screaming began.

Tess got up and walked out.

The video was almost seven minutes long. The man never faced the camera and he wore a mask. When it was done, Boone found Tess lying on her bed listening to the iPod.

'How'd it end?' she said, pulling the earphones out. 'They fall in love and live happily ever after?'

'You don't have to look at any of it. Sorry, kid. I should have checked first.'

'You ever seen anything like that before?' Tess said.

'Day of my accident wasn't a million miles away from it.'

Boone leaned towards compartmentalisation. She boxed away the horrors of her life and used them as fuel. She'd find these men. There would be a reckoning.

She made more coffee and they sat on the sofa going through the pictures. Most of them were like the ones they'd skipped through already – head or full-body shots of girls, some naked, all posed simply. Like Roo had said, a catalogue.

Some were not like the others, though, they were photos of

photos – snapshots of Polaroids that had bleached and faded with time. There were half a dozen like this, four of them of girls, a couple of them obscene. Children, eleven or twelve, nude. Two were simple group shots of girls, dressed, standing outside in a garden somewhere.

In one of the group shots there were two men. One wore a heavy coat with a scarf wrapped tightly about his neck, but was turned away from the camera, his face not visible.

The other was in his fifties probably. Neatly dressed in a grey suit, distinguished-looking, possibly even important but in a largely forgettable way. Forgettable, that is, if it hadn't been for his ears. They were giant things, hanging like fronds, as if a child had drawn them on.

'They look old,' Tess said.

'Twenty-five, thirty years, I'd guess.'

There were also a handful of other phone-camera pictures that weren't like the catalogue shots. Girls in sexual situations, like the video. Probably taken in the same place, but they were too dark to be sure. There was a strangeness to them. Either the angles were unusual, most of them weirdly low, or the image was obscured by something covering part of the lens.

'Almost like someone was hiding the camera when they took them,' Tess said. 'You think these were what they were looking for, searching Milan's flat?'

Boone nodded. 'Probably. I didn't see a computer or tablet there. These days, who doesn't have at least one of them? Someone took them.'

'You think someone would kill him for these? For having taken them?'

Boone's eyebrows furrowed. 'I'm going to watch the other video,' she said.

'Want another whisky?'

She nodded, and Tess took her glass to the kitchen area.

The second video was different to the first. It featured a blonde girl Boone recognised from one of the candid photos, but this was in a different room to the first film. The quality was bad, the only light narrow shafts of sunlight from a window high in the wall, semicircular and segmented like an orange.

'Wait, stop it there,' Tess said, half-full tumbler in her hand.

Boone paused it and took the drink from her.

'Go back to the light,' Tess said.

Boone skipped back to the semicircle of light coming into the room.

'I know that,' Tess said.

'You know where it is?'

'I know those windows. Or ones like it.'

She told Boone about Dave Fallon, a boy at school who had been smaller than any of the girls and would make up for it by bringing in tools from his father's shed to impress the other boys. Bolt cutters were a good one. Stephen Woodson, who was smart and good at football and got into real music before anyone else, took them from him and they all went out to the mine and cut their way through the fence. The abandoned buildings fascinated them. Huge and hollow, like the skeletons of megafauna.

'There's a series of smaller buildings, away from the mineheads and the washery. Some were tooling shops, some were storage or office buildings. Like long brick huts with pitched roofs, and each end they had windows like that up in the gables.'

She brought up a map of the area online.

'Quiet,' Boone said. 'Isolated. You could do what you like in a place like that.'

They watched the rest of the video. The girl was dressed, standing in the dark room talking with two men. The sound was bad, the conversation indecipherable, but clearly she was upset and crying. One of the men, a big man, listened to her until he'd had enough. He struck her, open-handed but it cleared her off her feet and she fell to the floor like a doll. The man turned, face covered by a balaclava, and walked by the camera.

No, he didn't walk, exactly.

He lumbered.

Boone knew immediately, and with absolute certainty, that this was the man who had been in the flat that day.

The day of her accident.

THREE

A HALF-PROMISED LAND

21

Boone woke with a start, face pressed against cool glass. Her neck was stiff and screamed when she moved it. She didn't know where she was and in a flush of paranoia she thought they had found her, the men from the video. They had found her just when she had discovered the first evidence of them, and they had taken her again. As soon as she thought it, she knew it was nonsense. If they'd found her, she'd be dead.

'We're here,' Mickey Box said.

The Mercedes was parked across the road from the house in Lark. There were no lights on. With the edge of her finger, Boone sawed drool from her mouth and chin, wiping wet from the window with her cuff.

'Cheers, Mick.'

'Uh-huh.'

'Be back soon as for the Saab.'

'Uh-huh.'

Recognising the men in the video had shaken Boone. She hadn't told Tess she knew them, but had treated the shock with a stiff drink. Then several more stiff ones, knocking off Tess's Scotch. Things got a tad messy. Tess had told her to crash in the spare room but, for reasons known only to a drunk, Boone had insisted she wanted to go home and tried to get into the Goose. Tess had to get Mickey Box, who agreed to drive her home when she still wouldn't see sense.

She clambered out of the Merc and waved as Mickey Box spun round, speeding off. As quietly as she could, she unlocked the door and went in. She wanted to appear plausible if Jack was still up.

A pale glow emanated from the sitting room out back, next to the kitchen.

Jack had said it had been listed as a *keeping room*, like they were buying a nineteenth-century New England farmhouse. Quin was on the sofa, one leg under him, big headphones on, spraying machine-gun fire in a video game. Boone edged into the room until she appeared in his periphery, and he pulled the cans off his head sheepishly.

'Hey,' he said.

'Late,' Boone said, wagging a finger. 'Wotcha doing?'

He gestured at the screen like it was self-explanatory.

Boone nodded. 'Drink?'

'Can I have a beer?'

She narrowed her eyes. 'I think it'd be wasted on you.' He wasn't impressed by that. 'But,' she said, 'we may have something better.'

She went to the fridge and found a bottle of cider Jack had ordered over the internet from some place in Somerset. Up in a high cupboard she found a mottled two-pint beer glass that he had taken as a souvenir from Oktoberfest in his youth and probably never used since. She half filled it with ice and poured in the cider, stabbing a straw in the middle.

Jack was partial to a fancy drink. Boone danced through to the front lounge, *the reception room*, and from the oak drinks cabinet took a bottle of 1969 Balvanie overproof that he'd paid a ridiculous amount for and never opened. Tonight was the night.

She threw some ice in a tumbler with a heavy tunc and splashed a generous measure over it, carrying both glasses (and the bottle under one arm) out to the sitting room.

'There,' she said. 'Grown-up fruit juice.'

'I don't want a straw,' Quin said.

'Course you want a straw. Who's having more fun than the fella supping cider through a straw?'

Quin considered the irrefutable reasoning behind that and fixed the straw between his lips.

'That's Dad's special bottle,' he said, nodding at the Balvanie.

'Your father would keep a unicorn in the zoo,' Boone said. 'I'd rather ride her bareback across the purple veldts.'

Quin laughed. Boone took a long drink.

'Now, teach me this shooting game.'

Quin fetched another headset and another controller and for the next half an hour ventilated his mother over and over with a liberal amount of lead.

'This isn't how shooting works,' she said, scrutinising the controller. 'Or dying, for that matter.'

Quin had a second cider, arguing that it would only be wasting the remaining ice if he didn't, and when half of that was gone, his trigger reactions had lengthened noticeably.

'I have something to share with you,' Boone said. She found

her iPod and held it up in front of her like a candle. 'How do we listen to this with two headphones?'

'Here,' Quin said. He fiddled about with the RF receiver and the stereo and the iPod and hooked it all up in that easy manner boys had with the sorcery of consumer electronics.

Pressing play on *Singles Going Steady*, which Tess had steered her towards, Boone got up and danced, swinging her hair about, and then dragged Quin up with her in a manner that would have mortified him if it wasn't for the cider. Holding a finger up like she had an idea, she opened the doors out on to the decking. Skipping forward to 'Why Can't I Touch It?', she yanked the RF receiver out of the headphone port on the stereo and the sound spilled out loudly into the house.

'This is the remastered version,' she yelled over the music. 'Don't tell anyone, but I prefer it, because they goosed the bass and because I'm basically an infant and don't remember the original. And because it makes me want to spin around.'

Quin, delighted by Boone's pissed-up ways and general unmumliness, allowed himself to be led outside. There, holding hands, with him in his socks and her in bare feet, they spun round and round as fast as they could and leaned back as far as they could, faces starward, until they lost all track of the earth and spiralled out of control, collapsing in a giggling heap on the lawn.

Quite abruptly, the music stopped.

'Boo,' said Boone.

Standing in the doorway, hands on hips, was Jack's silhouette.

'What's happening?' he said. 'You'll wake up the neighbourhood.'

From the ground, Boone waved about her. 'There's hedges, and they're miles away. And also, fuck 'em.'

Quin laughed.

'Several hours past your bedtime, young man,' Jack said.

'But Dad—'

'But Dad nothing. Go.'

Boone cupped a hand to the side of her eye to hide a wink as the boy trotted off smiling and disappeared into the house. Boone spread herself out into a star on the grass. Jack shook his head and went in.

He was on the sofa when she finally came inside.

'Look at you,' he said.

She was covered in grass and dirt and other fantastic stuff.

'You let him drink?'

Boone clocked the unfinished cider stein. Denial was futile. 'Bit of cider's all.'

'He's supposed to have school in the morning.'

'Hey, Dad of the Year, he was up already when I got back.'

'Drunk, no doubt. Did you drive?'

'I did not. A gentleman friend dropped me home.'

'And this gentle—' He stopped dead in his tracks when he noticed the bottle of Balvanie standing on the floor. Picking it up by the neck with two fingers, he placed it carefully on the table, as if it was evidence.

'That's my Balvanie,' he said.

'Yes. Yes it is.'

'My special bottle.'

'Yes.'

'Do you have any idea what I paid for that?'

'In fact, I do. And having that information only made it taste all the sweeter.'

'I was saving that.'

'For what?'

'A special occasion.'

'Like what? The day you finally get that sense of humour?'

'Maybe. Maybe a day like that.'

'You'd always have found a reason not to open it. Christ, no wonder I forgot all about you.'

Boone immediately regretted saying that. His face, he was crushed. Everyone was a stranger to Boone, but to Jack this was still his wife speaking, the love of his life. Her face, her voice.

'I didn't mean that,' she said.

Jack stood up, nodding. He grabbed the bottle and carried it back to the cabinet in the front room, Boone trailing behind him.

'Jack, I'm sorry. That just sort of came out. I've had a bit to drink. Too much.'

He wheeled round, eyes wide and furious. 'You're not his cool older sister, you know. You're his mother. Or you're supposed to be.'

'All right, Jack.'

'Don't all right me. What the hell is happening, Abigail? We never see you, you're out all hours with this Boxall chap and his daughter, and the only time you can make for our son is a middle-of-the-night drinking session? He's fourteen.'

'We were having fun. He was laughing.'

'There's a time and a place.'

'I didn't realise fun had to be scheduled. Maybe you can pencil some in, give me an appropriate time.'

'Can you hear yourself? How many mothers consider boozing at three in the morning with their fourteen-year-old son to be fun?

Get a fucking grip. Do you know what this has been like for Quin and me? Do you even—' Hand raised, he cut himself off.

'Go on,' Boone said. 'Tell me about it. Tell me all about how me being abducted and thrown off a balcony has been for you. I'd love to know. And then I can tell you what it's like to live in a house where everyone wants you dead.'

'What are you talking about, dead? Nobody wants you dead. You're my wife, Abigail. I want you well. I want you back.'

'That's it, though, isn't it?' Boone said. 'Don't worry, Abigail. You'll be better soon. It'll all come back. Things will return to normal before you know it. Because you see me as something that needs fixing. There's some previous state you want everything returned to, because I'm not *her*. I'm not Abigail, am I? I'm not the person you think should be inhabiting this body. And everyone thinks the sooner things return to the way they were, the sooner Abigail returns, the better.'

'I just want you better. Quin just wants you better. We just want what's best for you.'

'No. You want what's best for *you*. I feel just fine, thanks. But that doesn't suit you, does it? Because I'm not the person you married. Not the person you started a family with. I'm a parasite. You wouldn't concern yourself with what became of me if that other Abigail Boone suddenly returned.'

'You are that Abigail Boone. You're the same person.'

'Am I? Then why are you so upset?'

Jack touched her arm, held her bicep. 'Look, we're going to have . . . teething problems. But this is something we're going to work through. It'll be a process.'

'You don't get it, do you? You won't see it.'

'See what?'

'She's gone. She's not coming back. But you just presume that she'll gradually return to you, and that I'll gradually fade away. What's worse, you just presume that I should help you with that. No problem, everyone. Remain calm. I'll just commit suicide by recollection.'

'What on earth are you on about? Abigail, this isn't a war. You *are* the woman I married. This isn't zero sum, it isn't you or her. You're the same.'

Boone shook her head. 'That's not how it feels. I don't remember *being* before any of this happened. And I'm certain, absolutely certain, that I won't *be* at all if the memories of those things, of that life, return. I'll simply cease to be. And I cannot accept that.'

'What can you accept then?' Jack said. 'If you don't want to be the wife you were, and you don't want to be the mother you were, then what are you still doing here? It's easy to say you don't want this and you don't want that, but it seems to me that no matter what you say, you keep on coming back here, to the only home you have.'

He left her with that and went upstairs, Boone standing there addressing the space he had been in.

22

Boone woke up with a tongue hairier than a hog's back. She was on the sofa in her bedroom, apparently not having made it as far as the bed, though if the empty bottle of overproof on the floor was any indication, she had managed to find the drinks cabinet again at some point.

Half a dozen missed calls on her mobile, all Tess.

'Boone?'

'Yeah.'

'Jesus, you sound shit.'

'Yeah.'

'I thought vomiting in my shower might have cleared the system.'

'Possible I continued when I got home.'

'I see. So, visiting The Sink can wait?'

'Ugh. I have to come and get the Goose. I don't think I should drive for a while yet, though.'

'Mick said I can have the Mercedes. Said I should come and get you and drive you about. Bring you back later to collect the Saab.'

'Really? What's got into him with all the munificence? Especially after last night's unscheduled taxi driving.'

'*Noblesse oblige*,' she heard Mickey Box say in the background. 'Plus it gets this one out and about.'

'There you have it,' Tess said.

'World of good, out and about in the fresh air,' Mickey Box was saying.

'I think I'm going to throw up,' Boone said.

She sat under the shower for half an hour and then had two cups of coffee, thinking about toast but deciding against it. By the time Tess rolled up in the Mercedes, she had perfected her looking-sorry-for-herself face.

'What did you do?' Tess said.

'Played video games and danced with Quin. And possibly gave him cider. And then had a row with Jack.'

'Well, that's not too—'

'Then told Jack it was no wonder I forgot him and that I didn't want to remember any of our life together.'

'Oh. Well, on the plus side, you got fall-down drunk and didn't forget anything new, so . . .'

The Sink was boarded up. Standing on a road between places of no particular import, nothing near it for a mile in either direction, it sat there with its doors and windows shuttered like eyeless remains. Junk was scattered about the empty car park and the great wooden cross post stood naked, its hinged sign taken down so it no longer creaked in the wind. Boone found it lying flat at the corner of the car park, dented where someone had stomped it.

'Hare and Hound,' she said.

'That's what they changed it to. New ownership. Wanted to get away from the teenage pilling and pulling crowd. Went gastro. Didn't last long, and the old name always stuck. Always will.'

'Memories flooding back?'

Tess pointed to a low rail-fence at the back of the car park, a field beyond it. 'I tugged off Jeremy O'Brien standing against that fence. Back in my carefree days.'

'So much more responsible now,' Boone said, rubbing her belly.

'Shut up,' said Tess softly.

'Don't remember my first time. Or any time, come to think of it.'

'You haven't . . . you know, since?'

Boone shook her head. 'Who would I with?'

'I thought maybe Jack. I know you have different rooms and that, but . . .'

'He broached the subject a couple of times. I shut it down.'

'So it'll be like the first time all over again. Except it won't sting.'

'I can feel this bloody pin in my leg digging into my bum when I sit down wrong. God knows how it'd stand up to hanky-panky.'

Tess laughed. 'Such an old fuddy-duddy. Do you need me to explain the birds and the bees?'

'It's like a lot of other stuff. The thing itself feels familiar, but I can't recall a single specific time doing it.'

Tess sidled up and slipped her arm through Boone's. 'I can introduce you to some suitors. Lovely men, really.'

'Men aren't the answer to any questions I have,' Boone said.

The boarding over the front entrance to the pub was fast, bolted into the wooden frame. Round the back they found a loose panel. The lock on the door behind had been drilled, hasps and a padlock fitted, but the lock hung on the loop without the hasp fitted over it.

'Maybe they left,' Tess said.

Boone gently pushed the door open. It was dark inside and felt damp. Using her phone for a light, she edged along a narrow corridor to the bar itself, Tess shuffling along behind. A bed had been fashioned inside a window booth, and there were other signs of habitation – empty drink cans, food wrappers in a bin. They found a staircase and crept upstairs. It was a mess, carpetless, with the odd floorboard missing. Broken furniture lay in the hallway, smashed windows letting the chill in, and a mattress was propped up against the wall.

The first door swung open easily on its hinges, cracking against the wall. A heap of clothes and newspapers in the corner came to life and a man sprang from them, impossible to tell his age. He wore a winter coat with his hand tucked into it like Napoleon, a button left open to accommodate. His beard was matted and his grey hair stringy and unwashed.

'Easy,' Boone said, palms raised. 'We thought the place was empty.'

'Hey!' the man cried. 'Hey!'

He pulled his hand out of his coat and Boone saw that in fact he had no hand, his arm ending in gristled stump. Another man, younger, appeared in the hallway, hair shaved close to his scalp. A tattoo snaked up his neck past his collar, reaching behind one ear.

'Fuck are you?'

'Nobody,' Boone said. 'Thought the place was empty. Door wasn't locked. We'll be on our way.'

He stepped closer, hovering around the top of the stairs.

'Fuck are you?' he said again.

Lights flickered on downstairs, and a large man trudged halfway up the stairs before he saw them. His parka didn't quite close around him and his left arm was in a cast, hair pasted to his forehead with sweat. His eyes jumped rapidly between Boone and Tattoo.

'You go out and not lock the door, Chins?' Tattoo said.

'Got a paper,' Chins said, meekly offering up a copy of the *Mirror*. 'Wanted a Coke and a Crunchie.'

'You fat dickhead. Didn't you learn nothing?'

Napoleon clattered out of his room, a curtain rod with fleur-de-lis finials tucked beneath his handless arm, good hand brandishing it before him like some medieval weapon.

'I think maybe this is escalating quicker than necessary,' Boone said.

'Dal?'

A girl joined them from Tattoo's room, half dressed and honey-skinned, a coil of black hair falling over one eye.

'Go back in there, George,' said Tattoo, or Dal apparently.

She held his arm. 'Dal, what's happening?'

'Found these two sneaking about,' said Dal.

'We weren't sneaking about,' Boone said. 'We came here looking for a friend, and found the door unlocked. Figured the place was empty.'

'Fucking Chins left the door open again,' Dal said.

'Our mistake,' Boone said. 'No harm done. We'll get out of your hair.'

'Mercedes outside,' Chins said.

'Big car for poking about squats in. Paragon sent you, didn't they?' Dal said.

'I don't know who that is,' Boone said.

'Lot that own this place. You're with that security firm. Trying to get us out.'

'We're not leaving,' cried Napoleon, waving his pike clumsily.

'That's right,' Dal said. 'We're a family. Look after one another.'

· Napoleon took a step forward with the pole and Boone stepped in between him and Tess.

'You come closer with that thing, I'll take it off you and break the one good hand you have. You'll need to beg one of these bug-fuckers to wipe your arse. Think you're family enough for that?' She turned to Dal. 'I don't know what Paragon is, and I don't give a shit if you live here or not. I'm looking for a missing girl called Sarah Still. I was told a man called Luke Rayner might be able to help and that he might be staying here.'

'There's nothing here for you,' Dal said. He spat on the floor.

Boone pointed at Chins. 'We're leaving. Dunno how quick the rest of them are, but if you try to stop us, I'll thumb your fucking eye out of your head before any of them get to me. I promise you that, chubby.'

Chins looked up at Dal. Boone had Tess's hand and was already leading her down the stairs. Chins pressed himself into the corner where they turned and Boone pushed Tess past him and back down into the lounge.

'Place hasn't changed much,' Tess said.

Hurrying between tables and stools towards the door, they became aware of someone else in the room and turned to find a young man fiddling with a backpack, fawny dreadlocks creeping out like vines from under his hat. He looked older than his years, not mature but worn out. Used. Less a person than the detritus of a previous existence.

'Luke?' Boone said.

He looked up, startled, like a cat caught with its nose in the cooking pot.

'Don't run,' Boone said. 'I'm a friend.'

He moved quickly, putting a table between them, eyes darting around for an obvious escape route.

'I'm a friend of Molly Still. I'm looking for her granddaughter, Sarah. I just want to talk.'

'I don't know,' Rayner said.

'Just want to talk. I'm not here to make trouble for you.'

'I don't know where she is.'

'Okay, fine. But you've seen her?'

That was when he ran, making headlong for Boone and shouldering her hard, sending her toppling backwards over a low stool.

'Wait!' yelled Tess, stepping out in front of him, waving her hands about.

Rayner stopped, knees bent slightly and fists raised.

'I look like a threat to you?' Tess said, palms out.

'Hey,' Boone said, picking herself up.

'You better get aw—' was as far as Rayner got before Boone whipped out a finger jab to his eye, the heel of her other hand following it quickly, driving into his septum.

His head jolted back and he dropped his rucksack, falling to the floor in a sitting position just as Boone kicked him in the groin. He yelled and curled up.

'Jesus Christ, Boone,' Tess said, grabbing her arm and yanking her away.

'I'm calm,' Boone said, and she was.

'Bastard,' Rayner spat.

Blood streamed from his nostrils and he caught it in cupped hands beneath his chin, as if contemplating some future use for it. His eye was red and watery and he couldn't blink it away.

Tess knelt beside him.

'You're going to be fine,' she said. 'Just breathe.'

She touched the back of his neck and tilted his head back gently, a finger under his chin.

'Let me look. I don't think anything's broken.'

She offered a tissue and he held it to his nose as she helped him off the floor and onto a stool, chin still raised.

The girl, George, came down from upstairs, demanding to know what was going on. For all their earlier bluster, Dal and Napoleon hung back in the hallway at the foot of the stairs.

'It's fine,' Rayner told her. 'I'm fine.' He pointed at Boone. 'This one's a lunatic, though.'

Boone unfolded the page she'd torn from the school yearbook.

'This is you?'

Rayner swatted the sheet away.

'Fuck off. I'm not talking to you.'

Tess took the sheet from Boone, giving her an unambiguous glare in exchange. 'Molly told us this was you. She remembered you from when you were at school with Sarah.'

Rayner peered down his bleeding nose at her. 'She sent you after me? Two girls?'

'She didn't send us after you.'

'She's a drunk, you know. Anything she says—'

Tess touched his arm. 'We don't care about that. We only want to find Sarah.'

'We ain't seen her in ages,' George said. 'Couple of months probably.'

Boone showed her a picture of Sarah Still on her phone.

'This is her?'

George nodded. 'Hair's a bit different. She's thinner now.'

Tess showed Rayner.

'Yeah.'

'What happened?' Tess said. 'She just left?'

Rayner shook his head.

'Luke, if she was in trouble, we're no part of that,' Boone said. 'We want to help.'

'She left a while ago,' Rayner said. 'Said some people were looking for her and it was best she didn't stay anywhere too long. That was weeks ago. Couple of months maybe. Haven't seen her since. She was pretty strung out, so I didn't know how much of it was real. Honestly, I didn't believe any of it until that fella come here looking for her.'

'What fella?' Boone said.

'He means the big Paki,' Dal said. 'Security or something.'

George rolled her eyes.

'You saw him?' Boone said.

George nodded. 'He was big. Huge. I was in the bogs and heard him. Looked out through the door, but he never saw me. He broke Chins' arm. Just twisted it till it snapped. Dal said he was from Paragon—'

'He weren't from Paragon,' Rayner said. 'He asked for Sarah by name. Why would Paragon know her name? Why would they send someone to break arms? They don't do that.'

'He been back?' Boone said.

Rayner shook his head. 'Dal told him Sarah hadn't been here
for weeks at that point. We haven't seen him or Sarah since.'

'Wouldn't let her back even if we did,' George said.

'George . . .' said Rayner.

'I know you're silly for her, but she was horrible. Mardy cow,
right up herself she was. All her stories about this and that and her
rich boyfriends.'

'George,' Rayner snapped.

'What?' George said.

'Rich boyfriends?' Boone asked.

'There was a guy in the paper. I dunno who he was, but she
recognised him. He was some muckety-muck. The stories I could
tell, that was what she said. Then didn't tell none.'

'She say a name?'

'Nah. Someone she'd known forever, she said. Probably a line
of shit. Most of it was with her.'

'She tell you about any of this, Luke?' Boone said.

He shrugged.

'Luke?' Tess said.

'She said she could get money from someone, some guy. I know
the stuff she used to do, so I figured it was some bloke she'd been
with. But then she sent me to her gran's to ask for money, so I
thought whoever it was must have blown her off.'

'She didn't tell you anything else?' asked Boone.

He hesitated. 'No.'

'No?'

'Not really. She gave me something. I thought it was just to
keep hold of, but she's never been back.'

'What?'

He shook his head. 'No.'

'Luke . . .' Boone started.

'You know, if she'd given me the money, Sarah's gran, I'd have got her away. She wanted to leave. But she was afraid someone would be watching the house.'

'Watching Molly's house?'

Rayner nodded.

'She could have called,' Boone said.

Rayner shrugged. 'We were going to go to Ireland. She didn't have a passport, but there's a ferry up north goes to Belfast. We were going to drive south after that.'

'Sounds nice,' Boone said.

'I don't know where to go now.'

'What did she give you, Luke?' Boone said.

'A grand,' he said.

'What?'

'A grand. Cash. I'll show you.'

Boone laughed. 'You must be joking. How about you give it me, or I kick you in the bollocks again? Put my heart into it this time.'

'Boone,' Tess said.

'I don't know you,' Rayner said, standing up. 'I'm not giving you shit.'

When he bent to pick up his rucksack, Boone reached out and tweaked his nose. He screamed, dropping slowly to his knees with his hands together before his face as if in prayer.

'Boone!' Tess protested, stepping between her and Rayner. 'The hell are you doing?'

'Fucking bitches,' Rayner said forlornly, all women part of some conspiracy to ruin him.

'A grand?' Boone said, looking Tess in the eye. 'No.'

Rayner took his opportunity and, pack slung over one shoulder, legged it towards the door.

'Shit,' Boone said, starting after him, but she wasn't built for sprinting any more. Pushing past the boarding outside the door, she pulled up in a limp and watched him vanish across the car park and into the trees. 'Dammit.'

Tess followed her outside. She walked by without saying a word and got into the Mercedes. George slipped out past the boarding and stood in bare feet scanning the trees for any sign of Rayner.

'He'll be back when we're gone,' Boone said.

She offered George a score. The girl considered the note like she might refuse it, but took it and wadded it up tight in her hand.

'You okay in there?' Boone said. 'With them?'

George made a face. 'I know how to handle Dal. Besides, this is just till we scrape some money together. I cut hair. Not professionally like, but I'm going to get my City and Guilds. Dal used to be a plumber's mate. We want to open a place ourselves eventually. Unisex. That means men and women.'

'Well, best of luck with that. Tell Luke I'm sorry about the nose.'

Tess sat in the passenger seat, scowling.

'He'd already knocked me over once,' Boone said. 'I wasn't going to let him—'

Tess raised a hand. 'Do not.'

'What?'

'Do not tell me that was for my benefit. I saw you, the look on your face.'

Boone thought again of breaking Ingram's finger, how it felt. She was only mildly surprised to not find shame waiting there for her.

'Look, since we're here, why don't we drop in on Molly and—'

'Just take me home,' Tess said.

Boone drove them back to the Medway to pick up the Goose and, since Tess ignored her the whole way, passed the time thinking about George and her hairdressing and the lies kids tell themselves to fill their need for truth.

23

They left the Mercedes outside the cottage and Tess dropped the keys in the fruit bowl in the kitchen. When she came out, she got into the Goose beside Boone.

'You want to kip over?' she said. 'Avoid the hubby?' First thing she'd said since The Sink.

'Oh God, yes please.'

'Didn't think you seemed too eager to go back.'

'Embarrassed.'

'Must have had a barney before.'

Boone shrugged. 'Couple of little flare-ups. Nothing major. Before *everything*, I guess we had some rows. Not that I remember, though. And it's different when you know someone. Like, *know them* know them. Making up isn't hard, you know how things work.'

'You know how things work,' Tess said, giving an air blowjob.

Boone elbowed her in the side.

'I'm blaming you,' Boone said, thumbs hard at work texting Jack. 'You and your inability to look after yourself.'

'You know that he knows you're hiding, right?'

'Of course he bloody knows. But accepting each other's lies at face value is the first step to familiarity.'

Back at the caravan, Tess fixed up toasties – she and Boone disagreed on whether this constituted cooking – and pressed two mugs of coffee. Tess was still quiet. Boone could sense there was something she wanted to say but let her get round to it in her own time, which wasn't until she'd munched her cheese and ham Brevilles and one of Boone's on top. Committing early to the whole eating-for-two thing.

'Ask you something?' she said finally.

Boone nodded.

'You think they're dead?'

'Who?'

'Girls in those videos. Those men killed that girl in the flat with you, and they were going to kill you. And the one that went to The Sink broke that boy's arm for nothing.'

'I was a problem,' Boone said. 'What happened in the flat was them cleaning up problems. What happened at The Sink was . . . You know the Americans refer to enhanced interrogation? What was happening in that video was different. That was fun. They were doing it for fun. Probably do it all the time.'

'The masks, though.'

'Wouldn't surprise me if those girls knew exactly who they were. They're the kind of girls, nobody would believe them if they said anything. Who'd believe they didn't go willingly? Men like that rely on two things. Fear, firstly. And secondly, the fact these girls have no voice. Nobody cares what they say. People only start listening to girls like that when their dead bodies turn up. The masks are something else. You look at a person's face, you don't only see something you can recognise later. In a fraction of a second you start making judgements, not just on who they are but what they are. Their gender, age, race, mood, even if they're rich or poor, sick or well, mean or timid. Masks don't just hide identity – they hide a person's humanity. Hiding that gives them power, makes their victims feel powerless.'

Tess nodded. 'I need some TV.'

The news flickered on silently and it was the usual. Tess flicked idly through the channels until Boone stopped her.

'Wait, that's Barbara Stanwyck. I fucking love Barbara Stanwyck.' The holes punched in her semantic memory were large and arbitrary. She maintained a rough-and-ready history of the world at large, the Tudors and Stuarts, the Reagans and Thatchers, but culture was different. She knew who Cary Grant was, but couldn't recall having seen any of his movies (a situation Tess rectified by buying piles of second-hand DVDs the pair of them spent months watching). The experience of reading books or listening to music was also absent, though she could name bands and authors in the right context. She chose to take the silver-linings approach to all this – she'd get to see, read, and hear all of her favourites again as if for the first time. Her love for Barbara Stanwyck was one such recent discovery.

Henry Fonda fell over a couch and Tess giggled, and they settled in for what remained of the movie, Boone vowing to track it down on DVD to watch the whole thing and Tess telling her it'd be online somewhere. Boone was unsure about the ethereal nature of the digital economy. She was certain someone someday would take it all away and preferred to have the merchandise in her hand.

24

Morning, and the sun rose behind clouds and marmaladed the horizon, signalling rain. Again Boone hadn't made it to bed, dozing off on the sofa watching Richard Widmark playing a wanted murderer aiding the survivors of an Apache attack in *The Last Wagon*.

Something about the old ones. She hadn't watched a single film made since her accident, or even many from her lifetime, but felt comforted by the old Hollywood pictures. She wondered if it was simply a habit she and Tess had fallen into together, or if it was something she'd done when she was younger, with her uncle perhaps. Something speaking to her from her past life.

Tess came through looking like Boone felt. Maybe it was the baby or the pills or the lethal combination of the two, but she wasn't having a good morning. Boone showered and they had coffee for breakfast, and Tess surprised her by offering to accompany her into coal country to see Molly.

'What did you want to talk to her about?'

'Something from yesterday,' Boone said. 'What George said about Sarah knowing some rich guy. This muckety-muck.'

They left the Goose in a pub car park in Kearswood, walking
through to The Groves and rapping on Molly's door. She opened
it looking almost sober. The house was clean and tidy and Boone
saw no empty bottles or signs of booze whatsoever.

'You're dry?' she said, making three cups of tea.

Molly laughed. 'I'll never be dry. But I got rules now. One,
don't drink in the house. And two, don't go anywhere they serve
booze and you can sit down.'

'That doesn't leave much.'

'I get up, have a shower, blow-dry my hair, get dressed. I sit and
have a cuppa with a slice of toast. Then I walk down to the village
at eleven and pick up half a pint at the offie. I stop in the doorway
to the old post office. There's a field across from it, so when I'm
tucked in there nobody can see. I drink the bottle down and
dump it in the alley runs alongside. Then I come back here. Does
me for the day.'

'And this works?'

'It's worked for a couple of days.' Molly shrugged. 'Every time
I wake up, I only have to make it work for one more day.'

Boone nodded. 'Easier to act your way to right thinking than
think your way to right action.'

She brought the tea over and sat with Molly.

The dog loped in and hung its head at an angle, looking
between them. Then it looked up at Tess. Boone and Molly looked
at her too. Tess sighed.

'Come on, pooch. Morning constitutional.'

There was a scuffed leather lead on the kitchen counter and she
fixed it to his collar and led him out the back way.

'You got a purpose here,' Molly said, not a question.

'I found the boy who came to see you. I don't think he was lying – he had been with Sarah. Other people saw her too, at the squat.'

'She's not there now?'

Boone shook her head. 'They haven't seen her for a couple of months maybe.'

'Got herself in some sort of trouble. What asking for the money was about.'

'Yeah, looks like.'

'You really think you can find her?'

'I really think I can try. When I was here before, you mentioned the man you and your husband worked for. That he was good to you when Rodney got sick. Showed an interest in Sarah.'

'Very kind man.'

'Who was he?'

'Sir Alex,' Molly said. 'Alex Blackborne.'

'Would he take Sarah places? Trips or anything. Without you, I mean.'

Molly frowned. 'Not really. Of course, sometimes in the summer when I was keeping a close eye on her, she'd come to work with me. If Sir Alex was there, he might take her for an ice cream. Got her out of my hair. And sometimes Mark was there. He was that much older than my Sarah, but he was very good with her. I think she had a bit of a crush on him.'

'Mark?'

'Mark Blackborne. Sir Alex's son. I suppose he's Sir Mark now. How funny.'

'How do you mean?'

'When Sir Alex died. He was some kind of baron. The titles pass on, don't they? The old ones.'

'Blackborne is dead?'

'Such a shame when he passed. I remember reading about it. Very sad. Wish I had been able to go to the funeral. We owed him so much.'

'Owed him how?'

'What he did for us when Rodney got sick. This was the first time. He was ill a few times, kept coming back. That sort of thing does. There was some kind of insurance policy at the cement works. Sir Alex took care of it all, made it easy. We were worried how we'd get by, pay the mortgage and whatnot. We had Sarah by then. If it had just been the two of us . . . but a child needs security. The settlement took care of all that.'

'He was ill from the cement works then?'

Molly's mind had wandered. 'Such a shame I couldn't go. I wasn't doing so well then, though. Lovely service, I heard. Lot of people. He was very popular, Sir Alex.'

Boone nodded. 'You said that Sarah knew the son? Knew Mark?'

Molly got up suddenly.

'You must see this,' she said.

She went through to the living room and returned with one of the framed photographs Boone had seen on the shelf on her last visit, the one she thought had been Sarah with a cousin.

'This is Mark,' she said, pointing at the young man next to Sarah. 'They held family days for the staff. Food and drink and music. They were very good to us. Sir Alex took me to lunch at the

Kingsgate in Lark once. Can you imagine? They say it takes six months to get a booking there.'

Lark's swankiest hotel, the Kingsgate sported two restaurants, one so exclusive it was essentially a private members' club. All wing chairs and wainscot, the kind of place they didn't let women roam unaccompanied. Boone could see Molly sitting in Sunday best on a Tuesday afternoon at a table overlooking the sea, drunk with Victorian opulence. Finger bowls and fish forks, the place decorated like great rooms of Empire.

'Can I take this?' she said. 'I'll make a copy and return it.'

Molly nodded. 'If you think it's important.' She gazed at the photo.

'I'll bring it back, Molly,' Boone said, removing it from the frame.

She found Tess out the back chucking a stick. The dog stared at her. 'Listen,' Boone said, 'this mine of yours, the one you mucked about at as a kid, that might be the one in the video? It's around here, right?'

Tess nodded. 'Over that way.' She pointed.

'Within walking distance?' Boone said.

'Sure. You have to go through the woods any way you approach it.'

'Let's take a quick look, see if it's the place.'

Tess shrugged in agreement. Beyond the fence at the back of the garden, behind The Groves, earth that had been cleared for the estate's construction had been pushed into an artificial rise, evenly grassed. Concrete steps had been built into the side and a gravel path ran along the crest, shuttered by timber boards.

They walked out the alley beside the house and back around.

From the top of the rise in one direction was a view over the estate to the old Kearswood village. In the other lay allotments. Boone thought the place looked like a graveyard, the old bathtubs used for irrigation standing among the rows of fruit and veg like overgrown sarcophagi.

They followed a clay path through a wooded area and out into a vast meadow.

'This used to be the spoil tip for the Corringstone colliery,' Tess said.

A park had been made of it, reeds growing around the shimmering slurry lake, acres of grass and newly planted trees. Some of the land had been allowed to go to marsh, a habitat for birds and other small fauna.

'We used to ride our BMXs here,' she said, 'before they made it all pretty. The boys made tracks and jumps over the black heaps. Only thing that used to grow was dogwood.'

She recounted how in the late months, after leaf fall, the wiry stems of the dogwood would redden and stand out from the dark earth like fire. In winter, the spoil heaps would wear snowy calottes and the local children would pack the stuff in their hands, tossing it around drolly until the game turned serious and they played until they could no longer bear the cold, fingers blue and ears singed.

'We can follow the old railway,' Tess said.

She led Boone through a narrow strip of woodland to what looked like an ill-kept path. Used by the collieries decades ago, most of the track had long been removed, but the cutting remained visible.

'I'd come here as a girl to pick blackberries,' Tess said, grinning.

'Bundle them up in the skirt of my dress and walk home with my knickers showing. Little dark pawprints on my clothes. Seeds in my teeth. Drove Mum potty.' The smile fell from her face.

Blackberries grew still around the stone remnants of a bridge pier. Boone picked one and popped it in her mouth. Further down they came to a stretch of track bed with surviving sleepers and rails, their dull surfaces rough and orange.

'Oh my God,' Tess exclaimed, grinning. 'Come see this.'

A short way from the track stood a grand old beech that resembled several trees grown together. It had peculiarly small and prim roots at its base, like a Chinese concubine's bound feet, and in its elephant-grey bark were carved dozens of sets of initials.

'TB,' said Tess. 'That's me.'

She traced the letters with her fingers. Among the trees they heard the velocities of birds. Somewhere a woodpecker noddled.

They came to the halt, an abandoned colliery station where once coal had been loaded up and hauled off to the coast to be shipped. The buildings had been demolished, small heaps of broken bricks beneath the undergrowth, but the platforms remained, thickly mantled with moss. Box had completely engulfed one of them, its hard, slender branches green with velvet growth. The other side of a chain-link fence was the old colliery itself, its powerhouse still the tallest building for miles. It was a glum place, as if the sun wouldn't quite shine over it.

'Could do with your friend and his dad's bolt cutters,' Boone said.

'Boone, maybe this isn't such a great idea,' Tess said.

'Could climb it,' Boone said, grabbing the fence and rattling it. 'What if this is the place?'

Boone stared at her. 'That'd be great.'

'No, Boone. What if this is the place and they're here?'

Boone both had and hadn't considered this. Somewhere in the background was the constant concern that danger lurked round the corner, but she'd been aware of that feeling ever since she woke up in the hospital. It was all she knew. She had become used to not dwelling on the making of decisions themselves so much as the fact of carrying them out. She was here and she would find out if this was the place in the video.

'What are the chances?' she said. 'We'll have a scout around, keep it quiet. It's a reconnaissance mission is all.'

Now they had arrived, now the buildings were in front of them, Tess looked uneasy.

'We see anything out of the ordinary, we're out of here,' Boone said.

'You swear?'

'Swear on my life.'

Tess looked at her like she was weighing up how much that meant.

Boone walked along the fence. It had struggled with years of bored and adventurous kids and after ten yards she found a corner torn away from its post and curled like old wallpaper. She pulled it up and they ducked through into the colliery.

The roadways were cracked and overgrown, an honest-to-goodness tree growing through in one place, and the earth smelt damp and coppery. The lamp room and workshops sat in the lee of the looming powerhouse, the winding building behind that long shorn of its Koepe winder. They were all of the same red brick, faded now like an old photograph, like someone's memory of a mine. A red phone box provided the only real colour. Its receiver was torn out.

They paused beside one of the workshops and peered round the corner. Forty yards away stood a series of thin single-storey buildings, arranged in neat rows like a ghastly seventies holiday camp. In between was open space, dead land with a scatter of shrubs. Wire cages with latch locks had been fitted over the doors of the buildings and the windows were all bricked up, save the semicircular ones high in the walls at each end.

'See?' Tess pointed.

Boone agreed. They looked like the ones in the video. She went to approach them and felt Tess's hand on her arm stopping her.

'I don't like this place,' she said.

'There's nobody here,' Boone said. 'Listen.'

Wind rustled the trees and they heard the life living among them. No human sounds at all.

'Come on,' Boone said. 'This is silly.'

She set off across the open space. Everything seemed very bright and very close, and her mind burned with images of masked men watching her from the small windows, waiting in the dark for her. She rubbed her fingers together, feeling the dampness of her hands. She felt tight and rolled her shoulders, cracked her neck. This was stupid, she told herself. The place was clearly deserted. She looked back and waved for Tess to hurry, the girl catching up. They covered the ground quickly, walking between the buildings and looking for something that might point to recent use. One of them stood out. The latch lock had been replaced by a sliding bolt secured with a padlock.

'This one,' Boone said.

'Well, we can't get in there,' Tess said.

Boone grinned. Padlocks were piss. She kicked around in the surrounding weeds and came up with an empty Super T's can. With her pocket knife, she carefully fashioned a loid from the thin metal and quickly shimmed the U-lock with the tapered strip.

'The shit you remember and the shit you don't,' Tess said, shaking her head.

The main door was unlocked but stiff, and Tess shushed as it scraped along the stone floor. They left it ajar as the only light in the first room came from gaps worn in the pitched roof, like needles of light through bullet holes. The flat ceiling that had once hung below it had collapsed with water damage, bits sticking to their boots. The stony smell of outside fell away and was replaced by something moist and clammy.

'Doesn't look like anyone's home,' Boone whispered.

The building seemed bigger on the inside, with rooms off either side of a central corridor. Using the flashlight on her phone to navigate, Boone checked them as they went, most empty or containing only broken office furniture. Tess shuffled along behind, clinging on to Boone's arm. The corridor bent to the outside wall, the rooms in the rear half of the building being almost full-width. Light shone through at the very end from an open door facing them.

'Must be the window,' Tess said quietly.

Keeping the beam pointing down, Boone moved forward in little steps, eyes jumping between the floor and the light at the end of the corridor.

All she could hear was the air they took in.

Tess's breath.

Her breath.

Her mouth was dry, her lips papery. She tried to work up some spit. Some of the doors on their right were open. An old metal filing cabinet missing its drawers in one, a three-legged chair tipped over in another. Others were closed. Only when they'd passed a few did Boone think maybe they should be trying them, maybe someone might be hiding behind them. She shook the thought off as they approached the end room, the open door directly ahead.

She looked inside. It was clean and dry, the semicircular window gleaming high up in the wall, all the glass smashed from it. Other than that, she struggled to recognise the room. Cameras don't see the world as the eye does, don't hold light the same, and it felt like a different place to where the man and the girl argued in the video.

'What do you think?' she said.

'I don't know,' said Tess.

Boone went back out to the corridor and tried the next room. The door swung open quietly and there was nothing inside. She closed her hand round the handle of the next one and felt Tess behind her.

'We shouldn't stay here, Boone,' she said.

'We'll just check the rooms and go,' Boone said, turning the handle and pushing open the door.

Bingo.

A camp bed stood on its end in one corner, with a twin-head LED flood on a mast beside it. Its cables were wrapped round itself, trailing down to a generator in the corner. It was the room from the first video. Against the back wall stood an old Ratner safe, the shape Boone had been unable to make out on the screen. The locking mechanism had been punched out. She swung the door open but there was nothing inside.

'Hard to say if anyone's been here recently,' she said. 'Left the light equipment, though.'

'Come on,' Tess said. 'Let's go.'

They both spun round in alarm at a noise.

Way down the corridor, the front door scraped along the ground.

Boone switched off the light on her phone and pressed a finger to her lips to tell Tess to keep quiet. There was no way the wind moved that door, heavy as it was.

She peered down the corridor and waited.

Silence.

Then, with a scrape and a clunk, the front door shut and feet tapped along the floor. Boone was all heartbeat and tried vainly to dampen her breathing.

Tess was wide-eyed, terrified.

Boone touched her arm, tried to let her know it'd be okay.

Could be a tramp, or school kids.

Or the men who ended your old life and dumped you in this new one, come to finish their work.

Taking Tess's hand, she crept out into the corridor, taking small baby steps, hoping to get a few doors down. The darkness was conspiring to give her away, however, and she kicked something unseen along the floor, making a ridiculous racket.

She froze, Tess tight against her back, fingers curled in her jacket.

Silence.

Boone made fists, palms damp and clammy.

Her breathing moved the darkness around her.

Footsteps detonated, running towards them along the corridor.

Boone pushed Tess back into the room, sliding her into the black behind the door. The room smelt like piss and dead things and all she could hear were the footsteps, the footfall, the running, jagged breaths as someone ran past the door heading for the room at the end.

Boone thought about running. If she could get to the door, maybe close the padlock on the sliding bolt in the cage. If she could run. She knew that was hopeless. Just walking to the colliery she had felt her leg, felt that damned screw digging into her flesh.

She didn't have a good run in her.

But Tess did.

She'd have to battle with the heavy door to get them out, and what if whoever it was had fastened the padlock behind them?

The end door opened and closed again. Boone groped about in the dark for the standing lamp, running her fingers over it until she found the power switch and flicking it to the on position, the light still dead as the generator wasn't on. Gently she moved to the corner and found the generator, flipping the circuit breaker up and holding the power key between her fingers.

Another door opened, a couple down from them.

They were searching.

Boone grabbed Tess, pulled her close to whisper.

'You stand against the wall beside the door. Stay quiet. When they come, I'll move. You take your chance and run. Go for the door.'

'Boone—'

'No. You fucking run and you don't look back. You take care of yourself. I'll be right behind you.'

The girl nodded rapidly and Boone pressed her against the wall.

She pulled up her hood.

Her breath shortened, and the world suddenly felt a very small place, everything very near.

Everything was the present. The changes that had been and the changes that were to come were all shed from her and there was only now.

Only that room.

Only that door.

Only what came through it.

When the door swung open, she turned the key and the generator coughed into action, the floodlight coming on full beam. As the man turned his face from the light, eyes dilated big and black beneath his ski mask, Boone charged him, gouging a thumb into his eye, right into the socket, and he roared as he clawed at his own face. She felt his skin, scurfed and uneven.

Like tree bark but softer.

Like a burn scar.

She'd thought about how to hit him, go for the head or go for an ankle, but she fell back on the necessaries – eyes and balls.

Always eyes and balls.

Reaching down, she grabbed a handful of him, feeling him through his tracksuit bottoms and thanking the universe he wasn't wearing jeans. Gripping him beneath his cock, she squeezed with all she had, imagining crushing a peeled orange until pip and pulp squirted out between her fingers.

He howled a cry of the mad.

A cuffing blow caught her round the side of the head, crashing her into the door frame, but she didn't let go and he stumbled back into the corridor against the wall, sliding down to the floor, Boone still attached to his testicles like a dog with lockjaw.

She felt Tess leap by, heard her quick feet down the dark hall.

A fist slammed into the side of her head and then her jaw, and then clipped her above the eye.

She let go and pushed herself away from him.

Still blinking against the light, he vomited in his lap, and Boone was off as fast as her legs could carry her, hands out to either side tracing the path of the walls.

Round the zigzag and the straight shot through to the door. She felt cold. Wiping the sweat away, she realised it wasn't sweat but blood, as it moved quicker and heavier and was everywhere.

Her head thudded with life.

It was screaming, *This is better than the alternative.*

Up ahead, the door scraped deafeningly across the floor, its sweep recorded by a dark groove in the stone. She turned through it and crashed into the back of Tess.

The cage door was shut, the padlock fastened.

'Jesus, Boone, he locked it. He fucking locked it.'

Unhelpfully, the building door opened inwards, so couldn't be barricaded from without, but Boone pulled it closed regardless.

'Hold that shut,' she told Tess.

The shim was in her pocket somewhere, but her hands were not her own, her fingers slick with blood from her head.

Where is it, where is it?

Groping wildly, she found the sliver of metal and reached through the gap in the cage door around the bolt, turning the padlock upwards.

Slipping the curl of metal around the shackle, she pushed the tapered end down the shaft towards the latch. With the blood, her fingers slipped and the loid fell away to the ground.

'Shitting fucking Christ.'

On her knees, she stretched her fingers through the mesh of the cage, fumbling with the shim, trying to bring it closer.

'Come on, come on,' Tess pleaded.

Boone's fingers were wet, and dirt was thickening in the blood that streaked the cage door now. Catching the curve of the metal, she flicked it towards the cage and dragged it underneath. Cleaning it off with her sleeve, she curled the metal around the shackle once more and slipped it into position, disengaging the lock just as the man slammed into the door.

Tess screamed, trying to hold it closed against him, but he was stronger and the door shrieked open bit by bit, Tess's feet sliding along the ground.

Grabbing Tess, Boone shoved her out through the gate door. Letting the building door open a ways, she put one foot against the frame of the cage and pushed off with all she had, slamming into the iron door just as his face appeared in the gap. The edge caught him flush above the eye and he grunted.

Pivoting round, Boone flew out of the cage and closed the door behind her, sliding the bolt and snapping the padlock shut just as he barged into it. He was wild, rabid.

Screaming at them, he fetched about in his pockets for a key as Boone pushed Tess away the way they had come. She pressed the keys to the Saab into the girl's hand.

'Run to the car,' she hissed in her ear. 'Run to the car and get as far away from here as possible.'

Tess was shaking her head, but Boone shoved her away, so she turned and bolted, sprinting off between the colliery buildings and out of sight.

He just about had a key in the padlock when Boone charged the gate, throwing herself so her thigh crushed his hand where it reached through the door.

She didn't wait for a reaction, but took off in the opposite direction to Tess. Her leg was already there, tapping away at the back of her mind, and she knew she couldn't escape a prolonged pursuit.

Skidding round the corner of the vast powerhouse, she ducked through an archway, dancing over the broken bricks that had once sealed it up, and into the space beyond. Cavernous and stripped now of any machinery, it resembled a bare cathedral. Sun fell generously though huge skylights and saplings had sprung up through the floor.

In her best sprint, Boone skirted the great concrete pits cut into the ground and stooped beneath old chains hung with ivy. Pushing one aside, she disturbed birds that had nested far above and they fluttered with panic among the rafters. In the far wall was an empty doorway, a huge hook hanging above it from an iron pulley like a rusted uvula.

As she made for it, she heard him leaping through the archway behind her, the echoes of his feet clapping off the boundless brickwork. Outside, she made a beeline for the nearest trees, dashing between slender birches that offered little by way of cover. She was the other side of the colliery from the park and didn't know what lay beyond.

The ground sloped away to her left and she followed its natural declivity, moving faster that way but knowing he would do the same. The trees were white and straight, their canopy sparse, and it felt like winter in among them, cold and exposed.

She wondered if she'd even know if she was running in circles, and was struck by the terrible possibility of finding herself heading back towards the mine. She came to a road, unmarked and poorly maintained, an access or service lane. Birches leaned over from both sides, their entangled limbs vaulting forty feet above her. If she'd merely been lost she would have followed it, but she could see down it a hundred yards or more in either direction. He'd spot her straight off. Her leg was hitching and she thumped the side of it with her fist as though breaking down some plaque upon her joints. Diving through the trees on the other side of the road, she descended the steeper slope there like a crab, leading with her good leg to take the weight. There must have been the sound of the woods – birds and branches and the cornucopia of life – but she heard none of it. She heard her blood in her ears, her breath like an echo chamber, the swish of her jeans' fabric as her legs brushed each other.

When the stone rolled her ankle, there was something inevitable about it, as if with cosmic certainty she'd been waiting for it all along, and she tumbled almost gracefully into a rolling heap. She recalled having seen video of people chasing cheeses down a hill, arms and legs cartwheeling as they fell.

Coming to a halt where the ground levelled out, she found herself beside a ditch, perhaps eight or nine feet deep and banked by bushes and bramble. She could hear him shouting now, the words themselves lost in the trees, heard only as gusts of fury. With the noise came relief as well as fear. At least he had come after her and not Tess.

She dragged herself to the edge of the ditch through a gap in the bushes where the bank had fallen away. Swinging her legs over the side, she dropped down. The ditch was mostly mud, but twenty yards further down, the course had been dammed by a storm-felled tree and a thatch of branches and brambles. A dark and brackish pool had built up behind it.

Digging her heels into the almost vertical clay bank, Boone clambered past the barricade and waded into knee-high water. It was hard going, the bottom soft and slippery beneath her feet. She slogged onwards and came to another tree bridging the ditch where the bank had collapsed, exposing its roots when it toppled.

Hearing him hurtling down the hill in her direction, she eased herself into the water and shuffled herself beneath the bottom of the trunk. The cold was bone deep and there was only a few inches between the surface and the tree. She gathered about her a clutter of branches and debris, the door to a fridge and an old pram wheel.

Water lapped at her ears. Between its movements she could hear him above her on the bank of the ditch, hear his panting and his mumbling. She closed her eyes and pressed her face into the bark of the tree.

If she listened hard enough, she'd hear that soft hum of the engine of godly works.

25

When Boone finally hauled herself out of the mud, she'd lost her mobile and was soaked from head to foot. She followed the ditch back towards the park and eventually squelched out into a tarmac car park. One car waited. Its headlights burst on and flashed twice. Boone shaded her eyes against the bright and stood rooted. The door opened and Tess leaped out, running towards her.

'It's me, you bellend,' she said. 'Oh my God. You're bleeding. I didn't realise. Boone, you're soaking.'

'I told you to get out of here,' Boone managed through her shivers.

'I've been here and back to the village and here again, and I didn't stop moving once. Not even for lights or pedestrians. I was fine.'

'My feet are wet,' Boone said.

'Fucking feet,' said Tess, leading her back to the car. 'I'm taking you home, get you some warm clothes.'

Boone shook her head.

'Jack can't see me like this. I'll never hear the end of it.'

'You can't stay in those clothes.'

'The boot,' Boone stammered.

Tess popped the trunk and found some old tartan blankets in there. Boone quickly stripped down to her nethers and threw the muddy garments in the boot. Wrapped in the blankets, she got in the car and turned the heating up to full.

'So. Fucking. Cold.'

'Where are we going?' Tess said.

'Caravan,' Boone said.

The only sound was the chattering of Boone's teeth. She said nothing as they drove until she started to laugh.

'What's funny?' Tess said.

Boone shook her head, laughing silently but uncontrollably. Then it changed. Her chin tucked into her chest, she turned away with her face to the window, shoulders hunched and shaking.

Tess rested a hand on Boone's arm, left it there until she calmed down.

'You're going to need something to wear,' she said.

She stopped off at a supermarket in an old Victorian malting and picked up an array of cheap garments and some food, including crisps because Boone had said, 'And some of those posh crisps I like.'

She rolled the Goose up next to the caravan and Boone walked up the steps onto the decking in her bra and knickers and bare feet, boots hanging off her fingers, to find Roo sitting at the table swigging from a bottle of red.

'I have no key and am drinking to be warm,' she said. She looked Boone up and down, wet and shivering and bleeding, and shook her head. 'I told you this would end in you getting yourself killed again.'

'Tess, Roo,' Boone said. 'Roo, Tess.'

'Hi,' they both said.

'Get in here,' Tess said, opening the door. And they did.

'I'll turn the shower on,' she said, disappearing.

Boone stood in the middle of the living room and Roo followed her in with a suitcase.

'What are you doing here?' Boone said.

'What is it *I* am doing here?' Roo said. 'What it is *you* are
doing? Look at the mess you are. And why it is you are undressed
and bleeding?'

'It's okay,' Boone said. 'Looks worse than it is.'

Roo shoved Boone lightly in the shoulder, then again harder.

'This is what you want, I don't know why you mess around,'
she said, taking Boone's hand. 'Come on, we go outside now and
you lie down in the road. I'll run over you in this Goose of yours.
Easy as that.'

'Roo.'

'Gah,' said Roo, throwing her arms up. Silent tears ran down
her cheeks. 'You give me milk on my knees.'

Boone shrugged. 'I'm a different pair of sleeves.'

She grabbed Roo, hugged her tightly. 'I'm okay,' she whispered.

'You are cold and wet and mostly stupid.'

'Yes I am.'

'All right,' said Tess, holding open a fresh bath towel. 'When
you two are quite done, the shower's running. And then we probably have a few things to talk about.'

Boone stood under the hot shower a good long while, sending a
rusty whorl of bloodied water down the drain, her skin attaining a
sort of ruddy nimbus. She tried to wash it away with icy water in the

basin afterwards, leaving great swipe marks where she'd cleared the steamed mirror. She returned to the living room swaddled in towels to find Roo had polished off the red and moved on to another that Tess had picked up for Boone, the two of them having a right old knees-up on the sofa, tucking into several big bags of crisps.

'They're my fucking posh crisps,' Boone said. 'You don't have them for company. You have them for when you're alone and can lie to yourself that you're only going to eat a few.'

She sat in the armchair with her legs folded underneath her. Tess was drinking green tea and a mug of coffee sat steaming on the table.

'Figured you'd want something hot first,' she said.

'I keep my eye on her,' Roo said, 'and she follows the process to the letter.'

Boone cradled the mug in both hands, enjoying the warmth, as Tess briefly recounted their travails over the past couple of days. As she listened, Roo cleaned out and dressed the gash on the side of Boone's head and the cut over her eye.

'The head, it is okay,' she said. 'But this one, you may want a doctor.'

'Can Jack look at it?' Tess said.

Boone snorted. 'I can only imagine what his reaction to all this is going to be.'

'You say he knows you,' Roo said. 'Then he will understand. You have one of those faces people can't help but hit with their fists.'

Boone stared at her and then grimaced when she applied a plaster over her eye.

'Big baby,' Roo said.

'You warm enough?' Tess said.

Boone nodded. 'I don't even know how long I was in that ditch,' she said. 'Felt like hours. He probably left ages before I got out.'

'You knew his face?' Roo said.

Boone thought about the moment she turned the light on and went for him. She could see his eyes, black and wide. She could feel his skin, shiny and rough at the same time.

'It was him,' she said. 'The one I scalded with the water. Apparently he didn't heal too well.'

'Not like he could have gone to a hospital,' Tess said. 'They'd have been notified to be on the lookout.'

'Did he get a clear look at you?' Roo said.

Boone shrugged. 'It was pitch black in there. I had my hood up, and when I turned the floodlight on, it was right in his eyes. I don't think he saw either of us properly, but it doesn't matter. He knew it was us. Knew we were going there.'

'He followed us?' Tess said, alarmed.

'Luke said Sarah told him she thought her grandmother was being watched. They were waiting to see if Sarah went back there. Probably saw us when we went the first time.'

'You think they know where we are now?' Tess said.

'I don't know,' said Boone. 'I don't think so. Nobody followed us back tonight, and if they had the first time, I think they would have paid a visit before today.'

'How long do you suppose they've been using that place?' Tess said.

Boone shrugged.

'I used to play in those woods,' Tess said. 'A lot of us did. We explored the whole site. You think those girls were from the villages?'

'The only name they'd know is mine,' Boone said. 'They don't know who you are, so they don't know this place. At worst, they might be able to find me in Lark.'

Roo snorted with exasperation. 'I tell her, is stupid, looking into all this mess again. Is tempting fate.'

'Boone doesn't listen to mere mortals,' Tess said.

Boone rolled her eyes and changed the subject.

'You didn't hang about,' she told Roo, looking at the suitcase in the corner.

'You said you had a place.'

'Aye.'

'Well, I start at my new job tomorrow,' Roo said.

'What?' Boone said.

'You said to me – find job and I'll help with place to stay. You said that.'

'No, yeah, of course. But that was like the day before yesterday,' Boone said, thinking it felt like a lifetime ago.

'And you find place to stay. You want I wait a week more to find job?'

'No, I just – where did you find a job so fast?'

'At the library. I find the local paper online, jobs page. Dorothy's. I catch the train out this morning, and got the job. Part time and is shit money, but, like you say, shit money goes longer the further you are from London. So this is a start.'

'Who the hell is Dorothy?' Boone said.

'Laundrette and dry cleaner's in town,' Tess said.

'You're working in a dry cleaner's?'

'I know, it is unbelievable,' Roo said. 'I told them of my experience with serving food and the sexing for money, and was for sure they are to offer me a job as an accountant.'

'I didn't mean . . . It's sudden, is all.'

'The woman – you know, there is no Dorothy at Dorothy's? I
was sad to find out this. But the woman said could I start tomorrow, and I said of course, because who am I to set terms? The shifts
at the restaurant are whenever they like, so I call up and ask and
they say fine, you go. So I go. I am not so excited to take the train
from Lewisham in the morning, so I go back and pack up and how
the hell was I to know my good friend Boone would make me wait
outside in the cold while she tried to get herself murdered?'

Said this and a lobster and Pondicherry black pepper crisp hit
her in the head.

26

It was late when Boone got home, having swerved the wine so she could still drive. Three paracetamols and her head was a dull but manageable throb, but she was looking forward to bed. Tess had told her to stay ('The couch is comfy,' she said, to which Roo interjected, upon seeing her room, 'We have slept together in smaller beds than this, Boone and I,' sending Boone a bright shade of red), but Boone had lost her phone and didn't know Jack or Quin's numbers off the top of her head, and the house was ex-directory.

She was quiet with the door, but Jack was waiting for her in the study. 'I've been texting you for hours,' he said, coming out into the hall. 'Where have you—'

He was caught short by the state of her. The plaster over her eye, bundle of mud-soaked and bloody clothes in a plastic bag.

'Jesus Christ, what happened? You have a crash?'

He held her hand, examining her head, then led her into the study and angled a floor lamp to get a better look.

'You okay? Your face is swollen. And this cut back here – have you got a headache at all?'

'Jack, I'm fine.'

'Was it a crash?' He went to the window, peering between the curtains. 'The car looks fine.'

'It wasn't a crash.'

'Then . . . ?'

Boone dropped heavily into the club chair.

'It was them,' she said. 'One of them.'

'Them? Who the hell's them?'

'*Them*. The men from that day. The men from the flat. One of them anyway.'

Jack stood there looking at her. He said nothing for a good while, before walking round his desk and sitting behind it.

'You said you were just looking into things. The grandmother of the missing girl, this Bulgarian woman, things of that nature. You said there wouldn't be any going after the men. That's what you said.'

'Jack—'

'No.' He cut her off with a finger. 'Your exact fucking words. I won't go after the bad men on my own.'

'I didn't.'

'How's that?'

'They came after me.'

Jack stood up again, almost laughing.

'Oh well, that's just fine then. They're coming for you now. Alleviates all of my concerns, that does.'

'They're not coming for me here. He . . . I don't know. Followed me from Molly Still's place, I think.'

Jack walked over and picked up the bag of clothes.

'These are soaking. Where did he follow you to? Where did this happen?'

'The old mine at Corringstone.'

'What the hell were you doing there?'

'Long story. It was . . . reconnaissance. We were just looking at buildings. There wasn't supposed to be anyone there.'

'We who? You and this Boxall character? Or the daughter? Or the Bulgarian . . . woman?'

'Me and Tess.'

'Corringstone?'

'Yep.'

'Corringstone. That's what, five miles? Why didn't you call me?'

'I lost my phone in the—'

'Go on. The what? Fight?'

'The ditch. I had to get Tess away, distract him, make him chase me. I hid in a ditch, hence the wet clothes, and my phone must have fallen out. I don't know any numbers, Jack. They were on the phone, I never thought to memorise them.'

'Five miles. Could have been here in fifteen minutes. Get cleaned up, fresh clothes, and I could have looked at your head. But you went back to hers, didn't you? Went all the way to the Medway instead.'

'I thought if you saw me looking like this you'd—'

'I'd what? Be worried? Scared? Concerned? All of the above?'

'Upset,' Boone said.

Jack knelt beside her chair. Softly he said, 'You tell me, Abby, how does this end? Really? Where are we headed to? Say you find this girl, then what? Is that it, or do we have to find the men who took her?'

'Is that so wrong?' she hissed. 'They're the men who took me as well, Jack. The men who tried to kill me. The men who did this to me. Find them? I don't want them found. I want them dead.'

Rage was building within her again, but this was different to her familiar anger of frustration and isolation. This was born from fear. She had been scared, so very scared, and was enraged at the thought of that fear.

'Is that what this really is?' said Jack. 'You looking for one last confrontation? Finding the girl not enough, so let's see if we can't find some killers?'

Boone looked away, said nothing.

'This has to stop,' Jack said.

'I can't.'

'No. *I* can't. I can't sit here every night not knowing where you are, wondering what godawful state you're going to come through that door in. They must know your name, from the newspaper articles at least, if they didn't know it before. Are we even safe here? What happens if they knock on the door? Or worse, what happens if I get a knock from the police asking me to come and identify the body of my wife, Abby? What happens then?'

Boone shrugged. 'Maybe it wouldn't be your wife you'd be identifying.'

'Nice.' He shook his head. 'I don't get it, I really don't. You have a home here, you have a family. What is it you're after?'

She had no answer for that.

'I'm tired,' she said, moving to get up.

He placed a hand gently on her knee. 'You're going nowhere until I've looked at those cuts.'

'Jack . . .'

'I'll sit on you if it comes to it.'

Boone leaned back in the chair. 'Fine.'

Jack carefully peeled away the plaster over her eye and had a peek.

'Shit,' he said.

'Bad?'

He traced a finger round the edge of the swelling on her cheek.

'What am I going to do with you?'

Blood ran from the cut above her eye, down the side of her face, and Jack caught it with his handkerchief before it fluted off her jawbone. He ran it back up to the cut.

'Hold that there,' he said, guiding her hand to it. 'And try not to bleed everywhere,' he added, leading her to the kitchen.

She sat at the breakfast bar as he cleaned out the cut and looked at it closer.

'We might need the A and E with this,' he said.

'I can't be bothered with all that.'

'I think it needs stitches.'

'You can do it.'

'Jesus, Abby. You know how long it's been since I stitched any-thing up?'

'Come on. Think how satisfying it'll be, sticking a needle in me.'

He considered that.

'Mum?'

They turned to see Quin in the doorway in his pyjamas.

'What happened? You have a fight?'

'Knows you better than I do,' Jack said under his breath.

'Just an accident,' Boone said. 'I was in the woods and I slipped into a ditch.'

Quin looked at Jack, searching for reassurance.

'Worse than it looks,' Jack told the boy. 'And I'm going to patch it up good as new.'

He had Quin fetch the first aid box and some other supplies, whilst he mixed up two hydrogen peroxide solutions – one for the utensils and a weaker one to splash out the cut with. He soaked a cotton wool ball with the stuff and ran it over the thread.

'Quin, you should be in bed,' he said when he was ready.

'You are joking,' Quin said, perched on a stool with feverish excitement.

Jack looked at Boone, who shrugged.

'Okay then. But if you pass out, you'll be mocked mercilessly for a long time to come.'

'Let's do this,' Boone said, getting antsy.

'This is going to hurt you more than it hurts me,' Jack said, needle primed at her head.

He forced it through the skin and the pain was ecstatic.

She let out a little moan.

27

Roo went off to work each morning, eight till twelve, earning the appropriate amount so nobody was obliged to make pension contributions, and picked up a few shifts at The Yeast With Two Yacks, which styled itself as a conversational pub. Proud she had taken two jobs away from local go-getters, she was doing her bit to buttress popular opinions of her and her kind.

Tess slept a lot. Boone had arranged doctor's appointments for her and she'd been put on to a new pill regimen, one that made her even grizzlier in the mornings than the old one and kept her up as nightwatchman till the wee hours. Boone visited during the daytime, making sure she was back home for dinner each evening. She spent hours digging into the material found on Milan's phone, making a close study of the pictures and videos, until their horrors became almost abstract. Sifting through all of her notes again, nothing broke free, no new lead for her to act upon.

Without telling anyone, one morning she took a drive back to the colliery, parking in Litton, the next village, and taking the bus to the edge of Kearswood before walking around the long way to the abandoned buildings. For an hour she hid in the trees and watched, until she was happy nobody was there. The padlock was gone, and inside, the generator and lights had been removed. Only the safe stood there, massive and empty. She wondered if she'd always been this ineffectual as a detective.

She spent time online looking into the Blackbornes. Arriving home between shifts one day, Roo found her sprawled on the caravan's sofa, laptop on her stomach, papers scattered all about. A crumpled copy of a local Medway paper was open on the coffee table.

'That's him,' Boone said.

'What?'

'There,' said Boone, pointing at the paper.

Roo read aloud. ' "Councillor opens new petting zoo. Maurice Braithwaite, pictured left with Jacob the goat—" '

'Here, you idiot,' Boone said, jabbing her finger at a picture of several grinning men, suited and booted but with hi-vis jackets and hard hats, standing in front of a construction site. 'That's Mark Blackborne on the left.'

Roo read from the article. ' "Cornilo press ahead with new homes. Final approval was granted to Cornilo Construction to redevelop the site formally housing the Cornilo cement works, which closed three years ago. Two hundred new homes will be built, with fifty planned to be aimed at first-time buyers." '

'He is quite the big cheese.'

'Cheese? How he is cheese? This is more Italian?'

'No, that one's English.'

'Cheese is rich?'

'Might be from India, actually,' Boone mused. Like a lot of her thoughts, she wasn't sure how she knew that. 'Probably a corruption of something.'

'Cheese is corruption?'

'Yeah. No. The word. I mean he's an important man.'

'What it is he has to do with all this, you think?' Roo said.

'I don't know. Maybe nothing. Maybe everything. Maybe he's who Sarah was afraid of, who sent the men after her.'

'The same men who tried to kill me and you in the flat, and then tried to kill you and Tess at the mine.'

'Yes.'

'Well then. He is someone you should definitely be bothering. I can see nothing that might go wrong.'

'Listen,' Boone said, reading from stuff she'd found online. ' "Sir Mark Blackborne, 11th Baronet of the Blackborne baronetcy of Cornilo." He's half a noble or something. Usually it's politicians or moneylenders or other creatures of the realm that get a baronetcy, but this first chap, Geoffrey Blackborne, was some type of cutthroat in the French and Indian war, saved the life of a duke's son. He ended up owning a great estate near Boston, but when he died his son sold it to some lord or other and moved back to England, to Kent. All that land in Boston was taken by the Americans after the Revolutionary War. These wankers have been operator types for centuries. So look here.'

She brought pictures up on the computer of an older, ruddy-faced man.

'This is the father, Sir Alex. Died a few years back. Look at that face, there's some good drinking in that. The Blackbornes had lost all their money, but he became a big deal in the 1980s. After the mines closed, his cement works and chemical plant employed a lot of the colliery workers. Now they've closed down too, and Mark Blackborne is in the development game.'

'You think he knows where Sarah is?'

'I don't know. It's possible that she made contact with him, though. Rayner seemed to think so, that maybe he refused to give her money. Even if that's the case, it would be good to know for sure that she spoke to him. She might have said something, told him where she was going. Or what kind of trouble she was in.'

'Or perhaps he is part of that trouble.'

'Either way.'

'What are you to do? Knock on his house? Hello, Sir Mark. Can you tell me if you are involved in the kidnapping and the maybe murders of women? Thank you.'

'Like to think I'd have a touch more subtlety, but—'

'Yes, subtlety is written all over your face.'

Boone frowned, touching a finger to the cut over her eye. The stitches were just about due out, and the swelling had gone from the rest of her face, leaving behind a sickly patch of yellowed skin.

'I mean, you cannot go on your own to see him,' Roo said. 'You cannot be alone with him, you know this. How has this been working out for you so far?'

'I know.'

'You know. You say you know. You turn up half naked and bleeding and hiding in ditches. You know. Gah.'

'Look,' Boone said, turning the laptop to Roo.

The Cornilo website proudly announced that a show home was already completed and would be shown to the world at some kind of press event three days hence.

'Loads of people. Press, politicians, whatever. Finger food and fizz.'

'You will get an invitation?' Roo asked sceptically. 'How is this?'

'I'm going to walk right in. All about attitude. Act like you own the place.'

Roo had her doubts.

'Dressed as you, you will do this?'

'I may dress up,' Boone said. 'I'll have you know I possess very fetching ankles.'

'*Da*?' Roo said. She sat on the edge of the sofa and peered up the hem of Boone's jeans. 'Let me see. Is maybe where we will finally find your brains.'

28

Key in the door of the house at Lark, Boone stood there staring at the balloons tied up in the porch with a bow hanging below them, and honestly had no idea what they were for.

You've forgotten something, she thought.

Obviously you've forgotten some things, but now you've forgotten something new they must have told you about. She turned the key and went in, hoping she could sell them on her absent-mindedness. Wondering how much she'd played the victim already, whether there was still any slack left there.

Jack and Quin stood in the hall with stupid hats on and Jack fired a party popper, a clod of paper streamers landing in her hair.

'Happy birthday!' they said.

Boone stared at them.

'You forgot,' Jack said. He turned to Quin. 'She forgot.'

Boone said, 'In my defence, I've never had one before.'

'Oh no,' said Quin. 'You've had many, many before.'

'Thank you, Quin.'

'Dinner is ready,' Jack said, showing her through to the table in the kitchen.

The best china was laid and in the middle sat three large pizza boxes.

'Pizza,' she said.

'It's a thing,' Quin said.

'Few years ago we got a new oven,' Jack explained. 'Not *for* your birthday, but it came on the day. Got it all installed, fancy Italian one. Went to cook a birthday meal and . . . I don't know. There was a circuit board and a thing and basically nothing worked. So all our plans were scuppered.'

'Dad ordered pizza instead,' Quin said.

'And every year since.'

'Pizza it is then,' said Boone, taking a seat. 'We have wine though, right? The Italian oven didn't take the wine too?'

Jack pointed at the pizza. 'There's a pepperoni and I think other mixed sausages or something on that one. This one has chicken and chorizo and peppers. And that one is roasted squash, pear and caramelised onions. So, I was back and forth between white or red. Ended up thinking pink was the best option.'

Boone was staring at the pizzas. 'These didn't come on a moped.'

'That local place,' Quin said. 'The bakery thing up the road.'

Jack poured her a glass, saying, 'It's a Grenache and Rolle blend from Provence,' and Boone felt a bit of an arsehole for not knowing what that was supposed to do for her. It suddenly dawned on her that she hadn't taken any time to find out about the stuff Jack was interested in. Hadn't even pretended to care. The wine was pale, almost a buttery colour, and she thought she tasted strawberry, but didn't say anything. It was good and went down in gulps. So did the pizza, which she ate like someone was going to take it away from her.

'S'good,' she said, holding up slices of pear for close inspection before munching them.

Afterwards there was a cake, one in a box from a supermarket because that was how they saved the birthday the day the oven died. They'd stuck thirty-six candles in it, which was thirty-five more than Boone felt strictly necessary.

There were also presents. That was the worst bit. Neatly wrapped presents they had put thought into, presents that their Abigail Boone would have delighted in. They watched her for the slightest flicker, just the embers of remembrance.

Their every look larded with expectancy.

She wondered how much of what people felt for one another, what they called love, eventually boiled down to memories of shared experiences. She didn't feel any alchemy at work inside herself. When the chemical attraction or umbilical dependency was removed, what had been built together was what remained. With all of that obliterated from her mind, she instead found the place where love ends and something else begins.

Here be dragons.

29

The morning she was going to Blackborne's open-house event, Boone went to the caravan so Roo could help her decide what to wear. The coffee table bore empty wine bottles and foil takeaway cartons.

'Look at you two,' Boone said.

'She is showing me the movies,' Roo said. 'The Barbara Stanwyck.'

'She's my favourite,' Boone said, like someone was playing with her special toy.

Boone had brought a wardrobe bag with some clothes from her previous life, and she sat on the edge of Roo's bed watching her rifle through them. Roo pulled out several trouser suits, some skirts, various other garments, making faces as she shoved them all back.

'You did not wear sexy dresses,' she said. An observation, not a question.

'I guess not.'

'You want to wear a suit then, look like a business lady?'

Boone straightened out her legs and twisted her feet this way and that. 'Fetching ankles, remember?'

Roo held up the Sonic Youth astronaut T-shirt. 'Aha! The saint's shinbone. You are not to wear this, surely?'

'That's for you,' Boone said.

Roo held it up against herself.

'You said you liked it when I wore it before.'

'Is space people. What is not to like?' She pulled it on over her own T-shirt and nodded in approval. 'It is a good fit,' she said. Grabbing Boone's arms, she stood her up and compared their bodies in the mirror.

'Not so much different maybe,' she said. 'I have some things.'

She rummaged in the wardrobe and threw some items on the bed.

'Come on, come on,' she said, making a hurry-up gesture with her hand.

'What?'

'Take off the clothes. We see what we have to work with.'

She was holding up bras and knickers, matching them to dresses she had.

'I'm okay for that.'

'I have seen what is in your bag. There are men with sexier underwear. You want to walk into this place without anyone stopping you, then you are to look like everyone is wanting to do the sex. Helps you don't wear panties that sag below the dress.'

Boone started removing clothes.

'Hello. Where did they come from?' Roo said. 'You stick with your own brassiere, I think. Will be a battle to stuff those things in mine.'

Boone was appalled to find herself blushing furiously.

On one finger, Roo hung out a pair of knickers that appeared to be missing about two thirds of the requisite fabric. Lingerie wasn't something Boone had looked into since her accident, and if the floor had gaped open and swallowed her whole right then she'd have been absolutely fine with it.

'Turn round,' she said, snatching the knickers.

Roo sighed and turned around, hands on her hips. Boone slid her own panties down, stepping out of them and into the racier pair almost in one move.

'You know the door to cupboard is a mirror,' Roo said.

'Jesus Christ, Roo.'

'I would say it is nothing I have not seen before, but my God. Is not so much bush as rainforest.'

'Fuck off.'

Boone dressed and undressed in front of the mirror, Roo handing her different dresses in between. She found her a pair of opaque tights to try on too.

Boone pulled them on and examined herself in the mirror.

'Is working its way through,' Roo said in amazement. She got on her knees and played with the hairs poking through. 'A whole inch.' Looking at the packet the tights had come in, she said, 'Boone, one hundred den. My God. When it was the last time you shaved?'

'Probably the abortion,' Boone said, looking down at her hosed legs.

'The abortion,' Roo said.

'I wasn't sure on the etiquette. I shaved, you know, down there.

Left a little arrowhead above at first. Then thought maybe they prefer it all gone, so shaved it off and did the rest too.'

Still on her knees, Roo was holding onto Boone's legs. 'When, uh . . .'

'At the clinic, where I was recovering. Supposed to be recovering. They helped arrange it. Couple of months after . . .' and she made a clicking sound. 'The whole reset button thing.'

'I see,' said Roo. 'I am sorry. I thought that . . . I mean, you never said that they had done that. That anything had happened to you in the flat.'

Boone shook her head. 'The doctor told me in the hospital I was eight weeks, so it was from before.'

'Your husband?'

'I guess so. No other takers stepped forward.' With a shaky laugh she added, 'Can you imagine me with a little one running around?'

'Can't you?' Roo said.

Boone didn't answer. Roo gently patted her leg. She grabbed a tuft of hair that had sprung through the tights and tugged gently.

'Think I should have a shear then?' Boone said.

'Whatever it is you want to do,' Roo said. 'At this point I am more concerned about monkey genes.'

She ploughed through Boone's clothes again until she found a strappy summer dress with a floral design.

'Yes,' she said.

'Really?' Boone said.

'Not for you. For me.'

She wriggled out of her shorts and both T-shirts she had on, her naked body hard and frank, and pulled the dress on over her head. As she admired herself in the mirror, Boone took out her phone and snapped a picture. She took more as Roo swished this way and that, the pleated skirt playing around her legs.

'I think I am making a better Abigail Boone than you,' Roo said.

30

Boone hacked away at her thick fuzz with a pair of blunt-nosed nail scissors Roo had provided, then took a long, hot shower, shaving legs and pits and naughty bits. The caravan had no bath, and her leg precluded acrobatics, so she came out and sat on the toilet seat, feet up against the opposite wall, using a hand mirror for the trickier sections. Finally, after plucking a particularly rambunctious black hair that had sprouted beside one nipple, she was hairless from the brows down.

She let Roo do her make-up, applying some concealer above her eye where Jack had taken the stitches out. Roo worked her hair with the tongs, and on that side it cowled down around her eye.

'Is glamorous,' Roo said.

Boone resisted the urge to constantly brush it aside.

After all the grooming, she chickened out and plumped for a trouser suit. Took the best part of an hour for Roo to talk her into at least wearing a skirt instead, and she picked out a knee-length grey one with matching jacket. 'You were the one with the ankles all the time,' she pointed out.

In the mirror, Boone admitted it wasn't too hard to look at. The skirt was well cut to her form and she liked what the heels did to her calves. Walking around in the things was something else altogether.

'Think I walloped the ability to walk in heels out of my head,' she said.

'I do not know this wallop, but you wear heels like a man,' Roo said.

Boone had inherited a trove of shoes from her old self, but couldn't imagine when she would have worn most of them. These days she wore trainers or flats or low-heeled boots at best. After a few laps of the living room, she took to the stilettos just fine, but was conscious of her every step, and felt as if the skirt was riding up. Roo told her to stop fiddling with it.

The cement works site was across the estuary on the Hoo peninsula. As she drove, Boone practised the stories she and Roo had prepared to gain access, but in the end she breezed straight in without anyone giving her a second look. The show home appeared to have landed at the centre of a building site from outer space in its final form, with a faux stacked-stone and brick finish outside and rich stylings within. On the front lawn stood a Rolls-Royce, huge thing like out of the old movies, with steel bodywork in blue and black. It made the Goose look like a go-kart.

Guests were free to tour the whole house, with the open-plan downstairs living space the heart of the reception. Mark Blackborne stood at the centre of the room, barely moving as groups came up and greeted him before fading away to be replaced by others. People seemed instinctively to know just how much of his time to take up before moving on. He was the star around which their worlds revolved. He appeared popular, everyone laughing and smiling quite genuinely in his company, and Boone's first impressions, albeit from a distance, were positive. As people came and went, she became more and more prepared to believe that he couldn't be anything to do with the trouble Sarah Still had found herself in.

Then she saw him.

Among the crowd, a couple of faces remained constant. A young woman, whose suit made Boone feel like a geography teacher, ushering people to and from Blackborne's company, whispering their pedigrees in his ear. And an older man, seventy probably, wearing a suit not cut for him. Blackborne spoke to him briefly in between the handshakes and business talks, seemed to value his counsel. His face was mean and leathered, his mouth twisted into a permanent sneer, speaking out the corner of it as if a pipe were affixed to the other side.

And then there were the ears.

Boone recognised the sneer.

She recognised the ears.

Twenty-five years younger perhaps, but she'd seen him in one of the images of the Polaroids on Milan's memory card. He was the man pictured with the young girls.

Awkwardly she moved between small satellite groups of three or four people, hoping she looked as if she belonged. She wanted to get closer, hear the man speak or maybe catch a name, but she was useless at parties. She was fairly sure that had always been the case, but it was pathological now. She should have practised small talk instead of the tall tales she'd thought she'd need to get in the door.

She found herself constantly seeking cover, in a hallway or behind the table with glasses of complimentary bubbly, partly to avoid talking to people, but also so she could violently tug at her skirt where it painted itself to her thighs.

'You okay there?'

Mark Blackborne smiled at her as he picked up a glass of champagne from the table. He had an open, easy smile, and Boone knew instantly how people would tell him anything, how they'd want to laugh along with him and have him like them.

'I'd like to see men having to wear these things for a week,' Boone said, patting out the wrinkles she'd put in the skirt.

Blackborne laughed.

'Failing that, if someone could just find the man who designed them and bring him to me.'

'What if it was a woman?'

'Oh, it was a man. Trust me on that. Some things could only be designed by a bloke. That big wagon of a thing parked on the lawn, for instance.'

He smiled a cat-who-got-the-cream smile that broke across his whole face.

'That's my big wagon of a thing,' he said. '1938 Phantom III.'

Boone rolled her eyes. Boys with their toys.

'Honestly, I'm on your side on the matter. It drives like a container ship and costs a fortune to maintain. It was my father's. He paid a firm an eye-watering amount to reproduce the original coachwork. I would have sold it, but I've found it goes down well at events like this one. People cooing and aahing over it.'

'So popping down the local Waitrose, you drive something smaller, do you?'

'I have a hybrid.'

'Maybe you should design my skirts after all.'

'You know, I think I know everyone in this room,' he said. 'There's a few I met for the first time today, but I could have picked them out of a crowd beforehand anyway. However, you I can't quite place.'

'Don't surprises just ruin a day?' Boone smiled. 'Probably I should skip out, pretend the whole thing never happened.'

He laughed like someone had performed a magic trick.

'I bet there's a few here you don't know,' Boone said. She screwed her face in concentration and scanned the room. 'Him, for instance.'

She pointed at a large man in the window bay with a drink in one hand, a paper plate sagging beneath the weight of food in the other. His dark navy suit was rumpled and hung from him like curtains. His gut swallowed his belt and his tie was thinly knotted, as if a schoolyard bully had been at it.

'Even if I didn't know him, I'd know he was a local councillor,' Blackborne said. 'He's important for planning matters.'

'Okay,' Boone said. 'Her.'

A young woman, maybe not yet out of her teens, strode across the living room in dark trousers and a white shirt, her tightly tied ponytail whipping back and forth behind her.

'That's one of the girls helping with the catering,' Blackborne said. 'You may have me there.'

'Good excuse to go and ask her name,' Boone said.

Blackborne grinned, enjoying himself.

'All right,' Boone said. 'Redeem yourself. Him.'

She pointed at the old man, the one with the ears.

'Hanley?' Blackborne said. 'Come on, everyone knows Hanley. Well, Lord Moss, I suppose, to most people. He was an MP for years.'

'Here?'

'Down in Lark. Hanley Moss? When I was a lad, there was barely a week that old boy wasn't on the telly or in the papers. Of course, now they've made him a baron and packed him off to the other place.'

He stood close now, their shoulders brushing, voices lowered to a conspiracy.

'Maybe you do know everybody,' Boone said.

'Everybody but one.'

Boone laughed. 'I spent the morning rehearsing stories. How I might get in here, in case there were invites or a list or something. You're the first person to ask me who I am, though. All that effort wasted. I had a really cute one. I was going to confess, like I'd been caught out. Say I was the competition, putting together a development somewhere else. Come to see how you were doing it.'

Blackborne was still smiling, but it was a little skew-whiff now, some confusion in it.

'I'm here because we have a mutual friend, you see.'

'Who might that be?'

'Sarah Still.'

He frowned, shook his head. Boone couldn't tell, couldn't read his face. She showed him the most recent picture of Sarah.

'Doesn't ring a bell,' Blackborne said. 'She's a friend, you said?'

Boone took out another picture, the one of a younger Sarah with Blackborne by her side.

'Blimey,' he said. 'That's going back a way.' He scrutinised the picture. 'Yes, I sort of recognise her like that. Daughter of one of the plant employees, I believe.'

'Granddaughter,' Boone said. 'Molly Still is her grandmother.'

'Right,' Blackborne said, nodding. 'The husband had been in the pits. He worked here, didn't he? At the cement works, I mean.'

'That's right.'

'Got sick or something, poor chap. To be honest, I didn't really know them. I was still young, wasn't part of my father's businesses yet. He would have known all about them. He liked to know his staff like that. Better than I do, I'm afraid to say.' He gestured at the picture. 'That looks like one of the family days they arranged at the chemical plant. I must have had hundreds of pictures like that taken. Boss's son, you know how it is. I was that bit older than most of the kids at these things. I didn't really know them. I don't understand what this is all about?'

'She's missing, Sarah.'

'That's terrible.'

'I'm helping her grandmother look for her.'

'So you're, what? Some kind of detective?'

'I'm doing a friend a favour is all.'

'And I'm part of this favour?'

'That's what I'm finding out,' Boone said, smiling sweetly. 'The police didn't get anywhere. Didn't really try. Sarah was . . . troubled. So I'm running down any connection I can.'

'Of course,' Blackborne said. 'But I'm not sure I count as a connection.'

Boone was aware of someone watching them.

The young woman in the power suit – Blackborne's personal assistant, she assumed – was talking to a man in a police uniform. They spoke with heads bowed to one another, sneaking glances across at Boone and Blackborne.

The copper had collar patches and a hat with silver oak leaves on the peak, tucked beneath a stiff arm with martial ardour. The deeper meaning of such baubles had been lost in the soup of Boone's mind, but it couldn't be good.

'The picture,' she said. 'Like I say, any connection.'

'Well, I'll help in any way I can, but I'm not sure what use I can be. Frankly, I don't even remember meeting the girl really. The family story, I know the broad strokes.'

'You haven't seen her in the years since? She's never reached out to you?'

'Not at all. Why on earth would she? I only met her because her grandparents worked for my father. We weren't friends. I didn't even know she was missing.'

'Well, it was a long shot. Another lead I can cross off the list.'

'You still haven't told me your name.'

Along with stories to get in the door, Boone had tried out a few false names. Trouble with making up names, they sounded either too ordinary or too absurd. In the end, she didn't have time to chance one before someone else beat her to it.

'Abigail Boone,' said the baubled copper.

He had sidled over and stood before them now, straight-backed and chin raised. Boone suspected he had to restrain himself from clicking his heels. 'Sir Mark,' he added, shaking Blackborne's hand with a barely perceptible bow.

'John,' Blackborne said. 'Glad you could make it. You two know each other then?'

'Abigail here is an erstwhile detective sergeant of ours,' the copper said. 'Something of a hero, really. Rescued a young lady from a rather ghastly predicament, at some personal cost too. Isn't that right?'

'I . . . uh . . .' Boone stammered.

'Of course. How foolish of me. You probably won't remember, but we worked together a few years ago.' He offered a hand. 'John Bardin, Assistant Chief Constable. I was Chief Super back then.'

'Pleasure,' Boone said. Bardin's faux friendliness was barely covering what this was – a quite deliberate outing.

'Yes, I spoke to Zac afterwards,' Bardin went on. 'Most unfortunate business.'

He meant Deputy Chief Constable Sidel, the man who had quietly swept Boone out of the constabulary.

'Total retrograde amnesia I believe was the term he used,' Bardin said. 'I can't imagine how one would cope with such a thing.'

'So you are police,' Blackborne said.

'Not any more,' said Boone. 'And it's sort of like I never was.'

'What is it that brings you here?' Bardin said.

'I own a similar site,' Boone said. 'Old cement works. Was hoping to get tips on how to develop it.'

She was no longer amusing Blackborne, however. His gaze was already elsewhere, and Bardin was simply confused. The power suit appeared between the two men, each hand cupping an elbow.

'I wonder if I might steal these gentlemen,' she said, turning them away from Boone without waiting for a reply. She guided them smoothly across the room towards the fat councillor, who had worked several beige stains into his tie.

Boone felt a hand on her arm.

'If I might have a word,' said a small bespectacled man with tiny teeth behind his cold smile, gesturing with one hand towards a door whilst pulling Boone gently through it with the other. They were in a spacious kitchen where catering staff were uncovering fresh vol-au-vents to be laid out.

He grabbed a glass of red wine from the side before leading her across the room and out the back door into the garden. The newly laid turf was so bright it looked artificially green. A head-high gate opened onto a fenced alley alongside the house, where they found waiting for them a man who looked more traditionally muscle than Boone's new friend with the spectacles. Black and as tall as Boone in her heels, he stared impassively at her.

Boone was weighing up kicking off her heels, making fighting or running easier, considering what value they might have as a weapon with their sharp stilettos, when the short man tossed the wine from his glass.

'Jesus,' she said, startled.

He got her on the neck and across the chest, the wine soaking into a deep cranberry bib on her white tee. She wiped wet from her chin and neck, speechless.

'Oh, how clumsy of me,' the man said.

Boone looked to the other one. He wasn't young – in his fifties, she supposed – but was as solid as your average three-bedroom semi and spoke about as much.

'I appear to have ruined your top,' the short one went on. 'Wouldn't really do to be seen back in there looking like that. Probably best you head home and have it seen to. I'll be more than happy to cover any dry-cleaning costs, of course.'

His silent partner held open the gate at the other end of the alley, and followed a few paces behind Boone until she'd cleared the front lawn of the show home and was picking her way through the potholes and puddles of the construction road.

Looking back over the parked cars, he stood arms crossed at the end of the path leading to the front door. Was still stood there when Boone reached the main road. She walked out of sight to the Goose and in the back seat changed out of her suit and sopping wet top and into jeans and a sweater. She tied her hair back and pulled on a baseball cap. She had hoped to rattle Blackborne into doing something rash, perhaps follow him somewhere. But he was going to be at the open house for hours yet, and the whole thing was starting to sound like a movie plan anyway.

When she got back to the caravan, Roo had already packed her clothes up.

'Good timing,' she said. 'And good to see you are not murdered.'

'Uh, thanks. What's going on?'

'We are off out,' Roo said, handing Boone her bag and holding the door for Tess.

'Scan,' Tess said, rubbing her belly.

'I can give you a lift,' Boone said.

'Fitzy's taking us,' Tess said. 'You know what Mick's like. Protective.'

'Okay,' Boone said.

'Blackborne,' Tess said. 'Tell us about it tomorrow?'

'Yeah. Tomorrow.'

Boone watched them take the shore path behind the fields to Mickey Box's cottage. They laughed as they went.

31

It was early evening when Boone pulled into the drive outside the house in Lark.

Jack had the door open before she reached it.

'All right?' she said.

'We have a guest.'

She followed him through to the kitchen, where Barb was sitting at the table. She looked pissed. That was quick, Boone thought.

'Wotcha,' Boone said, exaggerating the leg as she sat down. 'They got you out here already?'

'What?'

'Whatsit, Bardin. The ACC. What did he do? Give Sidel a ring and tell him to warn me off?'

'I don't know what you're talking about, Boone.'

'Oh.'

She was a little disappointed. Would have been nice to have made an impression.

'Social visit then? Those mimosas?'

'If I run you through ANPR, what's going to come back?'

Boone considered her quietly for a moment. 'Why would you want to do something like that?'

'Sarah Still,' Barb said.

'Shit.'

The police didn't find missing people.

'She's dead,' said Barb. 'You need to come in for questioning.'

FOUR
AN END TO WISHING

32

'If it wasn't me, it'd have been uniforms with blues and twos haul-
ing you in a couple days from now,' Barb told her as she drove. 'A
right fucking mess you've got us into this time.'

Sarah Still's body had been found buried beneath one of the polytunnels at Scraycroft. Her hands had been severed, flesh cut with a
hacksaw at the joint and the job finished with blunt force according
to the pathologist, and her teeth removed. It had taken a few days for
the lab to match a DNA sample to the missing persons database, to
a sample from Molly Still and hair from a brush of Sarah's. They
were among the first samples ever entered in the database.

'How long has she been dead?' Boone asked.

'A month, give or take.'

Dead before you even started looking, Boone thought. This
time anyway – alive when you were getting tossed off balconies a
year ago.

'How long did it take you?' she said.

'How long what?'

'From finding Milan's body. How long to work out what happened to Sarah? I never even thought about excavating the farm. Not that I could have anyway.'

At speed, Barb swerved across three mercifully empty lanes of motorway and over the heavy white chevrons onto a slip road, braking hard and bumping the car up the kerb onto a grassy patch at the side of the narrow lane.

'Fuck-ing hell, Barb,' Boone said, looking agog at her friend.

Barb starting counting on her fingers. 'One: who is Milan? Two: where is his body? Three: who the *fuck* is Milan, Boone?'

'You didn't find his body?'

'No, Boone. We haven't found his fucking body.'

'So how did you get to Scraycroft without—'

'Are you somehow unclear on the relationship here? I'm the detective. You're the person helping me with my sodding enquiries. But we can make it the person under arrest if that'll clarify the situation for you.'

'Milan Jedinek. He ran an . . . an agency. An employment agency, ostensibly bringing seasonal farm labour over from the Czech Republic. But he was trafficking young women. They became sex workers.'

'This you got from Roo?'

Boone hesitated. 'She's not to be brought into this. Any way, shape or form, Barb.'

'If she's a witness—'

'Roo didn't tell me. Roo didn't say a word. I got it from a tramp in Lark. He was drunk and shouting at dogs and told me a story about a man called Milan.'

'Jesus fucking Christ.'

'Arrest me. I don't give a shit. Roo is not involved in this. Everything that's happened to her already? My God. Not a chance.'

Barb sighed. 'Milan.'

'He has a flat in Lark, up in the Carlton.'

'Fuck's that?'

'This trippy-looking block of flats on the sea. One of those sixties things all gone to pot now.'

'And you found him there how?'

'All I had was his first name and that he ran an agency. I looked up agencies until I found mention of one online, AnyFarm, that had a director called Milan. That stuff's all public info, Companies House and whatnot. Figured it was probably him, so I paid him a visit.'

'And he hadn't laid out the table, got the Kiplings in?'

'He was in his bathtub. Electrocuted, looked like. Been there a few weeks, at least.'

'When was this? Boone, when did you find him?'

'Three weeks ago. Ish.'

'Odin's cocking ravens,' Barb said, bashing the steering wheel and bibbing the horn.

'I thought someone would find him. The smell.'

'Why didn't you call?'

'I needed time. I don't think he killed himself. It was staged to look like that and I didn't want whoever did it to know that he had been found.'

'You're not police any more, Boone.'

'Police weren't going to find Sarah. Nobody gave a shit.'

'You weren't going to find her!' Barb roared. 'She's been dead over a month, Boone. She was cold and in the earth before you even started this craziness.'

Boone looked away, out of the window. The light was on and she couldn't see much past her own reflection. She felt like laughing. If life had any structure at all, it was that of every joke ever told.

'How did you find her?' she said.

'Owner of the place, man called Horton. Something Horton.'

'Geoff.'

'Geoff Horton.' Barb smiled. 'He said some mad bint with a limp had driven up there in a Saab tank and was asking about someone used to work there. Couldn't remember the name she gave him. When I heard that, I thought to myself, who could that be? Who could that possibly be among the countless psycho gimpy Saab-owning bitches with whom I'm acquainted?'

Boone shrugged.

'You think he won't be able to pick you out?'

'It was me.'

'I know it was you, fucknuggets. Why do you think I came to get you before someone else worked it out?'

'Horton found her?'

'His dog. Apparently the thing was digging up the earth. Probably smelt her. Ripped off a foot and deposited it in front of Horton like a cat might a dead sparrow.'

'Kaz,' Boone said, thinking about the huge Alsatian pawing at the ground when she visited Scraycroft. She was there all along, right beneath your fucking feet.

'What?'

'Kaz. Name of the dog. Kazak.'

'Seen smaller horses. Horton called the locals, and when the ID came in off the database, my shitometer redlined.'

'What have you told them?'

'Nothing much. That you worked on the case before and that you'd gone through the notes after your—'

'Accident.'

'Yeah. That you might be of some use.'

Barb turned the engine on again, looking both ways along the junction. 'Fuck do I get out of here?'

Boone glanced about. 'Roundabout bridge doobrey. Follow it round, we can get back on.'

'You said this Milan, his body led you to the farm,' Barb said, guiding them back onto the motorway to Maidstone.

'I found his car,' Boone said. 'There was a phone in it. Last place he'd looked up on the map was Scraycroft.'

Barb raised her eyebrows. 'I just give all that junk to the civvy tech dude. That wouldn't be half bad coppering if you weren't such a colossal pain in my fanny.'

'What are you going to do, Barb?'

'I don't see how I can explain any of this. Your presence at the farm, asking about Milan. Jesus, if anyone finds out you knew his body was there and didn't report it. You've dug us in good and proper here.'

'I'll say I was in London, that I spoke to girls on the street, Czech girls. One of them told me about coming over to pick strawberries or whatever. Told me where the farm was and gave me a name, Milan, and I followed up at the farm that way. I don't have to have ever been at Milan's.'

'Boone, I can't leave a body lying about the place.'

'Get this – you say you looked into these agencies and found one with a Milan Jedinek as a director. That's what I did anyway. You can create your own trail. Look him up at Companies House. Find the name of the company and the correspondence address he had listed. Go round, give him a knock. Fuck me, what's that ghastly smell, better put the door in, chaps. Bingo.'

'And you're not going to have left fingerprints all over?'

Boone gave her a look.

'Worrying how all of this comes so easily,' Barb said. 'Hope you're not thinking about changing sides.'

'There are no sides. Everything is a situation.'

'Thanks, Boonesattva. What about Michael Boxall? He a situation too?'

Boone said nothing. The men she sought operated outside the law, and so would she. There was something liberating about being an outlaw, in much the same way she imagined there had been something liberating about being police.

They turned into the nick in Maidstone, its countless windows turning the clear night's moon back on to them.

'What I was doing, Barb, I thought it might help,' Boone said.

'Police don't need help.'

'I thought it might help me. Looking into it was like looking into me, finding out who I am.'

'For someone who claims they don't want to remember who they used to be, you certainly wade through lakes of shit looking into it,' Barb said.

Boone couldn't answer.

33

There was no good cop, bad cop. The questioning was long and organised and tiresome, the same enquiries made over and over in the hope of chiselling out some small inconsistency to be worked into a wider crack. Boone had a peerless knack for creating her own realities at this point, though, and suffered through it calmly and resiliently.

Pains were taken to explain she was not under arrest, but that matters could and would be swiftly escalated if she did not help police with their enquiries.

Of course, no arrest meant no right to a brief, and Boone didn't fancy troubling Mickey Box to get one for her.

She was familiar to some of the detectives involved, even if she couldn't remember them, and this was to her advantage – they acted as if questioning the old Abigail Boone, as if there was something for them to leverage by knowing her. There was not.

She ran quickly through the story she had proposed to Barb, that a Czech tom had given her the name Milan and told her about the labour agencies, and that she'd been at Scraycroft looking into that when Horton came across her. They went through it again and again, sceptical both because it was their job to be so and because it sounded like complete horseshit.

Sometime after midnight, a female constable brought Boone a paper and some dinner (more droopy chips), and she was left alone for several hours, the door occasionally opening for a pale face to peer in at her and vanish again. When they returned to question her in earnest, it was Detective Constable Barry Tayleforth who led proceedings. Canter.

'Abigail,' he said, sliding into his seat as though he was going to be marked on artistic impression.

'Boone,' she said. 'Everyone calls me Boone.'

'Of course.'

She suspected he was the exact type of knobhead who used to call her Boone when they worked together and now thought it'd be funny to try it the other way.

'Boone,' he said, removing a photograph from a beige folder and pushing it across the table. 'Do you recognise this man?'

It was a headshot, looked like a blown-up passport photo.

'No,' she said, not lying.

'His name is Milan Jedinek. That mean anything to you?'

Barb had obviously worked quickly, establishing an independent link in the investigation to Milan. Boone took a closer look at the photo. She only knew him as the human soup in his bathtub.

'Milan,' she said. 'Could be the one I was looking for. Didn't have a second name.'

'And you're quite sure you've never met him?'

'I'm quite sure I don't remember ever meeting him.'

Canter nodded slowly. 'He's listed as the director of a company called AnyFarm, an agricultural labour agency, brings people over from the Czech Republic among other places. Strawberry-pickers, so forth.'

'That tallies with what I'd been told,' Boone said.

'By these sex workers you spoke with.'

'Yes.'

'Whose names you can't recall.'

'Whose names I never asked.'

He opened his folder and took out another picture, placing it next to the first one in front of Boone. It was of the bathtub, what remained of Milan. 'This is Milan Jedinek now,' he said. 'We found him a couple of hours ago, in his own bathroom. Been there a while, as you can see. Somewhere in the gunk that used to be a person is an electric heater.'

'Suicide?' Boone said.

'He lived in Lark,' Canter said. 'Block of flats on the front.'

'Britain today, eh? Quaint little seaside towns invaded by Eastern Bloc pimps. Thank God for the Ukips.'

Canter ignored her. 'Building is called The Carlton.'

'Oh aye, the funny-looking place? Always wanted to go in there. Nice, is it?'

'That was going to be my question to you.'

'Me?'

'No forced entry. But the place had been gone through. Suggesting it was either a murder staged to look like a suicide, or someone found him and searched the place before leaving without reporting the body. What would you say if I suggested it was you who had been there?'

'Wasn't me.'

'You've never been to The Carlton?'

Boone shook her head. 'Not that I recall.'

'Not that you recall.'

'Maybe he did kill himself but had been burgled prior to that,' Boone said. She sat up, as though inspiration had struck. 'Perhaps the burglary upset him so much, loss of family heirlooms or some such, that was the reason for his killing himself.'

He stared at her.

'You're the detective, though,' she added.

Canter dished out another photo, this time of a mobile phone. 'We found a car registered to Jedinek near The Carlton. This phone was inside. There was no memory card and very little data on the phone. The last location saved in the maps application was the farm at Scraycroft. In the flat, we found a power cord but no computer. So somebody removed a lot of potentially useful evidence.'

'Okay.'

'What would you say if I told you I think that person was you?'

'What would you like me to say?'

'You live in Lark, with your husband and son. Very nice house. He must do well for himself, Jack. Funny then that from what we can tell, you don't spend much time there. That you seem to spend a good deal of your time in a caravan with a Bulgarian prostitute and the daughter of a convicted criminal.'

'She's a prostitute? She told me she worked in a laundrette, bit of bar work on the side.'

'You know very well—'

'No, I'm saying if I'd known she was a tom I'd probably have asked for a rate.'

Canter said, 'I don't think there ever were any Czech sex workers.

I think Rumena Zlatkova told you about Jedinek. I think you went to Jedinek's flat, took his computer and phone. I think you linked him to the farm where we found Sarah Still's body. What I can't work out is why. At best, you broke into a flat and failed to report a dead body. At worst, you were involved in Jedinek's death and were cleaning house. What would you say to that?'

'I don't know what you're talking about,' Boone said.

'No? So if we search your house and the caravan, we're not going to find a computer or a memory card from the phone?'

'No. And I'd like to see you ask for that warrant with a straight face.'

'I'm two seconds away from arresting you, giving me powers of search and seizure.'

'You can search my home today if you like, Detective Constable. No need for arrest. The caravan isn't mine. I don't live there, and never have.'

'You don't think I could get a warrant? We know you've been there. Could have stashed anything. What if we have forensics go through Jedinek's flat with a fine-tooth comb? They're not going to find any evidence of you having been there?'

'I don't know.'

'You don't know?' His voice was rising. 'A minute ago you denied having been there, so how don't you know?'

'I didn't say I'd never been there.'

'You didn't say—'

Boone pointed at the camera. 'You've got it on tape. I said I didn't remember ever having been there. But then before a year ago, I don't remember a single thing about my life. I don't remember my parents. I don't remember school. I don't remember getting married, or giving birth to my son. I don't remember being a copper. So who's to say where my travels took me, or what forensic evidence might exist?'

'Oh, so in this former life you conveniently cannot recall, you might just have popped round to Milan Jedinek's flat? Spot of afternoon tea?'

'In that former life I was a detective sergeant in Kent Police, as you well know. And I was tasked with investigating long-term missing people, one of whom was Sarah Still, a girl whose death this Milan Jedinek appears to be connected to in some way. So it wouldn't be out-of-the-blue fantastic if I had run across him in some fashion, would it?'

Canter looked at her, mouth open. He was amazed. He almost laughed.

'That is the biggest load of bollocks I've ever heard,' he said.

'Yeah?'

'Yeah.'

'Prove it.'

34

It was still dark when Boone left. The incident room was humming, the excitement of new information going up on the wall. The police had vast resources compared to Boone, and maybe Molly Still would tell them something about her visitor. Maybe they'd piece together Rayner and The Sink. Boone was worried about Roo, though, especially now she was at the caravan. Canter could apply pressure, workplace visits and the like.

Barb found Boone in a brightly lit corridor and offered her a cup of machine coffee and a lift home. Boone accepted the latter.

'Should you be seen with me?' she said, getting in the car.

'I'm going to be getting it from Barry for days regardless.'

'He didn't seem pleased.'

'You as good as told him to his face that you were lying.'

'He as good as told me he was going to put me in the frame for murder.'

'Yeah. Well, there's loads to be getting on with, anyway.'

'All worked out. You lot know what you needed to know, and you looked good doing it. I'm assuming you made the link to Jedinek.'

'Was shitting it that it'd look too quick, that they'd see through the plan.'

'Too busy trying to fit me up for that.'

'Bardin was beyond pissed. He doesn't want to see you crop up in this case again unless we're dragging you in for charges.'

Boone smiled. 'Now I get it.'

'What?'

'The lift home. He sent you to tell me this.'

'His words – that bloody woman doesn't know who on earth I am.'

'I'm a multi-tasker,' Boone said. 'I'm capable of not knowing and not caring, all at the same time.'

'There are things that they're not going to just let lie, though. The laptop, for one.'

'That wasn't me. There was no computer in the flat when I was there. Whoever killed him must have taken it.'

'The phone is a problem too. They're wondering about an SD card.'

'It's an unregistered pay-as-you-go job,' Boone said. 'The location of the farm was all I got from it, and the numbers. But they're dead.'

She felt bad lying to Barb. She didn't know exactly what the photos on the memory card meant, but that Hanley Moss, now Lord Moss, was the man pictured certainly complicated matters. It would be catnip for the detectives on the case, but Boone needed more time to think it through. Self-preservation and making sure there was a lack of physical evidence connecting her to any crime scene certainly assuaged any pangs of guilt, however.

'Yeah, we didn't get much from the numbers,' Barb said. 'Tower information off the network has them in east London, but only for a few days, weeks ago. We couldn't narrow the area down to anything useful, given the location.'

'East London again,' Boone said.

'Canter has already noted that.'

'We'll be fine,' Boone said.

'Yeah, terrific.'

'Everything is deniable on your part. And I think I can keep Roo out of it. It'll be fine.'

'Boone, is there anything else you're not telling me?'

'My advice on this matter, don't ask questions you can't deny the answers to later.'

'This is a murder, Boone. Probably a double. It's large.'

'I don't have anything provable. Not even anything beyond vague connections and a hunch. I get something solid, I'll call you. Promise.'

They rolled up in front of the Lark house and Barb killed the engine. Lights were on in the lounge, and the telly flickered.

'Someone's waited up for you,' Barb said.

Boone sniffed.

'I saw the coroner's initial findings. Skull fracture behind the right temple, caused by something hard and sharp. Other facial injuries, bruises and a fractured cheekbone. They were ante mortem. Teeth and hands were removed post mortem.'

'Someone beat her and then didn't want her identified.'

'Looks like it. No other obvious signs of injury, but she'd been in the ground a while.'

'All right. Cheers for the ride. And when you see ACC Bardin, tell him to go fuck himself, yeah?'

'There's one other thing, Boone.'

'Yeah?'

'The coroner said there were marks, grooves on the inside of the pelvic bones. Parturition scarring, he said. She'd given birth at some point.'

Boone thought of Molly, of how she'd be burying her grand-daughter after all these years and now would be told of a great-grandchild she'd likely never see.

'Yeah, all right. I'll be seeing you, Barb.'

Jack got up from the sofa when the door closed. He looked like he'd been sleeping.

'So?' he said.

Boone shrugged.

'You weren't arrested?'

'I haven't done anything.'

'Uh-huh. So it's over now, yeah? Sarah Still found. Murder investigation for the police.'

Boone didn't speak.

'Abigail? It's over. Boone? You've solved the case.'

'I didn't solve anything. I went around kicking the walls until the ceiling came down on top of me. Finding a body isn't finding a person. Someone killed her, Jack. Bashed her brains in and then tried to make the corpse unidentifiable. That someone needs to be found.'

'Not by you they don't.'

'By me, by the police. By whoever.'

'What if it's not even them? What if the men who . . . who had you in the flat, what if they didn't kill her?'

'Then I'll have to find them too. I *need* to find them. These are things I can do. Things I will do.'

Saying it aloud, she knew this to be true. They were feelings that dampened down within her sometimes but that never left entirely, running on like an underground stream beneath everything she did, its current irresistible.

Missing or dead girls.

The people responsible.

It felt like purpose, like a life's work.

Her life's work.

35

Boone waited for everyone to leave before coming down in the morning. She decided to keep away from the caravan for a few days, just in case Canter got a bit zealous with his warrants. It was doubtful he had the manpower for surveillance, but she didn't want to drag Roo and Tess into things any deeper than she already had. She had called Roo the previous night to tell her what was happening. Hopefully she had told Tess, who would have the nous to clear the SD card and any computers out of the caravan and put them somewhere safe.

Sitting in the study with her first coffee of the day, she read articles about Hanley Moss. Lord Moss. She found an interview with him from his last day in Parliament. For twenty-seven years he had been MP for Lark, through, as he put it, seven general elections, five prime ministers and four wars ('Five, I suppose, with the miners,' he added, chuckling). He had served as a parliamentary under-secretary and a minister of state, before the young Turks of Westminster saw him put out to pasture in the Lords.

Great, now he was seventy-nine and only a peer of the realm. A man deeply connected in the highest reaches of British power, a man who knew MPs, senior police officers, prominent businessmen and other princes and pillars of the community. He'd been at it for a lifetime and had made a lot of powerful friends along the way.

She cross-searched Moss with Mark Blackborne.

'Brilliant,' she said, clicking on a picture of the two of them, arm in arm. She followed it back to the original webpage, a piece on the local paper's site from a year earlier, about the annual ball at the Blackborne mansion.

Something of a tradition apparently, a night-time boar hunt in their woods, followed by a daytime ball the following afternoon. The kind of event where men like Hanley Moss made friends who either shared their tastes or insulated them from the exposure of those tastes. Seeing who else attended these things could be interesting.

The photograph was credited to a Mark Hutchinson. Looking him up online, Boone discovered he was a freelance photographer, a mobile number on his website.

'Hutchinson Studios.'

'Hello, I'm looking for Mark Hutchinson.'

'You've found him.'

'Ah, Mr Hutchinson, I wondered if you might be able to help me. I saw a picture of yours in a local paper, taken at the Blackborne Ball last year.'

'Rings a bell. Think I sold a few from that day. That's with the boar hunt too, right?'

'Exactly. The thing is, my uncle was one of the guests and . . . well, he's since passed away.'

'God, I'm sorry.'

'What I was wondering, and I don't know if you do this sort of thing, but we don't have many pictures of him from recent years. When I saw your picture, I thought maybe you might have taken a shot or two with him in it that day.'

'It's possible. At a do like that I must have clicked hundreds of times.'

'He was an older gentleman, with silver hair and—'

'I'll tell you what. It'll probably be easier if I let you have a browse through them. You might spot him in the background or something, better than me. I shoot at a decent resolution, so we can blow things up if necessary.'

'That would be marvellous. I should come to you?'

'Oh, no need. I can upload the pictures from that day to an album online. If you give me an email address, I'll send you the link when I've done it. Might take me a few days to get to.'

'I would so appreciate that.'

Put on the spot, she riskily concocted a fake email address from the name of a character in a book she spotted in the bookcase by a dead author considered something of a writer's writer. She hoped it would be sufficiently under-read that no one would have snaffled the name for their email already.

The second she got off the phone, she set about creating the email address and was relieved to find the name had not been taken. Hutchinson hadn't commented, so as she made lunch for herself, and with no little delight, she judged him for not having read the book.

36

Sarah Still's funeral was a couple of days later. The crematorium looked modern, post-war, and resembled a scale model of a suburban Tube station.

'I shouldn't wonder if we destroyed so many buildings during the war that we flat forgot how to design them with any grace afterwards,' Boone said. 'Or maybe we thought it wouldn't be worth it, fearing the worst after a couple of right to-dos already.'

Nobody answered her.

'I said—'

'Bloody hell, Boone,' said Tess.

Boone had fetched Tess and Roo in the Goose, afraid to turn up on her own. 'I don't believe in funerals,' Roo had said, before Boone told her she had to go. It would be Boone's first funeral, first that she remembered anyway. Her first brush with grief, and she knew she wasn't going to understand a jot of it.

They got out of the car. A few spaces along, two men with short dark hair sat in a teal saloon.

'Police,' Boone said, nodding towards them for the others. 'Suppose Barb will be inside already.'

The entrance was a door at the side of a large porch midway along one wall. They approached from one end and around the corner, in the shadows' coolness, stood a man in a dark suit holding the leash to Molly's frowsty-looking dog. A dark patch on the brickwork betrayed where the animal had done its business. Another suited man held the door for them, nodding solemnly and murmuring something unintelligible that nonetheless conveyed an impression of sympathy. So familiar were these men with the grief of others that they had boiled the phonics of sorrow down to their simplest hum.

A tasteful sign directed them to the smaller of the two halls within the building. It felt terribly empty. Indeed, the three of them doubled the congregation. In the front of the dozen or so rows, each capable of seating maybe four people either side of a narrow aisle, sat Molly Still with a young woman Boone didn't recognise but wagered was a family liaison officer. Barb sat a row behind them. There had been no public notices for the funeral, as per Molly's wishes, and now as they entered, Boone wondered if they weren't making a dreadful intrusion.

Tess looked at her and with her elbow made a gesture towards a row near the back, on the other side of the aisle from the pitiful-looking party at the front. Boone nodded and they all slid silently into their seats.

'Has she no other family?' Tess whispered.

Boone shrugged. She was coming round to Roo's way of thinking. You had to live first in order to die, and so were smiled upon by the malicious joy of fortune by your very birth. This shabby affair made a mockery of that, though Boone wasn't convinced better attendance would improve matters any.

A local Anglican priest, who had previously met neither Sarah nor Molly, led the service, which was typically dour, with its kingdom and the power and the glory, but mercifully short. Molly was silent, shoulders shaking the whole way through, until the casket was drawn behind the curtain, at which point she let out a solitary sob and was caught by the young liaison officer as she rolled forwards slightly.

When it was over, Boone and the others remained standing at their seats as Molly was led out, hunched and frail, never once raising her eyes. They followed her at a respectful distance. Outside, once Molly had been reunited with her dog, Boone hazarded a quiet word, offering her sympathies.

Molly looked up at her, and it was as if a light had been switched on somewhere, a foul and lurid light behind her wild eyes. Boone thought for a moment the woman might go for her. Molly pulled her aside, and Barb and the other officer stepped away discreetly. From her bag she produced a package, a bubble envelope folded over and marked *Boone*.

'What's this?' Boone said.

'Came in the post the other day. From that boy with the hair, one what knew our Sarah. The note said it'd have a better chance of not getting lost with you than with the police.'

'What is it?'

'I didn't look. Don't want anything to do with it, or with you.'

'Molly . . .'

'I don't mean nothing by it, nothing against you. In my mind I buried her years ago, and now here we are again. Hope's worse than the drink. You find them what did this, I hope it brings you some satisfaction. But I don't want you knocking on my door again.'

Pulling her coat tight around her, she walked back to the liaison officer and allowed herself to be led to the waiting car. Boone slipped the packet into her coat pocket as Barb came over to her.

'Everything all right?' Barb said, looking back at Molly ducking into the dark saloon.

'It's only the saddest story ever told,' Boone said. 'We're going for a drink to get rid of the taste. Coming?'

'Some of us have murder investigations to wrap up,' Barb said. 'Any news?'

'None that I can share with you. If you were a fellow officer rather than a bothersome civvy who likes stepping in shit, I could have told you that DNA matching Sarah Still was found on the corner of a table in Milan Jedinek's flat. But you're not, so I can't.'

'So you're putting it down to Jedinek?'

Barb shrugged. 'Bit difficult, him having a severe case of being dead. Hard to establish a conclusive timeline, whether he killed her and died some time later, or they were both killed at the same time. Not that there isn't talk of laying her at his door and then guilt getting the better of him.'

'Neat and tidy.'

'I better be going. You still owe me mimosas, though.'

'Let me know when everything's quietened down and I'll buy you all the drinks you want.'

'Might even buy you one back, so long as you restrain yourself from sticking your tits into all this again.'

Barb waved to Roo and clambered into the unmarked police car. Boone drove the other two to a pub overlooking the old harbour that Tess had claimed with authority would be empty, it being a weekday afternoon. In fact, it was swamped with locals in the autumn of their lives enjoying the lunchtime specials menu.

'The crem should leave flyers in here,' Boone said.

She watched from the bar as the others staked out a table in the orangery at the back of the pub. An elderly couple sat before half-finished plates and swirled the dregs of their daily gin and tonics, and the women pounced when the pair eventually moved.

Boone returned with three glasses clutched precariously between her fingers. Roo raised her drink and said, 'In the arse of a whale,' to which Boone replied, 'There's no tripe for cats,' and Tess decided to write the pair off as a mystery.

In a corner, newly arrived and sitting alone with his drink at a small table, was an elderly man, his nose an extraordinary adjunct to his face, long and hooked as though straining to peer down into his mouth. He furtively watched the women with harried eyes that saw all youth as madness.

There was some talk of Molly and Sarah, each of them muttering bromide platitudes as their connections to the dead and living Stills were at best tenuous. Before an awkward pall of silence fell over them, Tess asked Boone what it was Molly had given her. Boone put the package on the table and tore it open.

Inside was a mobile phone and a note. *Only open on birthday*, in childish scrawl.

Boone turned the phone on.

'It's code-locked,' she said. She tried various combinations of her birthday to no avail. 'Bollocks.'

'What do you think is on it?' Roo said.

'Nothing good,' said Boone.

The three of them sat in silence and finished their drinks, Roo locating Boone's hand under the table and curling her fingers round her little finger.

37

Boone got it in the middle of the night.

Having dropped the girls home and made it back for dinner with Jack and Quin, she'd sat for hours trying to get into the phone Luke Rayner had left for her. Failing, she'd switched back to her case notes, trying to read them with fresh eyes, and out of nowhere she had twigged the obvious. The code to the phone wasn't her birthday; why on earth would it be? How would Rayner have even known what it was? It was Sarah's.

The phone's internal memory was packed with photos of girls. A full spectrum of teenage years, some of the fledglings not even that. Boys too. Photos of faces and photos of fucking and photos of walls and doors and tunnels. And there were photos of photos, colour-degraded Polaroid shots, snapped just off-angle with light sheening across their surfaces.

'Shit,' Boone whispered.

They were the same as the images on Milan's phone. The same faded Polaroids, and newer pictures taken on the phone's camera of the same house – recent images of windows and doors that matched the rooms in the Polaroids. There were also pictures taken in the colliery building that were a match for the videos on Milan's phone, and dozens of similar videos besides.

There were two saved numbers: a mobile and a London land-line. Jotting them down, Boone then crashed out and slept until the afternoon.

Waking to an empty house, she made coffee and looked at the numbers that were in the phone. The prepaid burner she'd bought had proved pointless for the numbers she'd taken from Milan's phone as they'd all been disconnected, but she about had a heart palpitation when she dialled the landline and it went through. After three rings it was picked up and a man grunted something that might have been a greeting.

'Hello?'

A pause. Then something foreign, unintelligible.

'Who am I through to?' Boone said.

The man's voice was faint, like he was holding the receiver away from his mouth, and the line went dead. She'd try it again later. The mobile number was active but unavailable, the handset turned off maybe. There was no voicemail. Taking Sarah's phone with her, she jumped in the Goose and headed for the caravan, hoping to find someone to bounce ideas off.

The sliding doors were open and she found the television on, Jean Arthur playing the piano.

'Hello?'

Roo's head popped up over the back of the sofa.

'I want to fly mail in the Andes,' she said.

'Of course you do.'

'I'm showing her the old ones,' said Tess. She emerged stretching from her bedroom, wearing the Sonic Youth astronaut shirt Boone had given Roo. 'She doesn't know any of them.'

Roo made a noise. 'I don't know *your* old ones. What it is you know of Nevena Kokanova?'

'Phooey,' said Tess, dropping down next to Roo on the sofa.

'Busy then, the pair of you,' Boone said.

'I have had a whole of a day off,' Roo said. 'I cannot tell you the last time this has happened. I have not left the sofa. It has been marvellous.'

'I'll make coffee,' Boone said, going to the kitchen counter.

There was some murmuring at the sofa and Tess ran back to the bedroom briefly. When she returned, she was wearing a different top. Boone didn't say anything. She poured two coffees and a green tea, bringing them over on a tray and explaining what she'd found on the phone.

'So it was Sarah who took the pictures, not Milan,' Tess said. 'She was there when they raped those girls.'

'She sent them to Milan?' Roo said.

'It makes sense,' Boone said. 'I couldn't work out why Milan would take them. Blackmail maybe, trying to extort the men in the videos. But they're part of the same operation, part of how he makes his living. Could have been insurance. Protection against anything happening to him. But if Luke Rayner was telling the truth, and Sarah wanted to leave and go to Ireland with him, then maybe she thought she could squeeze a few quid out of them. Last resort after she didn't get anything from Mark Blackborne and Molly didn't pony up.'

'This is why they killed her?' Roo said.

'Police are saying her blood was found in Milan's flat, on the edge of a table. Consistent with her skull fracture. She had other minor facial injuries. I think he finds out what she was planning. They fight, it gets out of hand, she hits her head a little too hard. Milan buries her somewhere he knows. The other one, the one who was asking questions at The Sink, breaking the fat boy's arm? If he'd killed her, why was he still looking for her?'

'For the phone,' Roo said. 'For these pictures.'

'But he asked for her. If he was after the phone, already having killed Sarah, and knew she'd been with Rayner, he'd have been looking for him, not her.'

'Milan killed her and the others didn't know?' Tess said.

'She sent Milan the photos,' Boone said. 'Maybe she wanted him in on it, didn't want to act alone. Which was daft. She only wanted money to run. What's he going to do, give up a lucrative set-up for a one-time bit of extortion?'

'Maybe there was something between them?' Tess said.

Boone nodded. 'Could be. Maybe she thought she could trust him.'

'So they argue, and things get out of hand,' Tess suggested.

'Now he has to get rid of the body,' Boone said. 'Maybe he doesn't know if she's already done something with the photos, so he tells the men about Sarah's plan in order to cover himself, but says he doesn't know where she is. If Sarah told Milan about the pictures, then maybe she told him about Rayner, or at least about where they'd been squatting. And Milan then tells them. So the big one, he's out looking for Sarah at The Sink, not knowing she's already in the ground. Not knowing Rayner has the phone with the pictures.'

Nobody said anything.

'Of course,' Boone said, 'if that is what happened, or something like it, we'll never really know because only Sarah and Milan would be able to tell us we're right.'

'So what else is there?' Tess asked. 'The rest is for the police, surely?'

'Steady yourself for avalanche of the bullshit,' Roo said.

Detachedly, as if it went without saying, Boone replied, 'These men need to be held to account.'

'Which is police work,' said Tess. 'Give all this to Barb, or send it in anonymously. Whatever.'

Boone shook her head. 'Too much of it is supposition. Things we think we know but can't prove. And there's Hanley Moss. He's a lord, for God's sake. He's in tight with Mark Blackborne, and the Blackbornes are connected to Sarah Still. There's something there.'

'Sure, but it's something the police can find,' Tess said.

'The same police who are sipping champagne with Moss and Blackborne at the open house?' Boone said. 'Those Polaroids, they don't actually show anything. So Moss was at this house, had his photo taken with some girls. They won't make a case out of that. They won't want to. How many times have they been bitten in recent years, investigating men like this but not having the evidence? Or investigating the wrong men?'

'You wanted to find Sarah,' Tess said. 'And you can make a plausible case for what happened to her. The man we think killed her is dead, killed probably by the men who had you and Roo in a fleapit room in London where they were going to kill you like that other poor girl there. To carry on now – I think it's about time you accept this is not, and never has been, about Sarah Still. It's about Abigail Boone and what happened to her.'

'What if it is? Isn't that something worth looking into?'

'What will you know?' Roo said. 'What will you find out that you don't already have a good idea about? These men's names? Their faces? Finding those things will probably mean you will die. Will probably mean you end up in another dark and dirty room . . .'

She tailed off, throwing her arms up in despair.

'But you will do what you will do,' she said.

Tess tried to defuse the situation. 'We're getting Chinese. Gonna watch a movie.'

Boone shook her head.

'I should get back. Jack will be cooking.'

'This Yellow Sea, they have the best seafood,' Roo said, already scouring the menu.

38

Fitz reclined against the Goose. He spat out a sunflower shell, which landed amid the crescent of others about his feet.

'Got a sec?' he said.

'For what?'

'Mick wants a word.'

They walked down the lane past the cottage and the scrapyard, out towards the tip of the headland. The place had its own smell, like rain-damp soil, that made it feel dangerous. Boone suspected Mickey Box had a stake in the ownership of most of the land out there, though actually tracing it to him would be next to impossible.

The lane ran like a giant horseshoe up one side of the headland and down the other, and where it began to turn back inland they left it and took a gravel path towards a wooded area. Two narrow strips of trees formed an L, growing so thickly that the series of low buildings behind them were completely hidden until you were almost upon them.

Mickey Box often spoke of 'going to the stables' and Boone had thought it was a euphemism, but the buildings had obviously been constructed for that purpose originally, though converted for more domestic use now. Through a window she saw a sparsely furnished living room, couple of sofas and a TV, with kitchen units at the far end.

Mickey Box was standing in front of a row of large raised beds, built from cuts of dark wood, where vegetables grew. He nodded to Fitz, who went into the building, closing the door behind him.

'This house guest I don't mind,' Mickey Box said. 'Doesn't seem to be much trouble. Police turning up would be another matter. You likely to be arrested again any time soon?'

'I wasn't arrested. I was helping with their enquiries.'

He stared at her.

'I went in with Barb,' Boone said. 'DS Bowen. She's a friend of mine. From before.'

'There for coffee and a Danish, was she? Non-official capacity?'

'It's nothing to worry about.'

'You're connected to bodies and to those who make people into bodies. That means police sniffing around my corner. I understand there's big money involved too, local snooties. Types who consort with brass and other men of rank. You know our agreement. Happy to have you around, acknowledging favours done in the past. Acknowledging they weren't small favours. But curious coppers are no part of that agreement.'

'You're right. There won't be bother from the police.'

Mickey Box nodded. 'You pursue missions of consequence, you have to expect consequences. I like that Tess has interests. Like that she has a friend, maybe even two. She's never much been one for friends. Few too many boys, one too many men. Not real friends though. I know that she cares deeply for you, and I see you care for her. She's going to need a friend or two. She's going to need normal stuff when her little prize pops out in a few months. Normal stuff is good. It's the abnormal stuff I need to know about. Pictures, little kids, nonce stuff, so forth.'

'How—'

'I don't keep Fitzy around for his nuanced take on culture and global affairs. He looks after my interests. And my most important interest is Tess, so he looks after her interests too.'

Boone was about to say something, but he raised a hand.

'Just hold on to whatever thoughts you have for a minute. Former constable and whatnot, I separated you from this side of stuff.' He glanced round the stables. 'You're not really separated though, are you? More like half in, half out. I've been thinking about that, and about this business with the missing girl and wherever that's taking you. When it's done, you thought about what you're going to do?'

Boone shook her head.

'Because I have some thoughts on the matter, but I'd need to be sure first.'

'That you could trust me?'

'More to the point, that you could trust me. So rather than hiding stuff, I'm going to do the other thing.'

'Which is?'

'Come with me.'

She followed him past the raised beds, three of them lined up one behind the other. The first two were growing tomatoes and peppers, but the third was empty. There was soil at either end, but in the middle was a manhole cover set into a square of concrete. He lifted it open, a ladder beneath it disappearing into the black.

From his jacket he produced a small lamp on an elasticated band and affixed it round his head.

'We going potholing?' Boone said.

'Pull the cover over after you,' he said, climbing down the hole and vanishing into the darkness below.

Clambering down as the headlamp flickered on, Boone found herself in a metal chamber with curved walls. It was widest at about waist height, tapering in at the top and bottom like a drum on its side. There was room enough for both of them down there, though the ceiling was only an inch or two above Boone, and Mickey Box had to stoop. The air was fetid. She covered her nose and mouth.

'Are we in a septic tank?'

'Uh-huh,' Mickey Box said. 'Have to crouch in this next bit.'

There was a door at one end of the tank that she hadn't noticed. It led to a tubular tunnel fashioned from a smaller tank, at most five foot in diameter, another one like it beyond that. After that, they stepped out into what appeared to be a shipping container buried beneath the ground. It was filled with cannabis plants, LED light panels above them. There were two further doors in the sides of the container and Boone discovered there were six containers down there, each packed with plants.

'You weren't fucking about when you set this up.'

'Lighting was the expensive bit. We had bulbs, but they were a pain and the electric was insane. Bills are a fraction with these panels. Paid for themselves in no time.'

He gently stroked the leaves of a plant, its chunky purple and orange buds smelling of pine.

'This isn't just your lazy super-skunk shite the slopes grow with chemicals and fuck knows what. This is pure indica, and we've got some hybrids. Royal Madre in the back container. This'll all be legal eventually, and people will expect choices. So I offer them now.'

'You'll go legit?'

'Fuck no,' he said. 'But when it's legal, selling it off-book becomes a tax issue, so I'll become a white-collar criminal. Nobody does time for that.'

At the back of one of the containers he had a table and chairs, a safe, and some monitors with greenish footage of the stables.

'Nobody can sneak up on this place,' he said.

Boone sat down at the table, looking about with something close to wonder.

'So now you know,' he said. 'And so will I.'

'So will you what?'

'Know for sure that your time with the Kent Police is done. See, you've done me good turns. Brought back to me that which I would miss most in the world. But you've also banged me up before. And now you say you don't remember any of that. Makes me nervous. Makes me think. That type of behaviour festers, up here,' he said, tapping his temple. 'Keeps me awake at nights. What's Boone's game then? What's she up to?'

'Be some long game,' Boone said. 'Throwing myself off a building and smashing myself to bits, just so I can fake memory loss in order to root out a small-time grower in the marshes. That's some fucking infiltration, Mick.'

'Yeah. And if I wasn't almost certain about you, you wouldn't be down here. This is just . . . peace of mind.'

'Hand me the keys to the kingdom and hope I don't fuck you over.'

'Handing you a home so you have no reason to. People that know about this place, they're family. One kind or another.'

Boone nodded. 'She's nowhere near doing anything risky, Tess. When she was riding with me before, that was strictly information-gathering stuff.'

'Running for your lives out at Corringstone aside.'

Boone didn't ask how he knew about that.

'You've strolled out into another blizzard of shit now,' he said.

'Yeah. I got Sarah Still's phone.'

'The dead girl.'

'Uh-huh. It has pictures on it. Videos. Horrible stuff.'

'And now you want the men responsible.'

Boone shrugged.

'Course you do. Might not be a copper any more, but there's still a detective in there somewhere. And these men have it coming.'

'I'll keep her out of it. When things happen, I'll keep Tess out of it.'

'Good luck explaining that without making one or the both of us look a cunt.'

'I mean I won't let her come with me if I pursue anything. I think she wanted to be involved. It was good for her.'

'It's good to be involved in that filth?'

'Not good exactly. Necessary. For her to be doing something, to help. She knows what it's like.'

'That was a long time ago.'

'It's never long enough.'

Mickey Box nodded.

'I'm not sure she needs it any more,' Boone said. 'She's fine, doing better. She's sleeping odd hours, but fine.'

He nodded again. 'New pills. Even keel?'

'From what I've seen she's sticking with them. Her routine will settle down. Until the little one arrives, anyway . . .'

'I try to keep an eye out, but don't want to look like I'm prying. Counting pills in bottles or anything.'

He sat down, found a battered notebook in his jacket pocket and began leafing through it at the table. Boone took it the meeting was over and got to her feet.

'This police mate of yours,' he said. 'You don't trust her with all this?'

'Her, yeah. The force, no. I found out who a man in one of the pictures is. He's not a fuckabout character. Has friends.'

'Snooty friends. Friends of rank.'

'Yeah.'

'How far back we talking with these things?'

'It's still happening now. But some of it also goes back a good while, I'd say. There are pictures of old Polaroids. The colour has faded on them. Thirty years wouldn't be a stretch. Others are much more recent, though. Digital. There are pictures of a house that seems to be at the centre of it all. I think it's round here somewhere, but . . .'

'You realise you have an in. One the police don't have.'

Boone frowned.

'Ingram.'

'Ingram?'

'Half a bacon, that one. Did a four for fiddling with a schoolgirl. Probably nothing David Bowie didn't do in his day, but she was a neighbour's daughter. Grooming, I guess they call it now. He was eighteen at the time. This was way before he had anything to do with Tess; she probably wasn't even at primary school yet. He did always like the teens.'

'You think he still does?'

He horseshoed his mouth. 'Pathological with these cunts, isn't it? They always have a stash somewhere.'

'Stash?'

'A collection. We're talking thirty-odd years back. Internet wasn't what it is now. He doesn't strike me as being smart enough to have been up with bulletin boards and the like. It'd have been magazines and pictures with him. Fucking die before he gives that shit up. He'd have known people who could get stuff like that. Worth a conversation, I'd say.'

'I'm ex-job. He's on licence. Fuck's he going to tell me?'

'That's where knowing me is advantageous. Have something that'll help him along, make him more compliant.'

'What? Like scopolamine?'

Mickey Box laughed, head tipped back. 'You've seen too many movies. No. I'm talking about Fitz. He's persuasive. My top nego-tiator, is Fitzy. Broker of deals. Keep it shtum from the girls. I'll have a word with Fitz and sort a time.'

'I don't know, Mick.'

'Your call. Looking for nonces, reckon you'll need someone familiar with the territory. Those ranks are closed to outsiders, especially ones look like you.'

Boone nodded. 'Why, though? Why would you help?'

He turned back to his notebook. 'Like I said, part of the family now.'

39

Boone walked back to the caravan to get the Goose. The sliding door was open and she stepped up onto the decking. The telly was on, Catherine Deneuve in bright pastel colours. Roo and Tess were huddled on the sofa, arms interlaced, debating whether *Umbrellas of Cherbourg* counted as a musical. Tess clamped a hand over Roo's mouth so she might better get her points across.

Boone got into the Goose and left them to it.

40

Next morning, Boone was woken by her phone vibrating on the bedside table.

'Muh?'

'It's Fitz.'

'What bloody time is it?'

'I'm outside, sitting at your table.'

The line went dead. Boone pushed herself out of bed and grubbed about for some clothes. Then thought, fuck Fitz, and had a shower instead.

Downstairs, she set about making coffee. Jack and Quin weren't even up yet. The sun was barely up. Out of the window she saw the back of Fitz's head where he sat at the table on the decking.

'Silly o'clock,' she said, popping her head out the door.

'Need a word,' Fitz said.

'Coffee?'

He nodded. Boone poured two and ventured outside wrapped in a towel, another for her hair. A small heap of sunflower-seed shells was piled on the table in front of Fitz. She sat opposite him and crossed her legs. She wished her shoulders weren't showing and briefly considered unravelling the turban and draping it around them.

Fitz looked at the damp footprints she'd left on the wooden decking.

'Always figured they'd be cloven,' he said.

'What do you need, Fitz?'

'Anyone else in?'

'They're asleep.'

He nodded. 'Seen much of Tess lately?'

Boone shrugged. 'A bit.'

'She doing all right?'

'Sleeps a lot, like a baby. A well-fed and possibly sedated baby.'

He nodded. 'New pills?'

'New pills.' Half a smile crept up on her lips. 'What's this new caring Fitz all about then?'

'Known her far longer than you,' he said. 'Nearly her whole life, most of my adult. She used to talk to me. Seems you get the honour now, or that other one.'

'Wouldn't take that personally. What's going on with her, having girlie friends isn't a bad thing.'

Fitz smiled, looked her up and down. 'Girlie?'

'Choose your next words wisely, Fitzgerald.'

'Ingram,' he said.

Boone put her coffee down slowly.

'When?'

'Now. Get dressed. We're taking your car.'

Half an hour later, Boone parked up a couple of streets down from Bewsborough Road. They walked round and made for a white

Transit across from the Regency Guest House. It was still early enough that most people hadn't shaken themselves from sleep.

Fitzy climbed in the driver's door. The side door was open on to the pavement and Boone got in, sliding it shut behind her. Mickey Box sat shotgun. The back was empty but had been hurriedly lined with plastic sheeting. There was no divider between the cab and the back, but the front seats were high so she knelt and poked her head between the headrests to talk to Fitz and Mickey Box.

'This looks like you're going to do a murder,' she said.

'Cannot be too careful,' Mickey Box said. 'Clever cunts abound.'

'Right.'

'Pays to prepare for the unlikely,' Fitz said. 'But the fact is, once we inject him with the scopolamine, we can just order him to get into the van if need be.' The two of them thought this great sport and laughed louder than it warranted.

'Funny,' Boone said.

'Heard the one about the guy who wakes up in an ice bath in a hotel with a kidney missing?' Fitz said.

Boone said something unladylike and sat back on her heels.

'We just going to wait for him?' she said.

'We know when he's coming,' Fitz said. 'Have his schedule.'

'How'd you get that?'

He peered back at her between the seats. 'I know you think you're the only one can solve a puzzle, but . . .'

Boone rolled her eyes.

'What if he goes somewhere after?' she said.

'He's on night shifts this week, at one of those supermarkets looks like an aircraft hangar. Gets off at six. Fuck's he going to go? Might stop at the garage down the road, get himself a Ginsters and a can of pop. Otherwise, he walks straight here and puts his head down.'

Fitz opened the door and stepped out.

'Told you, he sees everything that one,' Mickey Box said.

The three of them walked across to the guest house. The front door was unlocked and someone had left a bicycle in the hall. Fitz looked at it a moment before wheeling it back to the space behind the stairs. The rat-faced Manc wasn't in his hole in the wall.

'Where's the fella?' Boone said.

Fitz stared at her.

'Fella in the booth who signs people in.'

He winked. 'No idea who you're talking about.'

'Hush it,' Mickey Box said.

He took the stairs two at a time and they followed him up to Ingram's door. Fitz toed the loose carpet in the hall, maybe considering doing something with it, but in the end just smoothing it out with his boot. He produced a set of keys from somewhere and unlocked the mortise and latch, letting himself into Ingram's room.

Boone made a face at Mickey Box and he shrugged.

Fitz's face reappeared and he nodded for them to come in, shutting and locking the door behind them. The curtains were closed, and he left them like that, flicking on a shabby lamp on the bedside cabinet.

'Check the laptop,' Mickey Box told Boone, pointing his chin at the dresser where it sat. Casually he went through the wardrobe and a few drawers, not searching for anything in particular and finding nothing of interest. Fitz checked the small bathroom. Both of them wore leather gloves.

Boone snapped on a latex pair of her own and powered on the laptop.

'No good in a tussle,' Fitz said, glancing at her gloves. 'Tear too easily.'

'I think I can take the computer if it comes to a brawl,' Boone said. 'It's passworded, though.'

'Close it,' Mickey Box said. 'He'll let us into it.'

He dropped onto the bed and sat there quietly. Boone eased out the chair from the dresser and sat sideways on it, elbow on the back. Fitz flicked the lamp off and stood in the bay beside the dresser, looking out through a crack in the curtains to the street below. They each had their own thoughts.

'Man on,' Fitz said eventually, gently closing the gap in the curtains.

'Bathroom,' Mickey Box said, ushering Boone into the small room and standing beside her in the dim, door slightly ajar to the larger shadows beyond, which Fitz folded into.

They heard Ingram's hobbled walk on the stairs and then saw two dark patches in the trace of light under the door where he stood and slipped a key into the mortise. When he turned the latch, he barely had one foot in the door when Fitz grabbed him, a huge hand cupping his chin and twisting his neck, the other pinning an arm behind his back. Fitz checked the door shut with his hip as he pushed Ingram face down onto the bed. Mickey Box walked out and flicked on the lamp.

'Hello, Clifford.'

Ingram looked up, eyes like great lakes. He couldn't have struggled even if he wanted to. Mickey Box pulled out the chair from the dresser and spun it round. He nodded to Fitz, who hauled Ingram back to his feet and sat him down in the chair.

Ingram sported on his finger a DIY lolly-stick splint wrapped in gauze, souvenir from Boone's last visit.

Mickey Box leaned down, hands on his thighs, face close.

'I don't think you're going to make a fuss, are you, Clifford?'

Ingram shook his head in short, uneven movements, as if he had some palsy of fear.

'Hmm?' Mickey Box said, turning his ear.

'No. No.'

'No. Because how much of a fuss could you possibly make before Fitzy here started in on some diabolical violence, eh? A tiny fuss. A baby bird of a fuss. Not a fuss anyone is going to wonder much about.'

Mickey Box took hold of Ingram's knitted beanie and lightly pulled it from his head. A horseshoe-shaped scar curled from behind his ear round the rear of his skull and back to above his drooping right eye. Gently Mickey Box traced it with his fingers.

'I saw pictures,' he said. 'After they'd removed a chunk of your skull. Didn't look real. Like someone had monkeyed with the photo. Looked deflated, like a football after a dog's bitten it. See they put the bone back now.'

Ingram reached instinctively to the repaired patch of his skull, touching it gingerly.

'Hope nothing important fell out,' Mickey Box said.

Ingram saw Boone in the bathroom door, met her eyes.

'I didn't have nothing to do with T—'

'Don't even let that name pass your lips,' Mickey Box said.

'I've got nothing to do with her no more.'

'I know.'

'I never seen her.'

Mickey Box stood up straight. 'You never seen her?'

'Yeah.'

'Now that's not quite true, is it, Clifford?'

'It is.'

'To be clear, what you're saying is, you have not had relations with my daughter since you left prison.'

Ingram looked at Boone.

'Don't look at her. She's said nowt. Look at me.'

'I . . . No.'

'No, as in no you haven't?'

'No. I ain't saying that.'

'You're not saying you slept with her?'

'No. I ain't saying I've not.'

'This fella,' said Mickey Box, grinning. He clapped a hand to the side of Ingram's face. 'This fucking fella. You're a beaut, Clifford, you really are. I'm not an idiot. You've taken me for one before, and I had to remind you then of how things really stood.'

'She came here,' Ingram said. Spittle clung to his lips and chin and his eyes wetted. 'I didn't contact her. I swear I never.'

'Clifford.'

'I text her is all. It weren't even . . . I was just saying hi. I never come near her. Never even suggested it. She was asking me where I was staying and that, and I said about this place. And she said it must be awful, but it's better than a cell, like. That's all I told her. It's better than a cell. And then she turns up here out of the blue.

I never asked her. You can check my phone. Read the texts. I never asked her.'

'And then you fucked her. My daughter.'

Ingram hung his head. His lips were pursed, as if he was sucking on an invisible thumb, or trying to make the shape of words he didn't know.

Words that could satisfy this man before him.

Words that didn't exist.

'To answer the question you're asking yourself in your head, Clifford, this is not a will-he-won't-he type situation. I absolutely am going to hurt you. The only question is whether or not you get to crawl away at the end of it. That's the best-case scenario. It's all grist to the mill for me. Bringing you to an end would just be some seven-in-the-morning type shit. Only question that would remain is does your lovely old mum get something to bury, or does she just get one of those memorial services with no body, nowhere to lay the flowers. Maybe she doesn't get that even. Maybe she just thinks you took off without a word.'

Ingram's eyes were red, rims like filaments. A tear cut silently down one cheek, but he didn't beg or bawl, which Boone thought was more than she'd expect from herself in his shoes.

Mickey Box turned to Boone, nodded at the laptop. She opened it.

'Password,' he said.

Ingram mumbled it, and Boone got into the computer. She searched about but found nothing of interest.

'Nothing on here. Bit of porn in the browser history, pretty vanilla. Nothing illegal.'

'That ain't me no more,' said Ingram.

'Bollocks,' said Mickey Box.

'It ain't,' Ingram insisted. 'I was young.'

'Still like them half your age, though.'

And that differentiates him from the rest of you how exactly? Boone wanted to say, but knew better.

'Get him up,' Mickey Box said, and Fitz hauled Ingram out of the chair. 'Your old dear still live in that same one-bed by the railway line? See her much? Perhaps we should all go round for some tea, eh? Nice cup of tea?'

'What do you want?' Ingram said.

Mickey Box looked to Boone.

'You ever see photos, Polaroids, men with girls?' she said. 'Early teens, younger maybe.'

Ingram almost laughed. 'Have I ever seen photos?' He looked to Mickey Box, eyes desperate.

'Taken by someone local, we think,' Boone said. 'There might be a place. A house where men went, girls were brought there. Boys too.'

Ingram was shaking his head.

'This would have started a long time back, seventies or eighties even. But it's still going today.'

'It ain't me any more. It ain't me any more.'

'You were inside for it,' Mickey Box said.

'Not no more. There was only that one girl. Only her.'

'No magazines?' Mickey Box said. 'No pictures or videos?'

Ingram shook his head again, tears flowing now.

'I'm starting to get irritated, Clifford,' Mickey Box said. 'You were banged up before. And a longer stretch this time. Reckon you must need somewhere you can leave stuff. Somewhere secure. Somewhere you know it will be there when you get out. We're coming back round to that cup of tea at your old mum's again.'

Ingram was nearly hysterical now, shaking his head violently from side to side. He was standing only because Fitz held him up, slouched there as if the clothes he wore were hung on a hook.

'We'll all have a sit-down with her. Ask her if you might have left things there.'

'She don't know nothing,' Ingram said. 'There's nothing there.' He was sobbing now.

'Ask her about things like dirty books. Filthy pictures. Kiddie grot.'

'There's an allotment,' Ingram blurted.

'Now we're cooking, Clifford.'

'It was my dad's, but Mum kept it up. She grows marrows. She don't eat them, though. They're big, like, for this fair in the summer. If you try and eat them they're all sloppy inside, taste bitter.'

'Clifford.'

'There's a shed. Mum only goes in there for her tools. Dad used to spend whole days in there, though. Had a table and chair. There's all stuff piled up in there now, but under the table the floorboards come up and there's a space. Lined with bricks.'

'Told you,' Mickey Box said to Boone. 'Nonces always have a stash.'

41

Ingram allowed himself be led to the van and climbed in the back with Fitz. Didn't even seemed bothered by the plastic. Boone, who'd kept her hands in her pockets as they crossed the street so nobody would notice her blue nitrile gloves, sat up front with Mickey Box. He drove, following Ingram's directions, to an allotment that sat inside the wide fork of two quiet roads. Enclosed by trees on both sides, padlocked double wire gates stood in the mouth of a gravel track, a council noticeboard visible beyond it.

Mickey Box parked up a side street.

'He makes noise,' he told Fitz, 'feel free to find the most efficient way of shutting him up.'

Fitz clicked his fingers at Ingram.

'Keys,' he said.

Ingram held up a small bunch, just his door keys and two smaller ones. 'That's the padlock on the gates,' he said. 'And that's the shed. When you go in, the left wall is all shelves. On the top, up in the corner behind the door, there's a small tin box. It's black with gold on it. It's locked, but it's only a simple thing. Just turns to open. You can do it with a small coin. I ain't got a key. There's stuff inside. Foreign coins, bits and bobs. A few keys. One has black tape on it. When you pull up the floorboards, there's another hatch with an old door lock in it. That's the key.'

'You know anyone there?' Mickey Box asked.

Ingram shook his head. 'Used to, when I went there with me dad. Wouldn't know them now. Only been there once since I got out. Maybe a couple of times in the ten years before I went in. Just to check. That ain't me no more.'

'Aye,' Fitz said. 'Keep the stuff for sentimental reasons. Nostalgia.'

Boone went with Mickey Box.

The plot was near the front, tucked in where you had to turn back on yourself from the gravel track to get to it. Boone could see someone way down the far end, examining the heads of some kind of root vegetable. Ingram's shed was green, the curling paint showing the wood beneath. There was a small veranda at the front with a deckchair, its seat saggy and the fabric rotting through.

They found the hidey-hole right where Ingram had said, beneath the wooden floorboards. Under the hatch was a space about two feet square and two feet deep. At the bottom was a single paving stone, lined on all sides by unmortared bricks with some kind of rubber underlay behind them, pond liner or something. There were two items – a leather document holder sealed inside a plastic A4 wallet, and an old cardboard box from an early nineties games console.

Boone fetched out the leather folder and skimmed through its contents. Birth certificate, an expired passport, some old tax papers with the type faded beyond legibility. An envelope contained a bunch of photographs, what looked like Ingram as a child. One was taken outside the shed, with presumably his father sitting in the deckchair wearing trousers and a vest, Ingram beside him holding a bucket. He was perhaps eight years old, dressed in smart shorts and a shirt. She put it all back in the hole as she found it.

The cardboard box was heavier than it looked. The face of it was about the size of a dinner tray, but it was no more than six inches thick. Though dry, the box was warped where it had absorbed moisture in the past. It opened along one side and had once been secured with Sellotape, but that had since dried and peeled away. Boone found a couple of dozen magazines tightly packed inside. Each was protected by a plastic sleeve. Each featured a photo of a Lolita-like girl on the cover. There was also an A4 envelope thick with photographic prints, nubile shots of coltish girls draped over furniture in soft light, and pamphlets of picture stories created from similar images.

'Well, this is going to be deeply unpleasant,' she said.

'Bring all of it,' Mickey Box said. 'He's filth. Don't leave him anything.'

Leaving the place as they'd found it, they headed back to the van without being noticed. Ingram gave a start when he saw Boone put the box in the footwell of the passenger seat but said nothing. Mickey Box drove them north out of town, where the coast road was separated from the sea by an exclusive links course. The restaurant next to the members' club was a popular venue among certain sorts and the car park there was nearly full, but they went past that to a little-used spot near the furthest reaches of the course. The beach between the golf course and the Channel was accessible to the public, but at the north end it was thin and rocky and hounded by the wind, attracting fewer day trippers.

Mickey Box showed Ingram one of the magazines.

'Tell us about these.'

'They're old. I don't know why I kept them. I don't look at that stuff any more.'

'It's a collection,' Mickey Box said. 'Each one in its own protective cover. Look at the paper. Not a crease on them. Cared for. Treasured.'

Ingram shook his head violently.

'Calypso Press,' Mickey Box read from the back cover. 'Clever nonce was he, fella who ran these off?'

'No,' Ingram said. 'No, no.'

'No? Wasn't clever?'

'No, I don't—'

'You're about to say you don't know him. I'll stop you there, Clifford. Look at these here. You didn't walk into WHSmith and pick up a copy, did you? You and the likes of you, you're travellers who follow the same path. Local, was he?'

Ingram nodded.

'Could have told us this in your room, Clifford. Saved us a lot of fannying about.'

'I wasn't involved in any of it,' Ingram said. 'I swear I never was.'

'Involved in what?' Mickey Box said.

'I had my magazines, that was it. It was just a look. Just something to look at.'

Boone was looking through the magazines in the box.

'Some of these are old,' she said. 'Too old for you, unless you picked them up when you were ten.'

'They were his,' Ingram said.

'Whose?'

'My father. They were his. That ain't me no more.'

The pitiful truth of Clifford Ingram's life was coming into sharp relief.

'Your father built the hiding space in the shed?' Boone said.

'It ain't me no more,' Ingram said again.

Boone flicked through another magazine.

'Jesus,' she said, turning back and forth between a couple of pages, examining the pictures. 'I know this place. This is the house. This is where Sarah took the pictures.'

She got out her phone and compared the picture story in the pamphlet – a girl reclining on a chaise longue, her body clean and lithe, naked but for a silk scarf that came round her back and hung over the crook of each elbow. Her legs were pressed together, one knee slightly behind the other like a Venetian nude, a light fuzz between her thighs.

'The mirror,' she explained to Mickey Box.

Above the girl, the bottom of a mirror was visible, its frame a dark wood, cherry perhaps, with elaborate brass corner pieces. Boone showed Mickey Box her phone. One of the old Polaroids, an unsmiling girl staring into the lens. On the wall behind her hung the same mirror, not square on, so it didn't reflect the photographer but rather the window they must have been standing beside. She swiped through to another picture, just the interior of a window frame, one they figured Sarah Still had taken on her phone.

'Same window,' she said, scrolling between the images. 'Different curtains, but same sort of glazing bars.'

Each casement in the window featured a central timber bar that spread out into Gothic arches at the top. The paint curled off them in the more recent photo, the timber worn and dark with rot at the edge of the frame.

She showed the pamphlet to Ingram. 'You know who took these? Who made this magazine?'

Ingram recoiled as if the paper was searing, hyperventilating suddenly.

'No, no, no, no, no,' he said. 'It's not me. It's not me.'

'Fucking hell, Fitz,' Mickey Box said. 'Get a hold of him.'

Fitz twisted Ingram's arm behind his back and shoved his face into the floor of the van. He squeezed on his splinted finger and Ingram roared, tears in his eyes.

'Don't do that, for Christ's sake,' Boone said. 'He's having a panic attack.'

She clambered between the seats into the back and pulled Fitz off him, sitting Ingram up against the wheel arch.

'Hey, look at me. Look at me. Calm down. Breathe through your nose. Like this, take it in deeply. That's right. Keep breathing.'

Ingram gradually regained control of himself, wiping his nose on his sleeve.

'Do you know where your father got these from?' Boone said.

Ingram shook his head. 'There was a man, when I was a boy. He came to the shed. To the allotment.'

Boone recalled the photograph of Ingram as a boy, his father in the deckchair. 'You know his name?'

He shook his head.

'You recognised those photos, though.'

'Don't,' Ingram said. 'Don't show me. I don't look at them.'

'You've been there?'

He was crying now, face twisted in anguish.

'I can get it out of him,' Fitz said. 'Five minutes.'

Boone ignored him. 'Ingram? You remember where it is? The house?'

He was still shaking his head, great gouts of mucus hanging from his nose and lips. 'I was a boy. I was a boy.'

Boone showed him her phone, some of the pictures Sarah Still had taken more recently of the house, and a Polaroid of a young girl in a bedroom. There was another that she had found of Hanley Moss with another man whose face was turned from the camera. It was in a different room, but the carpentry on the door frame was identical.

'I need to know where this is,' she said.

'I don't know,' Ingram sobbed. 'I was a kid. Everywhere's miles away when you're a kid. It was night, in the country somewhere.'

'This is pointless,' Mickey Box said. 'Fitz.'

Fitz grabbed Ingram's wrist and twisted it round painfully.

'Wait,' Ingram said. 'I know the man. I know the man in the picture.' He nodded to Boone's phone, to the picture with Hanley Moss.

'Him?' Boone said, pointing to Moss. 'I know who he is. Can find him whenever I want. Bloody baron, he is.'

'The other man,' Ingram said, tapping on the man with his back to the camera. 'I remember him. I remember the coat and his scarf.'

'Who is he?'

Ingram looked at Fitz, who still had hold of his wrist.

'They got to promise not to hurt me.'

'Mick,' Boone said.

'They got to promise,' Ingram said.

Mickey Box nodded to Fitz, who let go of Ingram's arm.

'Promise,' Ingram spat.

'Fucking hell. I promise I won't touch you,' Mickey Box said.

'Who is he?' Boone asked again.

'I never knew his name,' Ingram said. 'But it was his place. Everyone called him sir. Even my dad.'

'Gonna need more than that,' Boone said.

'He was rich. Like, proper rich, country mansions rich. The house was his, he owned it. Ran it just for that kind of thing.'

Boone shook her head. Fitz took hold of Ingram's wrist again.

'And he drove a Rolls-Royce,' Ingram spluttered.

'Say that again,' Boone said, putting a hand on Fitz's shoulder to hold him back.

'He had a Rolls,' Ingram said. 'Massive great thing. Dad said it had an aeroplane engine inside. It was blue and black. Blue and black.'

Mickey Box looked at Boone, who nodded.

'There now,' Mickey Box said. 'Doesn't that feel good, Clifford? Getting all that off your chest?'

'You taking me back now?' Ingram said.

'I think maybe you'd benefit from a walk, Clifford. Exercise do you good.'

Fitz shoved Ingram from the van and steered him between the wind-bent bushes to the pebbled shore. Mickey Box walked behind. In the breeze, his hair was wild.

'What are we doing?' Boone said, raising her voice over the wind.

'Assuring clarity,' Mickey Box said.

'He told us what he knows,' Boone said.

Mickey Box smiled. 'You really think that's what this was about?'

Ingram stood shivering, hands plunged into his pockets. Fitz had stepped off a few yards, looking out over the sea as if events no longer interested him.

'None of this ever happened, Clifford,' Mickey Box said. 'We weren't here today. We never spoke.'

Ingram shook his head in agreement.

'You went for a walk after work. Bit of sea air. Something unfortunate happened, as it does to people like you. Anyone asks for details, it's all a bit of a blur. Jumped by youths, hoods up over their heads, so forth. Foreigners probably.'

Ingram's expression was vague; he wasn't following.

'Which is to say, what befell you was nothing to do with Fitz. Or myself. Just a tragic consequence of fate, I suppose.'

Ingram nodded, still not following.

'Because if my name, or Fitz's, ever crosses your lips . . . Well.' Mickey Box turned away, back towards Boone.

Ingram looked lost. Fitz came and stood before him, head tilted, and Ingram considered him almost with expectation, as if a favour of some sort was to be bestowed. Incredibly, he didn't see the punch coming, and he dropped like a bag of clothes, as though every tendon had been cut.

As he tried to sit up, Fitz's boot snapped his head back and he lay still on his side, stunned by the speed of things. He turned onto his hands and knees. Blood flowed freely from his nose and lips and he remained there, a trail of red spouting down to the pebbled ground as if chaining him to it.

Fitz dropped to his haunches beside him, grabbed some hair and yanked his head back. Ingram's nose was broken, flattened sideways against his cheek.

'Penny on a railway,' Fitz said, looking up and grinning.

'This'll be the last time we ever speak, Clifford,' said Mickey Box. 'No matter what happens in the future, no matter what you think it is you know, no matter what right or recourse you believe you have to contact my daughter, it absolutely will not happen. Are we clear?'

Boone could barely hear him over the wind, and Ingram's feeble noises of agreement were swept away completely. Mickey Box nodded and turned away, heading for the van. Boone hesitated before following him, glancing back over her shoulder. With Ingram still on his hands and knees, Fitz took hold of one of his arms and straightened it out behind him, so it was pointing straight up.

He was talking to him, but Boone couldn't hear.

Then he gently rotated the arm and drove the palm of his other hand through Ingram's elbow, folding the limb back on itself the wrong way.

She could see Ingram scream, his face breaking in agony, but it was lost on the wind.

42

The Yeast With Two Yacks was all craft beers and no music, a bistro bar in one corner offering a ghastly array of healthy cakes and muffins, one hot lunchtime meal option every day, and a very acceptable cup of coffee. The decor was a shitshow combination of modern and retro, but it had free Wi-Fi and a Roo behind the bar.

Tess sat in a window seat nursing a pint of Coke and a packet of scratchings. The only other punter was a young man in a suit supping a pint as he read his paper, strictly a sports-pages guy.

'You have the Goose?' Roo called from the bar.

Boone nodded.

'I bring you perfect soft drink for such a lovely day.'

Boone took a pew with Tess and watched as Roo brought over a glass of something that had almost enough colour but not quite.

'What's this?'

'Is elderflower.'

'Why is this happening to me?' Boone said. 'Why don't I get a coffee?'

'Because I cannot get rid of this stuff.'

'Marvellous.'

The door opened and Boone peered over to see who it was. She'd already imagined multiple cars following her that day, and now an old fella wandered in as if lost and she thought she recognised him. Events were doing funny things to her mind. Once the suspicion of being followed or watched set in, patterns could be seen anywhere. Paranoia's moonflower blooming in the dark.

The old man sat in a corner and ordered a tea and some kind of muffin, which Roo went off to prepare.

Boone toed a shopping bag by Tess's feet, big bags of popcorn and dolly mixtures visible.

'Movie night?'

'Do you know, she has never seen a single Katharine Hepburn film,' Tess said incredulously, hooking a thumb back towards Roo. 'That's madness. I mean, there simply isn't anyone like her around any more. Creatures like that no longer walk the earth. She's like . . .'

'A mastodon,' Boone said.

'Exactly. I dug the old box set out. People always say it's *Bringing Up Baby*, but—'

'*Holiday* is the one.'

'And that's what we're going to watch. I have toffee popcorn and everything, like the old adverts they used to run, you know.'

'Listen,' Boone said. 'I want you not to get angry when I tell you this.'

'An auspicious start . . .'

'I saw Ingram this morning. With Mick and Fitzy.'

'Fuck me.'

Boone recounted the whole sorry affair and Tess insisted on

going to the boot of the Goose to see the stash of magazines and pamphlets for herself.

'I didn't know,' she said, back at the table. 'That he had stuff like this. Ingram.' She kept her eyes out the window, avoiding Boone.

'I know,' Boone said.

'I mean, I knew he was a bit of a wrong 'un, but not this.' She scratched the tip of her nose. 'He must have been young.'

'Eighteen when he was convicted. These were from before. Some of them were his father's.'

Tess nodded, chin moving barely an inch up and down.

'The way people are,' Boone said, 'the way they become that way, these are things only they can account for. Coastal shelves and all that. Nothing he's done should make you feel guilty.'

'I know.'

'Do you?'

'Maybe.'

'So can I ask you something?'

Tess shrugged.

'Why'd you go to him?'

'Ingram?'

'Yeah. After what happened before. Why see him. Why—'

'Shag him?'

Boone nodded.

'I dunno. It was . . . familiar. Even if he is an evil prick.'

Boone looked down at her feet.

'What?' Tess said.

'Thought it might be something else.'

'Like?'

'To protect someone else.'

'By shagging Ingram?'

'By making Mick think he's the father.'

'Yeah.' Tess laughed. 'Smart plan. Pick the one fella Mick hates more than anyone else. Lot of fucking help, that.'

'There's something worse than someone he hates being the dad.'

'Yeah?'

'Someone he loves. Guess if the kid comes out with a sunflower-seed habit, then Ingram makes a decent patsy.'

Tess went pale. 'Jesus, Boone, you can't fucking say anything to Mick. He'd go nuts. Seriously. He'd kill Fitz. Might even kill me.'

'I won't.'

Tess looked over to Roo behind the bar, who, not knowing what they were talking about, poked out her tongue. Tess smiled.

'You and Fitz,' Boone said.

'Mick went up north, remember that? Left me in the cottage and had Fitz stay over, keep an eye on me. We've always been all right, Fitz and me. He's been around for donkey's, ever since I can remember. We had some wine and we were talking about you. Think he was doing due diligence. He wasn't at all happy about me hanging out with plod. So we talked a bit about you and all your tragedies, and then how I knew you from before. What happened with Ingram. We were drunk, and I was a bit upset. And it happened. Brilliant, I know.'

'Just that once?'

'Few times. Next couple of weeks. But it was weird. I know him, you know. Like, really know him. Felt a bit icky. He knew it too, and put a stop to it. I thought it might fuck things up. This is going to sound messed up, but Ford – Ingram – was the closest thing to a relationship I ever really had. Usually, few shags and I'd torch it.

Then they'd be on the phone all hours. Few even showed up at the house, until they met Mick. He called it PTTD. Post-Traumatic Tess Disorder. Fitzy wasn't like that, though. We're still mates.'

'And you and him thought this thing up, to blame Ingram?'

'Nah, Fitz wouldn't have had any of that, not even with a creep like Ingram. He'd have considered it . . . snide. Came down to it, he'd have copped to it and let things run their course with Mick. I went to Ingram. Knew I could bed him straight off, and I told Fitz on the phone after. He wasn't pleased. I was going to leave it a few weeks and then tell Dad. About the baby, I mean. The thing with Ingram was only if Dad pushed on who the father was. Except he had already figured the pregnant bit out, as I must have been an even madder cow than usual. Hated myself for doing it and then got in a bit of a mood. And then you turned out to be smarter than all of us.'

'Well, nobody'll ever hear it from me,' Boone said.

'I know.'

Tess played with the hem of her top, curling her fingers in it.

'How is he?' she said.

'Who? Ingram?'

Tess nodded. 'I don't mean how is he, like, what's he up to. I mean, did Dad kill him?'

'No. No, he's alive. Maybe not kicking, but alive.'

'Fitz?'

Boone nodded. 'Nothing life-threatening.'

'Bet they enjoyed it, though.'

'I'd be lying if there wasn't some delight at the idea.'

'Christ, this kid is going to come into some world.'

'Yeah, well. None of us live in a world of our making. Told me something interesting though, Ingram. Said the man who owned the house where the Polaroids were taken was rich and drove a Rolls-Royce.'

'What, like the one Blackborne has?'

'Not like it. That exact one. Blue and black, he said. The other man in the pictures with Hanley Moss is Alex Blackborne.'

'So what does that mean?'

'It means I have to go speak to Molly about her mortgage.'

43

Recalling what Luke Rayner had said about Sarah thinking Molly's place might be being watched, Boone left the Goose in the public car park at the spoil-tip park and walked through to the allotments and the rise behind The Groves. From up there she could see kids playing in Molly's street. Actually, not playing so much as coalescing, like a regiment awaiting orders, the odd bike circling the group.

She climbed down the concrete steps, coming out behind Molly's row. Like a puppy trying to climb stairs, she struggled over the fence into the garden, working up a sweat by the time she fell onto the grass.

A couple of lines of washing dissected the long lawn, fabrics clapping in the wind. Boone crouched as best she could to look for feet below them and found none. She rapped on the back door.

No answer.

She tried the handle but it was locked. The kitchen had an awning window that was pushed open a few inches.

'Molly,' she whispered tightly through the gap. 'Molly.'

There was a stink from the house, though not the stench of the dead. Not yet. It was dark inside and Boone couldn't see much through the small gap in the window. She was wary of attracting the attention of the nosy neighbour. She could have gone home then – she should have. But from somewhere in the wild trees at the back of her mind the killers of Sarah Still had been calling to her for too long. From the same place that religion spoke to some people, or booze to others, she heard them, their voices an echo of her own.

She pulled the window sash out hard, snapping the plastic tab that restricted it. Pocketing the evidence, she fetched a large pot from the alley beside the house and upturned it to climb through the window. Stepping awkwardly over the dishes stacked in the sink, she rolled gracelessly onto the floor.

She stood still and waited for a feel of the place. The washing machine door was open, the clothes inside beginning to mildew. Filthy pawprints criss-crossed the lino floor. She could smell old food and peelings turning in the bin. A pale glow flickered from the front room. On light feet, she moved into the hall and pushed the door gently with her fingertips, but it swung easily over the carpet's worn pile. Molly lay asleep on the sofa, shallow breaths moving her chest, a mostly empty bottle of vodka on the coffee table. The dog lay on the floor before the telly, its big dog eyes following Boone. What do you tell someone who has lost a daughter, a granddaughter, and a great-grandchild? Boone fetched a blanket from Molly's bedroom and laid it over her.

Sarah's room was still piled high with boxes, even more covering the bed itself. Boone began digging through them, locating in a far corner several boxes of old bank papers. Rodney had kept things in good order it seemed, though Molly hadn't continued the

practice. The statements were all at least ten years old. She dragged
the boxes out to the patch of clear floor at the end of the bed and
started reading. Everything was neatly ordered by date, including
what looked like every wage slip Rodney had ever received. The
dog wandered in and sat upright in the doorway, watching Boone
warily.

She found what she was looking for in 1996, the year after Sarah
was born. Molly had said an insurance payout, arranged by Rodney's employers at the cement works, had cleared the mortgage.
That had sounded hinky at the time, a company admitting liability
for his illness and paying damages without contesting it, and
almost a decade before Rodney passed away, but Boone hadn't seen
then that it was anything to do with her. Now she wondered.

The mortgage had certainly been settled in full like Molly had
said, but from their own joint account, into which a slightly larger
deposit had been made a week earlier by something called Omicron Holdings. Generic enough to be anything, but it sure didn't
sound like an insurance company, and Rodney's payslips carried
on up until 2002, so whatever the payout was for it hadn't pre-
vented him from working.

She folded and pocketed the statements, heaving the boxes of
documents back where she found them. The dog trotted into the
lounge in front of her and curled itself up on the floor beneath
Molly. Boone left by the back door, locking it and posting the
keys back through the window she had climbed in.

She bunked over the fence after a style and hurried away along
the ridge, the loitering kids still audible from the street, and back
through the allotments to the park where the Goose waited.

44

The abundance of information on the internet was bewildering. Boone recalled a line from somewhere in the soup of her mind about Maasai warriors with smartphones today having access to more information than Bill Clinton did when he was President of the United States just twenty years earlier.

Next morning, she googled the landline number from Sarah's phone. The only result that looked specific connected it to a kebab shop in Forest Gate called Tubby's. She found it on Street View online and it looked exactly as she expected it to. She called the number. This time when it was picked up, nobody said anything.

'Hello? That Tubby's? Kebabs?'

'The kebabs, yes.' Trace of an accent.

'I was wondering about your shish. Wanted to order for delivery.'

'No delivery, please.'

'Can I order to pick up then?'

The man said something in another language and the line went dead. Boone made a note of the address. One of only two numbers saved on the phone; there had to be something to it. She tried the mobile number but once again was informed the number was not available.

She spent the rest of the day searching for information on the company that had paid the Stills, sifting through online leak databases. There was an Omicron Holdings registered in Panama in 1996 and dissolved less than a year later. An Ian Harvey was listed as director. Omicron was also linked to an intermediary, a then privately owned bank in the Bahamas which later became a subsidiary of Coutts and was now a division of Société Générale, which was also connected to a couple of dozen other Panama-registered firms. One of them, Lamech Capital, listed Harvey as a director alongside Sir Alex Blackborne.

Proving ownership of Omicron would be nigh impossible. Off-shore companies were often controlled by bearer shares with no name attached to them – whoever was in possession of the stock certificate owned it. But the circumstantial was all there – Omicron making payment to the Stills, and Blackborne's connection to Harvey through Lamech Capital. It looked like Omicron was an entity set up solely to make that payment. Boone could see no legitimate reason for the whole affair to have been arranged through offshore shell companies in Panama and the Bahamas.

Having failed once to get a rise out of Mark Blackborne, Boone decided to have another run at him the next day, this time with more evidence in hand, and in the morning took the Goose out to the palatial country estate he called home. Cornilo House was buried at the heart of six hundred acres of private park and wood-land, half a mile from any public road, built on the crest of a rise. Once you broke through the burnt orange and reds of the pinetum the driveway crawled through, it loomed over you as the gravelled approach snaked up the incline. The place was a hive of activity. Vans and cars parked outside with people coming and going, carrying stuff into the house. They all had about them the purposeful look of staff.

Boone spun the Goose round the large decorative fountain outside the front of the house and left it facing back the way she'd come. Paid to be prepared for expeditious departures. The front door was open and transparent rubber mats lined the hallway specially for the salaried hordes bearing supplies and God knows what else. Boone swanned in among them like she owned the place. The main hallway, inside which Tess's caravan could have fitted several times, ran right through the house to a set of wide French doors at the rear that opened out on to a majestic lawn. She fancied she saw a peacock bob past. Most of the people trailing in and out headed that way. Boone popped her head into some of the many rooms off the hallway, but found nobody who looked like they lived there.

She wandered outside. The lawn was only the start of it – perfectly manicured gardens stretched off to one side of the house, and beyond them the land swept down a gentle slope to where she saw the glittering of water. Between the gardens and the water lay a vast hedge maze that branched off into dozens of pathways. Directly behind the house, the lawn gave way to the ancient woods that covered much of the large estate.

'Can I help you?'

She turned to find a woman with a shotgun broken over the crook of her arm. It was hard to pin down her age. Boone supposed she was in her sixties but how you would expect a movie star from the forties to look at that age. She was tall, probably five ten in her chestnut leather boots, and wore a tailored tweed shooting jacket

and herringbone breeks that were trimmed with something pre-
posterous like ostrich skin. Beside her stood Hanley Moss, also
dressed as if about to fend off a pheasant invasion.

'Hard to say,' Boone said.

The woman was smoothing out a pair of suede gloves in her
hand and that was where her eyes went when she spoke.

'There's a fellow out front coordinating things,' she said, glancing at Moss.

'Perryman,' Moss said.

'A Mr Perryman,' the woman repeated. 'He'll tell you where
you're required.'

Not needed or wanted, but required.

'I'm not here for any of this,' Boone said. 'I'm looking for Sir Mark.'

The woman looked up and met Boone's eyes, considered her
for a long moment.

Boone had particular thoughts on chickens. She hated them.
Their eyes had a blank, alien gaze and behind them was an endless
kind of stupid. This woman's gaze shared that alien quality, but
with something quite different behind it. Not merely an intelli-
gence but an assuredness of superiority, as if she was laying eyes on
a different species. There was something atavistic in it, something
older than names or money. Something that had been on the land
since back when it was still the way it had been made. The way the
woman looked at her was, Boone supposed, the same way she
herself regarded chickens.

'Why?' the woman asked.

'It's a private matter,' Boone said.

The woman almost smiled. 'Mark has few matters about which
I'm ignorant.'

'I imagine he should decide whether this is one of them.'

Moss leaned in behind the woman's ear, whispering something.

'You were at the open house,' she said. 'You were asked to leave.'

'Oh no, you're misinformed,' Boone said. 'Someone rather carelessly spilled red wine on me, so I left to take care of it.'

'My son isn't here at the moment, Ms Boone. Perhaps you'd care to walk with me for a spell?'

It was one of those invitations that was really a summons.

'You have me at something of a disadvantage,' Boone said, struggling to keep up with the woman's stride as they set off across the lawn. 'You seem to know who I am.'

'Mark is my son, Ms Boone. I'm Lady Theodora, but that sounds absurd. You can call me Teddy.'

'Boone,' said Boone.

'Hmm?'

'What people call me. Just Boone.'

Teddy apprised her once more. It felt like an ongoing process with her.

'Your leg,' she said, modulating her pace to accommodate Boone.

'I injured it a while ago. The fix hasn't really taken.'

'Yes, I read about it. You're that police detective.'

'Not any longer.'

'Yet you still ask questions like the police.'

Boone glanced back at Hanley Moss, who had fallen in a few yards behind them.

'There isn't much that happens within the ambit of my businesses about which I remain unaware,' Teddy said.

'Your businesses?'

'The men of the family are figureheads, Boone. All of the Cornilo industries are run by me. Always have been. My husband had the name and title, but no money or ambition. I had the ambition and cunning, but no name or money. Together we put all that right and made a lot of money. Women terrify men, however. It's why they do deals in shabby little boys' clubs. So it's easier to keep a man in the hot seat.'

'Not exactly leaning into it,' Boone muttered.

'I don't represent womankind, Boone. I represent myself. My family. My name. I'm extremely rich and extremely powerful, and nobody knows who I am. That's the way I like it.'

They'd cut in through the treeline at the verge of the lawn and walked among the woods, the din of whatever was happening at the house receding behind them.

'We have a hunt tonight,' Teddy said. 'Under the full moon. Boars are nocturnal animals so a day hunt is usually a waste. Then tomorrow there is the ball. I cannot abide those women who hover about over the preparations of such events. The point of being rich is you have other people to do that; why on earth waste your own time watching them?'

'I'm always worried the peasants will steal from me,' Boone said.

'Hmm,' Teddy said. 'Humour.'

She fetched two cartridges from her coat pocket and slotted them into the barrels, closing the break with a clunk.

'You were asking about that girl,' she said. 'The Still girl.'

'I was?'

'Come on, Boone. I think I've demonstrated I know who you are. You ask my son about the girl, her body turns up, and now you're here.'

Boone heard Moss's gun click shut behind her.

'Shouldn't we have dogs and beaters and whatnot?' she said.

'I don't like driven shoots,' Teddy said. 'I prefer to stalk and kill myself. We've had a lot of muntjacs in recent years, breeding like vermin. Tonight's hunt will be a circus, with guests and charlatans everywhere. Hanley and I like to get a proper shoot in first. Do you shoot, Boone?'

'I shoot. Don't hunt. Not animals, anyway. Never found much sport in it.'

'Oh?'

'Not like they can hunt back, is it?'

Teddy laughed. 'You should join one of our night hunts. A boar is not to be trifled with. Surprising animals.'

Boone jumped when a shot fired behind her, exploding against a tree twenty yards to their right. Moss stood aiming his piece, searching the woods over his sight.

'Doe,' he said. 'No tusks. Might have clipped it, or a splinter hit it. Thought it had a limp as it scuttered off. Lone doe with a limp won't get far out here.'

Teddy shook her head for Boone's benefit.

'An injuring shot is so frustrating,' she said. 'An animal can skedaddle and go to ground hurt. Often they die where they hide, and nobody'll find them out here. I bring dogs when it's pheasant. Sod all that searching about.'

Moss discharged his weapon again and whooped as if in celebration before lolloping off out of sight between the trees.

'What were you going to ask my son?' Teddy said.

'It wasn't anything urgent.'

'Ask me anyway.'

Boone was certain the guns were theatre.

Probably.

Teddy had to know people had seen her at the house, seen her walk off into the woods. Her car was parked outside and she could have told any number of people she was coming here. Nobody was going to shotgun her in the back and claim it was a hunting accident.

Probably.

'The girl has been found,' Teddy said. 'After a fashion. What more do you wish to know?'

'It was a small thing,' Boone said. 'Just clearing up an old matter. Curiosity, really.'

'You were at the mother's yesterday,' Teddy said.

That stopped Boone short, for several reasons. All this information Teddy had on her, it was more than Moss could have whispered to her. It was like she had a file. And now she was watching her? Or watching Molly. Moss had glided back to them, standing a few yards off. Boone was out of her depth here and would have to rethink her approach. She wondered what Mickey Box would do. And then she knew exactly what Mickey Box would do. Divide and conquer.

'I wanted to follow up on something I spoke to your son about previously,' she said. 'A technical detail, really. Regarding a company that had a connection with the Stills.'

'Oh?' said Teddy.

'Yeah. Omicron Holdings?'

It was slight, but she caught a glance from Teddy to Moss. More a flick of her eyes.

'Omicron?' the older woman said.

Boone shrugged. 'One of those Panamanian jobs.'

'Can't say I recognise the name.'

'Really? That's funny.'

'How so?'

'Well, your husband was involved in it, along with another man who was the director, Ian Harvey?'

Teddy had recomposed herself, and now the Sphinx had nothing on her. Face as immutable as ancient stone.

'I think I would know about that. Who is this man Harvey?'

'Well, he was also a director at Lamech Capital. As was your husband. But then, if I understand things correctly, he was only a figurehead?'

Teddy watched her carefully and Boone began to feel like a chicken again. One headed for a pot, perhaps.

'And you spoke to Mark about these matters?'

'Oh yes. We had a good old chinwag over some vol-au-vents before someone with particularly peasanty manners tipped a glass of plonk all over me.'

'Lady Theodora.'

They turned to a suited man carrying a tablet, an earpiece to complete the look.

'Mr Perryman,' Teddy said.

'Begging your pardon, the police are here. A walk-through for the night hunt?'

'Of course, Mr Perryman.'

Boone was already taking the opportunity, hobbling off as fast as she could and calling back over her shoulder. 'Well, thank you for your time, Lady Theodora. Much appreciated. Shan't detain you any longer.'

The Perryman character sort of fell in beside her, unsure whether he was supposed to plough on ahead or do the gentlemanly thing and escort the gimpy commoner back to the house. He opted for the surety of middle ground and maintained a safe lateral distance whilst matching Boone's more measured gait. At the back doors to the house he made something that might have been a gesture inviting her inside before him, or he may have been stretching.

In the main hallway, Sir Mark Blackborne was talking to a young woman who looked like staff. Boone hovered. Her phone vibrated in her pocket, new emails arriving. One was from Mark Hutchinson, the photographer who had covered last year's Blackborne Ball for the local paper. She was confused for a moment, forgetting she had used a fake name and set up a new account specially for him.

Dear Miss Raunce, yadda yadda, see link below for gallery of all the pictures I took.

'Hello again.'

Blackborne had sidled up, the rumour of a smile on his face.

'Sir Mark.'

'Abigail, wasn't it?'

'Boone,' said Boone. 'Just Boone.'

'Right you are.' He swivelled on his heel whilst leaning in conspiratorially, and pointed at the girl he had been speaking to. 'Fiona,' he said. 'In case you tried testing me on names again. I won't be caught out this time if you stray from the pool of guests.' He straightened up, looking around as if just that second realising where they were. 'What on earth brings you here? I thought they found . . . I mean, I read in the papers about the girl. Sarah. Heartbreaking story. But if they found her, you can't be here about that, can you?'

'Everybody does seem to want the matter to go away now. I

would have thought the discovery of a young woman's corpse would be the beginning of it, not the end. Perhaps that's just the latent copper in me.'

'So you came here to – what?'

'Actually, I thought of a better game for us. Instead of pointing people out and asking who they are, how about I give you a name and you tell me all about them.'

'I don't understand.'

'Starter for ten. Who is Ian Harvey?'

If she'd sliced his femoral, the blood couldn't have drained from his face any quicker. He looked over her shoulder to the back lawn, searching for his mother probably.

'I've already seen Lady Theodora,' Boone said. 'Great chums, me and Teddy. Whale of a time. I ask her about Omicron Holdings, then she tries to scare me with a shotgun. Such fun.'

'Christ,' Blackborne said. 'I really wish you hadn't done that. Here, come with me.'

He ushered her into one of the rooms off the hallway, a delicately period-furnished parlour whose newest item only went back to when Boone's family tree was a sapling.

'None of this is what you think it is,' he said. 'Look, take a seat for a moment. I'll be back as quickly as I can.'

Boone perched bird-like on a chair that belonged in a museum, and Blackborne closed the door behind him. Off to find Mummy, no doubt. She returned to her phone and read through the email from Hutchinson again, clicking on the link to the gallery. She waited patiently for the images to load before scrolling through them. When she reached a particular picture, her entire world imploded.

'What the Jesus fuck?' she said, standing up.

She sat back down.

Then stood up again and paced one way and the other.

She stared at the photograph but could make no sense of it.

It might as well have melted her brain.

Pinching the screen, she zoomed in close and squinted, as if it might change what she saw. The picture was of an expensively tailored and well-coiffured young couple whom Boone didn't recognise, but in the background could clearly be made out Mark Blackborne, standing in conversation with one Abigail Boone.

She'd been here before?

Didn't remember that.

She'd met Blackborne before?

Didn't remember that.

More to the point, at the open house he'd acted like they'd never met. Could he have forgotten? Surely not. She examined the picture again. She was in one of her trouser suits, something she wore when working, so she must have been here on official business, before her accident. Even if Blackborne hadn't remembered her at first, he must surely have known once Assistant Chief Constable Bardin had outed her as a former copper.

Boone flicked back through a few of the photos, looking for herself. Then forward to the ones she hadn't yet seen. Nothing, nothing, nothing, fuck my ungodly life.

There, plain as day, an old-timer in shooting apparel, great beak quivering as if already on the scent of his quarry. The same old-timer she'd seen at the pub after Sarah Still's funeral, and again in the Two Yacks with Tess and Roo. She'd dismissed it as paranoid fancy at the time, but now, seeing him for the third time, she was quite certain it was the same man.

A mild panic fluttered in her chest, but was quickly growing into a full-sized pigeon. These pictures were from a year ago. Was this man always in the Blackbornes' hire? And how long had he been following her? She hadn't noticed him until the day of the funeral, so since the open house perhaps, when she had revealed herself to Mark Blackborne. Jesus, where else had he followed her? Did he know where she lived? Did he know where the caravan was?

Boone didn't hang around for Mark Blackborne to return. Almost running from the house, she fumbled with her keys and got into the Goose, clutching the wheel as tightly as she could to counteract the shaking. With ferocious concentration she hurtled down the gravel drive, leaving the house behind her, and sped north for the marshes that Tess and Roo called home.

She stopped at the cottage first, though, asking Mickey Box for a favour.

45

It must have been written on her face, how shaken Boone was.

She'd found Roo on the sofa, kicking about in joggers and a band T-shirt, on her feet a pair of black and silver snakeskin Christian Louboutin stilettos she'd just dropped the best part of a fortnight's wages on over the internet. She had them up on the coffee table, ankles crossed, twisting them this way and that.

She dropped the display when she saw Boone.

'What is wrong? Your face is funny.'

Boone explained what had happened and thought for a moment Roo was going to pull off her new shoes and beat her to death with them.

'Why would you go to this place alone?'

'I saw fireflies instead of lanterns.' Boone shrugged.

But Roo was not in the mood for their playful patois. 'This is getting past the point of foolishness with you.'

'I wasn't alone, Roo. The place was crawling with people for this big party they're holding.'

'You knew this?'

'Well, no. But the point still stands.'

Roo shook her head like she couldn't be bothered any more.

'Nice shoes, though,' Boone said, cutting a route back to safe ground.

'Hmph.'

'And they're second-hand?' Boone clarified.

'Yes.'

'And they cost three hundred quid?'

'Yes.'

'More must have fallen out of my head than I thought.'

The tan shoebox was open on the table, tissue paper and red dust bag spilling out. Roo slipped the shoes off and carefully packed them away again.

'They'll certainly class up the Two Yacks when you're pulling pints,' Boone said.

'These shoes are not for working, I think. Good shoes, new shoes, they make you find new places to go to show them off. This is how they make your life better.'

Tess didn't quite beat midday, emerging from her room yawning and fingering sleep from her eyes. Roo immediately explained to her how disgusted she was with Boone's latest safari, illustrating the story with faces and eye rolls.

'He works for the Blackbornes then, this man?' Tess said.

'Looks like.'

'You know how long he's been following you?'

'Nope. Only remember seeing him the twice, but I have no idea what vehicle he was in or where else he has tracked me.'

'So he could know about Roo being here?'

'I think we have to assume he knows where we all are.'

'Jesus,' said Tess.

'What does it mean, you being in this picture at the Black-borne place?' Roo said

Boone shook her head. 'I don't know. I must have made the connection between Sarah Still and the Blackbornes back then. Confronted them about it maybe?'

'There's no record of any of that, though?' Tess said.

'Perhaps it was only a suspicion. Or I just had questions at that stage, the kind of questions that ended up with me unconscious in a flat in east London.'

'Any question that leads to that is the wrong kind of question,' Roo said. 'And now you are having not only the wrong kind of question again, but a few wrong kind of answers. The kind that will maybe get you disappeared with someone hiding your body under an old farm.'

'Maybe,' Boone said.

'So it is obvious you are to continue with these wrong kind of questions,' said Roo.

'It is, yes.'

Not for the first time, Roo shook her head like she was looking at some ageing animal in a zoo.

'Don't say it,' Boone said.

'I will,' Tess said. 'You should give this all to Barb. It's getting too dangerous for you on your own.'

'This all what? We don't have anything. We *know* what happened, or a decent guess, but what can we prove?'

'They are the police,' said Tess. 'They have the ability to find more than you can.'

'They are the police,' said Boone. 'They have the ability to brush all of this under the carpet.'

'Not everything is a cover-up,' Tess said. 'The man Hanley Moss, he will go down at the very least.'

'For what? Having had his picture taken? He isn't doing anything in the photo. We don't know where the originals are, or even where they were taken. And the only man who can identify Blackborne in the pictures doesn't actually know it is Blackborne and is a twice-convicted sex offender who I've assaulted and who Fitz has assaulted. He's not going to say anything to the police that isn't going to jam us up.'

'So what then?' said Roo.

'So we need more,' said Boone. 'And I might have something.'

She told them about the numbers on Sarah's phone, and about the kebab shop in east London. Tess brought a map up on her laptop and they explored the street online, the three of them staring at the wholly unremarkable shopfront.

'Not so very far from where we met,' Roo told Boone.

'There's no sign,' Tess said.

It was a thin shop in the middle of a three-storey block, made thinner by the door to the mangy-looking flats above. The shops around it were other food places, a mixture of Asian and Afro-Caribbean or halal, a few cargo services and wire transfer kiosks, a franchise bookie's, a cash-and-carry – and then this place with bare bulbs and wires above the door where a sign had been removed or fallen or maybe just never put up in the first place.

'Number is listed as a business called Tubby's,' Boone said. 'Spoke to a fella there a couple of times and he didn't seem too keen on new business. Mostly he spoke in another language and hung up on me.'

'Well, if you called me and started rabbiting away in Gaelic, I'd hang up too,' Tess said.

There was a metal table outside the shop, two chairs at it, but they couldn't see in the windows.

'It's what's next door that interested me,' Roo said.

The shop beside it was a minicab firm, a faded sign above the door reading RADIO CARS and three numbers, still with the old 081 London exchange code.

'Opened sometime in the early nineties, those numbers,' Tess said.

'Sign went up then, anyway,' Boone said. 'Something you said once, Roo. About how cab drivers ferried you around on jobs and whatever.'

'This might be the firm?' said Tess.

Boone shrugged. 'Kebab place could be somewhere the drivers hang out. Maybe take calls there for certain types of jobs. Be interesting to find out.'

Tess pressed her eyes shut. 'Jesus. You're going to go there, aren't you?'

'For sure she is,' said Roo. 'Latest chapter in this long suicide attempt of hers.'

Boone rolled her eyes.

'Well, I'm coming with you if you're going to look at this place,' Tess said.

'Not a chance.'

'Boone . . .'

'Not a single fucking chance in hell. The only place you're going is the cottage.'

'What?'

'You said it yourself. We don't know what they know. You both could be in danger here.'

'Unbelievable,' Tess said. 'You've already spoken to Mick, haven't you?'

'He agreed it mightn't be a bad idea to spend a few days there. Both of you, he said Roo could have the spare room.'

'And what are you going to do?' Roo said.

Boone raised a finger and from behind the sofa fetched what she had picked up from Mickey Box before she arrived at the caravan – a long black case.

'Jesus Christ,' Tess sighed.

'What it is?' said Roo.

'It's a fucking gun,' said Tess.

'No,' said Boone, producing a shotgun. 'It's a Mossberg 930 twelve-gauge semi-auto.'

'The guns are illegal here,' Roo said.

Tess snorted. 'Didn't you know? Boone's out there all the time, keeping the vermin down.'

'Waterfowl and the like,' Boone said.

'You are killing people now?' Roo said.

'Always aim for centre mass,' Boone said. 'Or a little lower.'

'I don't think the Metropolitan Police would approve of you shooting the dicks off a roomful of men in a kebab shop,' said Tess.

Boone put the shotgun back in its bag.

'Didn't mean for there,' she said. 'Meant for home. If the Black-bornes do know where we live, then the others might too. The men from the flat.'

'Again, forgive me for stating the obvious,' Tess said, 'but the police are better equipped for this.'

'What do I tell them? I think I might be under threat from parties unknown who you previously failed to identify, who might now be taking instructions from a sitting lawmaker of our great nation? Please help? I need to find out who these men are. This shop is the best lead I have.'

'She's right,' Roo said.

'What?' Tess and Boone said together.

'You are right. You should go to this shop, and I should go with you.'

'What? No,' Boone said.

'What is the good in you going alone? Do you know any of them? No. If the drivers are there, I will see and know them.'

'That's exactly why you're not going. They'll know you too.'

Roo grabbed the laptop and swung the view round to the other side of the road. 'Look. Across the street. A sandwich and coffee bar. There are stools and a counter in the window. You can take me for lunch and we watch out of the window. Nobody will notice us, and we can see who is coming and who is going.'

46

Next day the traffic was thick and a constant stream of people crowded the pavement. People entered and left the takeout across the street, even a few men from the minicab place, but Roo recognised none of them. They'd ordered coffees first, making a pretence of deciding on their lunch. After sitting in the window for an hour and a half, Boone felt they hadn't learned anything they didn't already know. Or not know.

She had saved the two numbers they found on Sarah's phone onto her own, the landline to Tubby's and the mobile number that was always off. She tried the mobile number again but hung up when it went to voicemail for the fiftieth time.

Roo was looking at her feet.

'Cannot believe you wore the shoes,' Boone said. 'I thought they were for special occasions?'

'Please, tell me what special occasion there is going to be. I work in laundrette. I work in bar. This is special occasion.'

'Thought Tess could take you somewhere.'

Roo was quiet a moment. 'This is why you have not been around so much? Tess and me?'

Boone shrugged. 'None of my business.'

'You think that your friends are no longer your friends? Or is it something else?'

Boone said nothing.

'What I think,' Roo went on, 'is that you do not know yourself. Do not know what you want. And I cannot be, how you say – a guide?'

'Jesus, all right. Stop.'

'I have been with people for too long only on their terms. I need something for myself.'

They sat in thorny silence and Boone wished someone, anyone, would come out of the kebab shop across the road. One of the men from the flat, the big one perhaps, could come out and recognise them. Throw a brick through the window at them. Anything like that.

'You know that you are still my very best buddy,' Roo said eventually. 'You saved my life, even if you do put milk on my knees.'

'Maybe on your ankles too,' Boone said, looking down at Roo's new shoes. 'With my ankles, I think they'd look better on me.'

'Pfft. You have skis for feet. You would never fit.'

'I don't have skis. I have elegant feet.'

'They are diving boards.'

'I . . .' Boone stopped and narrowed her eyes. 'I have the perfect comeback to that but I'm saving it for a more appropriate time.'

'This is a question of goat's wool.'

'Up a whale's arse.'

'We need to put more in the parking soon,' Roo said, glancing at her phone. 'The scratch card runs out in twenty minutes.'

'Fuck it,' Boone said. 'I'm going in there.'

'That is exactly what you are not going to do,' said Roo.

'I've got a hat,' Boone said, pulling on her woolly beanie. 'I'll go in there, order something. Hang around for a few minutes. I don't see anything, I'll leave.'

'And if you do see something?'

'I'll leave quicker.'

'We both go.'

'No. If there is someone in there who's involved, a driver or one of the men from the flat, there's a better chance of you being recognised.'

'But with you and your magical hat, they won't suspect a thing.'

'Exactly.'

'This is more of why I call you stupid.'

'Yes. Thank you. Go get the car. When the time on the ticket is up, drive round. I'll be waiting down on the first corner past the kebab shop. Pick me up there. Anything happens sooner, I'll text you.'

Roo took the keys, shaking her head.

'Lunch is on you,' she said.

Boone watched Roo leave before paying the bill. She wrapped her scarf tightly round her chin as she crossed the road. The kebab shop was doing a reasonable lunchtime trade, with two men waiting for their orders at the counter. Out back there were maybe eight tables, all but a couple with people sitting at them. All the customers were men.

She ordered pakoras and a can of Coke. The man heated a pan and it spat angrily when he tossed in the tikki.

'Can I take a table?'

Without looking up, he waved a hand at the seating area. Boone took her Coke from the counter and sat in the far corner, back against the wall so she had a view of everything. Not ideal, but the only other free table was between two groups of four men. Although nobody was paying her any attention, she felt terribly exposed, and pulled her hat down slightly.

The man brought her food in a polystyrene box.

On his way back to the counter, he stopped beside one of the groups of men. None of them had food. Coffee cups sat before them, and the owner refilled them from a pot behind the counter. When he spoke with them, it was as friends, laughing and jeering. They were dressed casually, jeans and shirts; one had a hoodie pulled up so Boone couldn't see him. The others had dark hair and complexions, Middle Eastern or south Asian.

A phone rang, a landline behind the counter. The man answered it and turned to face the wall. Boone couldn't hear him over the general din of the place, couldn't even tell if he was talking English. It was a short call and when he replaced the receiver he barked something to one of the men he had spoken with. He scribbled something on a notepad and tore the sheet off. The other man got up and took it from him. They shared a joke about something and the man left, not through the front of the shop but via a door at the rear, in the wall Boone sat against.

He didn't return.

Boone picked happily at her food and sipped her Coke. She pretended to read something on her phone. The other table of four men finished up and left.

They didn't speak to the man at the counter as they went, didn't seem to know him. More people came and ordered food to go. They talked mostly in a language Boone didn't understand, but the interactions appeared to be solely about the food. She checked the time on her phone. The parking time was up and Roo would be starting the Goose. It was only a couple of streets away and it wouldn't take her much time to pull round.

Eyes getting the better of her stomach, Boone popped one last pakora in her mouth. Idly she tried the mobile number from Sarah's phone again and this time it rang. She stared at the handset, absolutely no idea what on earth she was going to say. Somewhere across the room another mobile rang, and when its owner answered, cutting off the ringtone, the line opened on Boone's phone.

That had to be coincidence.

She thought of UFOs and socialism.

Confused, she hung up. Roo would be outside any second anyway. She got up to leave and the phone rang in her hand. The hooded man at the other table turned and looked up at her, phone to his ear.

There were creases around his eye like bad ironing, and a patch of pocked and shiny old-man skin spread across the side of his face and down his neck.

She didn't know his face, or his movements, or anything about him, but she knew it was him. Knew it was the man from the flat whose face she had scalded, the man who had chased her through the woods at the colliery.

He said something she didn't understand, and the other men stood, looking at Boone with as much confusion as she looked at them. He barked at them now and they fanned out from the table, approaching her slowly.

There was no way past them and out of the shop.

She didn't hesitate for a second. Dragging her table over on to its side between her and them, she turned and bolted through the same door as the man who'd taken the note.

A narrow hall led to a kitchen of sorts, chrome fridges and counters for preparing food. Against one wall stood several storage units, white plastic tubes that fitted together and supported shelves lined with bottles and jars of all varieties.

Boone grabbed at them as she ran past, bring them crashing down behind her. A door at the other end of the room led to another short hallway with a small office to one side and a further door that opened into a small yard. She stumbled through it and looked both ways. To the left was a wooden gate leading to a wide alley behind the block. She made to go that way but a car with minicab decals on it pulled up right there. The other way was a black iron staircase, a fire escape from the flats above.

She took the stairs as quick as she could, hearing the door bang open behind her. At the top was a wrought-iron gangway that ran the length of the flats, each with a rear door opening on to it. There were a couple of other staircases leading down from it further along.

The door to the nearest flat was open. Hearing feet on the iron stairs below, Boone plunged through the door and pulled it shut behind her. Rushing through a galley kitchen, she found herself in the lobby of the small flat. Through an open door, an elderly olive-skinned woman looked at her from her armchair and began screaming. Boone hurried on, slipping out the front door into a poorly lit corridor that evidently ran between the front and rear flats.

A young woman with a buggy and several shopping bags stood outside the next flat, door open. She looked at Boone and then towards the door and the noise the old woman was making. Boone barged past the young mother and into her flat, shutting the door behind her and locking her out. The woman pounded on the door and Boone heard other voices, male voices, join her in the corridor. Someone booted the door and the frame bulged and then splintered on the second kick. She found the back door but it wouldn't open. Sliding bolts top and bottom slowed her down and she heard the front door give just as she stepped out onto the iron concourse. There were no men out there and she hopped down the next set of fire stairs to the alley. It was wide and gravelled and lined with big wheelie bins. At the end she could see a side road off the high street, perhaps seven or eight shops away.

The man with the burn scars appeared out on the fire escape. Even with a head start, Boone knew she didn't have the running in her to make it. She ducked into the back door of the nearest shop unit.

Some kind of cool room, storage for foodstuff.

It was dimly lit but she could see plastic strip curtains leading out to the bright front of a grocery shop. She was surrounded by wheeled storage trollies, and beside her was an aluminium shelving unit, others like it in a row behind. She limped past the furthest shelves and, bracing her shoulder against them, shoved with everything she had. The unit rocked and on the second go toppled and knocked over the other two lots of shelves, blocking the back door.

Hiding behind a stack of cardboard boxes near the plastic curtains, she heard voices as staff came in from the shop floor to find out what the racket was.

At the same time, men were trying to force the back door in

but struggled to open it against the fallen shelves. As the two groups yelled at each other through the blocked door, Boone sent a text to Roo.

GET OUT OF HERE. LEAVE NOW! I WILL FOLLOW LATER.

She slipped through the strip curtains into the surgically bright store and nodded to a cashier, who watched her limp out into the street. Once outside, she broke into a kind of skip, swinging her gammy leg out to the side to get it going quicker, eliciting a few looks from other pedestrians.

Ahead, up at the next corner, a flash of iridium blue.

The Goose.

Roo had come round the block and was facing the main road. She reached back and opened the rear door from inside, beckoning Boone towards her. 'Oh Jesus, no,' Boone hissed, trying with all her might to run like a three-legged dog.

She heard a commotion behind her and glanced back, seeing the scarred man skidding out of the front of the kebab shop, pushing a young couple out of his way. He looked both ways, catching sight of her and taking off.

And could he move.

His trainers slapped the pavement, two, three steps to each of Boone's. The street was full of people, bystanders and witnesses. Surely nobody was going to let this happen here. It wasn't the woods, she wasn't fleeing alone and lost.

She tried to wave Roo off, shoo her away.

'Go,' she pleaded, frantically waving her arms. 'Drive.'

Roo couldn't hear her and she waved back, smiling.

The Goose suddenly shunted forward, rear-ended by a white

van. Roo looked back over her seat to see three men exiting the van and swarming her car. Boone was screaming incoherently. Her leg was murder and she was twenty yards from the car, eighteen yards, fifteen yards from three men dragging Roo out by her hair and arms and legs, ten yards from them bundling her into the side door of the van.

When the scarred man tackled her from behind, Boone saw Roo's face as the van bumped up onto the pavement to get round the car. Saw her terror as the door slid shut and she disappeared, the van crossing the high street and vanishing down the opposite side road.

The scarred man's fingers dug into Boone's throat and he raked her face across the paving slabs. His weight on her back squeezed out her lungs and everything was terribly close all of a sudden, close and soft as she lost focus. She twisted and turned and tried to gouge his eyes but he beat her with his fists. He punched her in the side of the head and the face. He hammered on her chest.

Boone had fallen limp by the time two men intervened. Someone had called the police. The scarred man was off her and she was free and began crawling towards the blue car. She'd make pursuit, catch up and rescue Roo.

She'd have to.

The driver's door was open where they'd pulled Roo out, and Boone hauled herself in behind the wheel.

Fucking keys were gone.

She screamed, her wailing heard down the street over the incoming sirens even. Her foot brushed something and beneath the seat she found the Christian Louboutins in their red dust bag. Roo had taken them off to drive.

FIVE

HOME TO ROOST

47

Sitting in the back of the ambulance, Boone remained stoic as a paramedic tended to her face. It wasn't too bad. A welt had come up beneath one eye and she had some bleeding in her mouth but no loose teeth. Her ear was sore and she had bruising around the neck and chest. Her knees were grazed from the pavement. She was still holding Roo's new shoes, and when the police learned where they were from, a female constable almost had to prise them from her hands as evidence. Two detectives she didn't recognise, and who apparently didn't know her, took her to give her statement at a nearby station, a large red-brick building, stone-banded on the lower floors.

Boone gave the detectives Barb's details at Kent Police. It was time to spill everything she had. She told them about Sarah Still, about the Blackbornes, about Milan Jedinek, about what happened to her in the flat a year ago and about the men who did it. The same men who now had Roo.

She told them about Hanley Moss and the photos and videos on the phones.

She told them about Roo, everything she knew about Roo.

It felt and sounded like a confession.

She asked to make a call and dialled Mickey Box.

'Mick?'

'Uh-huh.'

'I'm at a police station.'

'Uh-huh.'

'Roo's been abducted.'

'Uh-huh.'

'So, I'm going to have to come clean to them. They're probably going to want to search the caravan. You need to make sure you've got eyes on Tess at all times. Sorry, Mick.'

She waited, listening to him breathe. Finally, he said, 'You need a brief?'

'They said they're not arresting me. Interviewing me under caution, though. If I have to come in again, then it'll be time to think about representation.'

Boone spent the day at the station. The scarred man had escaped, nobody had seen in which direction. The kebab shop owner turned out to be an eighty-year-old woman in a care facility who knew Saturdays were beefburgers for lunch but couldn't tell the detectives anything about the business. The shop itself was locked up when they arrived and forcing entry yielded no further information. The office at the back was used for storage and there was nothing to identify anyone who had been there.

Some of the minicab drivers from next door acknowledged that they picked up a bite to eat in there occasionally, but none of them knew the man behind the counter or the man with the scarred face.

The white van had vanished. Various witnesses offered partial plates, but nothing matched and ANPR picked nothing up. Detectives who had worked Boone's disappearance a year ago joined the investigation, but since they had found out almost nothing back then, they had little to offer.

By the time Boone was free to leave, it was evening. In the lobby at the front of the station, sitting with his legs crossed and reading a slim paperback, was Fitz.

'What are you doing here?'

'Heard you might need a lift home,' he said. 'Seeing as your Saab got smashed up and they're keeping it for forensics or whatever.'

'Did they show up at the caravan?'

'You mean the men in those little white fairy costumes who turned the place upside down looking for evidence of unicorns?'

'Shit.'

'Aye. Shit.'

'Mick pissed? They didn't try linking it to the cottage or the scrapyard, did they?'

'How would they do that?'

'Well, Mick—'

'Michael Boxall lives in a cottage. He doesn't own any other property. The caravan and the land it's on is owned by a shell company. The scrapyard's mine. Well, technically it's owned by Medway Salvage and Scrap Ltd, but I'm employed to run the place by their director. Who lives in the Bahamas. And I'm fuck-all to do with this mess you've dropped on the floor, so they won't be coming near it.'

'Mick's going to shoot me in the face, isn't he?'

'Mick would never do that,' Fitz said. 'He'd ask me. Merc's outside. On the way home you can tell me how thankful you are that I didn't leave you to find your own ride.'

Getting in the car, Fitz tossed his book and a bag of sunflower seeds on the passenger seat. Boone picked them up and opened the glove compartment to put them away.

'You're sitting there?' he said.

'Yeah. Why?'

'Not in the back?'

'Why would I sit in the back?'

'Mick sits in back, is all.'

Boone got in beside him. He sighed and started the engine.

'Crowding you?' Boone asked.

'It's fine.'

She was nervy, fingers fidgeting, tapping on the armrest and on her knees. The glove compartment hung open still and she helped herself to a couple of sunflower seeds. They were hulled and roasted.

'These are – unusual.'

'I roasted them in cannabutter and sea salt.'

'Jesus, I knew there was something about these fucking seeds. You're always shovelling them in your face. You just drive round the place lit as fuck?' She was speaking fast, barely coming up for air.

'I was trying something,' said Fitz calmly. 'Usually they're regular seeds.'

Boone picked up the book. *'Morgue pleine,'* she said, flicking through it. 'This is by a Frenchman. It's a French book in French by a Frenchman. You speak French?'

'I speak four languages.'

'Fuck off.'

'French, and Spanish, and Italian too.'

'I know some Italian. *Non avere peli sulla lingua.*'

He glanced at her out of the side of his eye.

'It means without hair on your tongue.'

He took the bag of seeds from her and slipped them into the storage compartment in his door.

'It's a thing,' she said.

'Yeah.'

'There's this book, like a phrasebook for Italian, and the author had a list of idioms. And other people had pencilled in other ones too. And we'd recite them. It was like a bit we did, me and Roo. And . . .'

She trailed off, gaze lost out the window somewhere.

'They don't know anything, the police?'

She shook her head.

'And you?'

'Me what?'

'What do you think?'

'I think they're going to kill her, if they haven't already.'

'They'll want to know a few things. How she found them. What she knows about their operation. What you know. You have to assume she'll give them everything. They don't strike me as men who fuck about.'

'You think they'll come after me? Jesus, Tess. They might come for Tess. Christ.'

'Tess will be fine. She's in the cottage. Anyone who comes for her there will have the very worst and very last day of their lives. Shouldn't you have other priorities?'

Boone looked blankly at him.

'That husband and boy of yours?'

She recoiled, turning glumly to the window, quietened by a double stab of guilt. Firstly for forgetting Jack and Quin, and secondly for the flashing thought of them as an obligation.

'Might want to think about going into hiding,' Fitz said.

'I'm not going to hang around waiting for them.'

'Exactly.'

'No. I'm going to come for them.'

'Boone, they could be anywhere. And how many times do . . . You know what? Forget it. You're clearly a maniac.'

'I have to find her.'

'They could take her anywhere. Look where you were found. Some abandoned flat, boarded up and empty. How many places like that are there in London? In the whole south-east?'

Boone shook her head. 'After I was found, the Met hit hundreds of places like that. Thousands. All the decanted estates, any houses they could find that had been empty for more than a few months. It was a huge search. A police officer was missing. Remember? I don't think they'd risk using a place like that again for a while. I'd bet anything they're at that house, Blackborne's house. They know it well and they were still using it very recently. It's safe ground for them.'

'You still don't know where that is, Boone.'

'I'll go to Blackborne. Tell him I'll stop it all if he gets them to let her go.'

Fitz snorted.

'I'll offer myself then.'

'You won't get near Blackborne after this. Not if he knows any-thing about it. Not within a million miles.'

A police car was parked outside the house in Lark when they got back, all the lights on inside.

'You're on your own with this lot,' Fitz said.

'Yeah.' She opened the door and had one leg out. 'Fitz?'

'Yeah?'

'How's Tess?'

'I wouldn't show your face for a while. Not unless you find the other one and bring her with you.'

'Tell her . . . tell her I'm . . . Fuck it. What's the point?'

Jack opened the door. He touched Boone's arm lightly and made himself scarce. Barb was sitting in the kitchen nursing a mug of coffee. She rose when Boone came in and went over to her without saying anything, wrapping her arms round her.

Boone let her cheek fall on her shoulder.

'We'll find her,' Barb said.

Boone was shaking her head. 'No you won't.'

'Boone . . .'

'A year ago I was missing for over three days. I was a police detective and nobody found anything. How is it going to be dif-ferent for a Bulgarian former sex worker?'

'This was done very publicly. There are premises to look at. There's more to go on than we had before.'

'You track the van?'

'Not exactly, no.'

'What does that mean?'

'There's a camera right where it happened, on the junction with the main road. But the men were masked and there were no plates on the van. It went straight across, into the residential streets behind the main road. All the cameras in the surrounding streets have been checked. We think we have it again about a mile south-east. The van looks the same. It had plates but they're from a Peugeot Bipper owned by a plumber a couple of streets away. We think they stole them on the hoof. They were improvising, but this sort of thing isn't alien to them. ANPR picks the plates up twice more. Once near the North Circ, and again further east near an industrial estate on the river. After that, nothing. Maybe they switched the plates out. Maybe they have premises around there.'

'Fucking maybes,' Boone said.

'It's a white van, Boone. You don't need me to tell you how many of them are picked up on cameras out there. If they managed to get to friendly ground, then they could have cloned plates waiting. From what you tell us about these men, it's likely they've taken people before. They know how to cover their tracks. How to go to ground. We're looking at all the footage from the QE Bridge, in case they headed for Kent like you think.'

'Could have swapped vehicles by now.'

'Could have.'

'Or circled back and taken a different route.'

'Or that.'

'You came alone? You didn't search the place?'

'Should I have? Jack gave me the phone.'

Boone had called and told Jack where the phone Molly had given her was, and to expect Barb to collect it. She shook her head. 'The phone is it.'

She dropped onto the sofa in the sitting room. *Keeping room.*

'I need to be out looking for her.'

'Boone, you need rest. And where would you even start anyway?'

'Blackborne. I need to get to Blackborne.'

'Yeah, about that,' Barb said. She sat beside Boone. 'I've been at that pile of theirs most of the day.'

'Make a complaint, did they? I'm harassing them, I suppose? Unbelievable. Click their fingers and the police are over there and haven't they got some la-di-da daylight ball bollocks today anyway?'

'Boone, Mark Blackborne is dead. He was shot last night.'

48

The Blackborne Night Hunt was divided into two groups. The first shot by moonlight alone, targeting baited boar from high seats. The second stalked the animals with lamps, usually a less successful and more dangerous endeavour. Sir Mark Blackborne had been with the second group. After a long and fruitless hunt, a boar was finally shot, at a range of ten metres, with a solid slug from a shotgun (though not without some controversy, as the animal appeared to be a sow with a couple of squeakers). It was field-dressed and the decision was made for the party to head back to the lodge – a former stables that had been converted with changing facilities and bunks.

This was the point at which Sir Mark's absence was first noticed. With dawn an hour away, the party returned to the lodge, reassembling at first light to begin a search as he still hadn't returned. Shortly before half past seven, a body was discovered in the undergrowth of a patch of land the hunt had passed through. It was identified as Sir Mark on site. He had been shot by a solid slug round that made an entry wound in his chest about the size of an apple.

Both rifles and shotguns were being used, with members of the party frequently switching firearms. The shotguns were loaded with saboted slugs. The outlook for identifying either the shooter or the weapon used was not optimistic. These were the facts established by the attending detectives, SOCOs and the coroner.

49

'Hunting accident, it looks like,' Barb said.

'Bullshit. She killed him. Or had him killed.'

'Why?'

'You ever meet her? I'm surprised she didn't eat him when he was young. Needed a male heir to act as her puppet was all.'

'You thought he was involved with Sarah Still. Now you're saying his mother killed him. None of it makes sense, Boone.'

'It doesn't make sense because we can't see all of it. Alex Blackborne was definitely involved. He owned this house in the country somewhere, held parties, young girls and boys. Sarah Still had been there. She somehow links Blackborne's world with those other two, the men who had me in the flat. Blackborne made a payment to Sarah's grandparents through a shell company. It's all hidden. There's the old fella in the pictures too. The one who has been following me.'

'What old man? What fucking pictures?'

'I found the photographer who took pictures for a local paper at the ball at Cornilo last year. I thought I'd seen this old man a couple of times. He was at the pub after Sarah's funeral. And again later. He's in a couple of photos. Must be employed by the Blackbornes. Something to do with them, or with Hanley Moss.'

'These pictures weren't on the phone we found here. Sarah Still's phone.'

'No, they're online. The guy emailed me a link.' Boone fiddled with her own phone. 'There. I downloaded the ones of interest. I've forwarded them to you.'

Barb clicked on the link on her phone. 'Er, Boone? You're in these pictures too.'

'Exactly. So I must have made the connection between Sarah Still and the Blackbornes before. Must have found something.'

'Any barrister Teddy Blackborne can afford would lap this up.'

'Fuck.'

Boone stared at herself in the night-darkened window. She felt exposed, as if someone was watching her. Getting up, she drew the curtains across the rear doors and closed the blinds on the windows.

'There's something else,' Barb said. 'You have to come in. Give a statement about the other business.'

'Now?'

Barb shook her head. 'Former cop, and with what happened today, I convinced them to let you arrange it, so long as it's soon. Get a solicitor and have them come in with you. I can sort out the whens and wheres.'

'Jedinek's flat?'

Barb nodded. 'You told the Met you were there. And his car. We need a statement on all that. Reckon I might give one myself.'

'Don't, Barb. Your story still stands up, finding Jedinek yourself.

I'll tell them what I already told the Met. That I lied, that I broke in and saw his body. I didn't touch anything, I just left it there. I kept you out of it. What you did is exactly what I did. There's no hole there to fill.'

Barb nodded. 'You need the names of some briefs?'

'Mick will get me one.'

'Jesus, Boone.'

'What? If anyone knows someone competent, it'll be him.'

'You're too close to him.'

'There's no too about it.'

'All right. What about security? You want, I can have a car outside through the night. Keep an eye out. They can be inside in thirty seconds if anything happens.'

Boone shook her head. 'We'll be fine,' she said, thinking of the Mossberg in her room upstairs.

Barb gave her a look that suggested she could read her mind.

'Well, sort out a brief,' she said, standing up. 'Call me tomorrow and we'll get you in.'

'You hear anything at all . . .'

'I'll be right on the phone.'

'Good.'

Boone saw Barb out. Jack came down the stairs looking worried, unsure of what comfort to offer.

'I'm okay,' Boone said.

He reached for her face but withdrew his hand before it got there. Tears silently cut down Boone's cheeks. What she wanted more than anything was to be held. Jack took a step towards her but Quin hung round the banisters at the top of the stairs.

'There's someone watching us out back,' he said.

'What?' Jack said.

'I was in Mum's room, looking out at the sea. He's been there since you got back.'

'In the garden?' Jack said, looking through to the kitchen.

'No. He's out beyond the fence. Other side of the coast road. Just standing there.'

'I'm calling the police,' Jack said.

'No, come on,' Boone said, taking his hand and leading him upstairs.

'He's gone. He was there,' Quin said, pointing.

Boone corralled them both into her bedroom's en suite.

'I want you to stay in here,' she said. 'Lock the door and keep the light off. Get into the shower cubicle so you're away from the door and window. Only open the door for me, understand?'

'Abby, what the hell is going on?'

'Probably nothing. Just give me a second to check it out.'

Retrieving the gun bag from where she'd stowed it beneath the bed, she loaded the Mossberg, one in the breech and two in the tube.

'Jesus Christ, Abby,' said Jack.

'Get in there and keep away from the door and window,' Boone said, pushing him back into the bathroom. 'Lock the door.'

She heard the bolt slide and ran from the room, hopping down the stairs and exiting via the front door, leaving it on the latch. She jogged round the house, straining to see in the darkness her eyes hadn't adjusted to yet, the night a moiré of tinged blacks.

The next house was some distance away and between them was a stretch of grassy common land cutting through to the coast road. Boone hurried across it and came out down the road a ways from the gate to their back garden. Sea air scrubbed the night, but she couldn't see anyone out there.

Keeping to the shadows, she moved along their rear fence and found the gate unlatched and ajar. Controlling her breathing, she followed the barrel of the Mossberg through the gate and crept up the garden.

The back doors were open, the curtains snapping in the night breeze. Stepping lightly onto the decking, she parted the fabric with the shotgun and sneaked inside. Moving silently, she settled her sights on the back of the head of the man standing in the archway between kitchen and hallway.

'I got three shots, and this girl recycles automatically, so you move and I'll have all of them in your skull before you have a second thought on the matter. Nobody'll hear it out here, and where I bury you, nobody'll find what's left.'

He raised his hands slowly.

'I thought you might have seen me out there,' he said. 'Thought you might have seen me on previous occasions.'

'In the pub after Sarah Still's funeral. And the Two Yacks a few days ago.'

He nodded. 'Don't move like I used to.'

'Might not move at all, depending on how the next few minutes go.'

His arms flagged slightly.

'I'd find some fortitude from somewhere, keep those mitts aloft,' Boone said. 'Everything that's gone on the last day or so, I'm inclined to get awful nervous here.'

'That's why I came. To explain.'

He turned slowly. He was a small man who wore tweed like he'd been told it kept germs away.

'Can start with your name.'

'My name is Tanner. Edward Tanner.'

'Well, Edward Tanner, you want to remove your coat for me there, thank you muchly?'

Tanner unbuttoned his winter coat and slipped his arms out, holding it to one side.

'Just drop it on the floor. Take three steps forward and go into the room on the left. You do anything other than what I've just told you and I'll put one in the back of your knee. This range, with the choke I got, knee goes like that and your days of sneaking will be at an end.'

Tanner did as instructed. Boone felt through the coat as she followed him into the study.

'I'm not armed,' he said. 'I have a wallet in my back pocket. Some keys. A phone.'

'Turn and face me. Slowly. And stand right there, hands busy and where I can see them.' She held the shotgun at her waist, aimed at his midriff. 'You work for the Blackbornes,' she said.

'I did, until today.'

'Yeah, I heard your employer came to a bit of premature misfortune.'

Tanner flinched, looked away.

'I knew that boy his whole life,' he said. 'Was with his father when he was born. Taught him to ride. Taught him to shoot.'

'You knew what he was then. His father too. The things they did.'

'You don't know what you're talking about.'

'Oh no?'

'No. That boy was nothing like his father. Or his mother, for that matter. And now they've killed him for it.'

'Wasn't an accident, like they say?'

'Of course it wasn't. But they staged it well. Brazen. Out on the hunt, with a dozen people there. Jesus, even I was there.'

'Who's they? His mother?'

Tanner nodded. 'Teddy. And Lord Moss. I don't know who pulled the trigger. Moss, most likely. Teddy fired me this morning, told me I was too old to manage a hunt and that my carelessness cost her son his life. Said she'd make sure everyone knew it was my fault. Looked out for that boy his whole life, when she'd have been as happy if wolves raised him.'

'You were following me for Mark Blackborne then?'

Tanner nodded.

'Why?'

'Initially because he thought you could find Sarah. When her body was found, I told him we should tell you everything. But he was still afraid. It was his family name. The story getting out would have meant ruin.'

'Who were you to him exactly?'

'I'm the gamekeeper at Cornilo House. Was the gamekeeper. I was there when it was known as Eastmere, the estate of Lord Pollock, Earl of Bewsborough. Went there when I was sixteen as a stable boy and was keeping game by the time the Blackbornes bought the place in 1980. They changed the name to Cornilo House. Sir Alex was insistent I stay on. He enjoyed all the trappings his new wealth afforded him and used the hunts as a social lubricant. He was a vile man, caged by his own perversities. But Lady Theodora,

Teddy, was the real devil. She ran the family organisation to all intents and purposes, and cultivated relationships to hide her husband's proclivities.

'Sir Mark knew nothing. He led a mostly cosseted upbringing, even after his father died. His mother still ran things, asking only for Sir Mark to appear at a handful of board meetings. But he began getting more involved, starting the property development himself. That was when he started looking into the family affairs a little closer. He noticed payments through various shell companies in Panama—'

'Omicron Holdings,' Boone interrupted.

'Yes. And others. Then he found out about Sarah Still.'

'I thought he knew her as a child?'

'Knew her would be overstating it. He had met her, family days at the business, things like that. I doubt he would have known her if he'd run into her in the street.'

'So what did he find out?'

'That she was his half-sister.'

'Alex Blackborne slept with Molly Still's daughter?'

'That's one way of putting it. Savagely abused her would be another.'

'That's why she left?'

'Left?'

'Australia, Molly told me.'

'She was a troubled girl, but what happened pushed her over the edge. She was institutionalised for years. One morning they found her body in a pond. It was winter and the water had frozen and there she was, looking up through the ice. They had to cut her out.'

'Suicide?'

Tanner nodded. 'It was all covered up. The place where she was, it's privately funded. A closet for the rich to hide their skeletons in. The police were never called, no death certificate issued. She just . . . disappeared. As though she had never even been. Teddy had already arranged for a payment to the Stills. They concocted this story about an insurance settlement. I hadn't heard the Australia story before. I suppose the family needed something to tell people.'

'I don't get it. Teddy killed Mark because he knew about Omicron? *I* know about Omicron, and I told Teddy I know. Why not kill me?'

'There's more.'

'Such as?'

'I don't know what you know about Sarah. How much the police told you.'

'I know she died from a blow to the head. Probably from Milan Jedinek. I know she'd had a child.'

'It was Alex's.'

'What was?'

'The child.'

'But Sarah was . . .'

'Yes. He would see her from time to time when she was growing up. In her teens he started buying her things. Expensive things. She attended parties he threw, and they began a sexual relationship. She ran away from home shortly afterwards.'

'Did she know?'

'That he was her father? I don't know.'

'How do you know all this, about Sarah having Blackborne's child too?'

'She told Mark. There was an attempt at . . . blackmail, I suppose. We only have her word for it, but the pieces fit.'

'Jesus. I thought she was blackmailing him over the parties Alex held. I thought Mark was covering up for his father.'

'Far from it. Mark wanted to help Sarah. He thought she deserved to be part of the family. I don't think he fully grasped who she was, though. He had some ludicrous idea about having a new sister, but I think by that point Sarah was . . . I don't know. The things that had happened, who knows what that does to a person?'

'The parties. Where were they?'

'I don't know. Not at Cornilo, that's for sure.'

'No, there's another house. It is somewhere round here, though.'

'If it is, I never knew about it. Neither did Mark.'

'Abby?'

The study door pushed open and Jack appeared.

'Who the hell are you?' he said, looking at Tanner.

'Mum?'

Quin stood in the doorway, staring at Boone holding the shotgun on an old man, face screwed up with incomprehension. To teach a boy the harsh lesson that nothing is for ever, take his mother away from him. To teach him about cruelty, give her back to him with everything that made her who she was scooped out.

For the first time, Boone saw something of herself in the boy. Who she was, what she had become, everything she had brought into his life. It might have been close to an epiphany had it not been so horrifying, the dawning realisation that the defining sensation of her life now was fear – a fear of knowing people and of being known by them, a fear now reflected in the face of her son.

'Quin, I . . .'

The boy looked terrified.

'You need to leave, before I call the police,' Jack told Tanner.

The man looked suddenly so old and frail to Boone, cowering before her shotgun. How had she got this so wrong, so very badly wrong?

Tanner stared at his coat on the floor at Boone's feet. Quickly she lowered the gun and picked the coat up, proffering it to him. Hands still raised, he moved gingerly towards her and whipped it from her as if it dangled in the jaws of a trap. Slowly he circled round Boone and, with a nod to Jack, slipped out of the room.

'What the hell were you thinking?' Jack said.

'I had it under control,' Boone said.

'Put the gun down.'

Boone stared at the Mossberg as if only just realising she was holding it.

Ejecting the shells, she made it safe and stood it against the wall.

'Under control?' Jack said. 'You've been down a police station all day, again. Your friend was abducted by the men who almost killed you a year ago. A man broke into our house, and you have a shotgun just lying around. I'd say things were pretty fucking far from under control.'

'Jack, I can—'

'No. I really don't think you can.'

Boone nodded.

'I can't have this sort of thing,' he said. 'Not with Quin here.'

She stepped towards the boy, but he moved behind his father, out of her reach.

'Jack?' she said.

'I think it's best if you go,' he said. 'Until we sort this out.'

Picking up the shotgun, she said, 'I'll get a bag.'

They followed her upstairs and watched quietly from the door-way as she stuffed a few things into a shoulder bag. It had all been so easy to rebel against because she had taken it for granted, assumed it would always be there – a husband, a son, a house.

A home.

She slid the shotgun back in its case. When she went for the iPod in its dock, Quin reached over before her and took it, putting it in his pocket.

'It's mine,' he said.

Boone nodded. Finishing hurriedly, she headed downstairs, husband and son escorting her to the door. Looking at Quin, Boone tried to imagine him as a little boy, and before that as an infant. Imagined how it must have been that he came into the world. Her throat thickened.

In his face she finally felt that which she had lost. Some intrinsic and essential thing that was gone for ever, without her even knowing what it was, without having a name for it. There would be other losses, but none greater.

50

Outside, Boone got on the phone to Barb.

'Boone? Everything all right?'

'Listen, your offer for a car to be stationed outside.'

'Changed your mind?'

'Yeah. Stupid. It would be great if you could sort that.'

'Done. I arranged for someone to drive past every hour anyway. I'll get them put outside full time.'

'Cheers, Barb.'

Pocketing the phone, Boone slung her bag over her shoulder and tried to formulate a plan. She had no idea where she was going. She started down the road but stopped after a few paces, turning back to the house. The door was closed. She was having difficulty breathing. Putting down her bag, she slowly lowered herself onto one knee. Air shuddered from her as it must have when she gave birth. A wave of despair broke over her, so completely was she lost, so surely did she believe herself damned.

'Excuse me, are you all right?'

Tanner was standing in the road, the other side of a parked car.

'Shit,' Boone said.

'I have a car. Is there anywhere I can take you?'

Boone stared at him, his questions making no sense. She'd been fully ready to unload the Mossberg into his chest not five minutes earlier. Her phone was ringing somewhere and she searched her pockets. It was Tess.

'Tess?'

'Where are you?'

She looked up at the house. 'Home.'

'Fitz said you think they'll have taken her to that house?'

'I . . . Yeah. Probably.'

'So how do we find it?'

'I lost the phone. Sarah's phone. The police have it. I need the photos.'

'I have them. Can you get here?'

Boone looked at Tanner. 'Yeah. I think so.'

'Good.'

The line cut off. Boone got up and grabbed her bag.

'I need to get to the Medway,' she said.

Tanner shrugged. 'You're the one with the gun.'

'Look, I . . .'

He waved her off. 'Too many people have been hurt in all of this already. You need to get your friend back.'

They spoke sparingly in the car, and lulled by the soft purr of the engine, Boone felt suddenly exhausted. In her jacket pocket she found her headphones, unconnected and useless now, impotent without anything to feed them music. She slipped the buds into her ears anyway, to dampen the sounds of the road, the clamour of her mind.

51

At the kitchen table, Tess had the photos from Sarah Still's phone up on Mickey Box's laptop. She was all business. Boone desperately wanted to tell her about Jack and Quin, and in turn be told what she should do, receive some kind word. There was a gulf between them now, though, like there was a gulf between Boone and the world, it seemed.

'You made copies,' she said.

'You didn't?'

Boone sipped her coffee. Tanner sat very straight at the table with a cup of tea. He was uncomfortable, both under the gaze of Mickey Box and Fitz, who stood over them all, and looking at the images taken from Sarah Still's phone. He had been adamant he knew nothing of any other properties owned by the late Sir Alex Blackborne, but had agreed to go through the images in the hope he might recognise something.

'So your boy wasn't in on the nonce stuff?' Fitz said.

Tanner shook his head.

'He's okay, Fitz,' Boone said. 'Leave him be.'

'Some of these images look very old,' Tanner said.

'Over thirty years some of them, we reckon,' Boone said.

'So almost the whole time I knew him, then,' said Tanner. He took his time, clicking past each image once he'd scrutinised it, occasionally leaning in for a closer look. He said little, but his expression betrayed all. Some things could never be unseen.

Frowning, he removed his spectacles and peered down his great aquiline nose, shuffling his chair closer to the table to get nearer the screen.

'Something?' Tess said.

'Can we look at a detail?' Tanner said. 'Move in on a particular section?'

'Whereabouts?' Tess said, taking the mouse.

'The mirror here,' he said.

It was one of the first images Boone had found, taken from the memory card in Milan's car. A young girl standing in an upstairs room, a mirror on the wall behind her.

'That's how I knew Ingram's magazine showed the same place,' Boone said. 'The mirror, and the window frame reflected in it.'

'It's what's outside the window that interests me,' Tanner said.

Tess zoomed in on the mirror, and in further to the window frame, and further still to what lay in the distance. A grey shape, vaguely triangular, possibly metallic, but muddied by distance and age.

'A building?' Tess said.

Tanner shook his head. 'I believe it's the headgear of a mine pit. Specifically, the A-frame structure at Corringstone. It was the only colliery in Kent that had this type of headgear. There was a fuss when they took it down; people wanted it preserved.'

'Can't reopen a mine with no stock,' Mickey Box said.

'Exactly,' Tanner agreed. 'The picture must date to the eighties. Mine closed in '89, and the stock was pulled down not long after. Capped off the shafts and then left the rest of the buildings to rot.

'Jesus,' Boone said. 'That means this place must be in Kearswood. All the times Sarah went there, she was just round the corner from home.' She got to her feet. 'I need to go out there,' she said. 'Find this place.'

'It's the middle of the night,' said Tess. 'You won't find anything in the dark. And what are you going to do anyway, knock on every door and ask if she's inside?'

Boone looked at the picture again.

'The window frame,' she said. 'And the view.'

The casements featured ornate Gothic arches, unlike the houses built for miners, and the headgear was visible above trees and bushes. 'Has to be on the edge of Kearswood. A place on its own.'

'It's not in Kearswood,' Tanner said.

'Of course it is,' said Boone. 'You said yourself, that's Corringstone.'

'I know Kearswood quite well. Many years ago I stepped out with a village girl. From the high street, you could see the colliery across the fields.' He pointed at the picture on the screen. 'It's the wrong way round there.'

'Yeah, but it's a reflection,' Tess said.

'Aye, but what I mean is the stock didn't face that way. It stood with the winches pulling east to west, so from the village you saw them head on. Not from the side like this. The picture must have been taken from the north or south. And see this here.' He pointed to a blurred shape at the leftmost edge of the image, what appeared to be a conical tower. 'That's the thickener for the washery. It was to the east of the shafts. So if this was in a mirror, the window must be north-facing. There are several lanes meandering around the south of the site. Can't say that I know them at all, but I'd guess the place you're looking for is down that way.'

Boone picked up her bags.

'You need sleep,' Mickey Box said.

'Let her go,' Tess said.

Boone searched the girl's face but didn't find anything telling.

Off some unseen signal from Mickey Box, Fitz had departed. Tanner made his excuses too.

'What are you going to do?' Boone said.

'I have a small place in Pembrokeshire,' he said. 'I'll lie low there.'

They heard his car start up and his lights faded away down the drive. Boone looked at Tess, willing her to meet her eyes, trying to find some opening with her. There was none to be had. Finding her earphones in her pocket again, she fiddled with them, slipped them into her ears. She fingered the gold plug at the other end.

'Not sure you're grasping how those things work,' Mickey Box said.

Boone smiled. 'Lost the iPod.'

'Oh aye?' he said, indifferent.

'Well, Quin took it back. It's his really. I left home tonight. Jack wasn't happy with the way things were going, and what with Tanner dropping by and me with the shotgun. I think I really scared Quin. It's mine, he said, and took it.'

'Well,' Mickey Box said, feelings and the like not being his forte.

A dark van rolled up the drive and Fitzy stepped out. They joined him outside and he tossed the keys to Boone. Mickey Box walked her round the vehicle, pointing out this and that.

'Looks like shit on the outside, but it's rebuilt under the bonnet,' he said. 'Friend of a friend in Swansea, so it's in the system. Can't be traced back here.'

A windowless Transit, you wouldn't give it a second glance. Few dents here and there, rust on the arches.

Pulling her aside, Mickey Box said, 'I can send Fitz with you. This is madness on your own.'

'Someone needs to be here watching Tess,' Boone said.

'I'm doing that.'

'And someone needs to be here watching you.'

Mickey Box bristled. 'Perfectly capable of dealing with anyone stupid enough to come here uninvited.'

'I find it, I'm going to call Barb,' Boone said. 'She'll have vans of tooled-up coppers there in no time.'

'Guess them cunts have to serve some purpose.'

Boone touched the side of the van. 'Mick? Thank you.'

'We'll talk about it when you get back,' he said.

Tess lingered when Mickey Box and Fitz went back inside.

'Probably he meant the music,' Tess said.

Boone frowned. 'What do you mean?'

'Quin. He meant the music, not the player. He's fourteen. Why is he listening to loads of bands from years before he was born? You're always saying you and he have nothing to say to each other, but talking isn't the only means of communication. He was listening to those bands because it's your music. He was exploring your life because you'd lost it. He was sharing it with you, and sharing part of himself at the same time. It was a gift.'

Boone twisted her bottom lip between her fingers. She said nothing. The central fucking pain in the balls of life as she saw it was you had to live it forwards but it could only be understood backwards.

52

Tired, she took the motorway down to coal country, peach-lit in the cool night. Kearswood reared up out of nowhere like it always did, and Boone parked the van in the gated mouth of a field fifty yards shy of the first buildings on the main road. Fervent with fear and fatigue, she studied online aerial maps of the wooded expanse south of the colliery for possible locations. There were several likely-looking lanes.

She yawned like an old cat lying in the sun. She couldn't remember sleep, hadn't had any since before Roo was snatched. The world had changed in the meantime. She closed her eyes. Just for a moment, just to clear the old noggin. A tractor passing brought her to with a jolt and it was bright, morning sun bringing the world into sharp silver focus.

'Fuck,' she said.

Almost nine. She'd slept for hours. The van rattled into life and she swung it round in the wide gateway and headed back to the first turning, looping round to the roads south of the colliery.

The first place wasn't a house at all but an old granary built on staddle stones that resembled toadstools. Its roof was long gone, and even from the roadside Boone could see its timbers were dark and damp with rot.

With the headstock no longer standing, it was difficult to gauge her exact position. The next place she came to was an old thatched cottage called Little Ecks, but the windows didn't match, and the place was largely obscured by mature trees, which wouldn't have afforded much of a view of the colliery buildings. Further down the hedged lane she found a heavily rutted track cutting off into a wild wood, a Mohawk strip of grass growing high down the middle. It wasn't marked on the maps. It was deeply potted, some of the holes half filled with gravel a lifetime ago, and moving at more than a couple of miles an hour looked impossible without her head snapping back and forth.

Moving on down the lane, she came to another route branching off, a grassy patch formed in the fork between the two roads. Leaving the van there, she took the gun bag and walked back to the unmarked track, heading in for a closer look.

It had rained recently but now there was only dripping in the woods. The damp was close, not fresh, and the green seemed drawn on. She followed the track from about ten yards inside the trees, considering how nature conspired against a stealthy approach. Remain among the trees unseen but every step a crackle and snap of twig and growth underfoot, or walk soundlessly along the track for all to see.

The first she knew of it was the smell of the fire. Not rich like woodsmoke but a dark and toxic stench. Black wisps coiled around the trees. The woods darkened beneath a thick canopy and the track was all but vanished beneath the undergrowth when she saw the white walls flicker in the interstitial gaps. After years of neglect the woods had closed upon the house, branches pawing at windows and roof, creeping things attaching themselves to the walls and strangling the chimneys. What light was allowed to fall upon the place came indirectly from the north, where a meadow opened up behind the house. A large place, built not by a farmer but with merchant money, though now in some disrepair.

Boone hurried further into the woods and approached in a wide curve from the side. Out behind the house, two steel drums smoked furiously, flames sawing across their brims as a hooded man squeezed fluid over them from a plastic bottle. She crouched, gammy leg stretched out to the side, and watched in stillness. The man stood for minutes before the fires, fast and pyrolatrous. What looked like shoeboxes were stacked at his feet, and every so often he tossed one into a drum to feed the flames.

The ground behind the house was open and Boone couldn't circle it that way without risking being seen, so she returned the way she'd come and crossed the track back out of sight, coming round from the other side. A blue Transit was parked tight to the side of the house beneath a small window high in the wall. Not the vehicle Roo had been taken in.

Keeping as low as she could, she scooted up for a closer look. Staying on the far side of the van from the house, she peered through the driver's window but couldn't see anything that gave it away as being the men she was looking for.

A door opened and banged shut. She hurried into the bushes and pressed herself flat on the ground behind a tree. Lifting her head, she moved it enough for one eye to see round the trunk.

The big one was there.

She ducked involuntarily when she saw him come round the front of the van, held her breath as he looked round, casually scanning the woods. He was lighter-skinned than she remembered, so much so that she wondered if it was the same man.

That walk, though.

The way his bulk swayed from side to side.

Thick-wristed, with hands like the blades of shovels. He lumbered round to the driver's door and hauled himself up into the seat, the whole thing rocking as he did. He hit the horn, long then short, and the other, the one with the scars, came running. The van moved off, pitching down the track, in and out of its potholes.

Retreating into the woods, Boone called Barb. The reception was patchy and she was almost back at the road when she got through.

'Boone?'

'I've found them.'

'What?'

'The men. They changed vehicles, they have a blue van now. I don't know if Roo's here. They're burning things.'

'Where?'

Boone told her where the house was, explaining as best she could without knowing the names of any roads.

'I've got people coming, Boone. Don't go in there.'

'Yeah.'

'Listen to me, Boone. Armed officers are coming. They'll do it right and they'll do it safe. You stay away. Go back to the road and wait there. I'm coming too. We have to find the place, though.'

'Can you track the phone?'

'Someone's looking at it.'

'I'll leave it on then,' Boone said.

She placed the handset on the ground and began moving back through the woods towards the house, Barb's voice dying in the air behind her.

53

Boone unsheathed her shotgun and loaded three shells, more in her pockets. Scurrying up to the front door, she found it locked. Hitch in her step, she skipped round the back where the drums smouldered still, and rattled the back door, also locked.

'Fuck it and bollocks.'

The windows were gunmetal blue where they reflected the greying skies, and she had to press her nose against the glass to see through. The house was dark, the furniture unchanged in the years since the pictures she'd seen of it. One window was open slightly, fixed on the first hole of its brass stay. The gap wasn't enough to get her hand in to reach it, but with a found branch she lifted the arm off the peg and pulled the window wide.

She clambered into a dusty parlour, with winged armchairs and small wooden tables. Pieces you'd find in a doll's house. The downstairs was as empty as it was uninteresting, the only sign of recent activity a small safe, conspicuously modern among the other furnishings, door open and emptied of its contents. The furniture was old, the upholstery dusty, and though well used in the past, it gave the impression of not having been sat in for years. The whole place felt abandoned. There was a kitchen with darkly tiled floor and walls, and squatting within a huge bricked-up hearth was a fat iron stove.

Behind the kitchen was a small room, a drain at the centre of its stone floor. The only furniture was a heavy wooden table, dark stains in its smooth top. A limescaled tap protruded from the wall, its constant drip wearing away the stone beneath and trickling through the grouting to the drain.

Clearing the downstairs, Boone turned her attention to the upper floor. Keeping to the outside of the steps, feet in the white paint that would have bordered the runner had there been one, she climbed them slowly, looking down the barrel of the shotgun. A few of them groaned in argument still.

The small landing at the top was bordered by two further steps up to the doorways to three rooms, and a short passage to two more. A cardboard tray containing bottles of lighter fluid was pushed against the banisters, its shrink-wrapped caul ripped open. Perhaps they planned to burn down the entire place. She paused, palm flat to the wall to mask her shakes, sure that the clapperings of her heart would give her away to anyone who might be waiting.

She crept to the first door and leaned into it, listening.

Nothing.

She tried the handle, round and brassy, dulled by time.

It turned loosely, its mechanism sprung, and the door pushed open.

A rudimentary bedroom, undressed double divan with no accompanying furniture. Thick floral curtains were tied open, but the encroaching trees allowed little light to pass into the room.

She crossed the small landing to the room the other side of the stairs. The door was ajar and revealed a similarly spare bedchamber, but Boone recognised the view from the window, shorn now of the solid presence of the headstock in the distance. She edged into the room, the wooden furniture and wall mirror from the old Polaroids long since gone.

As she moved to the third room immediately off the landing, the small step up to the door reported like a gunshot underfoot.

Boone froze.

Imperceptibly, she raised her foot, as she might from a landmine, but it creaked all the louder for her caution as it rose back into place.

She remained still, waiting for someone to burst out of a door or charge the stairs two at a time.

Nobody came.

Her hand closed silently round the handle and gently tried it.

Unlocked.

She opened it and went in fast, keeping low and sweeping the space with the shotgun. The room was different to the others. Against the wall to the right was a shelving unit that housed an array of media equipment, cameras and screens and rows of tapes in their cases. Behind the door was an elephantine old cylinder-top writing bureau, its desk a clutter of yellowed papers and sunbleached card folders. In another corner a television sat atop a large upturned wooden crate, component cables dangling down from plugs behind its open fascia.

The videos on the shelves were labelled by date only. There was no VCR so she assumed the cables connected to the telly were for a camera that doubled as playback. The papers on the desk were years old and of logistical interest only, receipts and the like. She checked the top drawer and stood up straight from what she found. Polaroids. Probably hundreds of them, chucked in there in no discernible order.

Some were like the ones she'd seen already, unsmiling children posed against walls, everything in their faces contracting down to the pinpricks of their eyes and the small black idea of terror that lay therein.

One in particular bothered her, a young boy with a scar across his chin, staring in fear at something behind the camera.

Others were of a magnitude of horror she wished she'd never seen. She dropped them back and held her fingers out like something was on them.

Something that would never come off.

She was backing away from the bureau when she heard a sound.

Wet, raspy, a human sound.

Not loud, maybe not even deliberate, but definitely close.

One of the last two rooms.

She got back out onto the landing and stayed close to the walls, creeping into the short hallway leading to the other two doors. The first was wide open, a bathroom. Stripped down to bare walls and exposed plumbing, the tub plugless and stained. The toilet had no seat.

The last room was at the end of the hall. The door was shut and a small bunch of keys hung from a nail hammered downward into the wall nearby. Boone tried the handle anyway, knowing it was going to be locked.

The sound again, inside the room.

She slid the key into the lock and the tongue slid back with silent heft.

When the door opened, for a moment she was unsure of who it was. She lay on the spring wires of a bed, no mattress, wrists cuffed to the head of the metal frame. Her nose, or the first inch of it anyway, had been severed, exposing the nasal cavity with swinish abruption. Her head was shapeless with violence, one eye bulging in terror and the other absent, a pink slit narrowed amid the swelling. Bruises marbled her flesh deeply, her skin gouged with jagged cross-hatches.

'Roo,' Boone whispered.

She ran to her.

The sound seemed to be coming from what was left of her nose.

'I have you,' Boone said. 'I have you.'

She touched Roo's chin gently, about the only part of her face that didn't look broken, and looked into her good eye to let her know.

'It's me, Roo. It's Boone.'

The sound was different now. Roo's lips moved, but her mouth was full of blood and bits, most of her top teeth sheared off at the gums. Boone put her ear to the bubbling gap.

'Up a whale's arse,' Roo managed.

Boone grinned and cried all at once. She shook off her jacket and covered her friend's exposed body. Laying down the gun, she ran to the door and snatched the keys from the lock, fiddling with them, but her hands simply would not stop shaking.

'Stupid fuckmitts,' she said, fanning the keys out on the ring.

One was small enough for the cuffs. She hurried back to Roo and went to work on the bracelets, freeing her hands. They'd broken a ring of skin around each wrist, bloodied and beginning to scab.

Boone cradled the girl's hands in hers, her fingers going like little pincers.

'Oh Jesus, what have they done, what have they done, what have they done.'

A camera stood on a tripod behind the door. Boone could see dried blood on the handle strap.

Roo's head lolled from side to side, and Boone slipped her hand beneath it and gently lifted it up. Roo made a noise of pain and Boone let her down again slowly.

'Okay, okay. You're okay.'

Her hand came away slick with blood. A pool of it had formed on the floor under Roo, some head injury Boone couldn't yet see. Then she heard it.

A drone.

A remote hum.

The rumble of the world coming to its inevitable end.

The van returning.

54

Roo's one eye looked as if it might pop from its socket as she craned her head towards the window. Boone got up and peered out. The blue van pulled up beneath her, the two men already getting out, the big one with a white carrier bag in his hand. Boone could smell the food.

'Roo, we're going to have to move. I know, I'm sorry, but we have to shift.' Clamping the shotgun under one arm, she held Roo by the elbow and braced behind her back, the girl clamping her eye shut as she strained to sit up. Her head fell limply against Boone's shoulder, and Boone got Roo's arm around her own neck and hauled her up to her feet. Roo was reeling, feet refusing to answer the call to duty.

'Come on,' Boone said, as much to herself as Roo, as she struggled to drag her friend to the door.

They got as far as the bathroom door, at the mouth of the short corridor off the landing, when Boone met his gaze. He was at the foot of the stairs, the big one, and a light from somewhere lent his eyes the shine of a nocturnal animal.

He smiled.

'Go, go,' Boone said, heaving Roo into the bathroom. 'Lock the door behind me,' she said, pulling it closed. The bolt slid shut and she raised the shotgun, letting off three quick shots where she had seen the face. Plaster powder exploded from the wall downstairs.

He appeared again at the bottom of the stairs and charged up them. Boone went to reload the shotgun, but the shells were in her jacket pocket and she'd put it round Roo. She ran back to the room where she'd found Roo and shut the door behind her. The keys were on the floor by the bed. She scrambled for them and rushed back to the door, trying to sort the one for the lock from the others, her mind a rush of thoughts all seemingly doing their best to prevent her completing even the most simple of tasks. Her hands were complicit in the betrayal, trembling, the movie of her world coming free from its sprockets.

She was moving at pace when the door burst inwards, the impact knocking her off her feet and crashing through the tripod and camera. The shotgun skidded across the floor.

Her legs never stopped moving, and as soon as she turned over, Boone was scuttling away from him on all fours, vaulting over the bed and pressing her back against the far wall.

Her fists closed around the bar on the head of the bed and she dragged it between them, a lame buffer that he tossed aside with one swipe of a giant hand, the frame flipping over and skidding on its side into the wall beneath the window.

He moved in on her.

Boone stamped down with her foot, outwardly onto the instep of his, immediately throwing an elbow into his head to follow.

He laughed.

A huge hand reached out and took her by the throat, raising her onto her toes. She thought her entire head might fit inside that hand. He balled his other fist and struck her below the eye, hard and repeatedly, before throwing her back into the wall.

A funny sensation took around her eye, as if something had suddenly grown in there. She tried to blink it away, rolling her jaw and clenching her cheek, trying to work it out.

There was no time for that.

She was being dragged across the floor by her hair and she was being punched. She was being punched in the face, she was being punched in the breasts, she was being punched in the belly. She didn't know how long this was taking; time was no longer of importance. She couldn't see properly any more.

She lay on her front, his breath on the back of her neck.

'I'm going to break every bone in your face. Break everything about it. Then I'm going to kick down the bathroom door and get your friend. I'm going to burn her alive and make you watch. That'll be the last thing you see. That'll be how this ends.'

He twisted her left arm up viciously behind her back, lifting her a foot from the floor, and she cried out.

'You thought you were going to save Sarah? There was no saving to be done. She was one of us, not one of you. Who do you think found girls for us? Who do you think brought them to the taxis? She could have gone home any time she wanted.'

'No,' Boone shouted. She bucked and wrenched until he jerked her arm just a little harder. The wrist she'd broken before, in her accident. The wrist *he'd* broken.

An extraordinary pain cut off any thoughts.

Boone screeched, tears coming quickly. He released her and

she slumped back to the floor, arm still behind her. There was too much pain to try to move.

He dragged her arm back down to her side and rolled her over. Instinctively she tried to bring her hand up, but he sat astride her chest, stretching her arms out and pinning them down with his knees. The weight of him was excruciating, his bulk thick and suffocating. Her eye, the one that felt funny, had closed completely, and the other was dewy and she couldn't blink away the wet.

She never saw it coming when he smashed her mouth. Hard and sharp and chill, a spanner maybe, or a length of pipe.

One hand clamped round her skull, the other drove his tool of choice into her lips. Things tore and broke and she choked on blood running back down her throat, her tongue feeling out strange objects, hard pellets and soft ribbons. Bits of her.

Something inside Boone went. It wasn't a discernible process; nothing had broken or snapped. It was only the awareness that had come suddenly, that the truth she knew of the world was upended and that she welcomed death. No, yearned for it. It promised release, an exquisite relief. It promised grace.

The cheek of a blade pressed against the side of her nose. It turned, and she felt the quick of its edge, the curve of its belly, a fineness along the nostril. But as she felt the pressure change, some unthinking part of her raged against her capitulation and she struck out against the inside of his arm. The blade slipped and tore across her face, right down to the bone, and ran up to the outer corner of her eye.

'Cunt,' he spat.

Her face was slick and Boone couldn't tell what damage had

been done, which parts of her were still whole and which dismembered.

This was it. His sadism had harrowed a bottomless silence within him. There was only the breath shooting thick and fast from his nose.

The leaves against the window glass like tiny hands.

Fugitive light through the branches lambent across the flat of the knife.

There was noise. An explosion, and a rattle like hail against a window. She screamed, louder and deeper than she thought possible, so much so that she no longer recognised her own voice.

Except it wasn't her voice at all.

He reared back and swung off her. Through one eye, over his shoulder, Boone saw Roo standing there wearing her jacket, bloody and holding the shotgun. The shot loosened her grip on the gun and before she could fire again he lunged forward and backhanded her, taking her off her feet. His shirt was shredded at the back of the shoulder, sopped with blood already.

Crabbing backwards along the floor away from him, Boone banged her head on the frame of the upturned bed. Reaching into her mouth, she removed the broken bridge from the mess that was her teeth. She pulled herself up against the cool metal, something loose dangling against her arm.

'Where are you going?'

He loomed over her, hiking up his trousers and squatting. His injured arm hung uselessly at his side. She grabbed his other wrist, thick as a baby's neck, unable to close her hand around it. He laughed.

'What are you doing?' He spoke playfully, as if to a small pet.

Boone snapped the bracelet from one of the handcuffs on to his wrist and rolled away, hearing him pull at it, the bed scratching against the wooden floor.

'What do you think this'll do?'

As she fought to her feet, he lifted the bed frame in front of him and charged with it, running her into the wall next to the door. She felt it giving behind her, the lath and plaster caving in and leaving a Boone-shaped indentation.

He pulled back and came again, but Boone threw herself over the foot of the bed, landing on the wire mesh. Reaching out, she got hold of a leg of the tripod, swinging it round in a continuous movement and catching him upside the head with the camera end.

It wasn't much, but it was enough. He roared, face ceilingward, anger engulfing his sadism. Boone tumbled off the bed, snatched up the shotgun and with the same hand clutched Roo's arm, dragging her out into the corridor. Roo was barely there, legs dancing like a newborn animal, good eye rolling about in her head. Something up there was uncottered, mind freed from its moorings. He was after them, but the bed frame stuck in the doorway, too wide to come through flat. As he wrestled with the problem, trying in his rage to drag it through the gap any which way it would come, Boone managed to get a shell free from her jacket pocket before she pushed Roo back into the bathroom. Her arm was broken and doing everything one-handed was slowing her down.

A scarred face peered up from the downstairs hallway. He held his own gun, a double-barrel sawn down to about eighteen inches without a choke. Getting it from the van was probably what had delayed him. He went for the stairs at pace, raising the gun before him, as Boone reached for a bottle of lighter fluid from the tray on the landing. Squirting it at him and over the floor and walls, she crashed back towards the bathroom, working the shell into the tube of the gun with her good hand.

They fired simultaneously.

Everything happened at once. Little bites up Boone's thigh as she fell into the bathroom. She flicked her lighter and tossed it, flames rolling up the walls and over the floor with a *whoosh*. From the floor, she shut the door against the heat and slid the bolt across.

Another shot splintered the door above the lock, but it held tight. Voices beyond the door, frantic and foreign. A couple of thumps on the wood, and then nothing.

Her wrist didn't hurt any more, but the blood from her face was everywhere. She felt dizzy and sat back against the wall, trying to breathe steadily through her nose. She fingered the blood from the eye she could still see through.

Jesus Christ.

Hold it together, Boone.

Do not fucking pass out.

Roo was slumped on the seatless toilet, knees awkwardly raised as she sank into the bowl, conscious but unaware.

There was a window high in the wall, over the bath. It was small, but a person might fit through. The voices outside the door were gone, replaced by the crackle and spit of the fire now, a thing in the world, a real threat.

Standing one foot on either edge of the tub, Boone lifted the armbar on the window and pushed the bottom out. It wouldn't open fully, only to about forty-five degrees. She lifted the porcelain lid of the cistern in her good hand and hammered away at the frame, splintering the wood so the casement fell out, the glass shattering somewhere below.

Smoke fingered its way through the slender gaps around the bathroom door, and the bigger one made by the shotgun blast. Boone felt a ferocious heat behind it when she pressed her face in close. Thinking about the videos and pictures in the other room, she tentatively tried the door handle, but it was searing, and she tugged her hand away, leaving skin behind.

'Shite. They've lit the whole place up. Roo, we need to go through that window.'

If the girl understood, she gave no indication. Boone pulled her to her feet and tried to get her to climb up on the bath, but she seemed beyond even simple instructions. She cupped Roo's face with her hand, looked into her one eye, her wild and roaming eye.

'Roo?'

The eye settled on Boone, took her in.

'I need you to follow me now.'

She clambered up on the bath and, holding Roo's hand, pulled the girl up behind her. Roo's foot slipped off the edge, but Boone had her under one arm, barely able to support the weight. She leaned against the rough wall and hooked Roo's arm round her own neck. There was a unit at the end of the bath, half beneath the window, which would have held towels and flannels had there been such things. It was a good couple of feet higher than the tub and offered something to get a purchase on.

Boone steered Roo upwards, one foot on the cabinet, arms through the window like she was wriggling into a tight top. It was hard to see outside past her.

'Grab the pipe, Roo,' she said.

Roo twisted slightly and had her hands round the drainpipe next to the window. Boone shoved her artlessly through the hole, hoping she could hold onto the pipe long enough for Boone to be able to reach through and offer assistance.

She couldn't.

As her feet disappeared through the window, Roo swung down and lost her grip on the pipe. Fifteen, sixteen feet probably. Mercifully, she arced away from the concrete drain surround and a neglected flower bed softened the landing somewhat, hitting thigh-first into the weeds, arms up about her head. She rolled on to her back and didn't move much.

'Roo? Roo?'

The room was filling with smoke, making it difficult to see, and an amber glow flickered at the rim of the door. Boone was losing a lot of blood from her face, her top bibbed with red. She went through the window good arm first, knees on top of the cabinet. Clutching the downpipe, she hauled her legs through and managed to find a footing on a wall bracket.

Her grip held but the pipe didn't. It pulled free of the wall and Boone angled slowly away from the house, as if gravity's batteries were running down. Her legs came away from the pipe and the pain when her hip slammed into the edge of the blue van's roof was all-encompassing. She landed hard on the gravel beside the van and remained still, immediately fearing she had shattered her femur again, this time mangling herself around the steel rod that was still inside her. She could taste the iron of her own blood.

Blinking her eyes open, from where she lay on her back the smoke tumbled out of the house and away from her into the sky, knitting into the clouds.

Somewhere a window shattered; elsewhere flames licked at the panes.

The sound of sirens.

The leaves above her blushed blue, on and off, on and off.

She turned her head and searched for Roo, finding her heaped in havoc among the weeds and indomitable daffs. She was motionless except for the thumb and first finger on one hand, slowly furling and unfurling like the surviving legs of a crushed crab, semaphoring her distress.

55

They were carried in separate ambulances to the same hospital. Boone nagged doctors and nurses alike for information on Roo, barely able to make herself understood through the injuries to her mouth.

Roo's head injury was severe, she was told.

They would have to operate, she was told.

Yes, her head would be shaved, she was told.

Boone's face was a godawful mess, she knew that from the looks she got. Pure horror show. They did what they could, cleaning and stitching wounds. Surgery would be needed on her mouth and eye, and the knife wound. The swelling would need to come down first.

Her teeth were smashed, what teeth she had left after the first time. God knows what sort of dental prosthesis would be needed now. The whole way over in the ambulance, Boone had tongued away at the new landscape of her mouth, trying to make sense of it. Felt like she had four lips, as if it opened like a starfish. Nobody understood a word she said, even when she was merely repeating back what they told her.

The arm needed surgery, more metal inside her. Barb was waiting when the doctors were finished with her. Boone pointed to her mouth. *Can't fucking talk.*

Barb gave her a notepad and pen. She wrote, *Can't fucking talk.* 'Good job you're not a southpaw,' Barb said.

There would be many people and many questions and Boone would do much talking in the days and weeks to come, but for now she was silent. Barb told her they'd found a small van abandoned near a lock-up on the outskirts of Lark that wasn't covered by CCTV. They must have had it parked somewhere in the woods across the field at the rear of the house. Someone, possibly suffering the effects of a shotgun blast, had left behind a useful amount of blood in the back. It was being tested against samples taken from Roo. Beyond that, there was no trace of the two men. Vanished into thin air. The working theory was that they'd had another vehicle stashed at the lock-up, but analysis of local cameras had so far turned up nothing.

The house itself had been completely gutted inside, the floors collapsing and bedrooms falling into the rooms below. All the tapes and photos were gone, burned up in the fire.

Boone was only half listening. She tugged at Barb's hand and scribbled on the pad.

No visitors, she wrote. Then, *NONE*, underlined twice.

Barb said she understood.

Boone heard from a doctor that Roo had suffered massive cerebral haemorrhage and they'd had to remove part of her skull to relieve the pressure. She hadn't yet regained consciousness.

Tell me the good news, Boone wrote on her pad for her doctor. And he did. Her femur and thigh were not broken, though the end of the screw that protruded from her previous injury was a bit dinged up. He didn't think she needed the rod in her bone any more and, given her predilection for falling out of buildings (his words), he wanted to remove it to mitigate future and inevitable catastrophes.

It's fair, Boone scribbled.

Heavy bruising meant she couldn't walk for shit, so Barb rolled her to critical care in a wheelchair. She was allowed briefly to sit beside Roo and, on account of the fact she couldn't talk, psychically read to her tales of headstrong women in revolutionary Paris from a book Barb had brought for her.

After a while, Tess arrived, Barb having arranged for her to be allowed visitation. Pausing at the door when she saw Boone, she hovered for a moment, unsure of whether to come in.

Hey kid, Boone wrote on her pad, holding it up.

Tess's face broke into red anguish and she wept. Boone left the book on the side of the bed for Tess to read to Roo and nodded for Barb to roll her out. Tess didn't reach for her as she went by.

On the second day, Barb gave her an update on the investigation. She told her French police had sent pictures of someone possibly matching the description of the man with the scarred face. Under an Algerian passport in the name Abdelkader Belmokhtar, he'd boarded a ferry from Marseilles to Annaba. It was thought he had crossed the Channel undetected by ferry or the tunnel, and driven to the south of France. Barb showed Boone a blurry CCTV still, but it was enough to know it was him. Of the big one there was no sign.

'They made discoveries at the house, the SOCOs,' Barb said, settling down into the chair at Boone's bedside. 'The dogs caught a whiff of something. They excavated the grounds out back. Four sets of remains so far. One of them, they're saying it's a child of no more than ten or eleven. Down there thirty years they reckon from the clothing. At least one of the others is more recent, though, five or six years. We're waiting on analysis of satellite data before we continue searching. There's a firm coming in, they have ground-penetrating radar, magnetic gradiometers, equipment to measure electrical resistivity. We're expecting more remains.'

Ever the optimist, Boone wrote.

'There's something else too. A collapsed wall in the kitchen revealed a hidden space behind. They found an old soakaway in the floor with . . . biological materials.'

Biological? Boone scratched on her pad.

'Foetuses,' Barb said. 'Looks like they performed terminations, or had someone do them.'

Boone picked up her pen. It wavered uselessly over the page before she put it down again.

On the third day, Barb said Roo's family had been traced in Germany and were coming in on a flight that evening. Roo hadn't regained consciousness and doctors were hedging their bets.

An hour before they landed, Roo succumbed to post-operative pneumonia.

SIX

BLIND, WITH A GUN

56

The needed skill was patience.

Not a problem the first few months. The early days were crammed with appointments and consultations and interviews and interrogations. She did what the doctors told her and they said she might heal just fine, maybe. She answered all the detectives' questions and they told her she might avoid being charged, maybe. Tall tales of the Blackbornes and offshore accounts and paedophile rings involving politicians and industrialists were dismissed as baseless accusations, the evidence up in smoke with the house. Nothing linked any Blackborne to the property, which had been purchased decades ago by a Panamanian company long since shuttered. For the life of everyone involved, nobody could say who it actually belonged to now, so the local authority took control.

Full excavation of the site had taken months, revealing eight bodies in all. One, that of a girl of no more than ten, showed signs of injuries consistent with having been hit by a car. A couple sported fractured hyoid bones. Others showed no cause of death that could be discerned from skeletons alone. As far as Kent Police were concerned, the only suspects were the man who called himself Belmokhtar and the other man, the big one.

When the forensic work at the site was complete, the council bulldozed the ruins and turned over the earth. Out of sight, out of mind, like the headstock at Corringstone.

Intramedullary rod removed from her leg, Boone had asked the doctor about her limp.

'Wasn't the rod,' all he said.

Good enough for Boone, she took up a bit of jogging. Didn't do much for her knees, so she bought a bicycle, which she preferred. She lived in the caravan and biked the shore paths every morning, sometimes to the cliffs at Minster, or the marshlands on the south of Sheppey, where she could see great stretches with nothing human visible. She got a sense of the land as it once must have been.

The Goose was written off and Mickey Box let her keep the rebuilt Transit. She got to know the quiet lanes of the coal country, bike racked to the back of the van, and cycled the pitted paths running through the woods. Occasionally she drove to Lark and biked the coast roads, the salt surprising her every time. She took up photography, learned about telephoto lenses and F-stops and hacking firmware, and took pictures wherever she went.

She renewed her interest in shooting and became expert with shotguns, accompanying Mickey Box to hunts on private estates, where they shot quarry regardless of season. Gralloched deer hung on pagan-looking gibbets, smaller game alongside them, and wildfowl were strung from fences. She gained a proficiency with capping and roll turnover tools to fashion bespoke ammunition.

Tess lived at the cottage but kept a distance between them. Boone would catch sight of her, through the bloom of pregnancy and the flush of new motherhood, when she stopped by to see Mickey Box. Then it was Tess and Jim, who watched everything and grabbed at imaginary objects when he thought nobody was looking.

They rarely exchanged more than hellos, and Boone knew Tess held her responsible on two counts. Firstly for losing Roo, and secondly for failing to bring her back in one piece. Boone blamed herself for not having made anyone pay. She lived spartanly, keeping only practical clothes and essential tools. She stocked basic dry foods and bought fresh produce by the meal. Other than the ones she took, the only photographs in the caravan were the framed picture of Sarah Still and Mark Blackborne and a glossy copy of one of the snaps she had taken of Roo trying on her summer dress. The living were departed; only the dead remained. Evenings, Boone would pore over her own photographs or read books from charity shops and market stalls. She made no sense to herself. She was no good with people and in company she craved solitude, yet the thought of existing alone triggered a vertigo that almost levelled her.

Some nights, she thought of Roo. She recalled the movements of her face – a roll of the eyes, a twitch of the nose – and for a moment it would feel like she knew what it was all about. That the world had revealed its true name and she'd always remember it, even after death. The kind of trick of the heart by which the world lives within us.

Occasionally she'd sit out on the decking sipping a glass of red in the evening air, listening for the chuckle of the estuary against the shore. The nocturnal thrum she once had taken for the engine of godly works, she now knew to be nothing more than the veiled whirring of her own heart.

57

Boone awoke from the sleep of the just. Fetching her new bridge from the glass of water on the side, she slid it into her mouth. She rolled her gums, tongued round her mouth till it felt right. She cupped her hand and breathed into it. Sniffed.

'Ugh.'

After showering and brushing her teeth, she walked from the caravan to the cottage. The kitchen door was open, so she went in and began fixing coffee. Through the far window she saw Tess and Jim out on a blanket on the lawn.

'Saw the headlights across the field last night,' Mickey Box said. 'You got in late.'

He came in from the hall, sat at the table. She pointed at the cafetière and he nodded. She poured two cups and sat across from him.

'You need anything?' he said.

Boone shook her head.

'Missions of consequence all done and dusted?'

She nodded.

'Might be ready for some work then?'

Mickey Box charged her no rent and hadn't accepted a penny for the van, but her police pension wouldn't keep her aloft for ever. He had hinted at a few employment opportunities for her when the time came.

'Might be,' Boone said.

'She doesn't know?' he said, looking out at Tess.

'Nope.'

'You going to tell her?'

'Nope. Can't remember the last time we had a conversation anyway.'

'She's never been one to get over things quickly. Doesn't set things in stone, though. Her idea to have you in the caravan. You hear from your friend the detective?'

'They've basically wrapped it up. No headway. Algerian police never traced Belmokhtar, or said they didn't. His photo is in every passport office in France, but that almost certainly isn't his real name and he'll probably never use that passport again. The big one, they've never heard a thing about him.'

'Smart, he's out of the country and will never come back.'

Boone nodded, but some part of her wished a motherfucker would.

Tess came in the back door, baby Jim in one arm, tablet in the other. 'You seen this?'

The BBC website, a story with a picture of Hanley Moss.

'I just got up,' Boone said.

'Moss is dead. And Blackborne's wife.'

'Dead how?' Boone said.

Tess read from the screen. ' "Two bodies have been found in

private woodland near Lark. Police said a 67-year-old woman and a 79-year-old man were found with gunshot wounds on the estate of Cornilo House. The deceased were named locally as Lord Moss, the former MP for Dover and Lark, and Lady Blackborne, widow of the late industrialist Lord Blackborne. Kent Police said nobody else was being sought in connection to the incident." '

'Blimey,' said Boone.

'Nobody else is being sought?' Tess said. 'Hell does that mean? Another hunting accident?'

'Two people out hunting can't both die accidentally,' Mickey Box said. 'Murder-suicide most probably.'

Jim opened his eyes. He looked about and, not finding anything that a hundred per cent washed with him, squawked loudly.

'Needs feeding,' Tess said. She put the tablet on the table and looked at Boone. 'You look tired, old man.'

'Thanks a lot, kid.'

Tess nodded and carted Jim off to her bedroom.

Mickey Box leaned back in his chair and considered Boone. 'Better find you something to do, then.'

58

The morning Jack came, Boone was out cycling. She returned on the public pathway along the outside of the headland and saw the Lexus sitting there, Jack at the table on the decking. He stood when he saw her.

She hadn't seen Jack or Quin for over six months, not since before Roo died. They'd tried to visit at the hospital, but she hadn't let them see her. She hadn't offered a reason.

'Biking,' he said. 'That's new.'

'Every morning.'

She kept her head turned slightly, keeping her scar away from him as best she could.

'Sorry for just ambushing you. I know I should have called. I needed to see you, though, and I wasn't sure if you'd agree. I didn't want a whole to-do on the phone about it.'

Boone was sweaty and achy and smelled like dog most probably.

'I need to shower.'

'Yes, of course. I'll be in the car. Just let me know . . .'

'Don't be daft, Jack.'

A low wooden storage shed had been constructed beside the decking, and Boone rolled the bike into it and locked it up.

'I'll be five minutes. Make some coffee. Or tea.' She grinned. 'I'm particular about my coffee.'

She quickly rinsed off and changed into jeans and a sweater. In front of a mirror, she applied foundation to her cheek. The scar itself she could never conceal; its depth was as if someone had stitched it into the fabric of her face. It ran like a jagged hook from the side of her nose to the outside corner of her eye, and the skin inside the crook was pale and ashen, as if necrotic. She rubbed the cream in and brushed setting powder over it. Somewhere she had bags of cosmetics she'd brought with her from the house in Lark, but make-up was a different idea for her now.

The tea was too milky, as ever, but she slurped some down hot. Afraid of the inevitable awkwardness, she suggested taking their mugs for a stroll up the headland and back, see the sights. Hers was the marsh country.

Still early, tufts of wool snagged on the fence wire dripped with morning dew like the winter's last ice, and the Calvinist sheep pulled at greenish shrubs whilst maintaining its pastoral vigil.

They followed the path along the olive waters of the creek until it opened up into the estuary proper. The waters were as thick and brown during the day as they appeared at night, turning to mud and then to the marshes of the offshore islands. Out there stood the remains of old barracks and boom stations, eroded and reclaimed by the tides. Out there were buried the bodies of plague victims and Napoleonic prisoners of war. Out there were the waters of Nelson and Francis Drake.

Jack stole little glances at her as they walked.

Eventually, he said, 'Limp's gone, I see.'

She imagined him going through a checklist of her past and present symptoms, maybe trying to catch her out. She was trying to be less paranoid, though.

'Doctor told me it was all in my mind, and it just seemed to vanish after that.'

He laughed abruptly, unsure whether he was supposed to.

'How's Quin?' she said, figuring it had to come up eventually.

'Fine. He's . . . he didn't, uh . . .'

'Didn't want to see me.'

'Well, no. I mean, I don't know. He never really seems angry. Just . . .'

'Afraid.'

Jack nodded. 'Seeing you that night with the gun. And then hearing you were taken to hospital again. I think he's compartmentalising. Boxing the whole thing away somewhere in the recesses of his mind.'

Boone smiled. 'Dr Boone.'

'I was afraid of you too,' he said. 'Afraid for you, but also afraid of you.'

She stopped walking and looked at him squarely. She offered her cut cheek to him.

'They did this. Eighty-three stitches. The knife hit bone. They fractured my eye socket. Again. My nose. Cheekbone.'

Jack swallowed. 'I read about . . . your friend. They were trying to do the same? To cut off your nose?'

'To spite my face.'

She stretched her lips against her teeth.

'Doctors did good work here.' She turned her top lip up, showing him the scar running underneath. 'Thought that was going to be much worse, but it healed well. Teeth took another doing, though. This new bridge is special. Leg was badly bruised but not broken. They took the old metalwork out. Arm didn't fare so well, so I've still got plates and screws.' She touched a finger to her eyebrow. 'Still got the scar your stitches left me with too.'

'Stop it,' he said.

'We can joke about it or we can pussyfoot around it, but it's simpler to just report what happened.'

'That why you didn't let us see you? Your face?'

'No. Maybe. I don't know. I left you, Jack. I left you and Quin, and I did it because I was dragging this kind of thing into your life. Into Quin's. What landed me in hospital was just more of it, so it didn't seem the right reason to change what had happened between us.'

Jack was quiet a moment. He reached out, touched her healed arm.

'You'll still be setting off the detectors then.'

She smiled. Giving it back to her now.

They ambled back to the caravan and Jack stood at the door for five minutes picking off globs of yellow clay that had kicked up onto his trousers on the walk.

'You'll be fine, Jack. Just come in.'

'It's almost all off.'

She'd noticed him quietly seething as it was happening. She made him another tea, coffee for herself, and they sat down.

'I've seen a solicitor,' he said.

'I see.'

'I wanted to sort some things out. I've been seeing someone.'

'Oh, I *see*.'

'No – I mean I've been talking to someone. A therapist.'

'Right. Sorry.' She smiled. 'Physician, heal thyself.'

'For all my experience, I couldn't quite see straight when it came to you. Also, I think I make a lousy patient. They said pretty much what everyone else has. Workings of the brain, great mystery, could pop out of it any time. Yadda yadda.'

Boone nodded.

'It's not going to happen, though, is it?'

'I can't answer that any more than you can,' she said.

'And even if it does . . .'

'And even if.'

'More, it was useful for seeing it from Quin's point of view. The therapy, I mean. Finding a path forward, for all of us.'

Boone nodded.

'I really don't want to go through the courts over this.'

'Nor me.'

'I've got papers back in the car. A settlement. I think it's fair.'

'I'll sign whatever you want.'

'No, it's important to me we do this right. If . . . in the future, if things change. If you . . . you know.'

'Revert?' Boone said, almost smiling.

'Come back, I suppose I meant. Recover. I don't know what that would look like, in terms of us as a family. But I think it's right to be fair now. I can buy you out of the house.'

'Jack . . .'

He put a hand up. 'It's the only way I'll do it. I want to stay there, with Quin. He likes it. And I want to keep as much unchanged as possible. But I'm aware that it isn't just our lives that . . .'

'Blew up?'

'Changed. They screwed you on the pension, I know that. You should have money. Half of it is yours and that's all there is to it.'

'Okay.'

'There's one big thing.'

'Quin,' Boone said.

'I want sole custody. I'd never, will never, stop him seeing you. Whenever he wants. But I want it to be down to him. And me. I don't want trouble down the road.'

And like that, Boone signed away her only child. Her entire family.

Jack had always earned more money with his practice; they could have been more than comfortable on his salary alone. When she received the cheque, almost four hundred thousand, she banked twenty grand in her account and put the rest in a trust, her idea being that it should be for Quin if he needed it later. If he wanted it.

She tried to shake the suspicion it was guilt money.

Jack had filled two suitcases with her clothes, which he heaved out of the boot. There were also two taped-up cardboard boxes shawled with attic dust, containing bits and bobs from her child-hood. Jack said there was more stuff, but they never came to any arrangement about it. When he left, he poked his head out the window and called back, 'Goodbye.' They never spoke again, not in any way that mattered. Quin was gone a good while too.

Hours later, whilst putting her clothes away, Boone found an MP3 player tucked into a zippered compartment in one of the cases. There was no note or explanation, but it contained most of the albums Quin had put on the previous one for her, plus some extra stuff. Jack hadn't mentioned it, so Boone assumed Quin had snuck it in without him knowing. She connected it to the stereo and listened to *In the Aeroplane Over the Sea*.

Life can only be understood backwards, if it is to be understood at all.

All Boone wanted now was to leave everything behind her. The life she'd once had but could never know, and the other stuff too, the old men and young girls. What she'd craved as purpose, as a life's work. She had been waiting for herself to arrive at some notion of who she was, some idea of self. But self, she concluded, was an illusion. A lantern show flickering on the inside of her skull.

So she took jobs of a certain kind from Mickey Box, jobs that saw her on the road to the ends of the country. Operations, he called them, not missions of consequence. She was tired of consequences.

The lakes, the valleys, the cliffs, the moors. She wanted to get away from what had been, but just how far away she couldn't say. There wasn't enough road to get far enough; far enough wasn't a place within her reach. If she could never settle the restlessness within her, however, she could always keep moving and hopefully notice it less with forward momentum. She would become a prow cutting ceaselessly through the swell.

I am a woman with no more past.

I work at the end of the world.

Acknowledgements

I am not the onlie begetter.

Nicola Barr is my first eyes and last word, and as such has suffered more horrifying early drafts than any person ought. Though her knack for suggesting changes that settle in with a feeling of inevitability is peerless, the finest and most constructive criticism is that which cannot be written or verbalised at all, but comes solely in the form of a head tilt and all that is implied therein.

There is also the small matter of NBarr's advocating, along with everyone at The Bent Agency, which has brought Boone to print, here and in places further flung. Words cannot.

Toby Jones took a chance, and has worked with his squad at Headline to turn my book into our book and something more than it was. A challenging task that he has made look effortless.

Simon impressed upon me, mostly by way of expense accounted meals and insegrevious Titian-haired wenches, the advantages of being professional over a strictly skipjack existence. Orson. Pi

Jonathan said it would come to this.

Without Maddy, Roo wouldn't have milky knees or different pairs of sleeves. And then where would we be?

The unfailing support of my parents means more to me than anything. I love you. This paltry piece of work is for you.